THE ANARCHIST'S GIRLFRIEND

by

Susan I. Weinstein

The Anarchist's Girlfriend by Susan I. Weinstein
ISBN-10: 1-938349-52-0
ISBN-13: 978-1-938349-52-2
eISBN: 978-1-938349-53-9
Library of Congress Control Number: 2016946745

Cover design and illustration by Cathy Saksa Mydlowski
http://www.saatchiart.com/SaksaArt
Edited by Kelli Lapointe

Eat Your Serial Press Publication 2012
First Pelekinesis Printing 2016

For information:
Pelekinesis Publishing Group,
112 Harvard Ave #65, Claremont, CA 91711 USA

www.pelekinesis.com

The Anarchist's Girlfriend

Susan I. Weinstein

For Cathy Saksa, who knew well this New York and made such a perfect cover for *The Anarchist's Girlfriend.* In memory of Jean Michael Henshaw, who loved the soul of the AG. Thanks to Pete Cherches, who got me gigs reading the AG, to Art Murphy, who without fail, listened to my words, to Xavier Koller, who encouraged me to finish. Thanks to Eat Your Serial and Kelli LaPointe for resurrecting the AG and to Pelekinesis for this fine edition.

About *The Anarchist's Girlfriend*

"Uh-oh, Woody, Manhattan may be in peril. Pre-Internet, pre-Kardashian, pre A-Rod New York is the setting for Susan I. Weinstein's sneaky funny, ever-seductive, refreshingly unconventional novel, *The Anarchist's Girlfriend*. It's quite a head-spinning read. And no wonder, for Weinstein is a boldly creative, highly visual writer whose narrative moves with distinctive rhythms; she has a laser eye for hypocrisy and detail, and hits you fast with lots of stuff. Best of all, her imagined parallel universe here is occupied by a Rolodex of indelibly unique characters—starting with AG herself—unlikely to be found elsewhere. Well, at least not on this planet; UFOs come to mind. A truly original work."

—Howard Rosenberg, former LA Times TV critic

"Having lived in the East Village in the '80s, I can say from experience that *The Anarchist's Girlfriend* captures the spirit of the time, real and surreal. Like Balzac and Zola, it's the novel as social history, and like Don DeLillo, it captures that weird parallel universe version of a place that's frighteningly close to home. Fans of DeLillo in particular should be attracted to this work."

—Peter Cherches, author of *Lift Your Right Arm*

"What a puzzle box of a novel. The writing is very fine-textured and funny, but mostly beautiful. New York under siege. I guess in a way New York is under siege every day. I loved the character of the AG and didn't expect to. After all, there's that annoying trend in novels where the title is always someone's wife or daughter. *The Pilot's Wife*, the *Bonesetter's Daughter*, the *Pony's Aunt*. But the AG is like Fitzdare in *The Beastly Beatitudes of Balthazar B*, a beautiful book by JP Donleavy. New York is the only city where such a story could take place."

—Sally Eckhoff, author of *F*ck Art (Let's Dance)*

"A careening and suspenseful trip through not only pre-9/11, pre-cell phone Manhattan but into the souls of unforgettable characters...and further, into the world of ideas. Daring to delve into philosophy, metaphysics, politics, psychology, and even art, the author makes you think, feel, and ponder. Yet she's never, ever didactic, it's all part of the compelling story: a plot to create a horrendous event, and the love inspired by the title character—the luminous, lovely, and clairvoyant anarchist's girlfriend. In a way, this is also a coming of age story as even mature characters such as the Irishman anarchist; the Llama, a heavy in a church that will remind you of Scientology; and a deaf-mute writer make new choices for their lives. Don't be put off by the long cast of characters in the very beginning, or you'll miss the sights and smells of gritty old New York, the wonderful outfits the anarchist's girlfriend designs, and her apartment mate Sandy's bizarre collage. The writing is modern and hip; the surprises keep coming. *The Anarchist's Girlfriend* is a unique treat."

—Ann Schwartz, former copy chief at Grand Central Publishing

Preface to the New Edition

In 1976, when I moved to New York City, it was a far grittier and cheaper place than today. Artists of every kind, writers, performers, designers, from all over the world came to NYC, the Left Bank of the world. There were lots of creative people with passionate ideas and what they wore was often made up. From scraps of material and thrift shops to Patricia Field's St. Mark's store, Trash and Vaudeville, a pre-punk wonderland, and Unique Clothing Warehouse. It was a time of improvised looks and lives. What people were *into* was more interesting than what they *did*, day job or other improvisations. The concept of "Brand" was associated with mass production, conformity, corporate manipulation--not a term for an innovative way to sell, like "identity or angle." "Brand," like "content provider" for writer, was decades away. The reign of the Techie had not yet come to pass.

In this era, stretching from late Ford to early Reagan, the influx of young hip people intent on making their identity more than a pose coexisted visibly with the burn-outs and head cases, sellers of street drugs and addicts, especially in the East Village. In SoHo, still an urban frontier, artists opened their pioneer loft parties to strangers. You simply needed a password or the right gang. Art students, trailing savvy teachers, braved rickety fire escapes or creaky sometimes operational factory elevators to the lofts of Red Grooms and the less famous for drinks and hobnobbing. Colonizers were a select group, who liked isolation and social life as sporadic as their hot water and electricity.

Classes mixed at Max's Kansas City and later at the Mudd Club. Afterward there was Florent, an all-night French place in the smelly meat market. An oasis for hipsters, poets and transgender prostitutes of the West Side Highway, it was an outpost in a mostly deserted early morning. Uptown met downtown, mixing Harlem and the Upper East Side, Long Island and the Bronx. Renegade housewives socialized with art and drug dealers, musicians, and filmmakers. Cookie Mueller defied sexual labels. Jackie Curtis was a transgender star who didn't ask for mainstream acceptance. Straights were welcome to their shows, if they dared.

I lived in a loft on Cooper Square, where Hartz Mountain had stored birdseed. Our only windows looked into the men's dressing room of The Public Theater. Washing dishes, I viewed Keith Carradine in his boxers. Our loft, which came without sinks, toilet, bathtub or walls, rented for 1500. a month. We three employed young women carried our fixtures from Orchard Street, rented a sander for the floors, and practically slept at Phebe's across the street. Like the AG, who also spent time at Phebe's, our loft was situated between methadone and alcoholic clinics, so we traveled with denizens of both in the elevators. Privacy, like the AG's loft, depended on flimsy walls that did not reach the ceiling. But we had a swing.

Down the street, Nan Goldin once lived with her friends and eventually photographed her Ballad of Sexual Dependency. One of her roommates, Jan, drew amazing comic strips and made clothes of the future. An Irish Anarchist silkscreened peace posters in a basement down the street. I collaborated on an underground art zine, where "names" mixed with unknowns. It was like the lottery to become a "name" and often as not, those who did win weren't more outstanding, often less so than others who briefly shone before obscurity. Being a part of "the scene" was the point for a few years. I once met David Byrne in an elevator to see Philip Glass's Gandhi opera, so what? Friends put on "Night School", an absurdist fashion event, at Mudd. Someone had a show at Holly Solomon, everybody was equal.

To me "the scene" could deliver what you were curious to know. I was writing plays and listened to dialogue, so I went out and listened. In a pre-cell phone era, conversation was an art form and it was also improvisational, surprising, witty, as people competed to be entertaining. Topics could range from Plato's Cave vs. Camus' existentialism, the "Troubles" in Northern Ireland vs. the Vietnam War, the military industrial complex and the banking industry, to Russian poetry that sounded great, if you didn't know a word of Russian and actually made sense depending on what you drank. Never far from conversation was the recession hanging on from the early seventies. Wasn't it getting better? Take what money and jobs were to be had. There was a manic urgency about making life count, because who knew about tomorrow. There was also an intense curiosity about meanings, the point of life. Some of this was youth, but we all chose to be in a city where such discussions weren't pretentious but earnest. Part of the floating publishing and old art school crowd, I had survival jobs for years.

The bohemian "Downtown" New York was ascendant. Post-Vietnam, Nixon and Johnson, these low-key years of Gerald Ford and Jimmy Carter didn't transform to Reagan's America until around 1983. And though some people have thought of *The Anarchist's Girlfriend* as fantasy much that is described existed in that world, drifting toward the Millennium. While working briefly for *The Wall Street Transcript*, I began to write *The Anarchist's Girlfriend*, because I had read *The Idiot* and *Sister Carrie* and long puzzled innocence—found and lost—in the society around me. Dostoyevsky made his Mishkin a divine fool onto whom people project their emotions and motives. Eventually, he rises to consciousness. In a similar way, Dreiser's very American Sister Carrie is a materialistic lower class innocent. She only wants to better herself and means no one harm and, though uneducated, rises in society because of her beauty and charm. She's a wholesome variation on Zola's siren Nana, another lower class blonde, who ends up on the stage. The AG is closer to Mishkin. She is also a mystic, though not in the same Christian sense, unless you think of Gnosticism.

While the plot of the AG is largely invention, some devices are autobiographical. Around 1975, I worked in San Francisco as a switchboard operator. I had Sandy's clients, a church suicide prevention center, a prostitution ring, a dog grooming place. Mr. Dio was real, as was the Arizona Dust. I met him on a temp job, where he was an executive. He called me into his office to confess his fears that the dust used to store missiles would misfire. I once was crossing the street from Phebe's restaurant, when a Mayflower van stopped and the driver fell out in an epileptic fit. I was the person who directed traffic, until the Emergency team arrived.

Other incidents, like the Pigeon Drop, were reported in the papers. EST and Scientology were building empires, as was Phoenix House, a cult-like rehab center.

I am not nostalgic about the vanished past but it's useful to recall how people related before our devices became the filter for interaction. Today, young people still flock to New York and its environs to make their scene and live on the edge. The passage can be an awakening, devastation, or both. I see alarming numbers of young derelicts in Union Square and wonder whether the city was less a testing ground than the last stop. Yet others muddle through, move home, find employment, and ultimately, make their personal compromise between ideals and reality's demands. The AG's transformation is a mythology of this passage to maturity. And what she's lost and gained matter little in the long run. The forward motion of a life is an illusion, because we age. Yet in the AG, there's a fulfillment of character, a promise for good that forges a mysterious alternative path.

In 1964, media visionary Marshall McLuhan coined the phrase, "The medium is the message," and, in 1967, the term, "Global Village." It was his ingenious observation that the actual form of a medium, its imprint, is contained in a message. The essence of a cell phone or iPad affects how we perceive a message. He also saw a future where people would be part of an electronic "Global Village." It is irrelevant to say our electronic village is for better or worse. But it's historic fact that patterns from the past repeat—though never in the same form. *The Anarchist's Girlfriend* mirrors some of our former consciousness, before our devices became intermediaries. Our media filters, our devices, favor immediacy over introspection—speed over the slower filtering process of mental sifting of information and experience. This human processing system only peeks out of an Instagram.

2016 is a time of huge, pivotal transition. There is looming devastation from climate change that may bring mankind's sojourn on Earth to a close. Our "Global Village" has political and social threats to order and safety that seem without precedent. Yet the media hasn't the leisure to look back and digest, before seeking to understand the present. Only individual humans, like the AG, can choose to be apart in order to move forward again.

The threat of a new Dark Age of ignorance and violence is tangible. After *The Anarchist's Girlfriend* in the mid-1980s I began a cautionary tale, set in 2050 on the Earth's surface and in 3011 underground. Corporate business estates have relocated there, after the world is no longer habitable. The estates are called "Paradise Gardens" the title of the novel. I had read about the transition of feudalism to capitalism and imagined the reverse. It was the age of Reagan when I began to write about the devolution of democracy. With the magical thinking of all dreamers, I hope to wake up to the light of a new day.

—S.W.

The Portable Lower East Side is in NYU's collection of the lower east side art and literary movement.

THE ANARCHIST'S GIRLFRIEND

Somewhere along the Bowery, in a basement, a red-haired Irishman wears his eternal black suit.

THE ANARCHIST

The Irishman works without a green card in a health food restaurant. He likes beansprouts, nuts, and most goat cheeses. He also silkscreens posters in his basement at night. His long, white fingers are smudged with raw, red ink. The poster glows, DO YOU WANT TO KILL YOUR BOSS? It's very prettily designed, it's graphically appealing. It ends with a handshake.

The Anarchist examines the new poster, frowning at the quality. His silkscreen is fraying. He thinks of a specialist who prints offset, realizing there's a certain quality of poster you need in New York to be noticed. The specialist, who amuses the Anarchist, is fascinated by the "Spy vs. Spy" comic of the raincoated anarchist. His favorite episode is when the spy attempts to throw a sticky bomb with adhesive, ending up a very charred cartoon man. Once he embarrassed himself, expecting the Anarchist to agree to the cartoon's subversive nature. "I mean, it's anarchistic, even if the magazine still makes money on it."

The redhead laughed, "Anachronistic, you mean."

Chapter 10 -- Food For Vendettas

"Jesus has given me sa-tiss-fac-tion, yes he has, I'm telling you peo-ple...." In front of Federal Hall on

45

[Excerpted from the forthcoming novel of the same name.]

Summer 1984 debut issue excerpted "The Anarchist's Girlfriend" (Pages 45-49).

Contents

INTRODUCTION

Somewhere along the Bowery, in a basement, a red-haired Irishman wears his eternal black suit. Somewhere in Chelsea, a Russian defector has a twin brother. Somewhere in mid-town Manhattan, a switchboard operator is going on her night shift. She carries a little video camera. She doesn't know what it is filming. She assumes it will collage to a logical sequence of related images that will have meaning by juxtaposition. She doesn't know if this is so but it doesn't matter; not to this girl who lived for American rock 'n' roll blaring incongruously over a Greek coastal town. She doesn't matter to anyone in that isolated fishing village she left at seventeen.

THE ANARCHIST

The Irishman works without a green card in a health food restaurant. He likes bean sprouts, nuts, and most goat cheeses. He also silkscreens posters in his basement at night. His long, white fingers are smudged with raw, red ink. The poster glows, "DO YOU WANT TO KILL YOUR BOSS?" It's very prettily designed; it's graphically appealing. It ends with a handshake.

The Anarchist examines the new poster, frowning at the quality. His silkscreen is fraying. He thinks of a specialist who prints with an expensive offset machine, realizing there's a certain quality of poster you need in New York to be noticed. The specialist, who amuses the Anarchist, is fascinated by the "Spy vs. Spy" comic of the raincoated anarchist. His favorite episode is when the spy attempts to throw a bomb sticky with adhesive, ending up a very charred cartoon man. Once he embarrassed himself by expecting the Anarchist to agree to the cartoon's subversive nature. "I mean, it's anarchistic, even if the magazine still makes money on it."

The redhead laughed, "Anachronistic, you mean."

THE ANARCHIST'S GIRLFRIEND

The Anarchist's Girlfriend is from Brooklyn. She's apolitical. She works as a go-go dancer for sixty dollars a night. She sews unusual ideas of what people could wear, might wear, perhaps will wear in the next century at least. She can combine textures, styles, and periods to come up with any particular feeling in a short while. This is how she "positions" her creations. The Anarchist disapproves. He is very careful how and where he positions his posters.

"One must have the largest audience possible!" he often admonishes her. "Who will buy these?"

She always answers with conviction, "Museums of the Future. Underneath a holographic fashion cube, a small latex placard will say, 'ANONYMOUS DESIGNER, 1980,

DATE APPROXIMATE WITH TEUTONIUM 90.'"

The Anarchist's Girlfriend has short blonde hair cut like Kim Novak and a ski-slope nose under the largest, softest, otherworldly eyes. Though her heart is strong, she has very thin shoulders and delicate, highly-tuned nerves. Luckily, she is blessed with second sight. When the men hoot at her go-go act, she excuses their ignorance. In her mind's eye, she is wearing a demure black dress.

In accordance with her futuristic visions, she dropped her given name several years ago. She told her friends, "Oh, I don't have to carry it on, several others are listed the same way." To tell the truth, she believed there would be no such designations in the future. Presently she preferred the privacy of being known by how people referred to her. Since they often identified her by boyfriends, she became the AG, the Anarchist's Girlfriend. She doesn't mind the abbreviation as she treasures her friends who entrust her with all their tragedies.

SANDY

Sandy, the AG's roommate, works on an answering service under an assumed name. She changes services every week to another area of the city. Fortunately, she is, as yet only a personal nihilist, since her photographic mind retains much information.

Sandy records the auditory impulses of the city and the wires are long. Every tie-in has a magnate's love affair, a jilted mistress' confession that ticks off a multinational cover-up to be noted and diagnosed. Yes, Sandy knows her city and its moods. During full moons, the wires go wild with people seeking absurdly definite answers from their shrinks, clients, bosses, lawyers, mothers, brothers, and lovers. Sandy prefers the graveyard shift, when the board lazily lights up in a few spots, like the windows of a high-rise during a holiday.

Sandy takes and collages photographs that hang in galleries. They show anonymous limbs, faceless or masked people in strangely objectified compositions. She pastes when her switchboard is quiet. This evening, her subjects are magazine cut-outs of glinting chrome car bodies and "Town and Country" tweeded flesh. As she applies the glue, she wonders how best to use her video-cam's potential for arranging events. Sandy also wonders if the Anarchist can be manipulated. She knows that she controls the board. She has the right pigeonholes to stick the messages in. She cuts a hole in her collage of men and machines, tempted to go beyond art. It's a perfect square. It makes a great sunroof.

THE LLAMA

The Llama is a bald man with a broad back. His nose is flat, his cheeks are high-planed. His squint is evaluative. There is nothing of weakness in this man. There is something of self-delusion. He thinks his aim is peace through knowledge. It's really power through obligation.

The Llama's "Denotational Church" is based on his empirical concept of the universe. The Llama experienced an epiphany on the Santa Barbara Freeway during a traffic jam. This former life insurance salesman had more in common with Saul of Tarsus than just being a merchant. Not in the desert but on the highway, his eyes rolled back in his head, his mouth foamed, and he KNEW. Yes, there, in his car, on that freeway, he thinks he received the meaning of life. THE ROAD, he could get off one ramp and onto another, pass the speed limit or respect it. His reflection in the rear view mirror became his only icon.

Saul of Tarsus was an epileptic. The Llama is not. He postulated that all his mental logic was absurd in the overwhelming reality of the traffic jam. He gave no credit to the heat, which had so effectively triggered his vision. Still, he did recall the odd light around the circumference of his eyes before he passed out. Miraculously, when he came to he found himself on the exit ramp. Immediately, he went to Tibet for spiritual credentials and emerged several years

later with certain compatible age-old credos that were nothing new to the Anarchist's Girlfriend.

The Llama's Denotational Church offers a faith of demystification. Events have specific meanings. The truth is always in a homily. The Llama proselytizes in awkward homilies that are not important for inherent wisdom but for implications in context. They provide a through-line to life's incomprehensible mysteries. The future can be faced as objectively as death. Fragmentation is heresy.

Denotational journalists work in a loft in Chelsea rented

for the Llama by a pair of Russian twins. The paper is called "*The Printed World.*" The Llama uses it for political influence and as a source of new membership for his church. It preaches his pragmatism. It couches his homilies in the repetitive manner so necessary to reorder the mind's perceptions.

WAYNE

Wayne can stop on a dime. He's got a snub nose and good eyes. He can smell spilled milk from three days ago. He can sight a black cat at night. Still, he uses notes to talk.

Wayne is a deaf-mute, who parks cars in a pigeon-hole lot. He's also a floater on *The Printed World.* Both places are owned by the Denotational Church. Wayne is a devotee because the church eased his spiritual infirmity.

As a child, recovered from rheumatic fever, Wayne taught signing to his classmates as an elite code. He used his natural gift for mimicry as well. A popular boy, he was sought after as a man. He read gestures as speech. People found his attentions flattering, his understanding profound. Women anxiously awaited his notes, careful how they shaped their syllables.

Wayne became a gifted lover, a master of tactile sensations, who would select a scent, a cheek, even the turn of a heel for an individualistic approach to sex. Making love filled him with the soundless echo of a theme. But, he demanded ultimate content in an impossible compression of time. His mind and senses split. He went to too many parties. He read too much philosophy. Temporary illusion became his only goal.

At the age of twenty, Wayne was a nail-bitten sensualist—an indecisive intellectual obsessed with impossibility. An academic career seemed inane, the job market worse, his tolerance of boredom was very low. The Llama taught him a management system. Now, Wayne's smile rarely reflects that constant anxiety. In addition, the Llama has promised him an editorial column when he's firm in his faith. Wayne is grateful for the Llama's techniques but skeptical about his own potential for enlightenment. Sex, as transcendence, remains his first religion.

It was this reformed Wayne Niebold who took a drink of light coffee. He only drank it at night. It seemed to jangle his nerves. Wayne liked the effect, especially for a task as boring as proofreading his feature, "Helpful Hints for Citizens." Wayne compared the galleys with the corrected copy. The press proofs showed a neat line drawing of a woman in a very geometric kitchen. The pots on the stove had diagonal lines around them. Copy read:

MOTHERS! FOR SAFETY'S SAKE, KEEP
HANDLES INWARD AWAY FROM
CHILDREN'S ACCIDENTS!!!

Wayne decided the slant was right. The Llama would like it.

Somewhere along the Bowery the Anarchist's Girlfriend walks herself, her spirit taking her body. She wants to see the sunrise—the familiar landmarks that make her day. The lunatic placarded Socialist is on his corner at Fourth Street. Hung around his neck are various mottos: THIS IS YOUR WORLD, NOT THEIRS. THE KABBALA IS NOT A POP SONG.

The Socialist is old and doesn't see well. He thinks she's a debater on a soapbox with wheels, giving a Pearl Harbor harangue in Hyde Park. He shouts to get in the last word, "And I reiterate my friends, we are not sufficiently accomplished for apocalypse, we are not worthy!"

The Anarchist's Girlfriend smiles compassionately at such madness. She thinks perhaps he lives in the apocalypse presently. Paranoia? She smiles to herself at the term. It sounds too much like annoyance. Gingerly, she steps over the dubious puddles in her shiny yellow boots.

Chapter 1

SANDY BEFORE THE BOARD

FEEL GOOD! Wasn't that the current mode for urban living? Sandy sat before her switchboard collaging magazine images and thinking about the dangers of neo-narcissism. She was, she knew, beginning to believe that exterior reality conformed to her own visions. She was also aware of a new, maniacal sense of her life's destiny. Sandy distrusted but could not control these inclinations. Her collage, resting on the board, seemed terribly inadequate next to an ordinary ·plastic folder pocked with cigarette burns.

Through its transparent cover, she read down a familiar list of businesses: a call-girl ring, a doggie diner, an auction house, an information network, an international shipping firm, and eight other places. Each line contained a phone number and an assigned box number for messages. These lines of type made up the waking hours of Sandy's shift.

She put the collage in a drawer, thinking cynically, *Where are you random dialers? It's three AM – time for "Wire Songs."*

Buzz-buzz-beep.

A black hole lit. Sandy plugged, curious. She had never

before heard a beep in the ringing sequence. A breathy male voice asked, "Are you alone? Can I come over?"

The breathiness reached rhythmic hyperventilation:

"PLEASE LEAVE YOUR NAME AND NUMBER FOR me to make DI-RECT CONTACT ... Bweep!"

The tone was bad, nosily reverberating through a bad speaker. Sandy replugged with her best imitation of the tape: "IF YOU WISH to leave a message, SPEAK WHEN YOU hear the beep, you have THREE MINUTES TO complete this call… BWEEP!"

The tape ran over her words: "WE PHRASE MESSAGES TO REFLECT your most INTIMATE SENTIMENTS. If you prefer YOUR OWN WORDS AND DELIVERY, we provide equipment rental and UNLISTED DISTRIBUTION. BROCHURE AND CONFIDENTIAL

consultation available." The odd syncopation made her cringe.

Sandy completely detached the cord. How loony she had been to answer. Nothing as obnoxious as a random recording. She noted that machine-made solicitations added a beep to the ring. She lit a cigarette, hoping it and the call weren't a trend.

A red warning light took shape. She had forgotten about the new smoke alarm. With her keychain wire-cutter, she snipped the miniscule wires. Thanks to a matchbook electronics course, the operation was tidy.

Sandy wasn't a habitual smoker. Tonight was a night of bad habits surfacing, like her past. Unwelcome, a reminder had slipped under the door of the loft. The print was small, except for the return address: U.S. DEPARTMENT OF IMMIGRATION. The message was sinister: DEPORTATION. She had one week before the top deck of a cattle boat or a plush seat in a DC-10 with an officer padlocked at her side.

"Alexis Stanifraz," her real name, stared at her from the card, unfamiliar. Who would know it? Her friends only knew a few aliases. Sandy lifted a glass of water and slid the card underneath it. Rings of moisture on the board sometimes caused shocks. She realized that her dad had betrayed her. But that was not the issue. It was a matter of choices. Marry an American in a week? Go further underground? Sandy's mind blocked out the horror of deportation with an unprecedented result. She fell asleep at her board, sliding into a reoccurring dream.

She was a Cro-Magnon creature painting a mural on a cave wall. She used a porcupine quill brush and berry dyes. The brush was too thick to delineate gazelles. She loosened the gut, selecting one quill. Dipping repeatedly, she painted delicate legs and hooves. The scene took shape. A herd of gazelles were chased by a herd of buffalo. The buffalo were chased by a herd of hunters with flat spear points.

A yell! A rough group of Cro-Magnon hunters entered, sloughing a carcass on the packed dirt floor. One tore a limb, denuding the raw meat from the bone. It was a gazelle limb. Later, she knew the men would hollow the fine bone to make resonant flutes inhabited by the gazelle's spirit. Horrified, she threw the ravaged carcass into a pot of boiling water. The men had no sense of decency or of the purifying uses of fire. While they slept, she sealed up the cave. Outside the plain was burnt, the sun barbaric. Spear high, she pursued the massive buffalo, her blood richly primal with the challenge, her heart haunted by the dead gazelle. Sex role envy? Avenging maternal instinct? Neither. Sandy's parental halves warred in her psyche. The protector of the gazelle and the buffalo hunter were the same pagan God, the missing link of sexual androgyny.

Sandy woke ashamed of the raw primitive drama. It reeked of patricide and she had always loved her father, a G.I. deserter with a talent for impersonation and fishery. No one in that Greek village knew he came from Slovak stock out of the Minnesota heartland. No one that is but Sandy's mom, an Englishwoman who met her dad in the Athenian cafe where he first joked, "To hell with the war, I'll fish the Aegean."

Her mom thought it was a joke until their two-week honeymoon stretched two years past Sandy's birth. Her ticket to the States turned out to be a Greek enthusiast infatuated with living mythology. She found solace with a minor shipping magnate.

Sandy had been a motherless brash sixteen, rebellious enough to find him out. While shaving, in a clear American accent, he sang "Sweet Georgia Brown." Sandy caught him with other tunes. Her deafening rock 'n' roll became more than the usual teenager's taunt of hypocrisy. Fearful of exposure, her dad ranted against her and the country that produced such aural abomination, irretrievably linking both. Sandy exaggerated her alien half with short skirts, snapping fingers, and lipstick pre-smeared to infer usage.

But Sandy also had a secret, the pain of deep buckling cramps not unusual in adolescent girls. Her dad took her painful grimaces for arrogance, her speechlessness for censure. She took the ferry to Athens where a friend's doctor gave her some tiny pink pills. They came on a round card designating the days of the month. Her religious training declared Partum Novum contraceptives a sin, though Sandy believed they would regulate her periods.

Her dad discovered them during a fight. A slap, a slammed gate. He condemned her as a whore, never to come back. Sandy had been a virgin. She would be formed in exile.

Australia, Japan, the United States; she was lonely but it didn't pertain. She adopted a maverick's philosophy, a gritty teenage existentialism. "Object is Essence," became her rallying cry. She misconstrued a French philosopher, dosed it with German nihilism and passed across to post-'Nam New York, where she found herself at home in exile.

She had, she thought in retrospect, no more ill feelings toward her dad. There was something wild and testy about his adventurous self-exile, the same stubborn spirit she saw in herself. The problem was not with him, but the institutions he had fled. Nostalgically, she remembered him pretending to be sullen at getting up so early—secretly happy as he pulled in the gleaming nets. So what if he had blown the whistle? Maybe he just wanted to see her. Maybe he was growing old alone.

A brightening red light interrupted her reflections. It was Mr. Dio's client line. Sandy plugged immediately since he was her favorite.

"De Long Shipping."

"Hi, Sugar."

"Hi, Mr. Dio. How's your boardroom?"

"Good-looking, not bad, trading ups and downs, the deficit end of the cycle."

"Same here. How's the World Gazette, selling anything new?"

"We're stocking Arizona dust."

"A new Dust Bowl?"

"It's not funny. Good consistency. They use it for missiles. Seems the cleaning apparatus needs practice."

"Explain."

"I don't think listening to my problems is in your job description."

"So, I always do."

"Sandy, absolution is a scarce commodity."

"Go on!"

"Dust is used to test the circuitry in missiles. If a microdot is present in any electrical component, it could misfire to the wrong continent. But, it could never happen."

"You don't sound convinced."

"I've seen those designs in the drawing stages. Five by eights reduced and imprinted on film. The lines of the circuitry are transferred to plastic discs. The discs are scrutinized by lasers. The final product is inspected for dust particles by a negative ion light, and if defective, automatically discarded. So it'll never happen."

"Sure?"

"The problem is the cleaning apparatus and the apparatus used to inspect the cleaning apparatus are made up of the same sensitive circuitry. Now, if a particle makes the original apparatus defective, the rest of the process is ineffectual. It becomes a matter of form."

"What bar are you at Mr. Dio?"

"I'm home, actually. My warehouse is filled with Arizona dust."

"Why?"

"Sabotage."

Sandy lit another cigarette. "By whom, and for what?"

"We ship to all competitive global powers, depending on the guidelines set by multinationals for missile control. A Yugoslavian intermediary has ordered huge shipments of dust."

"What are you doing with it?"

"My peace plan. I've built a huge sandbox. I'm sitting in the middle of it. They won't proceed to assemble without my dust. Do you know it's the best test quality available in the world?" He sneezed loudly. "I'm also allergic to it. Isn't that ironic?"

"How much time do you have before they locate another source?"

"I have the monopoly. I can claim back orders for about a week if I keep dumping on private properties. Still, it's only temporary since they'll settle for an inferior grade once they realize I'm stalling. Dust as a weapon ... maybe I'm overexcited ... I know I'm stewed ..."

"Drunk. Mr. Dio, take a room away from the dust."

"A gesture, Sandy, an attempt at a noble gesture. I was always the kind who believed in…"

"I know that."

"I wanted to tell someone unconnected. If you can think of some way for the gesture to have relevance. "Mr. Dio, I have something in mind. I'll need collaborators. Are you game?"

"Give me a budget estimate."

"Soon." She unplugged.

There seemed a mystical synchronicity between the dust

build-up and her deportation. Her personal nihilism was easily elevated to a role larger than herself. The destruction of a city became the illumination of a nation. PHOENIX was her improvised code name for a mandala-shaped operation to be imposed on the city. Spokes, representing main arteries cut off by dump truck loads of dust, would radiate from her headquarters at Ad-A-Line Answering Service.

PHOENIX. Five grand might cover the operation, including dust crew, electronics experts, decoys for police, and media insiders. As the sole broadcaster, she would read a non-propagandistic statement, frightening for its lack of political affiliation. As people panicked, the socioeconomic fabric would be shed. Afterwards, during the rebuilding, a new ethic would be forged for the run-down city.

Abruptly, she was halted in her grandiose madness. An image of the AG had unaccountably come to mind. Wearing a futuristic gardening suit, the AG stood in the middle of the dust debacle waving a trowel. It would be just like her, Sandy thought.

She remembered the first time they had shared a bottle. Tenderly, the AG had turned over Sandy's right hand. Her voice was compassionate. "A Simian Cross. It's found on both hands in ninety percent of all Mongoloids.

On one hand of a normal person, it's the sign of sinners and saints, psychopaths with no conscience and the most dedicated of artists and priests. Those tortured by the pursuit of truth in good and evil."

"What does that mean?"

"Thought and feeling are compressed in one straight line. But an attempt is being made to release the tension. See how on your left hand the line forms an end for a natural heart line? Your inner self is more evolved than your actions may show."

Sandy recalled the fishing village that worshipped catastrophe as the just act of a violent God. Perhaps she was trying to become that same God? The insight repulsed her. No, she would disappear and start again. There were other towns to get lost in.

A buzz begged to be answered. It was Sandy's least favorite client. She plugged, turned up the tenser and said, "345-4621, can I help you?"

"Babykins," said a congealed voice, "It's Sid."

"You want your messages, Mr. Erickson?"

"Don't you want to hear about my week?"

"How was it?"

"The ponies been running good. Blue ribbons out front, daily doubles in the pocket. Sweepstakes tickets to Norway, the whole bonus bit. Honey, you ought to retire to something slow you can take lying down, like my stable. Yours is a high stress occupation. Only corporate execs and waitresses can claim ..."

"I've seen the reports."

"I'm a nice Joe. My girls get the best pastures, free health care /benefits package and your private life is private! I'm a modern businessman not a shrink."

"Stop pitching, Sid," Sandy said with instant regret, realizing a put-down would be encouraging.

"Tell me, are you blonde, brunette, redhead; weighing 105, 110, or 115? 5′1″, 3″, 5″, 9″?"

"Bald, 4′11″, and 200 lbs."

"Don't give me that!"

"I have, as you know, three minutes per call, ten seconds left on this one. You want your messages or not?" Sandy reached into box 621 and pulled out a slip of pink paper.

"9:20 Alma called. She said no straphangers or strap-ons, especially Japanese. There's an asterisk. She's surcharging you for the sex toys."

"No kidding! College girls have high expectations."

Sandy twisted the ear piece away from her ear.

"Sandy, don't you want some Big-A action?"

"Is that like reaction, what you want? Naughtiness is boring."

"You can't treat me like this. I want a fair tumble. Noon when you're off or I get you axed. Are we communicating?"

"Promises promises. Sid, you're in the dark ages. I can charge you for sexual harassment."

"I'll tell your boss you propositioned me."

Sandy disconnected. It paid to keep her responses consistent.

BUZZ-BUZZ-BEEP...BUZZ-BUZZ-BEEP. Sandy plugged, though she knew it was the random recording. She was too edgy to let it ring.

"WE PHRASE MESSAGES TO REFLECT YOUR MOST INTIMATE SENTIMENTS."

Sid came over the breathy voice.

"What do you really want but are too scared to say? Who do you want to say it to? I'll give you a free message just to ease my curiosity."

"Sid, that is you?"

"A subsidiary. I'm diversifying."

"Is that service used by police and public figures?"

"Some of them have even subscribed."

"I get a commission on Ad-A-Line's sales. I'll swap my client list, all the shifts, for yours."

"Only if you come with it."

"Nope. A straight deal, no fringe."

"That's a hard way to bargain."

"I'll send you a confirmation."

Sandy unplugged, glad to have Sid's list. The names,

addresses and sexual proclivities would be useful to her decoy squad.

Excitedly, Sandy pulled out the drawer containing her collage. It looked good. She HAD succeeded in transforming abstract pictorial units into a new form. The same could be done 3-D with the whole city! To hell with the AG. What did she know about the normal drives for wealth and power?

Struggling to run-down the AG, Sandy fixed on the glass of water on her switchboard. OBJECT IS ESSENCE, the existential phrase, came to mind. Though seemingly passive, the AG embodied a force and completeness Sandy lacked. She was like an inert drinking glass, yet she had more reality. Emphatically, Sandy drank her water and pushed the open drawer closed.

She turned down the tenser lamp and set up a projector to run the videotapes she shot all over the city. At intervals, she rested on key sites, the spokes of her mandala. These she marked with a red "X."

Chapter 2

GIRLTALK

Her loft building was in back of a truck rental place on Bowery and Fourth. The first floor was a specialty Volkswagen repair shop. The second housed a punk/folk band. The third was a plastics warehouse and the fourth was leased to the AG. It had two rooms separated by sheetrock partitions. The bathroom, once a telephone room, had a ceiling crisscrossed with colored wires.

The loft building had no doorman, intercom or alarm system. It did have aircushion locks, steel doors, and an out-of-service elevator. Those chased from the city's hot water pipes lodged in that elevator despite the telltale smoke from their cooking fires. These the Anarchist doused before retiring. He knew the residents of elevators were often less than discreet.

How the AG found this place was atypical. She had not used an agency, bribed a super or heard through a friend. She had used a mild form of self-hypnosis. After her mother's death, the AG lay down in the Brooklyn apartment newly aware of how tiny it was, how filled with her mother's Burberry scent. She could hear the words of that calm, patient woman. "My world was not yours. I retreated before you were born. Go find something else."

Mentally, the AG extended the walls and ceiling of the apartment. She felt herself in a huge cool gymnasium. She heard an irritated truck horn and zooming cars. The apartment was in a complex on a quiet cul-de-sac. The gymnasium was in Manhattan.

The AG got off the D train at Houston. She walked the gray Bowery blocks past the rock club marquees to the yellow awning of Phoebe's restaurant. From the traffic island across from it, she looked up at three weather-worn granite beavers that sat between each set of windows on the fourth floor. She asked about them at the truck rental place.

"Decoration. Astor built the place, fur trade. Had to do something with their money."

"Are any of those floors for rent?"

"Next door ask the super."

The super, a red-faced man with sparse white hair, talked out of the side of his mouth and looked straight ahead; never at the AG.

He growled, "Freight elevator's always out of order. Management's too cheap to fix it."

The AG didn't mind. Light poured from a wall of windows onto solid maple floors. The AG licked her index finger and removed a white circle of dust. Rich grain jumped into being.

"A coat of polyurethane will keep that," the super said.

The AG could see the bolts of many-colored fabrics that would fill everything.

"How much?"

"Six hundred a month, no fixtures. If you provide 'em, we install 'em."

"Fixtures?"

"Sinks, tubs, toilets, kitchen, refrigerator, stove ... We do give twenty-four hour heat."

"Can I let you know?" (The AG was slightly overwhelmed, she had forgotten those items.)

"Buying a sink's no hardship. It can be pretty cheap and you can use the basement. Guy here after the piecework shop did. He sold old clothes. He'd have given me a cut, if things had worked out. But they didn't and he's gone."

"And the lease?"

"Two-year ... option to renew. But, we can talk about that."

Regretfully, the AG said goodbyc to her dream gymnasium. She had felt herself living there but how? The rent was too high. The AG went to Phoebe's and took a table, knowing an answer would present itself.

***

Sandy had dragged into the States by way of Tokyo. She had stayed at the uptown Y for $40.00 a night, way too expensive for her. Desperately, she called listings for shares, sublets, and residential hotels. Possibilities were dim for an unemployed alien with some converted income and no references.

She checked out of the Y and wandered to the Bowery, considering the flops. Alamo on the Bowery, she romanticized about her state, no lower doorways than these. The self-pity passed quickly. Compared to Calcutta, the Bowery was no big thing. She would like living there. She would like living somewhere.

Sandy went to Phoebe's for some tea. She indecisively ordered a Tequila Sunrise, changed it to a gin and tonic and ended with a Heineken Light. She steadied herself by focusing on a pale blonde girl sipping a Coke. Suburban, she sized incorrectly. She looks lost. Maybe she'll buy me lunch if I find myself short. Sandy realized then that she was the lost one. She decided to skip lunch and maybe make a friend.

The AG was soaking up the sunset before work, thinking of a burger she might order.

"Mind if I join you?"

The AG smiled. The St. Andrew's cross on her palm was itching. It noted a gift for healing and Sandy was obviously in need.

"Of course," the AG said.

"Do you know of any cheap places to rent?"

"Yes, a loft across the street."

"Any living allowed?"

"Some. $300 apiece, and we'll have to get sinks and tubs."

"I'll be working at an answering service, so I should be able to swing it," Sandy improvised, wondering at the unquestioning naiveté of the blonde girl.

Sandy didn't know that the AG felt fortunate enough for her mother's directive not to question the character of her new roommate. Her third roommate, the Anarchist, came later. (The go-go club, Joe's Place, was a sanctuary for more people than just the AG).

Tonight, the Anarchist was dead tired. It was almost dawn. The sweat poured down his sides. Carefully, he stacked the silkscreen upright to avoid tears. On it was a cross-eyed portrait of George Washington made by printing his right profile twice. The original was in blue, the reverse in red; the halves separated by a thin white crack. The bold letters read:

AMERICA ! ! ! THIS IS NOT A BALANCED
FACE REPUBLICAN=DEMOCRAT

—Committee for Internal Anarchy

The message was classic, the method flawless, the materials superior. Still, the Anarchist tortured himself. He was only too aware of his hypocrisies, pretensions, and barren chances for real advancement. He hung the poster on the line. The bare bulb threw the yellow walls into relief. The Anarchist washed a squeegee in the chipped sink. His hands were cracked and stinging with acid.

Spatula-shaped, mechanically gifted hands, the AG had said; intellect applied to practical ends. *Yes*, he thought blackly, *I have little enough aptitude for people. Humanity and their petty manipulations for temporal satisfactions ... FREEDOM.* He reminded himself of his calling. Championing it was a real hardship when what he really wanted was a warm shower, a good night's sleep and the AG.

What hypocrisy for a wanderer, an Anarchist who strikes in the night. But the AG, here was real torture. Why should she disavow ownership, the transference of identity to objects, the joys of insularity? She said she didn't want it, but ... oh hell, how couldn't she? He paused. It WAS possible. She WAS freedom! If only she would marry him, then he could finally ... The Anarchist cut his finger on the ragged edge of the sink. What a stupidly acquisitive idea, he thought.

The shop was as the Anarchist had left it the previous dawn. The multilith printer sat unused in the corner. It was once a pipedream of prosperity; large runs, mass marketed T-shirts, and Vendetta incentive buys. The expert, who was to be his partner, promised the necessary funds next week, next month, next year. The Anarchist had appealed to local foreign agents for funding but been turned down for lack of a movement track record. He had tried for a third world neighborhood arts grant and almost got it, except for his dubious residential status. The Anarchist kept the multilith under wraps. It cost too much.

Tonight he removed the dust cover. Oil had darkened the bed and solidified in sections. He didn't take care of it, yet he hadn't the heart to sell it. The Anarchist had reached the end of the George Washington project. He always took stock before new work. He always decided that his posters were obsolete at the point of inception. He suffered a feeling of time passing, his own growing fatigue. The Anarchist looked to an inspirational postcard on the wall.

He had bought it in a thrift shop off Third Avenue in the fall of 1978. It was printed in Tacoma, Washington in 1920. The format was vertical with four frames drawn in fine cross hatching. The first one showed two pilots inside a nose-diving airplane. The balloons overhead explained the grim expressions on their faces.

"Well Jake, I guess this is it."

"Yeah, Matt. Who would have thought it starting out?'

"Every mission has its price. Guess it's worth it.

The buck rests with me. Good luck, Jake."

"Good luck, Matt. Maybe I'll see you on the other side."

(Laughs were simultaneous with the words BOMBS AWAY!!!)

The last frame was a second after impact. The plane was surrounded by flames.

The Anarchist was fond of this card, printed by an early Anarchist group against World War I. The group, devotees of Jack London, was united on the war issue. Afterward each returned to his wilderness outpost. The Anarchist envied that single-issue enthusiasm that made group action effective. He hated his own inability to sustain the urgency required for a lengthy struggle. Food for Vendettas, his own organization, had not lasted a year.

Usually, this card gave the Anarchist a lift. Tonight, it seemed decadent, definitely 'kitsch'. The word annoyed him with its neo-connotation of American chic. Anything over twenty years was an antique, a curio on a shelf of its own making. But process was purpose. He considered the mauled newspaper clipping in front of him. It had been in his pocket a week. It was just a line drawing with a little zipa-tone transfer for texture, yet there was a lot of active purpose to it. Had he the courage to begin? Was it possible to build a jerry-made affair?

The Anarchist, undecided, re-pocketed the paper and came up from the basement shivering. He crawled tensely into the loft. The AG had left on the hurricane lamp. Then, a rare occurrence, the Anarchist looked at himself in her mirror. He glanced from his ravaged frame to the lamblike AG pink with sleep, thinking— no accounting for tastes.

Sandy's area was dark, the thin sheetrock door open. A red light glowed through her bamboo curtain. It meant her tape machine was on and the Anarchist couldn't shower. The noise would be enough to set her off. When Sandy slept, which was rare, she defended it violently.

Wretchedly, the Anarchist dropped his clothes and crawled into bed far from the AG. She rolled into the curve of his back, breathing contentedly. The Anarchist felt her hair tickle his neck. Tenderly, he wondered of what stuff was she made?

Sandy was awake. She had a battery-run microphone hidden in the AG's bed. She was monitoring her recorder, hoping for an unguarded hint of the couple's processes. She used a two-tier system of sleep analysis to differentiate the REM cycle from deeper sleep. The first, which she called "Alpha", was of little use. It was the "Beta" from which she recovered obscure phrases and scraps of stories. She hoped to link these. Through the Anarchist's disturbed sleep, she could distinguish his uninhibited Irish, "Suurree as thur's a God in the heavens! This lad will come home!"

This did not seem to relate. Sandy wanted to know why the Anarchist was making posters. He wasn't founding an organization, mobilizing a task force, using them as a code for bombing sites, or really propagandizing anything but some esoteric societal complaints. Yet he was very serious. If he worked out of some misguided desire for transcendence, some introverted exhibitionism, he could be used.

Sandy listened to the "Alpha" level of his upper brogue, thick and incomprehensible "Burrrrssss" and "lorries" interjected by chattering teeth. After a second, he broke to a terse street lingo Sandy loved—"Yrr a routeen pieace of hurrssee's ass." She made a mental note to listen to some Gallic dialect records for exact origin. Then she allowed herself a cat-nap.

Sandy woke impatiently at 9 a.m. The microphone recorded the AG's idyllic breathing. How that girl could sleep! It might be two more hours before she woke. And then, the AG always took time to muse over her dreams in the most pretentious manner—eyes closed and meditative. The Anarchist, she knew, would be at the restaurant now, his hands ripping wrappers of fresh spinach. It was definitely time for the AG to wake up.

Silently, Sandy entered the darkened room. She opened the shades over the kitchen window, trusting the light to wake the hypersensitive AG. Then she returned to bide her time reviewing a portion of the tape. She skipped past the Anarchist's breathing to ... nothing. Though she'd need a meter to confirm it, she swore the AG slowed her functions past pulse beat. Once, holding a mirror, she could discern no breath. Alarmed, she had been relieved by the AG's shift into a baby-like sigh, whimper, or gurgle of bliss. Sandy remembered a rare feeling of warmth and protectiveness. But she could not think of this. She heard the Anarchist's brogue clarified with panic.

"No! I'll not get into that boat. I've done nothing to be 'shamed of! Bombs away!"

What did this fear mean? Sandy needed to know the perimeters of his mindset. With her timetable ticking away, Sandy heard the AG stretch and moan.

The daylight was orange under the AG's closed lids.

She savored the sensation a second before opening them affectionately on the Anarchist's ink-stained shape on the sheet. Poor Anarchist, she thought, so considerate of Sandy's sleep. He'd probably taken a sponge bath in the employee's sink this morning, before making dips for antipastos, forests of salad, bowls of Parmesan cheese and de-sodiumized bacon bits—all on no sleep. A smile strayed as she thought of the coming evening, after his nap. To the AG, passion and the Anarchist were synonymous. His tenderness had the tentative touch of suffering. His mood alternations were always a shock.

The AG pattered to the window and looked directly up at a rectangular patch of sky. A wet pigeon roosted under the ledge. The AG fed him a corn kernel. Pigeons were handy weathervanes. She thought of water, nature's perspiration, Earth's tears—liquid fluorescing in puddles, running to the water in an underground stream. She watched one drop expand and fall, transparently coloring from a sidewalk chalk drawing. Then, she turned to think what outfit she'd assemble.

Her loft was filled with colored clothes in various boxes, bolts of fabric leaning against walls, straw baskets filled with scarves, cubbyholes of hats, frames, feathers, and plumes. The AG considered a draped rocking horse. On it was an elegant Victorian dress, a practical Scotch coat, a Moslem headdress, and a circle skirt from America, circa 1952. The AG randomly thought of a polar ice cap, and then of the Bowery, knowing her one-piece rain suit would suffice — a bit of sci-fi humor from an unborn Galactic Age. Sandy's knock was too loud to her ears.

"AG, could we talk?"

"Of course."

Sandy sauntered in, struck as always by the AG's total indulgence. She was dressed near naked in the thinnest silk gown imaginable. Her wrappers were second skins in shades matched with how various seasons affected her. The AG shivered without understanding why. She sensed Sandy's disapproval.

"AG, what are you doing today?"

"I don't know. I'll see how it reaches me."

Sandy tried to think of another way to broach the conversation. The AG was so damned abstract.

"Is there something you want to know? I don't mind what you might ask."

Sandy was disarmed, as always, by the peculiar clarity of the AG's voice. She was unexpectedly frank.

"About the Anarchist. Why did he flee Ireland?"

The AG did not suspect Sandy of dementia. She would dwell on the positive aspects of her friends — the perfect irony of a laugh, an amused eye, an attuned ear. In short, all the things that are positive, noble, and endearing. Familiar with Sandy's inquisitive nature, she never hesitated to answer.

"My Anarchist, you mean?" she said searchingly.

The AG groped for his history; linear thought being foreign to one with her gift for associative, lateral thinking.

"Well?"

"He wasn't very popular there."

"Why not?"

The AG had some difficulty swallowing, as she recalled the Anarchist's horrors.

"He was the last son of his family alive."

"Think, you couldn't forget this!"

"No," said the AG, her mind rolling with images — the Anarchist covering his head from the sun with his arms, kneeling on the bottom of an oarless rowboat. The Anarchist in the middle of a club of boys. They praise his first silkscreen, an orange clenched fist wrestled to burial by a green. The boys are about fourteen. They cheer as he pulls the poster. The registration is perfect.

"You know how he likes health foods? He liked them a lot back then, too. And his town was at war, conflicting religious loyalties."

"What can that war have to do with health foods!" The AG was halted again—by a vision of a tanned,

healthy Anarchist planting in a small, square garden plot.

"He practiced organic gardening. It was very revolutionary."

"No!" Sandy laughed.

The AG was respectful. "On rocky soil it was genius.

He founded a nonpartisan co-op and ..."

The AG was interrupted by a seventeen-year-old Anarchist furtively postering on the corner of a wall. Quickly, he pressed the sticky side down the bend. Then, he worked upward in broad strokes until several hands gripped his arms. It was the boys from the club, only older. They were angry about the poster, which showed a miniature version of the torn town patched whole inside a huge, ripe tomato. Underneath it ran the words FOOD FOR VENDETTAS.

"He became an anarchist. His family was IRA. Though he made posters to appease them at first, after a while he had his own ideas. Both sides became confused and resentful and... violent. They shaved his head and put him on a boat shouting, 'See what you can grow in there!' The AG's voice trailed off. She was watching the vegetable-covered Anarchist being led to the shore by the outraged townspeople.

"He had no oars."

Sandy anxiously watched the AG's frail body shake with sympathetic paroxysms. The AG was reliving the Anarchist's misery. He used his body as a rudder— thrusting it forward, painfully, his arms moving in the water.

"He would move himself till he felt a current."

Sandy was glad to see the AG still, if looking very vacant. Two images had blended in the AG's mind. One was recent; the Anarchist holding her, his body drinking in the shivery wrapper ... "Soo,- suft you are gurl…" This, with him half-alive, being dragged with blackened toes to the shore at Liverpool.

"He made it to England. Frostbit."

Sandy would not have believed this story from anyone else. The AG, she knew, did not lie.

"Why did he come here?" Sandy asked.

"They weren't allowing anarchists in Africa. Besides, he thought he would have a better chance running a successful co-op in America."

Involuntary tears splashed from the AG. Sandy was relentless. "That was his total ambition?"

"Yes."

"I can't believe he'd make a stand like that for organic gardening! That's what he told you but there must have been another reason."

The AG spoke levelly, "You would find another reason."

Sandy switched tactics. "What happened to his dream?"

"He organized a group of members to grow on East Village plots, backyards, and vacant lots—no matter what the season. He also managed to rent a storefront to distribute his stuff."

"Do you have any names?"

"No, I didn't know him then."

You probably don't now, either, Sandy thought.

"They expanded enough to include bread, honey, and books on natural childbirth. But they were non-profit, non-granted..." she sighed, "non-neighborhood supported. The neighborhood was Czech, Ukrainian, fast-food oriented. So he sold out to the health foods restaurant, which, oddly, does well at the same location."

"That must be why they don't card him."

"I guess. He hates the sun and soil now. Spends all his time in that basement. He keeps sending tubes of posters to Ireland. They all come back unopened. It's so sad. He's so frustrated."

"What's he trying to do with them?"

"He consolidated his efforts to improve the quality of life by providing attractive posters with messages of a consistent thought-provoking ideology." The AG was tired. "Is that enough?"

"What does he want?"

"I think he'd like a shop not in the basement. He also wants a boy, an Anarchist Junior."

"Why not?"

"How could I? He's an uncompromising perfectionist. I couldn't do that to a child. Not now but he may change ..."

The AG was exhausted. She felt the weight of the Anarchist's bitterness and despair. "The child would be half him and he would hate that half. Sandy, he's desperate. Don't hurt him with your interest."

Sandy pretended anger at the implication. "How and why

would I hurt him?"

"I know you, Sandy, you cut the pieces to fit."

Sandy met the AG's timid guileless eyes. Did she somehow intuit her desire to use the Anarchist?

"I'm your friend. You know I'd never do anything to harm him."

The AG nodded acknowledgement. She knew Sandy would betray her, though, perhaps that wasn't the point. Sandy had never declared loyalty as much as independence. The AG had no reason to see a territorial infringement as betrayal. Even the concept was impossible.

But somehow inevitable, though not with the Anarchist. Sandy filmed to possess, then lost her plots in miles of tape.

"I don't know what I'm saying, exactly. Be kind.

He's a sincere man, the Anarchist."

Sandy shrugged, "You're very strange." She decided to humor the AG. "What are you going to wear today?"

The AG smiled shyly, "Whatever I feel like with what is on hand." With a generous sweep, she indicated the loft's colored expanse.

Sandy was amused, "Your emphasis on clothes is really too much."

The AG considered Sandy. It was beyond her to stop the vague and powerful force forming inside her. All she could do was issue not a warning, but a plea.

"Sandy, I love the Anarchist. Please don't hurt him."

"What would I want with him? I merely collect

sensations."

The AG faced the window, silent. She knew Sandy treasured last words. It was the way she revenged herself on the AG for often revealing her unconscious intentions.

"You are paranoid," Sandy said before leaving.

The AG put on her water repellent jumpsuit. She enjoyed the way the rhinestones glittered around the zipper. She put on a pair of silver-dusted transparent boots. She tied a scarf of a yellow shade slightly less delicate than that of her hair. The AG decided to give her melancholy fears to the clouds over the East River. A ritual was needed, since a chill of apprehension had pierced her warm, never oblivious heart.

Chapter 3

THE PRINTED WORLD

The Russian twins are called Bruno and Barry. They are of gypsy stock. When the Llama first met them, they played accordion and juggled in front of the main branch of the New York Public Library. They were about to be arrested for not having a street license.

"But we are emigrants. We are not vagrants!" they had protested.

The cop cracked to a friend, "Wear a sign."

Bruno displayed the one on his back: WE ARE RUSSIAN EMIGRANT DISSENTERS. WE ARE TRYING TO RESETTLE. HELP OPPRESSED EMIGRANTS.

The sign was true, except for some details. Bruno and Barry were not oppressed, though they were dissenters. They did not like to work and had never reported to their job assignments after schooling. The Soviets had given them multiple choices: work camp, prison, or exile. The twins chose the latter. They liked to travel. That day at the library, the cop did not feel menacing. He did feel he had a job to do.

"You're vendors, so you have to have some kind of a license," he said.

Barry spotted the Llama watching the scene. Because of the Tartarish cast to his features, he had embraced him speaking in Russian. The Llama, though ignorant of Russian, had nodded familiarly. To the cop's relief, he had vouched for the twins — admiring their convincing pitch and native charm. Later, he made them managers of *The Printed World.* The twins obtained the Chelsea loft, which is above the dry cleaning store. It was once a dance studio. They bought it very cheaply.

Besides an office for the Llama and one for the twins, the loft is filled with clusters of desks. Editors occupy them by day, proofreaders by night. The reporters are floaters. Wayne is a fledgling floater, calling in his stories from his proofreading desk at night. Like all staff, he is trusted since he is unpaid. The Llama uses talent employed elsewhere in his organization—working for *The Printed World* is considered an honor.

The Printed World costs fifteen cents. The front page is a relief from harsh headlines. It includes some downplayed international news, a smattering of national events, and in-depth local news. It runs obscure reprints from the National Geographic about the meat-eating Kookaburra of New Guinea and Australia. *The Printed World* also has two lovelorn columns. The one for teens offers sympathy and insight. Wayne's "Household Hints" are very handy. In total, *The Printed World* is uplifting, with an unfamiliar religious conscience. It was a hard paper to sell.

Bruno and Barry used a unique marketing strategy. For a week it was delivered free. Follow-up folks rang doorbells soliciting "suggestions." Subscription cards followed. Some people read *The Printed World*. Some used it to line their cat boxes. Some left it piled up in front of their doors, and some subscribed. During a newspaper strike, the paper gleaned many readers from the tabloids. Many stayed, finding it optimistic and unconfusing. The news was well-digested. The language was not tedious.

The Llama retains a controlling interest and an office. Pragmatism is his official watchword. This evening, the twins were in their office. They are both short, dark, and twenty-six years old. Bruno is heavier; his hair is thicker. He had his feet up on a desk.

"Barry, is he in?"

Barry eyed a white-painted toy troika. He thought it looked stupid on Bruno's desk.

"So the motherland is cute to you?" Bruno put his feet on the floor.

"He must be in, you're getting argumentative. You always do that when you're nervous."

"It has happened too fast, too easily. I keep waiting to be dispossessed."

Bruno had little patience with this familiar complaint.

"You want to be dispossessed," he said.

"It is in our blood. This alienation, this fear, this fierce love of our home. "

"Please examine your conscience elsewhere. The Llama doesn't require breast-beating."

Barry swept the troika off the desk and stomped it underfoot.

Bruno was irritated. "That's the second one this week. You must like the U.N. gift shop."

Barry felt silly. He decided he would approach the Llama about a program to manage this compulsion.

The Llama was in, though he ignored the Denotational Profile on his desk for a glance out along the rooftops. He was thinking of mankind, because a man in an army overcoat was asleep on a deckchair. The man, he mused, could be him — thinking, as he did, that all men are each other. The Llama doesn't really believe in the divinity of this kind of identification but he has transcended himself to a universal paternity. Still, he is not sure who he really is.

The Llama may look like a Eurasian, but he was born a blue-blood on Philadelphia's Line. The oriental cast of his face comes from an American Indian abduction of an ancestor and a habit of squinting he picked up on retreat under the harsh Tibetan sun. The Llama's mission is to free others but he has accepted his own psychological captivity.

There are no Denotational Profiles describing him because, unlike his followers, he cannot obtain consultation. It's difficult to be the sole source of enlightenment. Today he has transcended himself through the Profile of a church member. The Llama reviews each file personally, his sharp one-pointed meditation essential to each final recommendation.

The Llama's organization redeems societal outcasts by employing them in business projects. With the help of follow up observers, he monitors the effect of material security and emotional stability on criminal behavior. The file in front of him represents a rare problem. A couple running a garage on the Upper East Side would seem on the right path. But their observer suspected them of extracurricular criminal activities. No proof beyond overheard conversations substantiated his claim.

The Llama flipped through the couple's history. The man was an amoral klepto born and raised in a secure suburb. The woman was a conscious-stricken, but very compulsive sneak-thief. They had fallen in love on parole.

The Llama was on both boards when they elected for the Church's "wash," a procedure essential for all convicts entering the Church.

It disturbed the Llama to learn they were still more interested in scams than business. The report renewed his latent doubts about the odds for permanently reforming sociopaths. He decided to assign a watchdog to the garage before making final recommendations. The Llama was pleased with the next file, a list of names and short Profiles of new members not yet issued job assignments. He was completely absorbed.

Outside the Llama's office, Wayne Niebold sat in a deserted editorial cluster. He was bored with trying to think of new ways to keep kitchen sponges fresh. He picked up a syndicated story from a newswire service. Though material from the service was rarely useful for his "Helpful Hints" column, it was more interesting than sponges. The lead article might actually bear reprinting.

> PIGEON DROP SCAM FLEECING PENSIONERS
>
> "Pigeon Drop," a term used in skeet shooting, is the name for a notorious scam practiced on New York's Upper East Side. The "pigeon," often an old or naive person, agrees to deposit a bag of "found" money for an attractive lady just until the police arrive. The "pigeon" gives the girl an amount supposedly equivalent to that in the bag. Many people have been deprived of their life savings, since the bag has a layer of bills on top and nothing underneath. In other variations, the criminal needs an "inheritance" deposited quickly so she can hop a plane to an overseas fiancée or a family funeral.
>
> Sometimes, if the "pigeon" is unwilling to deposit the bag, the criminal suggests they wait off the street, in the "pigeon's" apartment, for the police. She calls her "boss," an accomplice who joins her in robbing the

> apartment. The chief targets of this scam are elderly pensioners or gullible youth, who sometimes believe they will share in the anonymous "found" wealth. Beware a lady with a Swiss Air Bag.

Wayne, who had never found the wire-service imaginative, found the scam fantastic. Could there be, in New York City, the most suspicious of cities, people capable of being duped by such a scam? Credibility, he decided, was a relative thing. Maybe he should capsulate the article for his "Helpful Hints"? Wayne dropped the piece, with a query, into the Llama's IN tray.

The Llama continued to face the window. His large red hands gripped the frame. The tightness of his grip revealed the man's emotional involvement. Upset about the couple at the garage, the Llama wondered if the man in the deckchair would ever awaken. Wayne tapped on his desk until he got the Llama's attention. He pointed to the article and made the sign for a question mark — palm curving, finger upward in space. The Llama tapped back— two fingers on his forehead indicating he was engaged.

After Wayne left, the Llama decided to assign him the garage watch. With relief, he made a note and inserted it in the couple's Profile. Though he intellectualized everything, Wayne would do fine. Maybe he should encourage him to undergo a "wash?" No, the Llama discarded the idea, Wayne's nervous system was highly keyed. He was too open to new ideas for old habits to stick.

The Llama glanced at his appointment calendar. Wes Mavine would soon be at the loft to make his presentation for the Llama's upcoming ad campaign. The Llama reviewed his knowledge of Mavine, a stockholder in his organization.

Wes Mavine had come to the Denotational Church via electronic media. Wes, a wealthy video artist, had pursued auditory/visual perception to a cerebral vacuum. He had discovered that thoughts were fragments of an unperceived total consciousness. The field of static caused by his electronic toys, video recorders, monitors, and mics haunted his dreams with fragmentation. His McCluenesque media martyrdom made him go beyond the ironies of social criticism to seek religion. Denotation became for Wes the Zen dialect of modern advertising lingo.

The Llama had met him at a viewing of his piece entitled, "Aimless Dialogues." Wes, intrigued by the Llama's Eastern appearance, had asked him for a visceral reaction.

The Llama had answered with two words, "Terminal Fragmentation."

"The inevitable," Wes had replied.

The Llama shook his head. "Entropy."

"And the force to disturb it?" Wes asked, feeling understood.

"Dialectical Will."

Wes took a card. Later, he became one of a group of cultural sophisticates who were invited to make an initial investment in the Llama's Church. The rest of the group included a ruthless builder of a soft-core porn empire, a conservative economist, a T.V. evangelist, and a labor organizer. They had all agreed, at the last meeting, that it was time for the Llama's organization to go public. The Llama was not exactly sure why. His tape recorder was within arm's distance. He pushed "rewind" and then "fast forward" until he found the transcript of the meeting.

"A modern religion married to the technological state. We are here today to revive the potential for private investment in this enterprise. Until now, our income has been sufficient to keep operating with modest profits. Because of our broad appeal and rapid expansion, it is necessary for us to go public, not as a church, but a taxable corporation. As we grow recruitment and increase grassroots political interest, our appeal has broadened to include a diverse national spectrum, much like this board. Denotation is becoming an American dialectical force as powerful as our old frontier fundamentalist religions, of which I am a descendant."

The speaker was a TV evangelist who secretly promoted Denotation. He felt a need to atone for the reactionary nature of his professional "calling." The Llama moved the tape up to Wes Mavine.

"Denotation provides a Way that is reasonable and dynamic. Our campaign's images will be familiar, made newly visible by the unique perception shift of which I am a master. The public experiences a "shock of recognition." I've rejected a Benson & Baily presentation that is similar to that of major oil companies, and one from Ogden and Nash that resembles the Mormon Church. Mine will not be similar to anything but the essence of The Denotational Church."

The labor leader interjected a question for the Llama, "Do you have an alternate end point, sir?"

The economist answered for the Llama, "The revolutionary process of evolution—the next logical step.

The Llama turned off the tape to think about Denotation. It was truly a wondrous theory, based more on inspiration than fact. Circumstances often colored logic and lent credence to many different perspectives. The Llama's highway epiphany had provided an unshakable foundation for Denotation. His situations ethics were formidable because his logic had the intuitive basis of genuine spirituality. He might weigh facts, think of context, time, and place but he always relied on his "gut" sense. It was this conviction which endowed him with the necessary charisma for media identification. It was this knowledge which also made him more akin to Machiavelli than he suspected.

From a low profile but influential religious movement, Denotation was becoming a national catch-word. The possibility excited the Llama so that he was unprepared for Wes Mavine's entry. Wayne should have announced him, the Llama mused. Perhaps he was getting too occupied with "Helpful Hints." An open-air job, like the garage would soon cure his imbalance.

Wes Mavine was dressed to cue in this year's ad-man suit,

a brown hound's-tooth, discreet and tiny. His beige shirt and pocket handkerchief were perfect with his accent, a thin plum tie. Wes' presentation was just as precise. He clicked open his case, synching double locks. He took out a three-color brochure and a giveaway pop-up creased for perforation. With a flourish, he propped the placard against the wall. "Billboard design," he said.

The Llama picked up the brochure. The cover showed an attractive young woman standing before a brownstone building on the Upper East Side. The back of the brochure showed another attractive young woman before an A-frame house overlooking Stinson Beach.

The copy on both the front and back read, "I used drugs to forget. Now I use Denotation to remember." Unfolded, the brochure gave the floor plans of both the Llama's Centers, including his Tibetan Garden on the Upper East Side. The inside copy listed the addresses and phones of the centers, along with that of *The Printed World.*

"You feel this will communicate my message?" he asked Wes, thinking the brochure's emphasis on reclamation was misplaced. Still, it was better to listen to the whole approach before discussing the parts.

Wes pointed to the placard, "Inside are subway posters, billboards for highway buses and signs for taxis. The idea is to prime people to look for the opening of our Denotation Centers in their own neighborhoods. It all ties in and acts as a teaser."

Wes propped up the subway posters. One was an infrared shot of a couple holding hands as they stepped into the silvery waves of a seascape. The sun, dropping into the ocean, reflected like a huge golden coin. The couple, naked, were seen from the back. Below, white letters proclaimed, "We were denoted through the church. We have faith in dialectic. It has given us a base of operations."

"Mysterious and catchy," Wes said, though the Llama had moved onto another poster; a child and his mother in a supermarket. The child, in a cart, is pulling a card from a shelf. His alarmed mother is half-turned toward him. The black copy read: "The truth can be found, easy."

The Llama took little notice of this poster, though the

next one he pondered for some seconds. The silence made Wes uneasy. "I followed your instructions…" Wes began.

The third poster bore a mystical logo the Llama had ordered. A paragraph in white was very intriguing: "A yellow line divides a circle in half. On either side are black bands. The upper half is filled with blue and one pointed star. The lower is filled with serrated green. The yellow is the highway, the green is the meridian strip. The blue is the sky, and the star is the Llama's link to Bethlehem's line. DENOTATE. LIFE IS VERY SIMPLE. LOOK FOR A CENTER IN YOUR NEIGHBORHOOD"

"I am pleased with this rendering. Show me the billboard."

A pretty girl in jeans smiled radiantly. She faced a huge sun that was actually the Llama's logo. The copy, sky blue, read:

DE-NO-TATION, SYN-CO-PATION.

"Listen to this," Wes said, switching to a tape of music featuring the lyrics. "Denotation, Sin-co-potion is the tune I'm dancing to ... It's easy once you see your way through ..." The Llama liked the tune: It contained his message and was danceable. He nodded, encouraging Wes.

"I have a film for people interested in our neighborhood centers. "How We Are" is a minor impact film about a man faced with narrowing alternatives, whose responsibilities are overwhelming. He's confused and can't see the consequences of different choices except in a negative light. Denotation removes the depression, giving him not just different options but a way to choose among them. The movie deals with his retreat, the 'wash' experience, and various Denotational testimonials."

"Here are dialectical progressions."

Wes handed the Llama a sheet of paper which read:

1. What you have just seen is an illusion
2. What I have just told you is true and untrue
3. Meaning lies in the juxtaposition of elements.

EXAMPLE: Your wife has left you. "What is the context?" "Was she with you when you lived together?"

"Were your genetics similar, your upbringing, value systems, and lifestyle?"

The Llama didn't like Wes' simplification of Denotational

dialectic. He resolved to gently inform him later to use examples the Llama had developed that were in the mainframe computer.

"Let me see your model for the drive-in centers," the Llama said.

The centers were rendered as large silver-metal boxes with one Plexiglas wall raised for an entrance. Inside was a computer confessional booth with a seat and a protruding speaker tube, extendable for the church member. The Llama's logo was subtly apparent on the roof of the center.

Wes was proud of the model. "The metal is almost completely deface-proof. I found an alloy which repels paint."

"It's a useful model. As far as the dialectic for your film, let our computer do the printouts for situation context, prescribed mode of behavior, and time projection. I also feel the brochure should only treat my reclamation centers in passing. The focus is on our aims and benefits for the average, well-adjusted disciple. I also don't want my building floor plans to be common knowledge. The Tibetan Garden is only for the inner circle. Please destroy any mechanicals you made for this brochure. And your posters need to emphasize the relief available for the confused and fragmented personality, with encouragement to come to our centers for a complimentary personality inventory. We are after a revolution of consciousness—the small deaths that knowledge brings, the small victories that leave the self full and integrated.

"'Do you worry about your job?· Your husband/wife/children? The future of our country? Come to the centers with the yellow center strip—the highway of our minds. We help you, in faith, to find your own answers, the ones that live within you but for the awakening. Fear is the cause of alienation and stagnation.' Print 'Denotation' above a picture of a nuclear family in front of their house, their arms around each other. Let me reiterate that Denotation is not for superstition or for those looking for gaps, breaks, or turning points. We are offering a consciousness of process. That is our essence, Wes. You've done well for a beginning."

Wes didn't understand the Llama's ideology, though he knew the man was Uber effective. He took a stab.

"Your poster wants a more intriguing image, perhaps a sci-fi effect — a golden glow surrounding an individual in the center of an alienated crowd?"

"We want to evoke mystery for the sake of demystification."

"You got it," Wes said. "When are the centers opening?"

"City-wide the end of this month."

Wes stared, though used to the Llama's impossible demands. That was his business—fulfilling the impossible. Just the challenge would charge him with new energy. Besides, he had done the legwork. Wasn't Denotation worth any effort? Effort-less, he thought.

"I am confident," the Llama said, "your campaign will be a success. Think of the illusionistic experience of demystification. Your own 'wash'.

Wes reiterated his objective.

"Our campaign opens the first drive-in, take-out church of the Denotation denomination. Absolution analysis done by computer will be offered. We will have a member march and a tithe-in with participating bank machines. A banner in red Gothic letters proclaims: ALL THINGS IN CONTEXT, THE BUILDING BLOCKS OF MITOSIS. DIVERSIFICATION LEADS TO PROGRESS, CHOICE, AND VARIANCE."

"Very good. We will meet next week at the half-way point."

"Very good," echoed Wes, bowing out of the office. Rock bands, television segments, soft-core magazines, the structure of media availability were apparent but exactly what kind of personal commitment might the Llama make? Ideology, no matter how enlightened, was irrelevant without a personal appearance, an interview, a write-up.

"I will do a Profile on the media campaign and give you a source print-out."

Wes left, relieved.

The Llama, feeling fatigued, went into rejuvenation mode. He propped his body against the wall in an upside-down position. He liked the feel of blood in his head.

****

In the editorial cluster, Wayne Niebold ignored new ways

to keep kitchen sponges fresh. Instead, he reminisced about the day he met the Llama. He had been riding a bus, or rather a series of buses, the classified section folded under his arm. He had ridden to several destinations but been unable to depart. The morning had been devastating, even for one with his checkered resume.

Wayne had done secretarial, construction, and gofer jobs. He had sold office supplies door-to-door, hauled cement bags, run errands for a nightclub entrepreneur, and swept up at a small ad agency bucking for a copy job. Each position was all right – at first. After a week, he saw the routine stretching out into the silent horizon of his life. After a month, the repetition caught with frightening impact onto his imagination. Wayne always managed to be fired for being too smart, too slow, too fast, too independent, or too much of a mimic. Unfortunately, unemployment made him claustrophobic.

Tightly, Wayne had held his manila envelope filled with fictional resumes and notepads. He was depressed. That morning, his personal charm had failed, though it was an asset he could have sworn by. He had walked into an office for a sales job he knew he could handle, despite being woefully inexperienced. He had planned an ice-breaker, a handkerchief he would change mid-sleeve to a white cloth bird. He never got the sleeve rolled for his magic trick.

The busy receptionist with her need for crisp summaries had offered him some change. He had tried to explain in gestures. She had called a guard. He passed her the resume for flower arranging, as the guard pointed to a "No Peddlers" sign, escorting him out. Wayne had begun to think maybe his speechlessness was a real handicap. He rode down Broadway on the 104 bus, spelling out in his palm the information on his sales resume. As the bus turned down 57th, Wayne noticed a large, square, Asiatic-looking man, who paused past his stop.

"Are you all right?" the man asked with too kind an expression for Wayne's mood.

"Sure," he gestured in a clumsy, half-hearted way meant to be casual.

The Llama signed, "You are a deaf-mute? "

"Not deaf, retard," Wayne signed, wanting the man to disappear. He despised people who treated him with special consideration.

"Looking for a job?"

"Know anyone hiring the handicapped?" he penned on the small pad he carried in a pocket.

"I'm not interested in disability. What can you do?"

"Anything," Wayne signed sloppily.

"Clarify, if you're serious."

Wayne wrote neatly, "I'M PHYSICALLY STRONG AND AGILE, MENTALLY CLEVER AND ORGANIZED. I WRITE LIKE A DREAM, RETAIN INFORMATION, AND CAN CARRY OUT INSTRUCTIONS WITH

LITTLE EXPLANATION."

The Llama wrote an address on a piece of paper.

"Report to *The Printed World*. If you volunteer, you might be paid with a job. We have a placement program through the Denotational Church."

Wayne was suspicious. He had heard the paper was semi-licit, subsidized by a foreign religious fanatic. The Llama was direct, *The Printed World* is my organ, nothing else. You might want to make it yours."

Wayne threw his classifieds away, along with his undefined suspicions. He received low-rental housing and food in exchange for volunteer hours and the community of followers that was such an integral part of Church activities. In addition, the Llama's techniques had been effective in integrating his thoughts and emotions. Along the way, he had even revived a slumbering knack of belief.

The Llama crossed to the editorial cluster and stood behind Wayne, looking over his shoulder. Wayne waited, pleased at the attention. The Lama's presence exuded a slow, effusive will. He reached with joy as the Llama handed him the Profile on the couple.

"Go to the garage tomorrow and ask for a man called Ray. There's a position open for an attendant. I want you to fill it. Your duties at the paper remain the same. A physical job will balance your cerebral activity. I will need weekly reports on the couple, who run the garage. They are rehabilitated and must not learn your purpose."

Wayne wrote on his pad, "CHECK. DO YOU THINK I SHOULD RUN THE PIGEON DROP STORY?"

"I will consider it," the Llama said, unsure about this reference. Questioningly, Wayne looked up at his impenetrable face.

"Anything else?"

"I am accessible."

After the Llama returned to his office, Wayne considered preservatives for artificial sponges that rotted quickly. The answer came easily: BUY NATURAL SPONGES. THOUGH MORE EXPENSIVE, THEY HAVE GREATER RESILIENCY AND BREAK DOWN LESS OFFENSIVELY. LET THE OTHERS ROT.

Chapter 4

THE PIGEON DROP

It was mildly drizzling. The AG stood by the East River watching a seemingly opaque sky. Actually, the clouds made innumerable formations. A stray jogger made a draft on her back. The AG didn't care. She was opening herself to the obscure pagan forces she believed to run the events of nature if not man. Her offering was for the safety of her Anarchist. Seething, he shuffled between the restaurant and the shop. Asleep, he'd grind his teeth, desperately wrapping his arms around her with constrained cries. Sandy would use his unrest. She would provide an event, some momentary promise of realization. Would he bend? The AG paused at the edge of a dock on the Upper East Side, wanting an answer, hoping he loved her more than a little. A tugboat chugged raggedly by. Its motor needs revving, she thought, ready for the trek home.

Wayne Niebold was also staring out onto the East River. He stood on the top floor of a pigeon-hole parking lot. The garage, run by a rehabilitated couple, was part of the Denotational Church. Wayne was taking stock of his "life situation". He pulled two notebooks from his jacket. The first, a "conversational" notebook, held the pages Wayne ripped for notes when sign language wasn't sufficient. The second was his life situation, chronicled constantly so he could forget about it on a daily basis. He looked over a half page he had written a week or so ago.

> I am a youth worker with the Denotational Church. I am a salaried garage attendant and a watch dog for the Llama and write "Helpful Hints" in *The Printed World.* I hope for a paid staff journalist job, retaining my column. Meantime, the managers of the garage make me uneasy. Can't say what, their routines are so repetitive, boring, I thought I had it down. But I missed the variation.

Wayne flipped to a page from his first week.

> PROCEDURES:
>
> 1. The lift is a red-painted box with a grille on the floor. It's mobilized by two metal cables wound on cylinders. It moves in either horizontal or vertical directions. Spaces were drawn ontologically by a Japanese engineer. The cars are driven inside a ruled box area painted on the ground floor.
>
> The lift sends out searching rods which lock under the wheels, drawing the car by the belly into the lift. I mate the cars to the lift and levitate them to the pigeonholes, pushing the levers. It's

> a pleasant ride, the earth recedes. I feel slightly ecstatic. The whole thing seems to me subtly sexual. It's probably because I'm 21 and still peaking sexually. I hope to be happily ascetic by 36.

(Wayne crossed out the last lines. He had "lost purpose in process," a Denotational sin. He flipped further back to the passages he had been ignoring, because Thursday still defined his insides.)

> It's the kind of chill morning that makes your blood run cold. I decided to embrace it. The river was choppy, the sky gray, business calm. I looked across the roof at a new, single-dwelling apartment house, the Dauphine Arms. Fleurs de Lise are on a billboard. The construction process was interesting; death, birth, filler. The fly ridden, swampy lot became a shanty town of catwalks and scaffolding. Poured cement pueblos grew and were molded to octagons with tinted, slit windows.
>
> The process was spare and modern. It's something I aspire to. I can complicate any task until it is an awesome project. The parking procedure in a pigeon-hole lot is very geometric. It takes a lot of precise notation, especially since my mind retains nothing but impressions...

(Impatient, Wayne skimmed on). That afternoon he had

been struggling with ways an old, peeling bathtub could be rejuvenated. The research had been technical. He cautioned against a mere cleanser and spray paint approach, since the paint would gunk up in spots and peel off. He had composed the copy in what he hoped was an amusing, zippy style:

"If it's time to re-enamel that unsightly bathtub, don't take the easy way out! Why spray-can it when, with a little more effort and less money, you can do a better job. Sand it yourself using several grades of..."

That was as far as he got. Wayne's distraction was in the next paragraph:

I am high in the lift here. Visual stimuli make it hard to concentrate. Rooftops sprout water tanks high on stilts, orange girder constructs, triangular elevator shafts, rock gardens, skylights and chimneys. Pools of water from faulty drainage systems burble. Vinyl bubble gardens seethe with vegetation.

Despite the drizzle, two men take turns lifting weights. One bends his leg at the knee, leaning forward onto his soles. His feet are spread masterfully. He grips the silver bar and hoists it onto his waist. His arms shake before a smooth swing over his head. He stands and faces his enthusiastically clapping friend. Before reversing the process, he pauses, triumph on every muscle, as though to say—I rule these buildings.

The man's white sweat socks, the silver pole—all the studied sensuality astound me. I wonder about sex in the city, its primal aim and current uses. Business seems a virile thing. Virility is big business. There was another note under a certain windshield today.

(Wayne put a red asterisk in the margin of the next section. It contained a reason he had been neglecting his reports.)

The car is a Citroën. The model is blandly beautiful, with an all-over tan, a well maintained perm, and a contorted soul. She said her name was Thursday, for the day I met her. She likes regularity in her sexual partners. The note is always the same: "5:00 IF YOU CAN. DOORMAN WAITING... THURSDAY."

> She has long, fine bones and eyes a refractory blue. Her fingers are the only unselfconscious part of her. Thursday had been a landscape painter at an exclusive Seven Sisters school. She had loved to contemplate the structure of a line. She had transposed this into a professional life. She exercised the line of her leg. Instead of mixing paint for a flawless shade, she groomed her tan.
>
> The last afternoon I'd seen her, she'd been haunted. When she took a drag of a thin cigarette, her lips half-rejected the filer. As she smoked, she'd stop at points, as if rooted by self-revelation:
>
> "It's odd being an object, know what I mean? Before I was a maker of an external object, now I'm in someone's commercial. Clichés aside, I am well-conceived but it's strange, being the girl in the ad. I've got to get out of this business."

> I went to her like a healer. My hand admired the curve from shoulder to breast. Her eyes softened a little, "You see, the money's good and I don't draw anymore..."
>
> I traced her cheek, loving the color gradation. My kiss showed compassion for her commercial sacrifice. You see, Thursday was a perfectionist. I always understood the part of her body she was most displeased with.
>
> I made this my center, righting the wrong she had done herself. It was an odd affair. She was "schizzy" I speculated (having never known a real schizophrenic) how a "wash" might dent her mindset. I mentioned the Denotational Church in passing to her. She let it pass. I did what I could..."

Between Thursday and the bathtub, Wayne hadn't been paying much attention to the managers of the garage, Ray and Zeke.

In all fairness, Wayne took notes. For instance, once a week, at precisely eleven A.M., they went through a ritual so familiar, he had mouthed the words along with them; unseen from his perch in the lift.

> ZEKE: I can't help being a criminal. I'm a genetic throwback to my great-grandad who fished the gutters for his fortune. He found a garment business. My dad ran it and then there's

me, back in the gutter.

RAY: What about evolution? You're third generation.

ZEKE: I'm a throwback. You can't deny history. (kiss) What about the Pigeon Drop?

Wayne knew from reading their Profiles that this ritual grew out of perversely reciprocal needs. Ray grew up in foster homes which severely punished behavior more than passive. Zeke was raised amid too tolerant affluence.

Their ritual was some twisted test of constancy. She would admonish him denotationally, "Actions bring consequences." He would reply, "You take them for me," reaffirming his freedom of choice.

For some reason, that morning, Zeke had said, "Damn the consequences."

Wayne, long bored with their routine missed it. He was busy juggling their cars. He was also noting his mistake, the infatuation that caused a serious failure of duty.

"The day was slow. Most of the pigeonholes were empty, so precision was not so important. A Fiat drove in. I should have started at the bottom and placed it laterally. I didn't feel like it and clamped, levitating into an upper right hand cubicle. The transaction was easy and gave me

> some time to enjoy the roof.
>
> The men were gone and Thursday had banished the bathtub from my thoughts. The Llama would consider her a negative pattern. I didn't even know her real name. The doorman let me in, and at first she always acted as though I was a stranger. It was stupid. I looked down the street for some diversion..."

The half page was unfinished. Wayne closed the book, remembering what had happened.

Ray, carrying a Swiss Air bag, ran out of the garage and frantically accosted an elderly woman. Ray had linked her arm in the woman's and walked her up the street out of Wayne's view.

Was she the young lady from the 'Pigeon Drop' article or was the odd newswire story haunting his imagination? On paper it didn't make sense – a nonobjective scam with an improvised closure. The perfect form for Ray and Zeke. But he was an attendant at the garage, a watchdog for the Llama.

He was not supposed to compromise his dual functions under any circumstances. He dismissed the incident until the next morning when Zeke teased Ray.

Bending his arms at the elbows, he flapped like a bird — pursing his lips in a round C-shaped coo. Then he smashed the fist of one hand into the palm of the other. Ray, upset, left the office before their customary exchange.

Wayne's rationalization didn't help him accept the fact that he had not followed Ray and the woman up the street. In fact, he had no definite idea of what had happened. He was derelict in his duty.

Today would be decisive. He looked at his watch and realized it was close to eleven. Wayne took a last look over the tranquil river. Something metallic caught his eye. He went down a few levels in the lift and saw the AG's silver suit.

"Extraterrestrial" crossed Wayne's mind before he saw her face, fifty feet below. He tried to think of an adjective besides "dazzling", which wasn't quite right. "Penetrating" implied an analytical element. "Wonder" combined with the others might be appropriate. She waved to Wayne, all excitement, indicating the pigeonhole lot.

Why, Wayne wondered, is she fascinated by the neatly aligned cars in this giant auto-mat — this brainchild of the egg crate. Had she never seen one before? Or was this some kind of odd come-on?

Wayne levitated downward, answering a vibration on the cord of the lift. The girl's face, growing nearer, was completely transfixed. As though she were viewing a supreme triumph of an ancient civilization, Wayne thought. He was intrigued.

When Ray entered the lift, Wayne knew something had taken place. Opposing emotions made havoc of her simple features. She shrugged her lower back into a small arch, her arms floating buoyantly to her sides. Wayne recognized this gesture of female capitulation and worried. He had seen the same gesture for years in restaurants, cabs, on dance floors. After the lift hit the ground, he followed her to the ladies' room signing: WHAT IS THE MATTER? Ray smiled and rumpled his hair, as if she thought he was asking a different question.

Through a small window, he watched her wash her face, brush ingénue bangs, apply a dash of lip gloss. She changed to a well-cut gray suit, and hauled a bulky leather bag onto her left shoulder. Stenciled on the side was Wayne's confirmation of his suspicions: SWISS AIR in red and white.

The AG was in the same spot. Several dogs watched her watch the lot. Ray brushed past Wayne and headed straight for her target. Wayne was paralyzed by ambiguity. His desired role in the event was less than clear. He thought of a theory, which held that 3D images were stored in memory on 2D structures similar to holograms. Maybe the waking mind, like the sleeping mind, pulled accurate images from memory and placed them in unfamiliar contexts. Maybe cause and effect was nothing but an interesting category for understanding— the same way chronological order gave meaning to the reports he filed for the Llama. Otherwise, weren't his notes mere images out of context?

Such abstract reasoning had little to do with decision-making. It only served to increase Wayne's anxiety and put him in danger of "fragmentation". What, Wayne wondered, was a mere recorder for the Llama doing in a criminal activity? There was, he realized, a difference between the Llama's and his own job description. He would have to satisfy both The girl's welfare and an accurate report were his responsibility.

Pulling his notebook from his jacket, Wayne wrote that the "Pigeon" wore a silver suit, purple suede boots, and a gold hairnet. No matter how Ray attempted to divert her attention, she remained glued to the parking lot.

Ray unzipped the Swiss Air Bag and showed the girl a pile of money. She wasn't interested. Ray scooped a few bills but the face that met hers was more than blank. Something else was present Wayne could not describe. From his viewpoint, under the garage, he could see two women in profile. two mouths shaped words. Ray's small, pointed features were molded in urgency, "The money! I found the bag. Two thousand just on top! I've got to get back to my boss. Can I leave the bag with you, while I get the police and call the office?"

"OH!" the girl said, rounding her word, but continuing to watch the lot.

"What is so fascinating about that parking lot!"

"It's so many things," said the girl, looking at Ray, who found herself avoiding eye contact.

"It might be a shoe rack for giants, housing units for an alien race..." the girl broke off, her gaze resting on Ray's little finger.

Ray involuntarily hid her finger, "Do you think I can deposit the bag in your account for safekeeping. Just give me a thousand for it?"

"There isn't a thousand in there," said the girl, acting as if the bag were transparent.

"Maybe we could go to your apartment and count it exactly. I could call my boss too."

"But that's far. I live on the Bowery," the girl said.

> Leave, Wayne thought, but instead she put her arm around Ray and suggested they call her boss from a payphone. He could meet them at the bank. That way Ray would have company on her way to the police.

Wayne shut his book, some people have to be protected from themselves, he thought. He trailed the two women up the street, hidden in the crowd of attentive dogs. Despite his commitment to the Llama to remain a spectator, he would protect the blonde girl. He would not be ineffectual.

Past the fifth phone booth, Wayne thought of his various deficiencies. Because of these, authorities had placed him in slow classes in grade school. Later, when he had proven advanced for his age, he was placed in accelerated studies. He discovered both the marginally retarded and the advanced had a sensibility in common. They took a considerable time to register the impact of an event but they rarely forgot it.

The girl's lack of comprehension must be the result of one group or the other. Whether brilliant or an idiot, she was choosy about her phone booths.

At the sixth booth, Ray stopped, saying she'd only be a few minutes. The girl nodded, scouring the high rises with the same absorbed look she had fixed on the pigeonhole lot. Wayne signed "hello" to Ray in front of the booth.

Ray was bad at hand signals but she made it very clear Wayne was to go away. He loitered, unsure of how to approach the girl yet convinced it was necessary.

"If you want to make a call," the girl said, "she'll only be a few minutes."

"What's your name?"

"AG."

"Is that a family name?"

"I guess you could say that."

The phone rang. Ray talked nervously. Wayne watched the AG pet the dogs. She was very fair. Each one in turn received the same amount of affection. He tried to follow Ray's lips behind the glass.

" Zeke, she's really nice and not very smart. She lives on the Bowery and I don't know about any cash on hand. She suggested her bank so she must have something."

Ray let the phone dangle and opened a crack. "My boss will hold the 1,000, while the police search for the owner. If they don't find him, we split the sum in the bag. We go to your bank, first, deposit the bag, and get the money. What do you think?"

Wayne held up a paper: ARE YOU GOING TO BE MUCH LONGER?

Ray was hostile: FIND ANOTHER BOOTH! I'LL WAIT AND TAKE THE CONSEQUENCES

Before Wayne could finish the message, the AG looked up from a black and white terrier. "Don't make him wait for the phone. I don't care about money. But, if you need an exchange, we can trade the bag at my bank."

"If you don't mind my asking, do you have a savings account? "

"Yes, a small one. "

"Great!" Ray said, picking up the dangling receiver. "I'll give you the bag for deposit and you can write me a check for the grand. After the bank counts the rest, you can let me know the balance. I'll trust you."

"I said we could deposit it but there's not that much in my account."

"How much?"

"Five dollars."

"Are you kidding? What the hell do you do for a living?"

"I'm a go-go dancer and," she blushed modestly, "I also design clothes, though I don't make much money on them."

The dogs had lined up. Ray and Wayne watched with wonder, as the AG carefully removed minute glass chips from the first one's paw.

"It doesn't matter much? The center of the bag is hollow,

anyway. It's just an empty shoebox with bills padded on the sides and top. There's tickertape below that."

"How do you know!"

"It's not hard to focus your attention," said the AG, examining the dog's paw.

"What a fool I am!"

The AG kindly objected, "Not at all. You're a decent person. You just have criminal tendencies." She paused to wipe the dog's paw with a tissue and some liquid from an antiseptic smelling bottle. "Your little finger is unusually small. In fact, it's undersized by a quarter of an inch and curves around the ring finger to hide in the soft Apollo mound. You're very easily influenced by love and beauty and, perhaps I shouldn't say it…" The AG broke off, sensitively replacing the paw on the sidewalk.

"What?"

"You're very easily manipulated. It's your thumb. It's small and not at all firm. That's your character. The clubbed end on the right one is an atavistic sign."

"Excuse me?"

"Not too evolved. You're gifted at deceit. You're not, I'm afraid, a poor girl who's unexpectedly found a fortune," said the AG politely.

"You're from the Church," Ray began defensively, "some sneaky test."

Wayne signaled NO, fuelling Ray's suspicions.

"She's a friend of yours and you're both from the Church!" Ray backed into the booth and picked up the dangling phone.

Wayne put his arms around the AG and turned her, pointing in the opposite direction and mouthed the word RUN.

The AG ignored his instruction and began to treat the next dog in line. Ray opened the door of the booth.

She mouthed the word TRAITOR to Wayne.

"I guess all this is a terrible experience for you," the AG said to Ray.

"Here, take the bag," Ray said. "I don't think you want to meet my boss. "

Ray had come to her conscience! Wayne felt very relieved. The AG seemed mildly confused.

"Your boss? Oh, you mean the man in the glass office above the parking lot. He's assembling a rifle. It's got a long lens. He's enjoying himself. I guess he hasn't done this for a long time."

"My God!" Ray said. "Get out of here, please!"

The AG, unconcerned, separated a painful burr from a mutt's belly.

" I'm in it," she said gently. "I can't disconnect from the flow of events."

While the AG checked the hindquarters of a Doberman, Wayne and Ray exchanged helpless looks. They had become allies.

"Don't you know this is a dangerous situation?" Ray asked the girl.

Wayne wrote WE WILL RUN TO THE CORNER MISS AG.

Ray, the bag on her arm, sped off into the distance, thinking the girl would follow. The AG held a finger in the air before the crowd of infatuated dogs. She turned it thumbs down on the sidewalk. The dogs retreated across the street, not crossing the spot she had marked.

Wayne found the girl's death wish hard to believe. She didn't seem a martyr, yet she knowingly chanced her confused captors. Not cold killers, they were nonetheless lethal. Maybe she believed some "good", some tangible will, would assert itself?

Random response, he wanted to say, can be another form of evil. He had no time to sign. The AG waved at the exact spot, where the window of the office would be. It was as if she knew the black pinpoint of the rifle was trained on her. The lens might have been her eyes.

High up in the office of the parking lot, Zeke was out of control. Rehab had not muted the violence of his fear of discovery. Wayne was a watchdog, whose report could be argued. But if the AG lived, the Llama would know all. Zeke pulled his finger back, but...at that moment...he was inconveniently flooded with a memory of the coral mouth and round eyes of a cardboard Christmas angel he had once received as a "Secret Santa" present in grade school. He fell in love again with the angel in the AG's face — understanding, forgiving. The Denotational homily: LOOK TO YOUR IMPULSES. IF EVERYTHING SAYS YES, DO IT. IF NOT, DON'T. COROLLARY— YOU DO KNOW WHAT

YOU'RE DOING came to Zeke's cloudy mind. The AG had tentatively fine hair. Zeke didn't want to touch it but he was afraid of prison, of losing the garage, of losing Ray, of losing...

A second before the shot, Wayne embraced the AG in a flying leap. The AG skinned her cheek on the cement. The bullet ricocheted off two bulletproof windows in the new apartments across the street, lodging in a third of cheaper glass. The AG emerged from under Wayne. She stood, brushing off her suit. Wayne pulled her down, too stunned to sign, but not to write: YOU'RE A BIT ODD. STAY DOWN UNTIL WE KNOW THERE'S NO MORE SHOTS.

The AG got up again, fearlessly smiling at the man in the pigeonhole lot. Wayne tensed for another shot. It didn't come. Ray must, he reasoned, have gotten to Zeke. A light rain sounded. The AG tilted her face up, seeming to enjoy the feel of it. Wayne handed her his pad. DO ME A FAVOR. WHEN YOU LEAVE, DON'T TALK TO STRANGERS. NO MATTER WHAT THE LINE.

The AG smiled, shaping her words so that Wayne could see

with little trouble.

"Thank you for saving my life. I'll try to return the favor sometime. If you see your friend, tell her there's a quick-change item I sew for people in her profession. If she's interested, she can find me walking on the Bowery most mornings."

Wayne, awed by her zany equilibrium, watched the AG cross the street to her dogs. He penned his last note for the garage owners:

I'M FROM THE CHURCH. THIS INCIDENT WILL BE FEATURED IN MY REPORT TO THE LLAMA. THIS IS MY LAST DAY AS ATTENDANT. FOR ANY NECESSARY COMMUNICATION, REACH ME AT *THE PRINTED WORLD*.

Wayne knew the message would not be news. He left the sidewalk, furious he hadn't found a way to head off the incident. If he hadn't been so preoccupied with Thursday, so bored with the garage work, he might have discovered the scam earlier.

Back on the lift, prepared to confront Zeke and Ray, Wayne looked on the city below him. With some astonishment, he noticed the "miracle" making her way with her dogs. She looked up at the garage, toward him, (he was positive) for one long moment. Then she divided her crowd of dogs into four groups – gesturing north, south, east, west. The dogs dispersed and she made her solitary way down the East River Drive.

Wayne was left with innumerable questions. Who was she?

Why had she so willingly accepted her role in the incident? Were they bound together in some inexplicable way? Had the Llama some knowledge of her and the scam? He would like some clarity. The Pigeon Drop was, he realized, a scam which depended on coincidence. It was unpredictable, since it lacked logic. He, Wayne Niebold, had done the best he could.

Intoxicated with this idea, Wayne made a note to confirm it denotationally, if possible. In the meantime, he looked at the world around him with open eyes.

The rain had stopped. The sun was setting. Along with the rainbow, it seemed a double bonus. He felt, pleasantly, not a shadow of a fear.

Chapter 5

REINDOCTRINATION

It was after five o'clock at *The Printed World.* Wayne Niebold, thinking of substitutes for expensive fireplace tools, was the sole inhabitant of the editorial cluster. A metal rod underneath his foot was set to vibrate with the buzzer of the elevator but he had forgotten all about that. He wasn't prepared for the elevator, creaking to the second floor of the Chelsea loft.

Inside were Ray and Zeke. Zeke was scared. He felt for Ray's hand. She gave it, withdrew hers, then sought him. It was she who knocked on the metal door, dropping Zeke's hand. She didn't want them to appear like guilty children. When no one answered the door, she panicked — anticipating another sleepless night before facing the Llama's anger. Luckily, she remembered the buzzer.

Wayne felt the annoying vibration, moved his foot and then recalled the elevator. He shuffled over the polished wooden floor to the window of the elevator and the penitent faces of his former employers.

"Is he in?"

Wayne brought them back to the Llama's office and disappeared to his cluster. He had made no signs of outward recognition. He wanted no further interaction with the pair. His report was filed with little doubt, he had acted in good conscience.

The Llama's door was open. His back looked immense. His voice, Ray thought, was more impassive than ever. It made her nervous.

"Come in," the Llama said, gesturing Ray and Zeke to the studio chairs across from his desk. "Wayne told me the outlines," he began sorrowfully. "For one thing, I'm very disappointed. For another, I'm disgusted. You have not lived up to the promise of your Profiles."

"It's my fault, sir," Ray interrupted. "I have not guided Zeke properly and he is prey to his desires."

"I am not a Christian, Ray," said the Llama," I do not believe the flesh is weak. On the contrary, it is the greatest strength we have. Nor are you weak but resignation has been a problem for you. BELIEVE IN YOUR OWN PROPAGANDA is an important tenet you seem to have forgotten."

"It's comforting to feel helpless," Ray recited. "You don't have to be responsible. But paralysis of the heart leads to fragmentation of the mind only Denotation can mend."

"Ray, I know you love Zeke, but it gets in the way, doesn't it? That is why I'm making you responsible for the garage, during the time Zeke undergoes reindoctrination."

The Llama opened a Profile folder on his desk. "You, Zeke, have gone from a marginal malingerer to chronic, completely controlled by your worst instincts. Despite the love of Ray, a job with potential and extensive reeducation, your character is totally fragmented. There is but one option left, the denotational corrections program.

"You sent someone to spy, because you expected me to be scamming. You never trusted me and I like to fulfill expectations."

"You were on probation," interrupted the Llama. "You cracked. If this wash is ineffective, you will not return to the garage. In the meantime, Ray will manage the operation and help you reintegrate later— if we see some plausible unity in your character. Since you have abused your authority, she assumes it. Under review, of course, since she did not prevent your actions. She does not seek authority, why this is appropriate."

Zeke nodded, though unsatisfied about Wayne. "Is that guy, your receptionist, on the premises?"

"Ray," the Llama continued, "you will work on floor plans for inner strengths. I expect you to write up your blueprints, after Denotational work. You must analyze the impulses behind your actions, delve into their origins and devise a correctional plan. I know it's hard for you. But your counselor will lay the foundation. Would you like to volunteer information about that?"

"You know my struggle. I have problems with Zeke and

find it easier to take the path of least resistance."

"YOU ARE YOUR GREATEST ASSET — have you Forgotten? You are too severe. It was partly your intervention that saved the girl."

Ray smiled for the first time, "Maybe that and her crazy ESP."

"Recognize the sabotaging impulses. But build on the positive, even heroic." The Llama smiled kindly.

Zeke eagerly injected, "Before I go into the state where I know nothing, I would like to tell you the odd projection I had on the girl."

"Yes?"

"She looked like a face on a Christmas card I got as a kid."

The Llama turned a half-inch toward Zeke.

"Truth, confirmed by your own technique. I reviewed the image and what had provoked it and traced back the original source. Both images related, though from two different contexts. When I pulled the trigger back, I paused to consider the image might have come from my subconscious to advise me against my action. But I was afraid she would expose me if she lived. She looked just like that angel. She made eye contact through a telescopic lens two hundred feet aboveground."

The Llama turned a full profile, thinking that Zeke had never been particularly imaginative. He faced Ray. "Can you corroborate her otherworldly character?"

"She reads hands and there's the dogs. A crowd of dogs swarmed around her. She treated them medically and she..."

"She saw where my lens was pointed. She looked at it."

The Llama turned a half-inch away from Zeke. "Let Ray finish."

"She said I had a weak thumb, that I was very easily influenced by love. She was right. I should have been stronger."

"It seems you did all right," the Llama smiled. "Wayne threw himself on top of her."

"Yes, but you allowed her to escape. That was a pretty definite stand. A dramatic commitment to your ideals," the Llama said, raising a brow. "That was the right thing to do, and you did not hesitate. Unity of character and purpose. What we strive for, Ray."

Zeke proudly kissed Ray, "You could have been killed."

"By you!"

"Tell him off," the Llama said.

Ray sighed, "It's the foster home biz. I've never been secure enough to tell off someone I love."

"Do it anyway. Zeke, don't reject her! But first, tell me what you think of me."

"I hate goddamn religious fanatics."

"Fine but I'm not that."

"I hate goddamn reformers."

" I'm not that, either."

"What are you?"

"Myself," the Llama said. "You're the fanatic and the reformer. YOU ARE YOUR BEHAVIOR."

As the Llama went through the familiar dialectic, he considered the enigma of the AG. Was she fearless, oblivious or both? Maybe the kind of naive individual animals reacted instinctually to. That kind of magnetism coupled with a pop-occult understanding of character could be formidable. In any case, she was a fortunate girl to have provoked a pause in Zeke's pathology.

"What was your projection on the girl, again?"

"She looked like an angel on my fourth grade Christmas card. How could I knock off an angel?"

"Your pause was a positive impulse."

The Llama walked to the window in order to steady his trembling hands, away from Ray and Zeke. He did not consider himself a suggestible man. The palsy was the reaction of a pragmatic soul to otherworldliness. His vision did not include the AG. Her very existence threatened the cornerstone of his life's purpose. Somewhere he hoped she did possess paranormal qualities. The hope went unacknowledged. It would mean self-sabotage.

"Zeke, you will report to the center today." Zeke lingered.

"Llama?"

"Yes?"

"She was highly unusual."

The Llama's fingers closed tightly over the edge of the windowsill. Though he wouldn't acknowledge it, he had hypothesized the existence of a being he termed a "clairvoyant dreamer". He ignored his desire for belief in such a being, assuming it derived from a human sense of personal limitation. But, Wayne's report had revived his inner fascination. SOMETHING IS NOT TRUE JUST BECAUSE YOU THINK IT IS. BUT IF TWO OF YOU, UNCONVINCED BY THE OTHER, UNKNOWING COME TO THE SAME BELIEF FROM A DIFFERENT BACKGROUND AND BLOOD TYPE, IT MIGHT BE A MUTUAL DELUSION. HAVE A THIRD, UNINFORMED, INVESTIGATE AND CATALOGUE THE BEHAVIOR. IT MIGHT BE NOTHING WITHOUT YOUR PERSONAL INVESTITURE.

Following this Denotational process, the Llama decided to assign Wayne to tail the girl. He would review that information and then—what? Maybe he could be of use to her? The possible historic -religious import (if she were a clairvoyant dreamer) brought back his palsy. He renounced this fantastic vanity. Shifting his thought to the concrete reality of his new Drive-In Denotation centers, he spoke benignly to Zeke and Ray.

"I appreciate your coming here. It took much common

sense."

Ray and Zeke moved toward the elevator with the relieved air of guilty defendants having received mercy—a just sentence. The Llama followed. He gave Zeke the password and address for the reindoctrination center and crossed to the editorial cluster.

Wayne Niebold had just discovered that an extended whisk broom, spray painted black, would make a fine fireplace implement. The Llama's hand on his shoulder sent a small shock through his body. The urgency with which he wrote on Wayne's lined pad was totally unexpected.

> WAYNE, ALL WE KNOW ABOUT THE AG IS THAT SHE WALKS ON THE BOWERY MORNINGS. I WANT TO KNOW MORE. IT MAY BE IMPORTANT.

Wayne took the pencil and answered, I'LL START AT THE BOWERY—SOAK UP THE COLOR. The Llama took the pencil from Wayne and leaned heavily on the desk so Wayne could see his seriousness about the project.

"I'm expecting something special in a clairvoyant way — a childish, naïve somnambulist. Her walk should be distinctive."

Wayne wrote WHAT DO I DO ONCE I LOCATE HER?

"Benign surveillance. Where she goes, what she does, who she sees. Also, help Ray with the garage, until Zeke returns."

I DON'T THINK I'LL HAVE TIME FOR BOTH PROJ-

ECTS, Wayne wrote, gambling which was more important. The Llama's silent disapproval made him regret his nerve.

CHECK, Wayne wrote agreement, expecting the Llama to leave. No movement. Surprised, Wayne made eye contact with the impenetrable face.

YES? he wrote.

> FORGET THE GARAGE. LET ME KNOW EVERYTHING ABOUT THE AG. ALSO, I WILL BE ACCESSIBLE.

Wayne forgot the fire tools and the garage. Happily, in his mind's eye, he saw his new assignment — the AG's open face, more than blank.

****

On the Upper West Side, between Amsterdam and Columbus, was the Llama's inner city villa. Except for corner wraparound apartments, it appeared a solid block of symmetrical brownstone houses. But walls for the living units had been removed. Large meeting chambers, small antechambers, and special rooms branched from a square corridor surrounding the center of the complex.

Hidden by a floor-to-ceiling brick wall, this center housed the Tibetan Garden, a site often used for "washes".

The garden had many rocks, a few shrubs, and several steep cliffs. The temperatures were maintained by an opaque plastic bubble. The climate exactly duplicated the weather conditions during the Llama's retreat.

Zeke did not remember the existence of this garden. In fact, he remembered very little about his previous "wash" so he rang the doorbell of the brownstone without apprehension. He had tried various methods of disorientation and felt the Llama's must be the best – an incredibly peaceful slumber of the senses, before he regeared to his usual manic machinations. The "wash" was a test to his genes, mental stamina, the whole history of his stock. His cranium must have thick walls, he thought. The early patterns had stuck. He wouldn't be permanently affected, just a little forgetful.

Zeke, as well as the Llama, thought he understood the effects of the "wash." What they didn't know was that each time, after the final "bliss-out", thought processes became simplified, solidified, and more dangerously brutal. The Llama thought he was breaking down thought structure for reindoctrination readiness. In a spiritual sense, he thought the "wash" provided the transcendence which criminals sought through crime. Both Zeke and the Llama were way off.

Zeke inspected the brownstone with a distinct sense of déjà vu. The marble steps were clean enough to show veins, the drapes were creaseless. A blonde woman in jeans came to the door with a dust cloth in her hand. She seemed vaguely annoyed. "May I help you? "

"I'm Mr. La Fourchette. Are you familiar with *The Printed World*?"

The woman smiled. "Come in, Zeke, I'm Elinor. We have something for you."

The voice didn't click in Zeke's memory until he saw her profile. Her name had been Jean the last time and she had been a redhead. A "diffused personality," she had cheerfully told him, had been the reason she had been a drug addict. "Diffused" meant she had an amorphous personality, not the same as a multiple, she had explained. Zeke hadn't believed her story. She seemed a pretty self-confident disciple for that.

Today, the story seemed plausible as Elinor took him through her apartment. Her bedroom was part of the dining room; her kitchen was half the living room. She had many restored antiques, a quaint Sears' Oriental, and a Deco clock. They walked through the eat-in kitchen to a cupboard wall, where she pressed a latch and a bell.

A smiling man in jeans greeted them from the other side.

"Elly! Keeping the home fires burning?"

"Sure thing, Ralph. When you get a break, come over for some java."

The man patted her arm affectionately before unlatching the cupboard for Zeke.

"This device may seem silly but we believe hokum has a function in all good security systems. What's familiar seems homey and safe."

"No argument here," Zeke said, more interested in the label on the man's jeans. They bore the Llama's insignia embroidered in multi colored threads. Zeke hadn't known the Church had diversified.

They walked down a black and white tiled corridor. Greek columns scarcely disguised a brick wall seven feet high. What was hidden behind it, he wondered, taking a right angle to a low-ceilinged door.

Ralph swung it open. "You should have everything you need."

The room was a perfect replica of a high-end motel room. The bed lamp was stainless steel. The desk counter was a white plastic "butcher's block". The rug was paramecium-patterned and very plush. The bed was a double. Zeke took off his shoes and turned on the television set. He lay on the bed. The wedge-shaped cushion perfectly propped his head. Zeke thought, "This is choice!"

On the TV was a 3D bucolic scene leased from Disney studios especially for religious programming. A tall shepherd in a Bible school toga rested wearily on his crook, watching an iridescent sunset. Sheep jumped over a rail, filling a small corral. A halo formed off the sunset around the shepherd, as the Llama's voice droned:

Home is where the heart is.

You are my guest, make yourself at home and forget Hey yahh you are all mah friend, howdy.

We're right glad to see ya! Come on now, forget Your troubles and get happy, we're gonna chase

All your cares away...sing hallelujah, the Lord is happy ...

The last hallelujah floated into a translated Buddhist chant:

"Glory to, victory to, the light within ... HOOOOMM-MEEE ... "

Zeke could sleep through anything. He dreamed of Ray, just out of the shower toweled dry and tan. It was familiar sex, except for the background of 3D mountains. They gave way to the East Side garage office, his rifle, and the AG — not in his sights but underneath him.

Zeke's muscles began to ache. He woke up, tense in a dark room filled with HOOMMEE. He threw the pillow wedge at the TV. It glanced off. He walked the length of the room, stopping at a row of creaseless curtains. He pulled the cord onto a seven foot brick wall.

Windows but no view. Damn, it wasn't like he didn't know it was a set-up. Zeke stood still, his feet twelve inches apart. He breathed deeply, watching the TV. The shepherd was in shadow, sleeping on his side under a very starry night. Above his head the lead star twinkled, then each smaller one in turn. Zeke's breathing became shallow. How could it work, he thought, a lot of 3D kiddy stuff? Zeke went back to bed. He fell asleep soothed, despite himself, by the word HOOMMEE...

Ralph checked the PRELIMINARY LINE on Zeke's chart and wrote in his progress:

> THE SUBJECT RESPONDED POSITIVELY TO LIGHT BOMBARDMENT OF CHILDHOOD RELIGIOUS ICONOGRAPHY AND ESOTERIC VERBAL REF-

ERENCES. RESULTANT BLISS-OUT AS EXPECTED.

Ralph decided this would be a smooth "Wash".

Zeke awoke to a starry night on the TV. He was naked on a moonscape. It was not a dream. He could tell by some loose pebbles embedded in his arm. He scraped them off and shivered, letting his eyes adjust to the dim light. It was damned cold and quiet. Somewhere in front of him, he could discern what looked like a patch of low grass. On his way to it, he stumbled into a puddle of something dark and sticky. The stuff tasted ominously salty. He crawled onto the patch and wiped it off his limbs, looking once at the dome of his environment. He guessed correctly that the stars were artificial. They were, in fact, pre-molded plastic protrusions filled with a permanent blue-white bulb. Zeke felt relieved about being in an artificial environment. It was a reminder, after all, that this was a controlled experience.

Immediately, the stars brightened and meshed into a painful white light. Squinting, Zeke saw the grass was an ochre carpet streaked with something like blood. On the carpet was his gun — in pieces. Next to it was a small religious card of a blonde angel. Zeke looked at the puddle with some fear. If they were trying to create a trauma, this wasn't a bad idea ... no! It wasn't blood, he decided, crumpling the card. He knew he hadn't killed her. "Almost" didn't count. Zeke assembled the rifle and waited for he knew not what. A slow, repetitive murmur, increasing in volume, put him on edge.

DEED AND INTENT, DEED AND INTENT ARE THE SAME!

Zeke stood with his feet twelve inches apart and tried some Tai Chi he used to take his mind off his environment. It was a long time since the exercise was fashionable, his adolescence in the late 1960s. Still, Zeke remembered enough to dim the relentless tape, until he felt a bullet graze his hip—then another. Zeke fumbled to aim his gun at something on that plastic dome. His eyes ached with the light. Another bullet whizzed by him and he realized they could kill him. Like another institution, the Church might have decided he wasn't worth the trouble...

DEED AND INTENT, DEED AND INTENT...

"NO!" Zeke shouted, shooting in all directions, "NO! I didn't kill her!" He emptied his rifle and fumbled on the carpet for bullets. He wanted to shoot out the machine—the tape. RAT-A-TAT-TAT... Zeke mashed himself under the carpet, away from machinegun fire. He could die. He tried to think of Ray and found he could only connect the name to the outline of a tan body and a beach towel. A commercial memory?

Shots... canned laughter. Blanks, Zeke thought, before a real one rang close to his head. The tape continued until Zeke knew not if it were off; he heard it inside his mind. Then he crawled out of the carpet. He lay on the top fetal-like and waited for the bullet that would conclude his life. They whizzed around him but none found a target. Was every other one real? Two in three? Naked and cold, he thought of Ray for comfort. Her name was comfort. Sex and death, deed and intent....

Ralph and other Denotational members looked through the Dome's telescopes at Zeke. When his fear of death peaked, he would be emptied of deviate behavioral patterns and achieve a critical "bliss-out". This would lead to the birth of a primary conscience. Ralph watched Zeke curl up on the carpet and pushed the button for the time-controlled tape. On Zeke's chart, he checked a line reading SUBSEQUENT ACTION. On it, he wrote: SITUATION CONTEXT HAS RECREATED THE SAME RANDOM TERRORISM INFLICTED BY THE SUBJECT ON THE INNOCENT PARTY.

Sustained physical terror and repetitive mental bombardment were the elements for the critical secondary "bliss-out." Ralph showed Zeke's chart to the two technicians in the control tower. They read reports of Zeke's progress into a teletype whose centralized memory was transmitted to the Llama's office. Then Ralph and the technicians retired for the night. Though each wash retained its unique procedure, the time sequences were infinitely predictable.

Zeke did not know if he was dead or alive. Had he killed the angel on the card? He couldn't recall, though prison was a memory he treasured in comparison to this hell. He had never experienced anything as terrifying as this field of fire; bullets true or false, real or blank ... DEED AND INTENT, DEED AND INTENT ... the tape buzzed inside him, filling everything. Zeke felt nothing but the sounds and then a catatonic state for an indefinite time. A light from converging stars opened his skull, pouring empty consciousness through him. Worse than death, he thought, was there a God?

A man with a flashlight opened a door vacuum-sealed from the inside.

"Time's up, Zeke. You killed her and your time is up."

Though unsure of his own name, Zeke knew it was true. He picked up the crumpled card on the carpet and tearfully unbent it. He followed Ralph into the pathway, ecstatically kneeling and kissing the black and white tile. He could not move from the spot where he knew he had walked before... alive.

Ralph placed Zeke's stiff legs into cotton material. Zeke followed him down the hall, mistaking Doric columns for heavenly hosts. Ralph left him at another low-ceilinged door. It opened inward.

Inside was a gray interrogation room with a requisite dangling light bulb. Five men sat in shirtsleeves around a rectangular table, looking hard at Zeke. Each harangued with the same speech loud and continuous. The voice-pitch of the men was an exact duplicate of his first interrogation before prison. The difference was the subject matter. Rather than merely deriding his character, this harangue involved Zeke's rationalizations for antisocial behavior, breaking them down one by one.

"Why do you, Zeke La Fourchette, insist on your convenient idea of heredity? You have stagnated the evolutionary process. Your genetic chromosomes contain no hostile 'X'—you have created the extra one. Why, Zeke? What are you?"

After each man had finished, a new harangue began. "Do you believe in man, government, rule of the universe, that you are a good man, a bad man, a disciple of the Llama?"

Zeke had tuned out faces—his own foreign-sounding name — voices were small pinpricks disturbing his floating self. The frequency doubled. His focus anxiously widened. Eyes, mouths, hands on a long table waiting to obliterate him. There was no escape—the LLAMA!

"Okay, Zeke, what's it going to be? Your circulatory system is functioning. You are alive."

One of the men took a large, thick book and threw it on the desk in front of him. It hit loudly and slid several inches into his chest.

"It's a phone book, Zeke. You have to dial every number and say you're sorry."

Zeke opened the book. The pages were blank. The men seemed amused.

"The Llama? Can I call...?"

A man rose paper in hand, as if sentencing Zeke. "What you have been through is an illusion. What

we've told you is true and untrue. Meaning lies in the juxtaposition of elements. Truth is always in context and it is up to you to frame that context. In other words, you're going in for life."

The man held a card which read: SITUATION CONTEXT EVALUATION. You will be required to fill this out, study and memorize the content. Examinations will follow.

The lights went out as a screen descended over the long table. A training film entitled AS WE ARE filled the total length of the tiny screen. A balding man with glasses sat in an office performing a desk-job for an unnamed company. He's a diligent man, a sincere believer in the work ethic, especially because he is divorced and managing the expenses of two households. He's laid off from his job, finds his skills are outmoded.

Faced with narrowing alternatives and overwhelming responsibilities, he becomes depressed. He can't see the consequences of any course in a positive light. His identity fragmented, without his occupation, he almost opts for death, but accidentally sees an ad in *The Printed World.* The ad elaborates on the free Denotational Counseling available at the new Denotation Centers. He goes to the Center, where a friendly, attractive woman counselor begins a Profile with the information he gives her about his life. The screen became filled with a SITUATION CONTEXT EVALUATION form to be used in conjunction with the Profile.

SITUATION CONTEXT EVALUATION

Problem perception=
List Alternatives

For each alternative listed predict:

Consequences

1.

2.

3.

For each alternative listed assign value of happiness produced

1. +++

2. —

3. +

Select Alternative with highest value for happiness=

The Denotationally Correct Choice is

Method is ineffective if:

(1) Subject is unable to predict consequences

(2) Subject is unable to access the problem

(3) Subject is unable to estimate happiness value.

The subject in the film is suffering FRAGMENTATION, his counselor explains. Fragmentation is the opposite of DIVERSITY, which is based on a unified personality. Diverse thinking is essential for creatively evaluating any situation context. She cheerily opens the man's PROFILE and shows him all the alternatives that may exist for him, based on his experience, potentialities, and interests. They busily fill out the form and then she waits until he has selected his alternative with the highest value for happiness. (The man decides to become self-employed and seeks a court order for his first wife to go to work while he continues his child-support payments) The counselor then hands the man a loose-leaf notebook filled with potential clients he can call on in his field.

All the lists in the notebook, she explains, are contacts pledged to aid Denotational Church members realize their assigned happiness value. The man is so moved, he shouts, "I have family again!" before the screen leaves him for mottos: DENOTATION REMOVES DEPRESSION. ALL THINGS IN CONTEXT, THE BUILDING BLOCKS OF MITOSIS. DIVERSIFICATION LEADS TO PROGRESS, CHOICE, AND VARIANCE. A voice over says, "Denotation is a blueprint for those who live."

Film off, lights on and Zeke faces the man, who had previously "sentenced" him. He jokes, "You like psychology? We do not reinforce the laziness of low self-images. We don't believe in 'bad luck', since Denotation incorporates the random element of nature. You have total responsibility for your life. How do you feel?"

"Absent," Zeke said, incapable of lying.

"Jail is the waste of time you fear the most. That's why you're always reliving it. You set up situations that demand sentencing. We are changing your blueprint. This is all history and it never repeats itself in the same form."

Zeke is handed a pile of books.

"You are required to read this material and report on it so a Context Evaluation can be relevant to you."

In Zeke's pile was a copy of the Origin of the Species, Mendell's bean experiments, and a manila envelope marked "La Fourchette". Zeke opened the envelope. Inside was a pleasant pen and ink drawing of his family tree three generations back. It identified the occupations of progenitors, excluding the ones he had chosen as his forerunners in crime.

Zeke's identity had been dissolved, but his personality reasserted itself. He had never heard of these relatives. "My family's my business. You can make-up as many trees as you like. I know who my relatives are and I never heard of these."

The men nodded to each other. The third one picked up the chart and wrote: NEGATIVE PERSONALITY REASSERTION.

The fourth man smiled pleasantly.

"You always say it's in your genes, so we've given you a new tree. As the Llama says, "Know thy illness. This is a management course tailored for your needs."

"Take me as I am."

The fourth pressed a button for Ralph and a hidden tape. The third man wrote: IDENTITY FORMATION IN DANGER. PERSONALITY REASSERTION IS CREATING A "SELF" IN-OPPOSITION.

With no resistance, Zeke fled down the corridor looking for an exit. People smiled in various rooms, glimpsing (as Zeke did not) Ralph behind him.

Ralph carried a tray with several wrapped packages, one of

which bore the word SLEEPYTIME.

Hearing Ralph's soft steps scurrying behind, Zeke attacked. He threw Ralph against a Greek pillar and the brick wall. But Ralph was well-trained. With a sharp blow, he warded off an attempted hammerlock. Zeke crashed into the wall, barely breathing and very bruised. Ralph pulled the SLEEPYTIME wrapper off the plastic hypodermic and reluctantly injected Zeke. He had been sure this "wash" would be smooth but repeat cases could be more difficult. He had misjudged Zeke's readiness for reindoctrination.

There is a pleasant subdivision of the Tibetan Garden, which the Llama created as a concession to his American origin. It has a lawn of well-trimmed grass. On the lawn, formed with marigolds, mums, or roses depending on the season, was the Llama's logo.

Zeke woke up on this lawn, groggy. By his side was a straw basket filled with bright blue paper. Zeke read the wrapper inside the paper: BOUNTY OF THE LLAMA. The hamburger inside tasted delicious. Zeke ate lazily and stretched out on the lawn, grateful for the warm sun. Somehow the logo on the lawn seemed synonymous with success. Whatever he had done was forgiven.

Outside the subdivision to the Tibetan Garden, Ralph observed. He filled in the few remaining lines on the chart:

> Medium success. Suspect backlash from over wash, this being the subject's third experience. Reindoctrination readiness, after personality

> reassertion, was chemically induced. Suggest permanent supervision for subject after reindoctrination

Zeke, feeling cheerful, was glad to hear Ralph's "HI!" from the brick archway. He remembered they had fought but couldn't imagine what about. Weren't they both members of the Church? Weren't they both recipients of its bounty?

Zeke followed Ralph out of the garden with many questions about the Reindoctrination Center. "How long have you been in the Llama's inner circle? How are the 'washes' planned? What position do you hold in the organization?"

Ralph laughed. "Everyone's 'wash' is a custom job. I don't remember much about mine but I know I enjoyed it as much as you. Besides my work here at the center, I have a rug cleaning franchise. I demonstrate rug shampooing techniques for the home. Our shop rents out the equipment at a pretty good price."

Ralph led Zeke back to the motel room, which had been altered to that of a dormitory room in a junior college. The TV was gone, replaced by a brown corkboard hung on the wall. The white butcher block table was also replaced by a Formica-topped desk. An electric typewriter and several notepads were on top. Maroon linoleum gleamed without the rug. The bed was a single. Above it was a poster of the Llama and a pendant with his logo. Over the desk were snapshots of Ray and one of the garage.

Zeke lay down on the bed, uncertain what was expected.

An exam? Zeke hated, envied, and feared intellectuals. He had always been a "closet reader", garnering half-understood ideas to back his own desires. He lay for a day, ignoring the Profile and books on his desk, wishing for the simple justice of jail. There you knew how much time you had to do. The absence of a calendar was conspicuous.

Every day Eleanor left his food on a tray. Once a week, she changed his linen. She also hushed him with an inspirational motto. Zeke was restless, the bliss-out from the garden had worn off. He pretended indifference to her remarks but made a list of them:

LOVE IS THE ANSWER IF YOU
HAVE NO QUESTION.

THE WAY OF THE WORLD IS
THE WAY OF NO FLESH

TWO AND TWO MAKE FOUR IF YOU
DON'T USE A BINARY SYSTEM

A STITCH IN TIME MAKES
A SAILOR'S KNOT

AN OLD SHOE HAS NO LAST

YOU CAN TEACH AN OLD
DOG OLD TRICKS

A WORM TURNS IN WARM SOIL

DUTY IS IN THE EYES OF THE BEHOLDER

THE LLAMA KNOWS NOTHING

Zeke supplied the answers in the complimentary Denotational catechism:

QUESTIONS ARE STUPID, LOVE LIKE
LIFE SHOULD BE ACCEPTED

THE WORLD IS SIMPLE,
PEOPLE COMPLICATE IT

WE ARE ON EARTH FOR THE DURATION OF OUR BODIES

WE CAN APPLY LOGIC FOR SENSE.

A STURDY LIFE HAS MEANING.

DISCARD OLD STUPIDITIES

YOU CAN BE YOUNG, IF
YOU THINK FERTILE.

HE WHO LIVES RIGHT IS HAPPY.

ZEKE CAN DO ANYTHING,
BUT IMPRISONS HIMSELF

The Llama, he thought, knows everything. Where had the answers come from? Eleanor's suggestion had helped them emerge, miraculously from his consciousness. Zeke felt happy and accomplished. Life was perfect after all. His subconscious held all the answers. If the exam was constructed on the Denotational mindset, he had no worries! Confidently, he opened his Profile to the appropriate mottos and catchwords for his life's course. The erring logic of his genetic argument was readily apparent. If he believed it, substitution was the preferable course.

In the manila folder, he found an uncle who had been a surveyor and a Yankee businessman in North Carolina. Pondering this personage, the old Zeke reasserted himself. "A carpetbagger!" he interpreted, halting this thought with a truism: AS THE WORM TURNS SO HE LIES. Knowing he needed work, Zeke opened the Origin of the Species, leaving his predilection for pop psychology behind.

Zeke's exam consisted of a computer print-out with 250 blank spaces. He was to write the correct Denotational questions in each one. Zeke, understanding the way they would build, passed, though a playful image slowed down his test score. The missing link to his former self was a broad, hairy man with the vested suit of a Yankee dude. His tilted straw hat shaded his ape face from the sun. He pulled out his pocket watch, admiring the inscription: fourteen carat.

Chapter 6

WAYNE'S ASSIGNMENT (EXCERPT FROM HIS JOURNAL)

The Llama believes a bad home is responsible for much criminal behavior. So he houses his people in good neighborhoods with subsidized rents. Some live in a converted hotel on Broadway in the '80s, some in a town outside Nyack, some share a complex on the East Side with former mental patients and others pair off for small attached houses in Yonkers. I, Wayne Niebold, sublet illegally in the West Village. I'm supposed to be the tenant's brother. In the sense of Denotational logic, I guess I am (by self-evident fact).

It's an apartment a man can live up to. It's on the sixth floor. One of my neighbors grows tomatoes. Another has a stucco-Venus on his terrace. I have my desk in the middle of my room surrounded by concentric circles of crumpled paper. No two contortions are the same. The outer circles are filled with blue lined yellow paper, the middle ones contain blue lined white paper, and the inner ones are plain bond. They represent the stages of my thinking – from inkling to idea. I mark the stages by color to keep them clear.

I turned on the hum of my typewriter for a fast tempo.

I wanted to clarify my thinking on the AG before setting out on the Llama's crazy assignment. I mean the Llama is fantastic. He teaches discipline, independence, patience, religious awe and business savvy. I respect his motive, but sometimes his procedures seem a little off base. Why undercover tailing of the AG when we've already met? I could learn more by asking for an interview and feel a lot less sneaky. It would definitely have simplified my task. I had little to go on. What did the Llama want to know and why? I needed focus. By Denotational ethics ("Meanings are always in context"), I knew I'd have to invent one. I started with my yellow notes on the Pigeon Drop: A SHORT, BLONDE GIRL WITH A TURNED-UP NOSE, AN UNCONSCIOUSLY SENSUAL STRIDE....

I crumpled this, remembering it had been written from fifty feet above when I saw something. I uncrumpled and read on: TO SAY THE AG IS DISORIENTED WOULD BE MISLEADING. DETACHED IS NOT RIGHT EITHER. SHE SEEMS AWARE, LIKE PLANTS, CHILDREN OR OTHER MINDLESS SPIRITS...

I recrumpled, assigning that paper to the outermost ring. Maybe she was a catatonic "Bliss-Out", the product of too many drugs or just a bit slow? (I doubted both of these). Maybe a victimizable innocent (this seemed fairly certain) with latent survival capacities. What was the mysterious protective device she possessed? It was more than luck. Her emotional directness, her very lack of confusion indicated a person very conscious of herself and her surroundings. Yet by her walk, I wondered how she did not bump into walls.

I read a white note: ABSENT, BUT TUNED-IN. That description and OTHER-WORLDLY were the keynotes the Llama had selected from my oral report. Searching for insight, I rested my eyes on the second-hand astronomy chart I had taped to my wall. The planet Uranus took on a new significance. It was related to eccentricity. She had looked like a sci-fi dream; silver suit, purple boots, gold metallic scarf and underneath it, the face of a blonde madonna. There was also her strangely light tentative walk and that trail of devoted dogs. I would make that walk my focus. I had studied some the psychological implications of stances and movements. To succeed as a shadow, I would need to recall this training. How far I had strayed from the Spartan teachings of Mr. Robbie; a militant mime, who taught an extension course in a continuing education program.

Robbie didn't use white face. He looked like a biker, wore studded black leather armbands, pants low on the hips and shirts high on the midriff. He had unwashed Prince Valiant hair on a pale muscular neck. Robbie came from Indiana, studied in Paris, and used his body as a point of contention for a Nietzschesque-Calvinist philosophy of art. He wanted to learn how to "sign", so he didn't charge me. It became an apprenticeship when no other students materialized. Robbie taught courage, as well as action, a unique educational experience. His movement lingo, the studied gestures of mime, was a medium for urban survival.

I met him at his rented loft for the first lesson. We were

locked out. He gestured to an invisible audience, "I seem to have misplaced the key!" The door had a pane less square window the size of a man's fist. He put his own through it, hoisting his body up the door. Long, snake-like, and lean, dead weight on his flexing arm. Upper and lower arm followed the fist through the square window. The left shoulder blade fitted through the opening. He collapsed his chest and the right shoulder blade followed. A graceful swoop and his head disappeared, then waist, pelvis, legs. I was left starring at a set of Herculean toes. I heard the door unlock and the thump of a handstand.

"If you need any other credentials," he said after this contortionist act, "they're taped on the wall."

I wondered what Robbie would think now, years later, of his former pupil. Besides the Llama, he had been my only mentor on survival. I well remember his introductory lecture.

"You need muscles, Wayne, especially if you're slight. Lifting an invisible object, you must feel the same strain as the real load. You will, if imagined correctly, develop the muscles as if the real object existed. You must be in perfect condition to live in society. Muscular readiness is the key to mental adjustment and vice versa. You never know what your imagination will call upon you to do."

A glimpse in my mirror confirmed what I suspected, a thin nervous guy way out of shape. Still, the superficials were all right for a shadow. I was nondescript. My Keds were classic.

The pinstripe shirt and straight denims were versatile. My close haircut could pass for nostalgic. I rolled my pants legs mid-calf, the shirtsleeves mid-arm. I smudged some ink under my eyes and made a cowlick with peanut oil. I beat up a manila envelope, adding some obscene figures. I wrote "Times Square Express" in the middle with marker. I tried to invent a walk for the Bowery, but was way out of practice.

With imaginative effort and muscular recall, I rehearsed Robbie's basic MOVES. I practiced dividing my chest muscles from my pelvic muscles. I revolved my limbs in their sockets. I broke down sequences into separate actions. In this way, I rehearsed the way a thing was picked up, how a surface was sensed and the shapes of objects. I learned to open doors invisibly and be unobservable while loitering. I could disappear very quickly. Robbie used mime technique as a subtle weapon. For a handicapped person, as I thought of myself at the time, it made me feel more than equal. Self-consciousness was transformed into a sixth sense.

My graduation piece was "A Subway Door". I had to externalize the environment inside a subway car and its motion. I entered the car, making my body a sidestepping pencil in a crowd (my hands were forced tightly against my sides). Tensely I gripped the floor, my feet several inches apart, and swayed with the motion of the car. When it stopped, I squeezed in to allow people to leave the car. I even grabbed the rubber edge of the closing door, so others could enter without being slammed.

The weight of the closing doors was an amazing strain. My

muscles shook as, Samson-like, I held them back before being crushed into a vertical line. Mustering additional strength, I hurled them apart and inched into the car and my original pencil stance. Grappling, I obtained a strap at the second stop. But the door opened I was expelled onto my face by the departing crowd.

Robbie leapt from a standing to sitting position, cross-legged on the floor.

"Fantastic! You see what you have learned?" Skeptical, I signed, "I DON'T UNDERSTAND."

From a split, he achieved a vertical position, and then a natural stance. "This was your walk," he said, walking thrust forward, his body forming a diagonal from head to toes. After a few paces, the angle began to straighten out. He seemed newly aware of his feet meeting the surface—how gravity strained his torso. The light, sensitive walk, the vertical stance, was what I had achieved.

"You are no longer leading with your head," Robbie said. "You must continue the warm-ups if you want to retain the orientation. The trick is to make the idiom a second skin and leave your mind free."

I had been sensitive enough to design walks for different parts of Manhattan. Great camouflage. I recalled my "St. Mark's Walk" and checked my mirror to see how it read. I emphasized my natural diagonal into a sullen slouch—centered by the heels with a pelvic dynamic. It wasn't bad. "Make the idiom a second skin and keep your mind free." Robbie's words gave me courage for my assignment.

I headed for the LL line, figuring to transfer to the Lex down to Astor Place. I practiced my walk in the tunnel, running an electronic tune through my system. It had a tense beat, my back ached. But it was the right feeling. A kid veered to my end of the tunnel, pulled something from his jacket and lunged at my chest. I bounced back from the wall, ready. He laughed, opening his bare hand. "Good reflexes, man."

After that, I resumed my old walk. It wouldn't do to practice in public tunnels. I wasn't ready yet. There were too many things to pay attention to. Since my internal conditioning with the Llama, I had only applied my sensory apparatus for sexual pleasure. Robbie, being an ascetic, wouldn't approve of that usage.

I came onto the platform at Astor Place and looked around. There was a ceramic tile in the shape of a beaver chewing a log. Upstairs, there was a black cube sculpture decorated by art students. Across from the cube was a parking lot and next to that, a prestigious off-Broadway theatre. I noted an old man leaning on a cane in front of the parking lot. I was too obvious. He called that he was down on his luck and would I give him a quarter? I doubted his line. His clothes looked too good. I picked up my St. Mark's walk, and he ignored me, soliciting other passersby. His grin altered slightly when an old hippie strolled over, picked him up by his collar, and said, "Hi, pops."

I was thinking of dropping my "cool" to help, when I saw

the old man pull out a five and mouth the words, "Earwick on the first." The hippie put the guy down, passed a paper, and left. The old man leaned on his cane, stashing it among a roll of bills. He noticed me, still across the street, and decided to give me another chance.

"Spare a quarter?"

I made the traditional deaf-mute signal and he immediately lost interest. I wondered if he was a simple bookie. Who knew about scams in the city? So many layers; scams for fun and/or profit, scams without object. In the East Village they seemed more on the surface. The slick fate of the West Village hadn't totally pushed them subterranean. Still, rents had gone up, stores took credit cards and matrons were visible among the runaways and sellers of badly-cut dope. I was watching this playtime in front of the St. Mark's baths when I saw the AG.

It was 4 P.M. when the dreamy blonde crossed to Cooper Square. She was dressed Rangerette style; white boots with pom-poms, a red satin cowgirl mini and vest, a silver belt, and a gray pull-string hat. One cur, a yellowish thing, followed her. I fell in line, pausing at a music store to offset any suspicions. The racks of sheet music were exhaustive. I waited five minutes before following her into Phoebe's restaurant on the Bowery. The dog waited outside.

I ordered a coke from an alcove, where she couldn't see me. I watched and waited, drinking in some local color.

Mostly black and henna red across from me. I noted a black

camera case, a zip portfolio, an off-the-shoulder T-shirt, and a man's skinny tie. One wore Helenca nylon stretch pants, the other a turquoise circle skirt. Both had burr haircuts and faces about twenty. Art students, I figured and smiled internally—unnoticed. They were discussing the sadomasochistic imagery of a Times Square peepshow. They decided it expressed a societal death wish, thus anti-woman in content. The one on the right was very pretty. Her lipstick glowed. She lit a cigarette. Her nails were the same hot pink.

Through the plate-glass, I could see the flop next door. A masturbator on the steps decided to make contact with the girls. His face, pressed against the glass, was distorted. The girl on the right shrugged to her friend, "What can you do? It's a natural outgrowth of gentrification."

I took a peek at the AG, sipping a coke at the edge of her chair. Her body was perfectly aligned, elbows directly above her knees. Her fingers tapped rhythmically on the tabletop. I noted the sequence before her eyes suddenly lost focus and her hand relaxed. A fit, I thought, wondering if she was epileptic. But no, she recovered as fast as· she had succumbed. She left Phoebe's and I kept her in sight through the plate glass window. Maintaining my disguise, I abstractly sketched a light fixture on a notepad. It was black enamel and only half-shielded a blue-white bulb.

A Mayflower truck pulled over at Bowery and Fourth. The door fell open. The driver fell out of the cab, writhing on the cement. Two people tried to lift the insensible driver. A waiter ran out of Phoebe's with what appeared to be a

#2 yellow pencil. All were stopped by words from the AG. Honking cars were directed by the two people around the driver. A cool white hand removed the pencil before it could dangerously be chomped in two. She put the waiter to keep the crowd at bay and kept him in her sights as…That same cool hand deposited a dime in the payphone over my head.

I went to the men's room to see her roundly shape the words, "Come to Phoebe's, Bowery and Fourth. A man is hurt, having a seizure. He may need some attention. Emergency, yes, he's having convulsions."

I returned, avoiding eye contact. Besides my orders to conceal my identity, I couldn't bear the profound worry in hers. The AG's genuine concern illuminated my own lack of feeling. Because of her fabulous eyes, I had been indifferent to the man's agony in the street. I had only watched him, looking for her. The Church says: CONSCIENCE IS EMBODIED IN A VICTIM'S PLIGHT — NOT THE CRIMINAL'S MIND. I felt both in that moment, unable to do anything but watch. Without a doubt, I suffered a paralyzing infatuation.

The traffic was backing up along the Bowery, as the waiter returned to work. The AG hung her hat on a parking meter and began to direct traffic. Cars slowed for her smooth, upraised palm. Unquestioningly, they navigated in accordance with her beckoning hand. Her arms sliced with total authority. I noted with asterisks her face, body, outfit, and actions—all beyond exclamation.

I paid for my coke as I saw a passing man take over the traffic. An oil truck refused to move. Was the driver, I wondered, as struck by the AG?

The crowd around the Mayflower driver now included two overly curious St. Bernards, a woman with a baby in a stroller, the two art students, the waiter, and myself. The AG mouthed that epileptics needed room to breathe and people moved away. She eased fears about his swallowing his tongue (only if he was on his back). In fact, the man was passively lying face-down on the cement—now covered with a towel—his convulsions quieted. The AG flagged the ambulance before it turned down Third Street. The doctors lifted him to a sitting position on the curb, checking for broken bones. He regained consciousness, protesting at the doctor's efforts. Reluctantly, he accepted a pill and boarded his Mayflower truck.

"You shouldn't drive," the AG said, timidly offering a remark.

"I could lose my job if there's a report," the man pleaded with the doctors, using the crowd as a witness. The doctors shrugged at his ingratitude and repacked their instruments. One handed the stricken driver a card, while he sat in the cab of his van, radioing a slight delay. The crowd dispelled. It was dusk as the truck barreled up the Bowery.

I spied the white boots and silver blonde hair of the AG on an island. She seemed amused at the traffic moving in two directions around her; carefree, as if it were a toss-up which way she might go. She wrinkled her nose, the delicate tip looking like rubber, then running a hand through her hair, she crossed. I grabbed the cowgirl hat from the parking meter and followed, close as I dared, to the side door of a loft building. It had a slow lock. I caught it, last chance. Abruptly, she entered her loft at the fourth floor landing I rested in the third floor stairwell, professionally pleased I had escaped detection. If quicker, and discovered, the charade would be over.

I was tired of being a shadow. I held the gray felt hat, feeling the soft material, wondering if she had liked me that time at the garage. A bald conceit but I wanted her to know me, trust me; depend on me. I decided to wait for her to come out of her loft, no matter how many hours. She would, eventually, come out.

Chapter 7

THE ANARCHIST'S SEDUCTION

THE LASER EXPERIMENTER'S HANDBOOK - McAleese, Frank, G.

LASER FUNDAMENTALS AND APPLICATION - Muncheryan, M.

THE LASER - Smith, William Vick

The Anarchist folded a paper with the above titles and put it in the same pocket which held a crumpled newspaper clipping. He had taken a sick day at the restaurant to do his research at the 42nd Street library. He found what he needed.

The Anarchist took the RR subway and got out at Broadway and 8th Street. He walked up 8th. It was a dark block. Smack in the middle, huddled in doorways, various Bowery musicians and suburban kids fresh from the rec-rooms played differing kinds of jazz. Saxophones crooked on thighs, tender trombones on arms, trumpets arched in the air — this was an ancient spot, a decade at least, of musicians on the rise and decline.

A player caught the Anarchist's eye. He was good. He had on a huge overcoat, '30s or '40s depression line with a slouch hat to match. The hatband was wide, the sleeves almost long enough to hide a pair of small, black hands. Square-nailed fingers pressed the keys—the mouth of the horn thrust open to the sky.

The weather was muggy, the street broken up. People poured out of the subways tired from work. The tune was not sweet but insistent. It moodily pierced the atmosphere. The Anarchist liked it. He dipped into his pocket, scrounging for a bill. The trumpeter coolly accepted it with one hand, playing on with the other. The Anarchist wanted to see his face. He lifted the hat.

Her hair was in a wild bun. She was black, fresh-faced about seventeen. Her cheek dimpled in a smile. She grabbed the hat back saying, "Thanks," mid-note. Another breath and she faced the wall, replacing the angle of her hat. Then she faced the street again, an old musician on the bum. For one quick moment, the Anarchist stole eye-contact. Sweet girl-eyes upturned in some private ecstasy, soon hidden by the hat's descent.

The Anarchist felt embarrassed about violating the black girl's public privacy. She made him think of the impenetrable mystery that was all women, especially the AG. It was a good topic for the evening. The air was close. The rattle of the train underneath him a sensual cry in the growing night.

From the third floor landing of the loft, Wayne felt the vibration of the Anarchist's lumbering climb. He hid, not wanting to provoke a possible outbreak of violent temper.

The discovery of strange people in one's home could be threatening. Wayne noted on his pad:

> He looks a sad, martyred type, perhaps a Scandinavian with a taste for tragedy. His red hair, black suit, green and orange scarf are worn like banners. I wonder what his relationship is to the AG.

The AG did not know Wayne was outside, though she knew she had been followed by a man. She made some tea, wondering what kind.

The Anarchist was thirsty.

"Ah, a spot of tea on a damp day, and you to pour it," he said, circling her waist. "Darlin' babe, you're much too good for a drudge like me."

"Oh, stop it."

"No, I'm serious. You'll be stepping over my body, shuddering for the man you used to know."

The AG took his face between her hands. "You won't remember me?"

The Anarchist unbuttoned his black jacket. "You are sweet."

She poured the tea. "You will not wind up anywhere, but where you choose."

"What worries me is what I choose. What I've chosen."

"Don't torture yourself! You've chosen by heart and not by

circumstances. You're true to your nature. What's wrong with that?"

The Anarchist rested his forehead in her hair. "My heart has no brains and that's the truth of it."

While they drank, the AG imagined the club and what she might need to bring. The fringe on her costume had torn and she would have to fix it.

The Anarchist thought of leaving her, but decided she would find him. Better for her if he could make her go. But how? He loved her too much to act unkind.

"I'm going early to patch my costume. Will you be working in the shop?" the AG asked, changing into a camouflage body stocking that took its color from the walls. He raised his empty cup in affirmation. He was thinking of the list of materials he would need to actualize the crude diagram he had clipped from the Times.

The AG picked up her bag as he asked, "Will Joe see you home?"

"Sure."

"Call if he can't. He might be sick or..."

"Yes?"

"Give him my regards. He's a decent fellow."

The AG, concerned, paused at the door unseen by the Anarchist. Manically, he ran his fingers through his hair, openly anxious now that she had left.

As the AG descended the staircase, Wayne saw another woman pass. She was about the same height as the AG but more solidly built with short, brown hair. She wore an army surplus pea coat, olive fatigue pants and red circular glasses. She was not pretty yet she had good posture and (he noted)… A KIND OF ARROGANCE THAT MIGHT BE TAKEN AS A CHALLENGE.

"Aren't you early, AG?" the woman said.

"I'm doing some patching. And you, Sandy?"

"Just a bite before the swing shift."

Wayne decided to first contact the AG, then return and observe her roommates. Damn journalistic objectivity and the Llama and his obtuse motivations. He would expose himself. Wayne sped up to catch the AG on the street. She was waiting.

He was nervous. He scribbled on his notepad and handed it to her with a pencil stub.

MY NAME IS WAYNE NIEBOLD

She replied, WHY HAVE YOU BEEN FOLLOWING ME?

(Because I love you, he wanted to write) IT'S MY JOB.

WHY?

Wayne couldn't answer for the Llama. He scribbled what sounded plausible.

I'M DOING A STORY FOR *THE PRINTED WORLD*. YOU WERE A VICTIM OF THE NOTORIOUS PIGEON DROP SCAM.

HOW ARE THE COUPLE DOING? DIDN'T YOU WORK THERE?

UNDERCOVER. THEY HAVE BEEN APPREHENDED.

"Oh," the AG said, thinking how cute Wayne was, but how tiresome to pass the pad. She let him keep it, after writing YOU ARE A DEAF-MUTE?

Wayne signed, YES and she smiled sympathetically, making certain she was facing him.

YOU WORK GO-GO, DESIGN CLOTHES, AND HANG OUT ON THE BOWERY. ARE YOU MARRIED?

"No. I live with the Anarchist and Sandy."

That explains the black suit, Wayne thought, lettering WHERE DO YOU WORK?

"Joe's Place in Brooklyn."

CAN I MEET YOU THERE, LATER?

'It is open to the public..." I UNDERSTAND

The AG blushed. "It's just that it's a really dumb act." THAT WOULD SUIT ME FINE.

The AG blushed harder. "I mean stupid, really. I'm not insensitive." She scribbled, TAKE THE D TRAIN TO

PEARL STREET. I MUST GO NOW.

Wayne waved, astounded at his luck. He found it hard to believe that she had consented to meet a perfect stranger. This was York City! Was it because he was a deaf=mute and "safe"? No, he decided, watching the AG emulsify into the green-tiled subway tunnel. She would not think in that fashion. Did her camouflage suit really create an illusion?

Wayne thought of the AG's epilepsy simulation in Phoebe's. Had she precognitively experienced the driver's disease? Or, was her "fit" some esoteric relaxation exercise? Coincidence of appearance or precognition, she had communicated an emotional state in a direct non-verbal way. That fact greatly intrigued him

Beyond mere infatuation, he thought. On stage, in a public forum, would he feel that same wave of comprehension?

Lifting the silver suit, Sandy had felt a traitor to the AG. Why did the suit tick off such a moral response? It smelled of Burberry, a scent Sandy recognized but couldn't identify. She resented such tugs, tagging them preconscious and dismissing them from her psyche. But now, standing outside the Anarchist's shop, she simply felt scared. Her deception was more than a performance piece. The suit was tight. Sandy unzipped it to the waist. That would be sufficient. Like most fanatics, the Anarchist was ideologically nearsighted.

Wayne Niebold, gathering information about the loft, saw a light in the basement from a ground-level window. He flipped his pad to a clean page and copied a slogan he could make out on a buff poster: THE POPE IS YOU. THE POPE ABDICATES RESPONSIBILITY FOR THE MASSES —

Committee for Internal Anarchy. The organization didn't register. He checked the opposite wall, where a group of yellowish posters were taped. One looked familiar. It showed an overflowing cornucopia in shades of brown and orange. He could not see the motto but he stopped trying. Neither he nor the Anarchist could believe the evidence of their eyes.

The naked magi! An image from an art reproduction stood in the doorway of the Anarchist's print shop. The AG's hair was wrapped in a gold-flecked turban. Her shoulders were squarer, her neck less delicate than the Anarchist recalled. It was also unlike her to be so dramatic. He put his arms around her. Her naked back against the front of his flannel shirt was very exciting. His hands travelled inside the suit, below the zipper's end.

"AG!"

"I couldn't stay away."

This surprised him. The AG never came to the shop uninvited. Perhaps, she also felt the bareness of their lives apart. He kissed her mouth, newly aware of how dependent he was on her for his tenuous happiness. It was an oddly objectified kiss. What was the matter? He opened his eyes in horror. Those looking into his were hazel, Sandy's. He pulled the turban off. Out fell Sandy's razor cut, spiked hair.

If the Anarchist was appalled, so was she. She had forgotten political manipulation in desire. Perversely, she would have to fight the feeling to achieve the same result. Political passion must be egoless. She dissolved the dichotomy with an appropriate visualization. She substituted an image from her schoolgirl catechism for an erotic image of the Anarchist. She saw a golden statue of St. Teresa clinging to an arrow through her breast.

Who would have thought they looked so much alike, thought the tortured Anarchist. He had cherished an ideal of spiritual love but the mere suggestion of clothes and he didn't know the difference! He wanted to shake Sandy but he was afraid to touch her. He now knew he had a problem with nuances.

"Joke's over," said the Anarchist. "It just goes to show how unobservant I am."

"It only shows not just how alike two women can be, but two people, a man and a woman. We're both aliens, aren't we?"

Sandy walked around the shop. The Anarchist found himself powerless to stop her. She paused at a postcard. He felt violated, it was a personal item.

"BOMBS AWAY*?* Is that a kitschy '50s catch-phrase?

I wouldn't have taken you for a nostalgia-collector."

"Sandy, get out."

Sandy sat on the bed of the multilith, her suit still purposefully unzipped.

"I need a collaborator for a planned political event. I want your membership list from Food for Vendettas. I also need your incendiary knowledge, organizational ability and moral support. I know you're interested."

"You're being thrown out."

"You care about your posters. You like doing them, but is it enough for you to spend your life and hers for?"

"I can't have this conversation with you."

"You would only have it with me now," said Sandy, indicating her naked breasts. "You're too embarrassed to throw me out."

The Anarchist had never liked or trusted Sandy. Still he had long contemplated an act of desperation. Such things, could not be spontaneous or poorly planned. News reports about any event were slanted but he could prove that terrorism came from others than deluded fanatics. It would be tricky, working with Sandy. She would have to go with the primitive laser he had chosen. It was his weapon of priority.

The Anarchist threw the crumpled diagram at her. It was a chance. Sandy took it as a form of consent. She zipped the suit down to her knees.

"What?" he asked in extreme perplexity.

"You're an idealist. I need a carnal commitment. Sex to seal the bargain."

"Why?"

“It’s an old device. It works with moral men.”

The Anarchist ground his teeth. He was a prude but how had she known that? Sex was an appetite he felt reluctant and grateful for. With the AG it was fun. What Sandy was referring to scared him like death.

“My word should be enough.”

“I need to temporarily fray your bond with the AG.”

“Impossible! We’re almost one person.”

“That was the point of my demonstration.”

The Anarchist didn’t like being manipulated, no matter how overt the attempt.

“What will I get out of this?” he asked, trying to seize the initiative.

“The notoriety of a true anarchist’s act and a safe escape route for you and the AG to be comfortably reunited afterward.”

‘”What guarantees do you offer?”

“My word,” Sandy said with a sureness that made the Anarchist wonder which of them was more insane. He wanted to be a mere printer and feel ink again.

“What’s the extent of time and damage?” he asked. “Desperate acts have their limits.”

“An event as a two-part act is what we have in mind. My backer has an inevitable source of global disaster, he wants to call attention to. I want an Event, which will add significance to my faceless deportation. My backer will guarantee your escape with the AG to a cottage in the south of France, or anywhere else you prefer. I used that example so you would know that money is not the object."

The act of a lifetime! If he could leave peacefully with the AG. if he had a real home...

With a measure of resignation, the Anarchist knew Sandy had him. His participation in her plot would be a small price to save the AG from the unrealized monster he was becoming.

"Your design is simplistic but it will serve as a token act," he said, planning the laser concession for later.

"It's more a matter of PR," Sandy said, stepping out of the silver suit. She kissed the Anarchist but he pulled away and faced the multilith. The press had a deep, dry bed. He could, he acknowledged, remain uncommitted.

Sandy took his belt out of its loops and carefully rolled it up. She unbuttoned his shirt. She unzipped his pants and placed her hand on his sex. The Anarchist was more than embarrassed. He had never seen a woman fuck with a battle plan. Suddenly, she lay down on the press bed, waiting.

The Anarchist was passive. He had never been unfaithful to the AG. He lay long beside Sandy. It was she who closed around him. Her head fit into his neck. Her knees bent to draw him in. Her exactitude stirred him. He entered her with firm, well-paced movements — the same way he smoothed a poster on the wall. The way she moved with him inside gave him the simple satisfaction of a job well done. Her body, he decided, was just a different kind of glue. A cry escaped her and he felt, unexpectedly, the master. Yet it was not more than a political act. Duty as pleasure had been forged.

The earth outside the loft building was very wet. It took Wayne many minutes to realize he would be very cold. He had been sketching two paths of arrows, which intersected at the multilith. The circuitous routes in the diagram showed enough indecision for Wayne to conjecture they represented a first seduction.

The AG's best friend and lover! Jealousy was probably not in her lexicon. Did she know? Wayne wondered this, visualizing her small form disappearing into the subway. No, he decided, the AG was an unwitting third party. He'd been involved in enough scenes to know. The configurations were not really endless. Despondent, Wayne left the Bowery. He continued to puzzle over the peculiar sexual union.

In the subway, he looked at a cigarette ad peeling off an ad for chewing gum. Half the rugged smile of the former was intact, a man's hand held a pack. The edge of the pack merged into the gum girl's vibrant grin. Refreshing spring water doused the cigarette smoke. Two faces absurdly united; Sandy and the Anarchist. It didn't go. Wayne looked at the other end of the train at an ad for chicken salad filler mix. Unexpectedly, it brought to mind a cornucopia and CLICK... he remembered the "Food for Vendettas" sign. It was painted on a wooden shingle over an East Village co-op he had stumbled upon seeking fresh vegetables. How was the Anarchist connected?

Wayne got off the "D" train at Pearl Street feeling better. He had an angle to field to the AG. He decided to keep her ignorant of the scene he had witnessed. First of all, he wanted to be her friend.

Sandy left the shop for the AG's closet flushed with victory. Fortunately, she had found the part of the Anarchist the AG had not satisfied. Her hand strayed on one of the AG's thin silk gowns. Sandy was struck by the amazingly delicate texture. She wondered how someone as vulnerable as the AG survived! She groped for the right hanger and rehung the suit, aware that her method was insidious. The end had dictated the means. And, if there were problems with her partnership with the Anarchist, compromise would not be one. She was the general. She would tell Mr. Dio it was a GO project. She would make calls, edit miles of tape, set up meetings. No more collages, she was finally LIVE!

The Anarchist sat on his bench still naked. He appeared thoughtful because his head was in his hands. He was really crying. He took his hands away and began to brood. Introversion can be a disease of the conscience, he thought, considering his recent act. Time alone in the shop had its price in reality. Mind and passion meshed in making a poster; the point where he became the object being made, a peaceful submergence into the interior.

But the more time away, the world looked stranger. His work absorbed him until he became nothing but process. Intimacy with another person? It's fantasy with me, he thought. In one insane act, he had alienated the AG. Obviously, if self-absorption were one side of the illness, self-destruction was the other. Still, it was done. He had collaborated. Grimly, he took out the New York Times clipping dated Sunday, February 10, 1980. Amazing, he thought. "A gas mixture, a fluorine, is burned within a hollow tube ...."

Chapter 8

SANDY'S STRATEGY, OR BACK TO THE BOARDS

Sandy let herself in an almost hidden side door in the Pan-Am building. She unlocked the tiny service elevator and pressed the button for the 93rd floor, barely conscious of her actions. Mentally, she was imposing a mandala on the city. The spokes radiated from her headquarters at Ad-A-Live, centering around the name, PHOENIX.

Five grand might cover the operation, she had decided, including the dust crew, media insiders, electronics experts, police, and decoys for politicians. Conceptually, the PHOENIX would be a wide-ranging umbrella operation subject to diverse interpretations. It would be a demonstration docudrama for and against nuclear power, corporate interests, genetic engineering, abortion, ecology, urban sprawl. Evangelists might even receive literature saying the operation was a symbolic timetable for apocalypse. Sandy wasn't sure if the interpretative aspects of the PHOENIX could be actually accomplished, but she didn't much care. What mattered was its execution and that was firmly under her control.

A small group of Vendettas volunteers would be recruited

and told the operation was a video recreation of a political takeover to be used for neighborhood safety purposes. Volunteers would be provided with video backpacks for documentation, walkie-talkies and Red Cross armbands to direct stray motorists to emergency centers.

She, Sandy, as the sole broadcaster operating in the city, would read a propagandistic statement that would be frightening for its very lack of political purpose or affiliation. The Anarchist would be responsible for organizing Vendettas recruitment and his ruby laser. Would he toe her line? He was monolithic in thinking, unaware of her obvious intrusions into his plans. Could she program him to propagandize properly and not self-destruct from hypocrisy afterwards? She would have to stress the "symbolic liberation of the act itself." It would be difficult.

Anarchists did not like the structure inherent in nihilism. He would have to cede her the right to clarify societal overtones. There would be no martyrs!

Sandy got off at the Ad-A-Live office on the 93rd floor. Since the board was on "aux" for auxiliary, she knew the previous shift had not shown. Sloppy, she thought, switching the "aux" button off. From the tiny refrigerator in the coatroom, she took a beer and imagined the city choked with Mr. Dio's dust. She could just see the AG walking along the Bowery, incredulous at the stuff. Sandy popped the can open and laughed at the AG, who would probably spend the day making some uniform for a futuristic gardener.

Sliding a message pad under the beer, Sandy took the Anarchist's old Vendettas list out of a manila folder.

Though it was two years old, it did include phone numbers and addresses. An update was in order and it was just as well. She needed some practice in public relations.

Sandy took a sip of her beer and blitzed through the first ten names on the list; sublet, moved, disappeared with no forwarding address. Damn, she thought, pausing before the next twenty names. New York was such a transient town.

On the twenty-first she got a live one.

"Burt, this is Sandy from Food for Vendettas. Do you remember the East Village co-op?"

"Yeah, the Irishman's gig. Too bad he couldn't make a go..."

"Some of the former members have formed a lobby for good produce. We'll also be taping a video film as a demonstration tool and wonder if you'd like to come to a meeting."

"I'm kind of apolitical. I moved to the upper West side and don't believe in macrobiotics anymore. I think it's more important what you think than what you eat.

Denotationally, 'The brain is not a porous membrane' ... know what I mean?"

"Not exactly. It says on your card that you were an electrical engineer and we could really use someone with your talents."

"Damn the electrical company. Hey, the Irishman wrote that stuff on cards?"

"You wrote it, filling out the members' cooperative service

policy."

"Yeah, right. Send me something. I'm non-union, so..."

"Did you get fired?"

"It was the serviceman's incentive that got me.

There's a special crew that gets bonuses for every service they turn off for nonpayment. But they don't get that to turn 'em on. The heat berets they call 'em, will go through broken basement windows for that bonus, but to turn-on — if you're not on the premises, forget it! Whole thing made me sick, so I made a stink and..."

"Burt," Sandy interrupted, "can I have your new address? You're exactly who we need."

Sandy got Burt's new address, noted his profession, and finished forty other names on her list. At 1 a.m., she decided it was too late for additional calls. Sandy felt encouraged. She would have a small but dedicated core group. Outside operatives might be more difficult. She would start with her "board" members, Ad-A-Live clients, and see if her contacts expanded.

From switchboard experience, she knew how an individual's influence could reverberate throughout the city to every possible enterprise. A marvel that with one network, you could run a simple operation that mirrored itself innumerable times. Despite the supposed control of city government, the real power lay in these informal networks of de facto self-managers. The last term made Sandy grin. Wasn't that, in truth, one of the tenants of real anarchy?

Encouraged, Sandy curved her cords, ready for her next blitz.

On Sid's line was a recording of ponies running a race at Belmont, before "This is Sid, leave your name for a front-runner every time…"

"Sandy at the boards. I have a proposition for you. Signal with your homing device."

She plugged her next line, "This is Reverend Ray, may the Lord bless you and keep you wherever you may be, whoever you are. Twenty-four hour evangelical music and cheer. If you wish for a pastoral consultation, hold for the beep and the operator will pass your message to our..."

Sandy skipped to the end of the tape, before it reverted to her line.

"Ray, it's Sandy at Ad-A-Live. I need your advice on a personal mission."

Next on Sandy's client list was Jack Duncan,

a network clearinghouse man. Formerly, as Duncan MacKenzie, he had been a troubleshooter for both the leftist radical SDS (Students for a Democratic Society) and the Klan. More from curiosity than commitment, as he told Sandy on a too quiet night, he had found himself in the middle of a personal political crisis, playing both ends against the middle. Now he worked for a MOR (middle of the road) media network and did a little gardening on the side. Sandy and Jack were intimate, though they had never met.

"How are the collages going, Sandy?"

"I've graduated. I'm going mainstream."

"It's about time — real estate?"

"Food for Vendettas."

"Can't say it's made a splash."

"Only a season in the East Village. I'm reviving it for video verity..."

"Don't be obtuse, Sandy."

"If you're tired of your garden, let me send you some material about a Vendettas meeting. I'm arranging a bit of urban paralysis. I need you for media access. You'll broadcast emergency material and my message, so if I don't show...it won't be a catastrophe."

"This is very funny but it doesn't wash."

"It's a re-creation of a takeover for political purposes.

No joke."

"Send me something. You're too glib to believe."

"You'll get a card in the mail."

"It doesn't exactly sound like public service stuff. You know I'm up for a real news job."

"Jack, there's an exclusive in it."

"You are hard-core, you know that?"

"I'm not bad. I get some looks in the street. Nothing big, but heads turn. Love ya!"

Sandy signed off with Jack and plugged into a lit green in-house line.

The message was obscene. She unplugged, but then remembered she wanted to talk to Sid. Quickly, she intercepted the tape.

"THIS RANDOM RECORDING WAS A PAID SEXUAL SOLICITATION FROM SID. IF YOU WISH US TO SERVICE A REPLY… "

"It's Sandy at the board. I need a contact at the city sanitation department and the number of Georgeanne's service. Thanks."

It was essential to her plan that she had an "in" with someone who knew the location of the city's snow removal facilities. She wanted to block their access after the dust was dumped. It was also essential that she contact Georgeanne. Sid's girl operated a stable of vans on the West Side highway. Georgeanne's girls would be an invaluable resource. They could decoy authorities, if she correctly budgeted the costs. It could be a problem to identify travel routes, but she had an idea of how to obtain that info. A call on client #573 might be a good place to start...

"Marzipol, this is Sandy at Ad-A-Live. If I had a copy of your client lists: pooches, frequency of visitations and treatments, I could actually anticipate some scheduling and cut down your costs. I know your customers are elite and confidentiality is a concern, but I speak to them quite often as it is and..."

Sandy had over pitched. Before she could finish the message, a tape squealed in her ears with a poodle's ggrrr and the background sound of splashing water. Marzipol's overly modulated voice said: MARZIPOL'S SALON: CUT, MANICURE, COLOR AND CURL. WE DO YOUR POOCHES VERY FINE. PARLOUR PICK-UP CAN BE ARRANGED BY DIALING ..."

Sandy hung up, irritated. The woman was such a snob! Still, one failure so far wasn't bad. She took a sip of beer, shocked that the groundwork for the PHOENIX was under way. Things would come off in 3D in the real world. And if the operation fell apart, it would be just as effective. That was the beauty of a non-objective operation. It always worked, as long as it wasn't discovered too soon.

The beer felt full in her stomach. Contentedly, Sandy allowed her mind to range through images of public officials, who were really unavailable for comment, bankers frantically trying to have Wall Street declared a disaster area in the aftermath of the laser. Dust settled all over the city, but no one could unearth the snow-blowing equipment. In the confusion of blocked subways and downed electrical lines, she would broadcast through Jack Duncan's offices.

Sandy's thoughts returned to her switchboard, because of a buzzing lit line.

"Sandy, its June. I couldn't make my shift. Did you cover

for me?"

"No trouble. By the way, could I depend on you to get sick another time, as a favor?"

"Sure. I like my sleep."

Sandy, pleased, hung up the phone and put her lines on aux. She had fifteen minutes before her meeting with Mr. Dio. She needed to run her slides without interruption.

Sandy ceremoniously wiped her fingers with film paper and took out her projector. She set the lens at magnify and ran her downtown footage until she came to individually X'd sites. Included were tunnels, bridges, and freeways, which gave access to Manhattan Island: Williamsburg Bridge, FDR Drive, Manhattan Bridge, Brooklyn Bridge, Brooklyn Battery Tunnel, Miller Highway, Holland Tunnel, Lincoln Tunnel, Henry Hudson Bridge, Major Deegan Expressway, Triborough Bridge, N. Astoria Blvd., Queens Midtown Tunnel. Dust would be dumped simultaneously at each site. The map framed all seventeen in the pleasing shape of an asymmetrical mandala. Mr. Dio entered the office, as she reached the last frame. Sandy held the image.

She offered Mr. Dio a chair and said, "Five bridges, three tunnels, three boulevards. It won't be easy, but not impossible. I estimate five grand for pay-offs, coordination, equipment, and other aspects of the operation."

Mr. Dio fidgeted uneasily. He found Sandy's "boardroom" eerie with the post-fluorescent echo of after-hours office wastelands. He was overly sensitive to such sounds lately.

He'd not given notice at his job yet, but they were beginning to talk.

Sandy waited patiently for an answer to her request, which made him once again question his own rationality. It had started with his laugh. Always a bit loose, it now trailed off indefinitely. His worn clothes were slept in. In his desk drawer he had placed a half-full bottle. The drawer was open so it could be discovered. A good alibi? He knew he had not stockpiled tons of dust without someone noticing the reroutes. There were 500 diverted trucks, numerous rented warehouses, townhouses and motels charged on his expense sheets. How more blatant could he be? Still, his corporation acted slowly, and he was too well-respected to be axed soon enough. It would take six months to process that he was out of hand, REALLY. As for now, no rebukes above the norm had been issued.

The thought crossed his mind that he didn't want to be stopped. Maybe he wanted Sandy's plan to succeed. It might forestall the eventuality his facts indicated. He had to Illuminate the impending missile disaster. Confess to someone, a voice on a line, Sandy. Mr. Dio decided that he was indeed sane. He nodded his assent to the young commandant coolly at his side pointing to certain X's.

"The trucks should not be uniform. The routes must coincide with driving time. It is important that the dumping be synched. Power lines will go except for my network contact system and emergency hospital equipment.

Vendettas volunteers, a citizens' group, will curtail early

travelers and relay to my network contact and ham lines through my center here at Ad-A-Live. The laser attack should, in implication, reverberate throughout the city from Wall Street."

"What about the missile question? I want the dust, its type and function, to be identified. People must know about the danger. That's the point of this whole operation?"

"That will be specifically spelled out as I clarify societal overtones. Remember, there are two phases of this event: the dust and the laser. The central command is comprised of you, me, and the Anarchist, who is working independently. The second tier is our support group, Vendettas Volunteers and our outside operatives."

Sandy pointed to several streets that had been X'd. "The quantity of dust needed to block each major subway should be estimated. Fire hoses will congeal the stuff in spots for safety."

Mr. Dio was visualizing, as Sandy talked. He could imagine an ice-cream truck, an armored car, a Ritter van — all at their assigned thoroughfares prepared to dump tons of dust. He could see weighted power lines crashing for a black-out, as lights extinguished everywhere (except for Sandy's board in the Pan-Am Building with her independent generator.) The operation would be short with minimal damage, but long enough to expose the city's vulnerability. Minimum destruction, a short paralysis, he told himself, would help a nation perceive a larger risk.

Yet, despite the obvious gain, the PHOENIX was a scary scenario.

Sandy stopped the projector to emphasize a point. "I decided against a vertical, monolithic structure to minimize the risk of leaks, sell-outs, potential for self-sabotage. Because we will be recruiting groups with differing ideologies, a mandala is more appropriate and manageable. All lines converge on the dumping of dust. If one or two tributaries are cut, the rest will be sufficient."

Strategic planning made Mr. Dio's skin crawl. His thoughts darted toward an obscure childhood memory. He was three, his sister five. They were fighting over a plastic signet ring, which changed from pink to green depending on how you turned it. He had found it on the curb. She cried, "You took it!" It was too small for him, so he had given it to her. This incident was, as he saw it now, the beginning of his commercial diplomacy. He had been a mediator between inventors and industry, suppliers and distributors, buyers and shippers. No matter how different the objectives, deadlines and inventories, conciliation was his mission.

He did not want to conciliate anymore. He hated compromise almost as much as he hated strategy. He would put himself in Sandy's deliberate hands and take orders. He was just a voice on a wire. While Sandy talked, he starred at her switchboard; the dark light of his office at the shipping firm. The mail box above it was numbered "509". A small area in her world, he thought. Mr. Dio leaned back in his seat prepared to listen, anxious to hear.

"We will broadcast emergency instructions, as an unidentified organization," Sandy continued. "Groups will not have media access to make contrary claims. There will be a sense of national relief. The collective 'people' believe in nemeses. The country believes in its eventual downfall. There will be a sigh that a catastrophe has finally occurred. Yet it's limited in extent and duration."

"It will mean all things to all people." This phrase of Sandy's pleased Mr. Dio, and he ignored the rest. In each successive contract, a bit of his personality had died. In understanding each point of view, he had lost his own. An arbitrator had no business with personal opinion.

Mr. Dio thought of his apartment. The furnishings didn't reflected him but a 'contemporary" decor of an immediacy quickly dated. He had several red curvilinear plastic chairs, a white shag carpet and translucent filament lamps, which hung upside down like plastic ice cream cones. The plastic had chipped badly. The original Italian designer lamp was delicate, uncompromised like the mass market knock-offs. But his walls were white. He had a sliding door to a small terrace. Thank goodness the intimidating stainless steel sink was now filled with dust. Mr. Dio had enjoyed erecting a sandbox for the living room with 2x4s. It was a crude job. He had dumped the dust over everything, feeling free. No more compromise!

He was disturbed from his reverie by Sandy's intense calculating gaze. He pulled out his checkbook and wrote her a check for the amount of five grand. He said to call if she needed more. She said she'd be in touch.

Sandy was glad to see him go — glad to pack the warm check in the top of her video cam. VICTORY!!

Oddly, acquiring the Anarchist had seemed more of a transaction than the financing. Sandy packed up her projector and slides. She kept the board on aux for the second shift. Their lateness was irritating.

At 4 a.m. it was cool outside. Sandy was careful not to vary her routine. Consistency allowed her more focus. She would need it to execute the PHOENIX. The streets were tinged with an aesthetically appealing mist. Sandy aimed her video cam up at the Pan-Am Building. She fancied she could make out the minute light of her tenser lamp on the 93rd floor. It was a fancy. She knew it was switched off.

The Pan-Am Building was completely black except for metallic letters, which read gray. The black-holed windows were another slick surface. Sandy imagined what it would be like to climb the front of the building; to dangle over recessed, tinted glass. She angled her cam to capture that sensation. Then she walked downtown.

Third Avenue and Twenty-Eighth Street was halfway to the Bowery, a Spanish singles' neighborhood. Sandy was looking into a shoe store window when she heard a faraway TICKA-TICKA sound. She saw a penlight, heard rubber on velvety wet asphalt. Then a silver spoke. A lone biker, thought Sandy, an eager-beaver messenger doing a dawn job. TICKA-TICKA-TICK-TICK-TICK, in refraction—a fender under pressure? Sandy shot in self-defense. She misjudged the distance. Against the traffic, parallel wheels careened downtown. Not two unicyclists but a motorized wheelchair with no reflectors. A lone car passed her on the curb. The wheelchair went for the car. The car had room to miss it. Sandy shot the near-miss.

The driver of the wheelchair was an amputee in a leather cowboy hat. He held a cardboard sign: HIT ME I'M A VIET VET. His black T-shirt bore an alternate message: I'M A VIET VET-SO WHAT?! Sandy thought the glowing letters might have detained him from his self-sought destiny. The Vet got his bearings and aimed for another car, kamikaze. The car wasn't moving fast enough. The chair only overturned. The Vet lay on the ground beside the spinning wheels.

"Want a hand?"

"Got one. Get fucked. "

He righted the chair with one hand. Sandy handed him his hat. Unexpectedly, he posed, actually wanting to be filmed. Sandy shot straight on, portrait footage. She scribbled on a piece of paper her phone number at Ad-A-Live and FOOD FOR VENDETTAS. He looked at her skeptically.

"It's a grab bag of groups."

"What for?"

"What you're doing, only larger."

Chapter 9

OUT OF THE CAGE

Joe's Place, on Pearl Street, was just over the Brooklyn Bridge and almost invisible to the uninitiated. Joe ran a clean show. A sign proclaimed: NO PASSES WITHOUT PROVOCATION. His customers didn't push it. Drinks were not exorbitant, sandwiches were well-packed, his beer and wine list thoughtful. And for Ladies' Night, every other month, he even had an exotic male dancer.

Joe had given the AG a job because he had loved her mother, sorry to realize it too late. She was, at first, just a faded blonde seamstress who came in for an occasional beer. Later her solitude intrigued him. Joe would speculate outrageously; she was a runaway wife or an ex-convict, or any woman down on her luck with a love-child. She laughed at these but in five years of shy friendship, he never learned her point of origin. He did become addicted to her soothing voice, which he fortified with strong red wine.

Towards the end, she asked him home. Though he knew of her illness, he went out of love, little prepared for her thriving imagination.

The seamstress had transformed a studio apartment into a luxury liner equipped with brass quoit portholes, records of ocean noises, salt scent and cool lace curtains. Yes, the seas had played a significant part in her life, she said, making love with the litany of the ship bound, "I will never see you again and we barely know each other. We have tonight."

Many women had treated Joe as if he were a shortstop to somebody else they would eventually settle for. With the widow, he had eternity. He guessed correctly then that she was a refugee from a coast or island What other immigrant would be sentimental about high seas?

In her memory, he was unquestioning to many who came for havens and stop-gap credit. But the Anarchist! There he had made a mistake. Joe groaned internally every time he thought of the misfortune of his surrogate daughter—did that maniac Anarchist treated her right? He would have liked someone else for the AG, but she was a dreamer like her mother. A crazy, bohemian girl, he thought fondly, remembering when she first showed up at the club wiping her red-rimmed eyes. Joe said he hoped she had not been crying too much.

"No, it's trying to sew straight seams," she had explained.

Yes, the AG's seams curved. She had inherited her mother's machine but not her knack. Joe had offered her the go-go job which paid better than waitressing. He watched over the rough spots when he could. The Anarchist was one that had escaped him.

Joe D'Angelo, half-Irish, half-Italian, didn't think he had any prejudices towards refugees. Even he was dubious the night the Anarchist had appeared, drenched in his black suit.

"You looking for the Bowery?" he said, not joking.

The Anarchist, still stunned from the cold water, was a red-skinned, glassy-eyed redhead barely standing upright.

"The Bowery? Beg pardon, man, just came from the bogs. Thought this was Brooklyn. I was told to go to Joe's. That he'd take care of me."

"Who told you that?"

"Guy at the dock said to ask for Belinda."

"BELINDA." A waitress turned. "Know him?"

"Luv ya, Joe. He's the founder of Food for Vendettas!"

"Never heard of ..."

"A cowardly lot if ever there was."

The Anarchist's temper had flared, "Horse's ass."

Joe liked his indignant attitude. Especially coming from someone who looked the way he did. He gave him a meal.

The AG asked, "Who is that guy at the bar?"

"Never seen him before. Is he bothering you?" "No. He just seems someone I might know."

"You're just like your mother."

"What do you mean?"

"Whenever she said something was in her head, it was real."

Looking out for the AG, Joe had started a conversation with the Anarchist about the waitresses. It was the wrong topic. The Anarchist said he'd seen hard-bitten women before. "Locals in the pubs, aye, women looking fifty at twenty with wailing kids and husbands blown sky-high but they were women! America must be a harder country than I heard. No religion but that's not the problem. You need more nutritious fruit and vegetables."

"Pipe down, boy, you'll never win 'em with that line."

"This couldn't be anywhere but Brooklyn, right?"

"Sure. Think there's joints like this everywhere?."

"Oh," said the Anarchist, sounding depressed.. "What variety there must be in such a huge country."

Joe was almost sorry for the ingrate, when the AG entering her cage claimed his attention.

"Does she have a name?" the Anarchist asked. "No."

"Are you her boyfriend or something?"

"No."

"Then she goes by..."

"She doesn't have a name right now!"

"Hasn't much identity has she..." the Anarchist began.

"Go to hell! She's a crazy nonconformist. She doesn't care about names!"

"Sorry," the Anarchist said in some confusion. He watched the AG dance, mesmerized.

"Wonder what she thinks of up there?"

"Who can tell?"

Afterwards, he approached her and said, "Hi. My name is...well, let's just say...I'm the Anarchist." He said it with a wretched mixture of shame and pride. (He could not yet give her the weight of his given name.)

"I'm the Anarchist's Girlfriend, I guess. Would you like to see the river? It's pretty at night. All lit up."

The Anarchist walked out, her tiny hand electric in his, wondering what they would do. They went to the river. The Anarchist slept alone at Joe's Place, though only for that night.

Joe hoped for the best. The Anarchist was not a bad guy just a fool. But he kept an eyes out. When she came in, he'd make sure everything was all right. A short conversation was enough. The AG didn't know how to lie.

The walls of Joe's Place were lined with gold-framed mirrors and painted a flat black. The seats were red vinyl. Square Formica tables were bolted into concrete stands. A revolving strobe hung over a narrow stage. It was the cages that stood out, homemade half-circles on either side of the stage. Joe perfectly drilled holes five inches apart for the whittled dowel sticks. More functional than slick, the cages even had blowers to relieve the warm spotlights.

The AG came in at about seven. Joe ordered her a bowl of tortellini in brodo (broth to the non-Italians who dared to ask). It was a good, nourishing meal before dancing.

"How's the fashion business?"

"Fine," the AG said, pulling her mending and acetate thread from her bag.

"Lots of production and no sales?" She nodded, threading a needle. "Are you trying?"

The AG began to stitch. "I'm not discouraging it."

"What about that boyfriend of yours, the freckle-faced madman?"

"Oh, you shouldn't talk about him like that. You know you like him."

" I'd like to know if you're okay. Is he taking care of you? When are you gonna tie the knot?"

" I can't say," the AG said, looking at the torn fringe. It was hopeless to stitch it. "Joe, do you have any glue?"

"Yeah, by the juke," Joe said, walking across the club, where his '50s record player stood. It was tinny but it worked for vinyl, Joe thought. He glanced with pride at his stock of Frank Sinatra. His juke was representative of the kind of homey atmosphere he liked in his club. With approval, he watched as Belinda brought the AG her soup. He was pleased to see her eat. He was also pleased the AG lived with a lady-friend, since she was short on common sense. Someone needed to watch out for her besides the Anarchist!

An early customer nodded and a new one. Joe paid attention to the latter, not too many of these. He saw a boy in his early twenties with dark blonde hair and eyes too sharp for Joe's taste, especially when he looked at the AG. He gave her a slight wave. Did she know the guy or was he just friendly? Damned if he didn't look like the press gone slumming. Joe dropped the glue on the AG's table and made his way to the bar. The guy was dressed wise-guy, not the style of his club despite Sinatra.

"What can I get you?"

GIN AND TONIC, Wayne wrote on his pad. "Laryngitis?"

PERMANENT. I'M A DEAF-MUTE.

Joe washed a glass, perplexed. An occasional Manhattanite would stumble onto his place, but he'd be damned if he knew how word had travelled to Wayne's population.

Wayne was not in the mood for conversation. Pearl Street had been a dark stop. In one direction, a vacant lot was defined by a broken chain fence and beyond that loomed the Brooklyn Bridge. The other direction offered nothing but closed warehouses. Nothing moved but him.

Wayne wished he had a street number and a flashlight. He got lucky. Two blocks down the slope toward the warehouses he saw the sign, JOE'S PLACE, shining in a freak streetlight. Wayne noted for himself:

A BIT SCARY ON PEARL. GOT HERE AT EIGHT. ONE GUY AT A TABLE AND THE AG EATING.

Joe brought the glass, trying to read over his shoulder. "You're not from the Voice, doing some kind of folksy article on a Brooklyn bar?"

NO. WHY?

"You look like a reporter."

Wayne, in his St. Mark's get-up, was almost flattered. Yet he wondered if this bartender really thought a deaf-mute was a real journalist? And so unfriendly!

"Manhattan spells death to a place like this. People there think everything outside is quaint, know what I mean? No one's making my place into a mausoleum of 'quaintness'."

Wayne wrote: COLLEGE STUDENT.

"Why I was suspicious." Joe pointed to the pad, "No journalist was ever that closemouthed."

Wayne and Joe stopped to watch the AG and a large girl in a raincoat disappear behind the curtain that led to the stage.

"Is the AG a friend of yours?" MIGHT BE.

"What did you say you wanted?"

GIN AND TONIC, Wayne wrote, tearing off the page for Joe.

"I knew her mother." WAS SHE LIKE THE AG?

"Yes. I looked out for both of them." Joe's hand hit the bar, face-down. Wayne wished he had a drink so he'd have something to slam too. He tested a stool further away. It seemed the safer course. Joe was a burly man — a mountain getting hostile.

YOU HAVE A NICE PLACE, Wayne wrote, CUSTOM JOB?

"I built it myself, just like Regines without the celebrities."

IS GO-GO STILL BIG IN THE SUBURBS?

"Since when is Brooklyn the suburbs!" Joe's knuckles rapped the wooden surface of the bar. Wayne, feeling nervous, turned the stool and noted the restaurant interior.

The walls were luminous around the edges. Day-glo under black. The cages were a real eyesore.

Wayne felt a heavy hand on his shoulder and closed the book, expecting the rest of the arm to do some violence.

"You know that bum, the Anarchist?" NO.

"You're an improvement over that one." THANKS.

Joe finally mixed the gin and tonic, wondering how the AG had met the amiable deaf-mute.

The walls of the dressing room, where the AG and Rhonda made up, were layered with jars of makeup and cold cream thrown in fits of tension. Go-go was rigorous. The job required emotional self-control, mental detachment, and good muscle tone.

Rhonda was a pro. Mental preparedness and physical abandonment were her strengths. She steeled herself by cleaning her mirror, layering her face and imagining a glamorous Rhonda who sang mezzo for the Met. She had always wanted to. She knew lots of arias by heart. But she had no voice. Besides, after years in the cage she was honest with herself, she craved admiration more than song. The act might be a 1960s relic but it filled the bill more than singles' bars with their status systems. Did her looks measure up—her job—her age? She had to be smart, look pretty and play quiet with good jokes to be appealing.

Rhonda had initiated many conversations. Many men walked away to a distant drink or a phony visit to a men's room. She'd see the same guy talking to someone else, looking through her attempts at eye contact. Now, she didn't care about the steady boyfriend she had once wanted. The cages were sufficient. Rhonda felt like a cliché. That was one reason why she worked at Joe's Place. It could be anywhere, and she could be anyone.

Lately, the music got on her nerves. This month's tape was unusually repetitive and one of the songs was scary. The rhythm was too violent, like some suicidal mating urge. Rhonda's shrink would disapprove but the choice was not her call. She put on her costume not questioning her motivation. It seemed the easier course.

With a green pencil, the AG emphasized the up tilt of her eyes. She also thought of her first night with the Anarchist.

"Where do you live?"

"The Bowery."

"Sure, that's where I'm headed," he said dourly, "from what I've heard..."

"I know you'll live there. I can read minds sometimes."

The Anarchist was superstitious. Even after Joe's talk about the unworldly AG, he was whitely afraid.

The AG filled in her lips with bright pink. She decided it looked okay, while she recalled her explanation about "sometimes."

"That's the problem with ESP. How to know what is genuine and what is imagined. It's a matter of 'feeling' the difference and knowing when it should be acted on." She acted intuitively, having long ago accepted the impossibility of analysis. Over time, the Anarchist had accepted her.

If only he could trust himself as well! Then Sandy would be no threat. While putting the top on her lipstick, the AG could sense her moving between them. She muted the painful sensation.

The AG peeked out of the wings pleased to see Wayne, her new friend. He was smart, high-strung, and sensibly self-confident. He had suffered into maturity earlier than most and it was this hypersensitivity that was his real handicap. All this the AG saw in side glances. It remained for her to guess what he was noting on his pad.

Wayne was holding his pencil stub and thinking about sex. Oh, for the delusion of a simple Madonna-whore complex. If he could just project guilt onto one woman he would be more considerate of all women. Custom-made satisfaction, his sexual obsession, became an addiction for his lovers. When a woman realized he had moved on, the hurt was worse. He was responsible. He was flagrant in his short-lived need to please.

Thursday, with her carefully delineated protocol for affairs, had made him an honest man. But since meeting the AG, he had neglected her windshield. Notes probably whirled in the street. He felt awful, but he just couldn't meet her. The AG occupied him completely.

Joe leaned over Wayne's blank pad, "You know, I'm well-known in some circles but I never want to become a popular interest spot—no matter how much business it would bring. After the noise died down, the guys I care about, the ones who helped me get started, would snub this place—talking about how great it used to be. You understand?"

Wayne curled his index finger and thumb to form something between an A-Okay and an imperfect zero.

About ten o'clock, the AG felt a little nervous. She wondered what Wayne would think of her. He would note the truth of what he saw and what, she asked herself, would that be?

Joe went to the front of the stage and raised an eyebrow to silence the crowd. Clapping ensued when he held up two fingers and said, "Ladies!"

The AG and Rhonda entered in pink mini Comanche outfits. Wayne thought the AG looked a ridiculous punk Pocahontas, until she struck what he noted as:

REMINGTON POSE. SHE ARCHES HER BACK, RAISES HER HAND RIGIDLY. HER FACE IS MEDITATIVE. "BRAVE COMMUNING WITH THE MOON BEFORE BATTLE?

Wayne was astounded. He had seen a girl in a G-string perform a one-handed upside down split on a poodle's perch. He had seen another girl bathe in a champagne glass. He had witnessed a bubble-gum competition involving two participants in a simulated sex act. Wayne could determine the AG's was not a commercial sex act. It certainly wasn't Go-Go, that job traditionally reserved for women with low IQs and matching self-esteem. The thing about the AG was assumptions didn't apply. She didn't seem to take her role very seriously. In fact, she didn't seem to be aware of it at all!

SHE IS NOT MENTALLY IN THE CLUB. SHE INDICATES A FOREST WITH TREES...SHE KNEELS, CLASPING BOTH HANDS TO HER BREAST BEFORE REACHING OUT TO THE SKY. SHE SEEMS TO TELL A STORY OF STAR-CROSSED LOVERS.

HAWAIIAN INTERPRETIVE (Wayne crossed this out.) NO. HORSE-OPERA KABUKI, IF SUCH A FORM EXISTS.

Rhonda, he noted, was a conventional contrast — a large-boned girl with huge breasts, long legs, and flat feet. Wayne focused on these. The veins were enlarged and purplish. The toes were bent under from years of high heels. These would be the part her lover should concentrate on, Wayne decided. He also noted how dull her eyes were.

He couldn't tell much else.

Neither could Rhonda, who was about to unleash some suppressed emotion. After a teenage abortion, she had groggily signed a sterilization paper. Originally, she blamed herself for naiveté about sex. After the paper, she blamed the procedures of welfare doctors. Subconsciously, Rhonda raged at society's sexual hypocrisy. She danced vengeance because she was impotent. This emotional drive made her a professional purposeful tease. Tonight she was exceptional — the bitch of all jilting girlfriends, untouchable Sports Illustrated poster fold-outs, newsworthy princesses in bikinis and manipulative soap opera queens. Rhonda provoked male malice. Her body was an arrogant thing they could want to abuse. She asked for it. Wayne wrote: SIREN.

The AG was towards the end of her tale, where the lovers part in a snowstorm. She was physically following the beat of a computer-refined tune. The climax was not strong enough, so she detached her vision, careful to practice imaginative control coming out. Slowly, Rhonda's cage took shape. The tables below it formed and the bar in the back gradually became unblurred and distinct. The AG was hyper aware of Rhonda's kewpie-doll outfit. She felt her own body dressed the same but imagined instead a black Victorian dress. It had a set-in waist, mildly puffed shoulders and a high white collar. She thought it was too long but didn't want to shorten it. She felt unexposed.

The crowd was rough and red-faced with too much alcohol. Wayne nervously wondered when the tension would erupt. Then he noticed Joe, unperturbed, mixing a whiskey sour. Wayne relaxed. Obviously a nightly saga?

The AG registered individual faces in the crowd. This guy loved his wife but not as much as he'd expected when he first married. That one was left in the lurch. Another was paying through the nose. The AG felt they wanted to get theirs, get somehow through it all. She was a pretty girl they possessed in fantasy as they drank. It was all very human.

They were very tired with long days of work behind them.

A new tune. The AG was a spineless, single-celled organism swimming upstream. She eerily reflected a brainless vacuum, feeling peaceful until she heard the dowel stick CRACK! Imaginative control lost, she instantly snapped back to her surroundings.

The new tune was the one Rhonda feared with the voice near orgasmic death. The cage became the operating table she would be obliterated on. Rhonda smashed through the cage, spraining her arm. She leapt into the aisle, goading the besotted crowd until the first man dropped his belt.

Wayne could not swallow his drink and didn't know what to do but scribble: GO-GO GIRL GOES BERSERK!

The headline simplified the story about a "train" that had to be stopped. Wayne remembered high school tales of girls who pulled gang bangs.

NOT ABLE TO RECORD, NONRECORDO (he wrote) AG!!! DON'T LEAVE YOUR CAGE!

The AG stood center stage, the strobe whirling confusedly over her. She closed her eyes in order to sense what to do. Hands clapped insistently. Wayne stood on a stool holding his notebook horizontally. It said: SING!!

He meant diversion. The AG had never sung before. "Do I have to?" she asked Wayne, without speaking.

Wayne nodded, folding his arms and swaying to indicate something soothing.

LULLABY! He thought the word.

The AG declined. Belinda went downstairs for Joe, who was looking for some missing Gin bottles.

DO IT!! Wayne thought.

Unexpectedly, the AG began to warble. Wayne visualized a place where a mountain stream ran. A bird shrieked about an avalanche — sorrowing among the rubble, looking for its buried mate. No one else understood this narrative. The men in line paused because the performance was strangely insistent, sad enough to quell bloodlust.

Rhonda sat up and drew her legs to her knees, wanting to believe that she had died. But the pain in her arm was too real. She let Belinda take her home as the AG finished her song. The dead mate ascended with the unborn birds and the dust finally settled over the mountain.

The crowd clapped, and the AG realized she was out of her cage. She was not sure what it was that she had sung. She thought perhaps it was not the usual. Joe put his arm around her, furious at his clientele.

"Okay you animals, I'm closing! AG, what happened to Rhonda?"

"She broke down to her components,"

"Huh? "

"She had a breakdown," the AG said, watching Joe's crowd depart with. His fear signaled the end of Joe's Place. Yet she knew he did not really want to retire.

"Joe," she said, "I want to conciliate...I really do."

Joe did not understand, but he could not prevent the AG from returning to her cage. Without music, to her own rhythm, she danced about women followed on dark streets; unloved wives, besieged secretaries, an off-balance barmaid shifting her tray from hip to hip. The AG did not dance ideology but conciliation and pain. She also danced the Bowery — of men with fired brains and wasted bodies searching for a means out; hating, avoiding, not being able to avoid a final hand-out.

Wayne caught the gist, though the crowd did not know or care. They liked watching the pretty girl. She was soothing.

The AG was in no danger. Mostly, Joe's Place attracted a moral crowd. They only wanted to defile what was already defiled.

Wayne wrote a word he'd last seen stamped on a soap package: PURITY

Once he'd broached the subject to the Llama, who said, "Aspiration, that's its function."

"Does it exist outside of that?"

The Llama looked long, "In relation to the impure." Wayne had felt it was precarious to press him.

Fragmentation would be the charge. Sometimes Denotation caused its own disease, Wayne thought heretically, scribbling INTEGRAL = INTEGRITY.

The AG absorbed the crowd's pent-up passion. She improvised a song of a leopard's desire. It was bizarre, incoherent and erotic. Wayne recorded the sequence as he "heard" it reading her inspired lips; knowing later he might doubt his own veracity.

SHE SINGS IN A WIDE RANGE OF GROWLS. THE LEOPARD'S MUSCLES ARE WELL-OILED, HIS SINEWS LOCK. HE LEAPS THE CLIFFS UNTIL HE SPOTS HIS FEMALE. THE SPACE BETWEEN THEM IS HUGE. HE SPRINGS INTO THE AIR, LANDING ON PADDED PAWS. SHE SHIES AWAY. THEY CIRCLE TENSELY. HE MOUNTS HER. THEY MESH IN PLEASURE, REACHING ORGASM— HERS A BIT AFTER.

FOR A SECOND THEY CANNOT SEPARATE. A TRACE OF FEAR ENTERS HIM. SHE PURRS AND RELAXES. HE EASES OUT, NUZZLING HER UNTIL HE PERCEIVES AN ANIMAL ON THE PLAIN BELOW. HE LEAPS AFTER AN ANTEATER, RETURNING WITH THIS LATE-NIGHT SNACK. NO ABSOLUTION NECESSARY. ANTHROPOMORPHIC?

Wayne underlined the last word. A key to the AG? She had touched his imagination so he did more than record. Perhaps a genuine leap into creative conjecture.

As Joe found the disco controls, the exhausted AG trudged backstage. The crowd ordered no drinks. They could do nothing but talk about the pale-haired girl. In truth, there had never been an act like hers.

Changing in the dressing room, the AG hoped some help could be found for Rhonda. But unfortunately psychiatry had its gaps. She would visit Rhonda soon. Tonight, she wanted to talk to Wayne. It might be a good time for confidences since the moon was three-quarters.

Wayne guessed that she would not be in the mood for his fake interview. Neither was he, so when she walked over to the bar he simply wrote on his pad: CAN I TAKE THE D TRAIN WITH YOU — YOU ARE A REAL SWEET SINGER.

The AG blushed, "I'm not a singer." DANCER

"No. Go-go girl."

DID YOU EVER HEAR OF THE AMERICAN LLAMA?

he asked her on the D-train. The AG said no but showed polite interest, though she did not understand the purpose of the Denotational Church or what a disciple did. Wayne used the word "follower," which only added confusion. The AG just said she hoped Wayne liked being one and slept on the train.

Wayne moved a stray hair from her eyes as the lids rose and fell in an optical heave. Amazing, Wayne thought, after the whole evening he still did not know any specifics about her. Who were her folks? How old was she? When had she developed ESP?

This last boggled him. What was the extent of it?

How was it used and controlled? Did she communicate with everyone in the way she had with him? An exclusive communication was one of his deepest wishes. His pad was a nuisance at best, his voice an unused humiliation. If she understood him, perhaps he also had ESP?

Suddenly aware that she was leaning defenselessly against him, Wayne glanced fiercely around the car. The only other passenger was a prone drunk. Relieved, he returned to her face. Her features were cookie-cutter clean. He tried to tap into her dream but had to resign himself. It was definitely a one-sided affair.

Wayne tried to imagine what it would be like to be different in some profound way. Maybe the Llama understood how such a person could exist. Hell, he was just a confused kid. Wayne woke her at Astor Place and walked her to the loft.

"How long have you been following me?" A DAY.

"What do you know, now?" the AG asked, opening her eyelashes widely.

EXTERIOR HABIT AND INTERIOR POTENTIAL.

"Have you watched the Anarchist and Sandy?"

YES.

"Let me know if you find anything unusual in his routine. I think Sandy means us harm."

Wayne was surprised. How could she not have anything concrete? If a medium, she was strangely insulated from her immediate environment.

"I trust you, Wayne," the AG said with quiet intensity, "I know you will tell me true things."

Wayne did not want to think of the Anarchist's seduction. He was afraid the AG would tap in. He wanted to think of anything else.

WHAT CAN YOU TELL ME ABOUT FOOD FOR VENDETTAS?

"It was the Anarchist's food co-op. I'm afraid his lack of success has made him bitter."

Wayne did not ask further. Her eyes were darkening with tears. At the garage door, he was ecstatic when she smiled.

Her face was incandescent.

"Will you be following me tomorrow?"

Wayne said he thought he would, unsure what the Llama would make of his report.

The AG kissed him on the forehead and said, "What he likes, I guess."

Wayne had not verbalized the question, he realized, back in his room. He hadn't even noticed. It had seemed so ordinary.

SURVEILLANCE REPORT ON THE BLONDE GIRL KNOWN AS THE AG:

I have been following the Anarchist's Girlfriend for a week and can determine few facts except that she is on the scene of various emergencies and manages to "save the day." In the time I've followed her, she arranged aid for an epileptic, who fell out of a van on a major highway, and stopped a self-destructive go-go girl from a "gangbang" with a weird spell-binding lullaby. Adding the "Pigeon Drop" incident, one can say the AG has internal antennae for such situations. This ability, however, doesn't extend to her own problems. She appears unaware her roommate has seduced her lover. Her surrogate father, who owns the club that employs her, has her interests at heart but is uninvolved in her home life. She could use help in this area.

CONCLUSION: The AG is an unusually perceptive but otherwise simple young woman. Much might be gained by a study of her paranormal abilities. Potentially, she's a valuable addition to our congregation.

PLEASE ADVISE FURTHER SURVEILLANCE PROCEDURE—WAYNE NIEBOLD

It was clear to the Llama that Wayne was backing off from revealing information about the Anarchist's Girlfriend. He had almost denigrated her gifts to coincidence and emphasized her "simplicity," a clue he was getting personally involved. Once that happened, his usefulness would be negligible.

Wayne, in his editorial cluster, was fiddling idly with his pencil. His concentration was not good. He had only attempted to deceive the Llama once before, during the Pigeon Drop incident. His lapse about Thursday had been indulged, but he might be less fortunate if the Llama saw through to his real feelings about the AG. Wayne felt eyes on his back. He turned to see the Llama wave him into his office.

"Have you had direct contact with the subject?"

"No," Wayne signed, "Makes it hard to get specific

information. Can I drop the cloak and dagger?"

"No."

"It's idiotic! I can learn more if I tell her I'm a reporter. She'll be flattered."

Wayne's hands got tangled up with his emotion. He reached for his pad and carefully lettered: PARDON, I'M A

BIT NERVOUS — TOO MUCH COFFEE.

The Llama waved the pad aside and warmly smiled.

"I can tell she's very charming, so I hate to refuse, but she might recognize you from the garage and become frightened."

Wayne twisted his hands in frustration. "Maybe it would help! If I can talk to her, I would know what I'm looking for!"

The Llama faced the window. "That is for you to discover by the means given. Wayne, you're on the right track with her paranormal ability but I fear for you. You're a soft-hearted man. If you get involved, you'll lose your budding objectivity."

"Not if I tried!" Wayne said, his fingers pointing like knives.

"I cannot filter truth through a change of attitude. I'm sorry, no direct contact or you're off the case. That would be unfortunate. I know how hard it's been for you to develop yourself and I do have an interest in clairvoyance."

The Llama faced him impassively and Wayne knew the interview was over. The benign smile and outstretched hand had the usual warmth but he was oddly skeptical. He tried to think of the Llama as a man with motivations and drew a blank. Wayne returned from the office to his desk. He put his embryonic "Helpful Hints" column (he hadn't been able to concentrate) in a drawer and took out the carbon of his report to reread on the way home.

The report was distanced enough, maybe too much...oh hell, it was a direct giveaway. As Wayne neared his mailbox he knew he would disobey the Llama. He didn't like the idea but appreciated the necessity. He would pad his reports with details of time and place, trivia about her outfits, with enough hints of the paranormal to pique the Llama's interest. Eventually he would announce she had discovered her tracker. By then he could introduce her to the Llama and expect a favorable reception. He briefly worried about the strain a lengthy deception would put on his relations with the Church. Oh well, he thought.

Wayne took from his pocket a small key, like the kind that came with a diary, and opened his mailbox. What treasure would he find beneath the circulars and bills? There were never too many of these, as Wayne lived minimally and wasn't on too many mailing lists. Today he found two ads for discount drugstores just opening, one bill for electricity, a schedule of journalism classes offered by the Denotational Center, and yes...unexpected treasure. A postcard, though Wayne didn't recognize it as such, from the Anarchist's shop. He looked at cartoon frames of World War I pilots and didn't get the humor. The message, on the other side was equally ambiguous.

OPENING: THE PHOENIX

A Non-Conceptual Event— "Movement in Action"

Contact: Sandy at Ad-A-Live for this Food

for Vendettas meeting and party.

How had Sandy gotten his address or even known of his existence? Was she also clairvoyant or had the AG engineered the invitation? It wasn't until his fourth flight of stairs that he remembered his name might have been on the old co-op's mailing list. Wayne entered his apartment with resolution. He would go to this meeting, permission or not. In fact, he wouldn't miss it for the (printed) world.

Chapter 10

FOOD FOR VENDETTAS

"Jesus has given me sa-tiss-fac-tion, yes he has, I'm telling you peo-ple..."

In front of Federal Hall on Wall Street, a rock evangelist sang with an electric organ. Her fervent "sa-tiss-fac-tion" tantalized the Anarchist. He put a dime in the girl's straw basket and, as an afterthought, a postcard from a brown-wrapped package he carried under his arm. Sandy could use such talent, he thought. The girl looked around for the card giver, but he was already climbing the impressive steps of Federal Hall. The Anarchist was wondering what such a grand building was used for.

The inside rotunda was bordered on two sides by bank vaults whose doors were wide open for tourists. A sign proclaimed: THIS AREA IS GUARDED BY SECRET SURVEILLANCE. They needn't have bothered. The place was a tomb except for a sallow, nervous guide in Betsy Ross calico who greeted the Anarchist with cheerful desperation.

"Welcome to the Treasury Building! On Wednesday, March 4, 1789, on this site, the government of the United States under our present constitution began to function. New York City was the first capital of the United States, and New York's City Hall, remodeled, enlarged, and renamed Federal Hall in honor of its national importance, was its first capital. It is the building in which Congress met for its first session with the Senate in one wing and the first House of Representatives in the other. It is here, also, that Washington gave his first inaugural speech. Our tapes catch much of the authentic flavor of that bygone era."

"How do you know?" asked the Anarchist.

"I was a history major," the girl flushed. "Not that that means much."

The Anarchist disagreed with her and said that it meant a lot, before he entered the side hall of the rotunda. The hall was lined with two glass cases. In the first one was two rows of figurines against a painted backdrop of colonial houses, carriages, and cobblestones. Minute Men and Red Coats twelve inches high faced each other with features of an identical cast. The Anarchist thought it was ill-fitting that revolutionists and royalists should bear such a familial resemblance. He abandoned the scene for the adjacent case. The contents better pleased him.

It held a miniature inauguration with enough color for him to imagine the real event. Painted spectators hung from windows and rooftops. After a few seconds, he could identify Adams and Franklin in two dolls. There was even a tiny red bible in the hand of a George Washington doll. The Anarchist pressed a button on the side of the case to see what would happen.

He heard the sound of carriage wheels and then a reverent voice saying, "Here on April 30, George Washington of Virginia, wearing a suit of brown cloth manufactured in Connecticut, with silver buttons decorated with spread eagles, and standing on a half-enclosed open air balcony on the second floor, took the oath of office and became the first President of the United States."

Though the Anarchist knew he was listening to a tape, the presentation was so "on the spot", he almost expected the doll's lips to move as the voice on the tape recited, "And I say to you, I have no experience in law, none in domestic affairs. I am not qualified for this office."

A second voice was identified as the Chancellor of New York. He administered the oath, "Do you solemnly swear that you will faithfully execute the office of President of the United States and will, to the best of your ability, preserve, protect, and defend the constitution of the United States?"

"I solemnly swear..."

"It is done!" cried the voice of the Chancellor. "Long live George Washington, President of the United States!" (Cheers in different voices were repeated.)

The Anarchist looked respectfully at the Washington doll, admiring its modest disclaimer of competency. He reflected on the revolutionary struggles of his own countrymen — the unthinking violence — feeling an irony in a museum representing giants of Washington's ilk with dolls. What an odd shrine, he decided, leaving the hall. The very principles the country was founded on were exalted, yet trivialized. The question why this was so occupied him on the steps outside. He answered it as economic, looking down Wall Street at a patch of river. Cynicism had its function in providing good, unquestioning workers for the marketplace.

Steps below the Anarchist, two boys coolly smoked a joint. Black box radios blared electronic minimalist music. A tune for marching, the Anarchist thought, as a boy addressed him in singsong, "Ludes, reefers, ups, downs, mesc-a-linee."

"Sorry, I don't have the coin," the Anarchist said, in all truth.

The boy imitated a well-known comic, "Heeyy, that's show biz."

The boy's intrusion into the Anarchist's thoughts about revolutionary leaders made him realize how alien he was to American culture. Like the statue of Washington, whether poured concrete or marble, both were irrelevant.

Around the statue, around the deserted museum, the business district throbbed. In its shadow, within the insistent beat of the black boxes, the Anarchist pledged to be a visible element of Sandy's PHOENIX operation. If this meant he would forgo a safe escape with the AG, so be it. He would not procreate generations to enshrine himself. Every man had his job. Washington knew he was to be no emperor. His destiny was to serve two four-year terms. Under Washington's statue was the right place to employ his laser.

Sandy would not be pleased, since Federal Hall was just a museum. It housed little of current interest or strategic importance. The Anarchist didn't care what Sandy thought. Washington's face carved in that statue and what it represented awed him. He saw the origins of a great country now in an atrophied state. He would illuminate the truth of the symbol by incinerating the statue. Long neglected and ridiculed as pop iconography, it was first left to identify greatness and integrate noble intentions. Then left to atrophy, the same fate as the American Revolution. His own act would lack the force of a revolution, but it might have an effect on the debris of ideology he lived among.

The Anarchist had made an irrevocable decision about his destiny. He turned his granite face toward Nassau Street. He saw from a bank's clock it was time to go home. He had to meet a new volunteer before the Vendettas reunion that evening. Identify, integrate, atrophy... BREAKTHROUGH, he thought. At just the same moment, the AG HIT THE CITY CASH MACHINE.

****

It was the kind of almost spring day that made the AG feel as if her shoes were carrying her inches above the ground. In actuality, she was walking through Washington Square Park in solidly cast rubber sandals, beige latex harem pants, and a cream-colored sparkle sweater which had once sprouted ostrich feathers. She was glad she had removed the feathers, she decided, on her way to the cash machine at La Guardia Place. They were too fragile to bear the weight of the canvas marketing bag on her shoulders.

When the AG reached the Urban Banking Center, she inserted her plastic card into the vacuum-formed indentation at the side of the brick building. With mild trepidation, she waited for the "buzz" that would jolt her senses before admitting her through a thin electric eye to the Quik-Cash Center. The machine inside was separated from the bank, which had not yet opened, by a seamless Plexiglas wall. The AG, waiting in line, appreciated the round Plexiglas screws that fitted so perfectly flush. Could not have been sanded down afterward, she thought. The Plexi was completely unmarked. At her turn, the AG dipped her plastic card into another premolded slot. The pleasant computer blinked its green display board welcoming her. She read the display:

> I AM GLAD TO SEE YOU! TELL ME WHAT LANGUAGE YOU WISH TO CONTINUE IN— FRENCH, SPANISH, ENGLISH, GERMAN, ITALIAN, GREEK, OR JAPANESE?
>
> AND MILLIONS OF OTHER CUSTOMERS FOR A ONE-YEAR PERIOD HAVE LED TO ONE CASH-O-LA WINNER EVERY SIX MONTHS. CONGRATULATIONS!

The green type blinked fast and bright. The cylinder rotated raucously back and forth. Money thudded onto the floor. The AG counted seven complete revolutions of the cylinder before it calmed down. On the display screen she saw a graphic of dollar bills floating in space. She picked up the gray customer service phone and waited for a voice. For 15 seconds she heard "Hey Look me Over, Lend me an Ear..." Then a tired, human voice said, "May I help you?"

"What is Cash-O-La?"

"Our mainframe computer's brain was recently transferred from our Las Vegas branch, where we have linked banking programs with legitimate gambling enterprises. We are attempting a transplant."

"There's been a mistake," the AG said. "Money which is not mine..."

"The L.A. brain is in a trial unit. The New York branch will soon link our banking system with legalized gambling. This is no mistake. You may keep the money. You have been chosen the lucky depositor of the past six months, while we test our equipment. It's a great promotion. This event has been videotaped. We will publicize your experience as a recipient in our statewide campaign. Please accept the cash, but make your deposit another time. We're having problems switching to normal functions after Cash-O-La."

The AG, stuffing bills into her marketing bag, realized that cash had suddenly become an object of some importance. Because of the unspoken estrangement with the Anarchist, she felt apprehensive. Money could change the exterior of things. It could also become another object between them, like Sandy's presence and the general atmosphere of suspicion which filled the loft.

Sandy believed in alliances, observations, recordings and conquest. The AG felt a strain in their living arrangement. She hoisted her marketing bag onto her shoulder and decided not to go shopping. Money was a valuable commodity, though its proper usage evaded her. Instead, she would go to Central Park and contemplate the changes it could bring to her life. The AG knew of a round pond perfect for absorbing transitions.

Riding the Lexington Line, she realized one had already occurred. Unlike the day Ray had approached her with the Swiss Air bag, she was now very concerned by the money in her marketing bag. The stuff had no real origin or history of ownership but money was a "standard." Being poor, her past and future had become integrated in a now of daily work and meals, never planning ahead. Money forced her to review the past and separate it from a new future. She might acquire property for the Anarchist but what else? She had never believed in spanking new things without subtle traces of previous ownership.

Sensitive with her new anxiety, the AG deeply felt the shock of the day's beauty. The air uptown, as she ascended from the subway, seemed exceptionally clean. The sunlight endowed people, buildings, cars, trees with unique clarity. She thought of buying a red wind-up toy from a sidewalk vendor, but became distracted by a man in a semi-formal suit hawking falafels from one of the most modern stands imaginable.

The AG lost herself in admiration for the chic aluminum stand with red-walled wheels. A bright yellow umbrella covered the whole cart. The falafels inside the gleaming deep fryer were perfectly asymmetrical and fresh smelling. The tomatoes, pre-cut in quarters, were scooped up by a dark man with a beautiful smile who said, "Whole wheat or white pita?"

"Yes, I would like one," the AG said without pause.

The man randomly took a white pita and scooped falafel and salad into a delicious wedge. "Hot sauce?" he inquired. When she demurred, he poured Tahini and wrapped the sandwich in wax paper and clean paper. The AG had never seen such a perfect falafel sandwich. She took a tasty bite and realized the immediacy of her possession. She had become self-consciously cognizant of such transactions. Possession, the possibility of enjoyment, heightened her sensuality. Was money really its own Magna Carta?

A black man with a boutonnière in an impeccable pin stripe suit watched the AG eat and said, "So, you like this food? He's been trying to get me to try it but I won't."

"Oh, you should," said the AG, enjoying the man's very red carnation boutonnière. "They're delicious and healthful and taste so good!"

The proprietor bowed imperceptibly, pleased by the AG's testimonial.

The black man bowed pointedly. "I am the ambassador from Guyana. Your country has much to answer for. Patronage of immigrant food-stands scarcely fills the bill." The AG was not ignorant of the excesses of neo-colonialism. She bowed markedly, feeling the weight of her marketing bag on third world countries.

"I can only answer for myself. Others are rarely somewhat aware."

The ambassador handed her his carnation, "You must visit my country some time. It is very beautiful... like you."

The AG shook his hand and headed for the park, her consciousness stirred. Yes, her money did have a social purpose. It could be used to alleviate future pain but the Anarchist would need to help with its distribution. She could never choose among the world's needy.

The AG walked past decorative carriages to her round pond. The water was still, though trees rippled ecstatically in a strong breeze. The AG watched the water's minimal movement and an old lady in a print dress with expertly rolled sweat socks. The woman ran laps in the opposite direction from an old man of about the same years. They crossed, their circles overlapping where the AG sat on a bench. The woman, without breaking stride, inquired of the man, "How many laps, Mr. Phelps?"

"Six."

"I'm doing ten."

"Beat ya."

"You think so, Mr. Phelps?"

They crisscrossed smiles of playful competition. She quit at six.

"Better wind, Mr. Phelps," she gasped.

"Wait for me, Marge," he said at a slowed trot. "Ready and waiting," she said, taking a seat next to the AG.

The broadening shadows of the couple circling the pond made the AG think of the distance between the Anarchist and herself. They were running in opposite directions but no longer intersecting. Slowly, imperceptibly, each had lost sight of the other's stride.

Was it just Sandy's doing? Maybe the AG had been less than understanding of his troubles, less than resourceful in helping him resolve them. A small pain in her chest came with a sincere need for reassurance. Did the Anarchist love her as profoundly as before! What difference did a windfall make to this estrangement? It would affect the Anarchist more. Antimaterialism was an ideology he had accepted, though it went against his instinctual desire for perpetuity. He liked fine, beautiful objects – objects with historical import that could be passed down.

Perpetuity and procreation were things he valued. Maybe, with coaxing, he would learn to enjoy himself and put the money to personal use? As for herself, it was getting on towards dusk, and soon she would need to go to work.

Luckily she had left her costume in the dressing room and wouldn't have to make an extra trip back to the loft. This evening was not the one to show the Anarchist the contents of her marketing bag.

The Anarchist had taken great pains to insure she would not be home. He had taken inventory of her possessions, making sure she had all she needed for her go-go act. He was eating his dinner out, he said, so she should not bother to cook when she returned from the market. Even so, she had seen the postcard on the table. She knew there was a meeting in his print shop to which she had not been invited. She hoped, with all her being, Wayne would attend.

The AG wondered how people coped with anxiety. She decided not to let the unpleasant feeling darken her day. Clarity was not to be lost. Spring was a treasure and she carried it's materialization in her marketing bag. What was luck, after all, but an aspect of time?

Philosophically, she took an upward path from the pond. A boy with bad skin and a few teeth fell into step beside her. Moved, the AG noticed his sneakers were in tatters. She perceived his nature was not evil but stunted. She was prepared, when he jeered, "Where you going, doll? You're gorgeous. How would you like me to call you up?"

The AG knew how much he hated himself, how he cultivated rejection by acting offensively. Why the AG wondered as the boy mounted his verbal offense, did he set himself up for abuse?

"Nice ass..."

"You need new sneakers. You must have walked very far with these."

"Yeah, you wanna massage my..."

"Could I give you money for a new pair?" the AG asked with gently. "Would that make you feel better?"

"No, just your ass," the boy said evasively.

"You never saw it," the AG said sincerely. "We've been walking side-by-side."

The boy nervously jumped from one foot to the other, "Smart, how 'bout I use my knife…"

"Why? If you want money," The AG unzipped her bag. "I have a lot here but would appreciate your leaving some for me."

"You're a cop," the boy said, backing away. "It's entrapment or you're nuts. No one goes around talking to people like me!"

The AG watched him retreat, thinking how odd and sad some people were in New York. She realized she might have been risking harm by not giving him his usual abuse, but she had wanted to offer recompense. Some people were so suspicious!

The AG exited the park at the Plaza and walked up toward Fifth Avenue. She saw the boy navigate the thick crowd intent on a girl in a green raincoat. She heard "Hi, gorgeous!" before the pair disappeared. The AG hoped he would find satisfaction. It was a matter of inverted ambition. She had been too receptive, even tried to reward his initiative.

The incident showed her windfall was no cushion from the aggression of those less protected than herself. She had never desired money for the purpose of social insulation. All she ever liked to buy, she thought with childish joy, were exotic foods, feathers, beads. Her enthusiasm for varieties of trivial goods might serve as a temporary balm for her anxiety, but so what?

On her way to Joe's Place, she thought about life's uncertainties, glad she had taken a little peace of mind from the park.

****

FOOD FOR VENDETTAS

The Bowery businesses were bustling to the end of another workday as the Anarchist headed for a small, triangular park across from Cooper Union. Surrounded by a wrought-iron fence, the park was barely deserted at night, barely inhabited during the day but never really empty. Art students and derelicts coexisted around the statue of an eminently unremembered personage, which had resisted the graffiti and pickaxes of the idle and deranged. The Anarchist sat on a bench under this statue and opened a brown paper package filled with postcards.

Glossies! He rubbed his finger over the lush surface.

No smudging! Photo-litho on cardboard plates. The specialist had finally come through. The cross-hatching was as sharp as the original. BOMBS AWAY in red was a real eye catcher. On the flipside in bold Helvetica he read OPENING—THE PHOENIX—A NON-CONCEPTUAL EVENT, "Movement in Action" Contact: Sandy at Ad-A-Live.

Sandy had sent out half. The rest had been circulated by the Anarchist through the old members' network. The Anarchist, after admiring the cards, rewrapped the package and waited for his contact. Recruits could be safely and singly met in the park, right under the gaze of stray neighborhood cops. He was just another bum hanging out The Anarchist was glad to be making contacts again. The meeting gave him an excuse for a reunion with many old friends.

One, who worked at a clinic down the street, was due very soon. The Anarchist was surprised he had followed-up on Sandy's call. He had always seemed a sensible, moderately liberal person. He had channeled his idealism in a dedicated career as a social worker. Why would such a man consider the PHOENIX seriously enough to request a private meeting with the Anarchist? They had been friends but became distanced from varying interests and attitudes. Regrettably, the Anarchist thought, that was how one lost contact — points of variance more frequent than intersections. It was a facet of life in New York City.

The clinic had a modern-esque door that never locked properly. The tile was turquoise in the lobby, set in half-inch squares all over the walls, ceiling, and floor. It was the American Byzantine style popular in the 1950s, when gold paint was mixed in the mortar. The floor also contained yellowish puddles and plastic cups littered in circles. This lobby was the battleground, where the methadone clinic on the fourth floor trafficked with the alcoholism clinic on the first floor. Though once a day the floor was swept and mopped, the odor still remained — the plastic relics reappeared.

Unwashed clothes, yes, that's what the lobby smells like, thought the social worker getting into the elevator.

Heroin and alcohol. Two different drugs, two different sets of addicts.

An alcoholic wandered into the elevator and greeted the social worker with a bold face bloated beyond lines. The man wanted to get off at the methadone clinic, whose door the social worker had just locked.

"The clinic is closed for today, and don't you want the one downstairs?"

"Don't people live here on the fourth floor?" the alcoholic persisted.

"Not in the clinic."

"Do you live here?"

"Not if I can help it. I'm a worker."

"Can I join and live here, too?"

"I don't think so."

"Why not? Aren't a man allowed to live…"

"Look, I don't want to talk. Do you mind?"

"Not if you give me a cigarette."

The social worker didn't smoke, so he offered the drunk a quarter. The guy refused it saying, "I asked for a cigarette. Not money."

Different populations, the social worker repeated to himself, wondering about his own motivations for offering the quarter. He'd forgotten that alcoholics were a different species of addict, more grandiose and somehow more human, though he was prejudiced after all his years at the methadone clinic. His gesture was an unprofessional act, some kind of alienated liberal leftover. It was the liberal leftovers in his character which made him agree to Sandy's solicitation. He had always liked the Anarchist. The guy was serious about his statements. "Last stand" was one that was currently in the social worker's vocabulary. He figured they now had something in common.

Just that week, the social worker had been informed that the clinics were being kicked out of the lofts for luxury conversions. The alcoholism clinic could relocate but the methadone clinic had completely lost funding. That meant more bodies on benches, more deadly dealing. Hoarding already caused the street value of methadone to balloon. Plastic cups were glutting the few clinic outposts left. The Anarchist's friend would fight the loft conversion and the funding cut, but he feared it was a losing battle. He would become an unfunded sociological priest. Eventually, after unemployment and nonprofit organizational leads ran out, he would redirect his counseling skills to a public relations firm or some philanthropic organization funded by an obscure eccentric for esoteric studies or...He would rather talk to the Anarchist.

Three o'clock. The Anarchist saw the time on the clock at Cooper Union. He didn't have long to chat, since he was to meet Sandy at four o'clock about the logistics of the meeting. With some relief, he watched the social worker approach. There was a "gameness" about him he had not noticed before.

"What do you have there?" asked his friend, pointing at the brown-wrapped package.

"Like one?" the Anarchist offered, slipping a card out and handing it to the social worker. "You might find it a good time."

His friend, perplexed, turned the card over, only increasing his perplexity.

"I don't get this."

"Look again," said the Anarchist with a grin. "Have you ever known me to have a sense of humor?"

"This isn't a joke?"

"Nope, it's purposefully obtuse. I can't afford humor,"

"You pay for that perspective in time wasted."

"Cultural release?" the social worker laughed. "Adaptation, survival—are preached as a supreme virtue to hide the fact that to have 'survivors', there has to be an incident of devastation, unless the whole society is just that."

"Propaganda," the Anarchist shrugged. "You're in the reclamation business. Besides, really, who are 'they'?"

"Government, private industry, powers that be— authorities. When they talk survival, they mean kissing ass and knuckling under. I'm losing my clinic and I'm not the only one."

"This meeting's in my shop, the basement of the loft," the Anarchist said, pointing across from Phoebe's. "Come tonight and make whatever commitment you can."

The men crossed arms and shook hands. Then the Anarchist was alone. No one watched them, he was certain. The social worker should not be seen with him, just in case. For all he knew, some "authority" might be taking the Phoenix seriously.

****

Wayne Niebold, returned from the Vendettas meeting, took off his St. Mark's outfit. He smoothed down the spikes of hair and washed off ash he had smeared into his sneakers. Out of a battered manila envelope, he took the folded invitation and a copy of Sandy's questionnaire. He wanted to make some sense of the experience. What was he committed to? The Questionnaire was as straightforward as a management seminar:

1. Have you ever committed a radical act? If "yes" list dates and type.
2. Are you proficient at firearms, electronics, munitions,

propaganda or video equipment?

3. Do you need a definite object for your actions; financial reward or personal value?

4. Would you volunteer time for the new Food for Vendettas? How many hours a week?

5. Food for Vendettas is a fully responsible, unstatused organization dedicated to internal political anarchy. Would you be responsible for its acts or protection? Is your participation contingent on certain conditions?

6. What kind of monetary contribution would you be willing to make? Amount?

7. If you were asked to leave now and return the form, would you comply? If not, please explain.

8. Does commitment to an ideal mean action? Do you feel a need for either?

9. Does acquiring goods and services in a never ending variety and quantity seem a suitable objective for your life? What role do you assign it?

Wayne, of course, had filled every question in the time allotted. He described himself as skilled in nonverbal communications. He said he knew something about commitment; had a religious orientation and acrobatic skills. He volunteered an afternoon a week and specific weekends. He was lucky, when he thought about it. Sandy had allowed him into the meeting. His nervousness might have made her suspicious. She had singled him out at the door, where she collected invitations and checked off names. He ran his finger down the list and crossed off his name. Sandy handed him the questionnaire and a cover sheet. The cover, printed as a gallery opening, was very good. The flipside contained a price list for the Anarchist's posters.

"Don't talk much?" she had challenged him.

Wayne had shrugged poker-faced. He didn't feel, under her pressure, like saying he was a deaf-mute. Her aggression inhibited him from revealing anything she might construe as an advantage. Yet she had singled him out.

After the "opening" part of the evening, she and the Anarchist had collected pencils and questionnaires from opposite ends of the shop and met at the front. For a podium, she overturned an orange crate next to the printing press. She stood on it.

> "The opening part of the evening is over now. Thank you for coming and we greatly appreciate any purchase of posters. Anyone who wants to participate in the Phoenix operation will be assigned a port-a-pack and walkie-talkie. The Anarchist will instruct on their usage."

Sandy discarded cards as people left. Wayne saw her mouth to the Anarchist, "I hate to waste my breath."

Randomly flipping cards, she singled Wayne out from the small group that remained.

"Wayne Niebold, why are you here?"

Wayne had hastily scribbled a page in large block letters. He tore it off his pad and waved the page with OUTRAGE.

"Have you taken a vow of silence?"

Wayne, reluctantly, signed a typical deaf-mute's NO, thinking the sign common knowledge.

"Deaf–mute" the Anarchist clarified.

"Do you have a background in outrage?" Sandy asked, undaunted.

Wayne decided to have some fun. He took his folding chair and smashed it on the floor, succeeding in breaking one cross-bar of wood.

Sandy approved. "Good response," she said, making an okay sign.

"Now an intro for all who remain. The Anarchist is my associate. I am the coordinator. The scope of this operation is Manhattan Island, but it will serve as a symbolic national paradigm. I have your cards and you will be contacted if you volunteer. For your own protection, no volunteer will be told more details than they need to perform their tasks."

"What kind of thing are you doing?" asked a red-haired girl from the back.

"This is the opening of 'The Phoenix,' a non-conceptual event. Movement in action is our vernacular. The Phoenix is really a radical act. This will not be a psycho-drama or a recreation but a live guerilla-strike, documented in video-verite style. Make no mistake. My name is Sandy and I am a terrorist. Immigration is familiar with my identity. We will be staging our event like the ones created by mainstream cultural institutions. We want to show the vulnerabilities of urban defense systems and the lack of a coherent, consistent ideology, which serves the people. For example, let me talk about one absurd practice of the so-called public utilities."

Sandy went on to describe how the electric company had a special squad who were paid bonuses to turn off the service of people who were late in payment. She related the boast of an employee, who climbed into a basement through a broken window on a rickety ladder to turn electricity off. Turning it on was a "routine" operation. Employees received no incentive and, in fact, were encouraged not to go out of their way. Even so, she raved, you were supposed to identify with the company's right! It's a subtle process of intimidation.

Wayne found Sandy and her mysterious operation more melodramatic than threatening. He was surprised when her request for testimonials of this "process" provided stories: a stockbroker told of false stock manipulations and what they cost the country in economic stability, a chemical engineer told of incentives to develop compounds dangerous to humans but lucrative to business, an ex-Krishna told of the extensive corporate investments of his organization, despite the celebration of poverty in recruitment policies.

Litanies of bad and dangerous working conditions, unemployment, evictions, price-fixing, and lost pension funds were commonplace. How, Wayne wondered did these people accept this and continue to feel at all. Were they numb or deeply cynical or just without hope? But they had showed up tonight.

If Sandy was the evangelist, the Anarchist was the resident sage. A rare man with the internal resources to resist absorption in external ideologies. Had he been manipulated by someone as obvious as Sandy? Since Wayne had entered the shop, he had wanted an answer for this question. He had noted all data, relevant or seemingly not; how the Anarchist tilted work lights to display his posters as at a real art "opening." He greeted guests and poured wine, near someone with a watch, of whom he repeatedly asked the time. The Anarchist smiled and shook the hands of curious college kids, sullen art students, post-'60s organic food consumers, Ukrainian neighborhood folk, a few desperate but tidy corporate men and one woman in a gray flannel suit—who didn't seem to take herself seriously at all. Friends of the Anarchist crowded around the posters. Some bought and left. The basement smelled dank.

Despite this observation, Wayne was unsure what he thought of the Anarchist. His initial impression of a hot temper was muted by a shy cynicism apparent in compressed lips and lowered eyelids. A girl in a halter dress halted the Anarchist's tense prowling.

"You're printing these! How nice. I've seen them around town. They are very idealistic."

"Your choice," the Anarchist said, smiling shyly. "Three

dollars or free."

The girl took out some singles and asked, "Is your friend serious about her 'Phoenix?'"

"Just a tape and take-over to be exact."

"I'm not too action-oriented," the girl apologized. "I better go."

"Stasis, an intelligent course," the Anarchist said wistfully, giving her the poster. "A body at rest stays at rest."

At nine o'clock, the Anarchist told people the "opening" part of the evening was over and began to set up rows of folding chairs. With angry precision, he formed rows, straightening each chair. His clean, white shirt didn't camouflage the impression he hadn't slept in days. He drifted over to the apple juice table and picked up Sandy's cards. The Anarchist took a back seat.

"Walk through that door if you are merely curious," Sandy said. "If you have families, leave also. Those who remain can take a questionnaire card and review the material carefully. It will help you determine if the Phoenix is the mission for you."

Watching the Anarchist pass out lined index cards, Wayne was impressed by his purposeful self-control. A complex man; the cynicism of a few minutes before now seemed a cover for an earnest fervor. Wayne understood why the AG had chosen him. He felt a need to strike this man with the force of his own character, make him realize that Wayne Niebold was worthy of notice. He listened to Sandy, waiting for such a moment.

"Each of you is to list the acts you have performed which qualify you for this event."

A neatly-dressed man in a V-neck sweater stood up. The Anarchist, Wayne noted swiveling in his chair, showed a strain of recognition. A friend?

"My name is Ralph. I'm involved with a methadone clinic soon to close. I know there are two sides to the argument, whether maintenance is better than..."

"Ralph," Sandy interrupted, "what do you offer?"

"Munitions, hand to-hand combat and," he laughed,

"counselling people who don't fit. I began with myself, after I shot my battalion leader in Vietnam."

"Sounds good but I also want you to list practical skills – like truck driving. Give your card to me or the Anarchist before you leave."

After Sandy's line, the Anarchist buttoned-up his jacket for a hasty exit. Wayne followed the angle of Sandy's open mouth from the orange crate to the door of the shop.

"Where are you going?"

The redhead turned reluctantly. With the barest of courtesy he said, "Out for air, gurl."

"No. Your pledge and presence are a necessity."

Reluctantly, the Anarchist found verification in the faces of the expectant audience. He joined Sandy at her podium. She kissed him hard with solid possession.

"This man's integrity and dedication are known to all in this neighborhood," she began.

The Anarchist silently went along. What made him a mark for someone as obviously unscrupulous as Sandy, wondered Wayne. Maybe there was something fragile underneath his committed ideology, some naive vanity stirred at the thought of being essential to the PHOENIX. In any case, Wayne wanted to help the Anarchist and not just for the AG. He wrote a note at the door of the basement, where Sandy and the Anarchist embraced the departing recruits. Wayne passed the note in his palm to the Anarchist and lingered behind the last recruit. YOU WILL NEED AN ASSISTANT. I WOULD LIKE TO WORK WITH YOU read the Anarchist.

Sandy regarded Wayne with some hostility and spoke of him in 3rd person to the Anarchist. "You don't believe he's a deaf mute, do you? He's too fashionable."

The Anarchist released anger. "Enough of your suspicions. This man wishes to help me in my work."

"I'll not discuss sensitive issues before I know he's dependable. By the way, did you like Jack's Krishna impersonation?"

(She aimed her last remark at Wayne, hoping to see disillusionment.)

"I think your friend, Ralph, will be useful, but him," she gestured toward Wayne.

"I want a report on all your activities with the Anarchist."

"NO," said the Anarchist. "I will not be monitored."

"I want to keep an eye on him, not you. If he proves a spy, if the Phoenix is miscoordinated or falls apart, all the better."

"What," The Anarchist said, "are you talking about?"

"No one important will believe it's real."

Was the operation a hoax, Wayne wondered, later at home, or did she want him to suspect that? Why risk the well-being he had recently created in his life? Why had he volunteered for such craziness? Something to do with his need for commitments—the way he joined organizations because of individuals he admired. Denotation might have given him a way of life but wasn't it the Llama he adhered to? And now the Anarchist? Why did he gleefully smash the chair?

Sinking into his platform bed, Wayne practiced self-analysis by free-associating Denotation-style. He thought of his childhood and the suburban family left behind. Wayne's adolescent rebellion had not been severe. Only a coy, occasionally clever joke, like when he referred to a suburban center for mass consumption as a shopping MAUL. Such cute witticisms became family jokes, still causing ripples on his infrequent holidays home.

His father, who had once made a living repairing electrical appliances, now sold components for stereos in his own chain store. He was, Wayne realized, a man who changed with the times. He showed his approval of Wayne's journalistic aspirations with technical talk about available word processors.

On Wayne's last visit, the family posed for a Polaroid.

Wayne's brother-in-law held the camera. Wayne was installed, in chronological order, between his two sisters. His father wore a spacey metallic cap. He handed it to Wayne, who put it on his head just before the SNAP! The family had been preserved in natural daylight without a flash. The world was not picture-perfect in the suburbs.

His father might be progressive but he had never remarried after Wayne's mother died. The family portrait was not sepia-tinted. Who knew how Polaroid developer would wear in ten years? His father was sad without a wife. Perhaps, he thought optimistically, the picture would form its own aftertint. Transitory items, such as space hats and Polaroid shots, made the suburbs fun but seemed part of a matrix of hypocrisy.

People only talked about "pleasant" subjects — a new car or baby, an engagement ring, or a perfect haircut. He grew up among serious discussions of daily tragedies—mastectomies, cancers, car accidents, heart attacks, divorces, and robberies. Horrors were whispered by his sisters, under the oppressive "pleasantness," which had to be maintained against any evil. Wayne was taught to cultivate an attitude of well-being, equilibrium, "normalcy." He must keep it up at all costs!

Maintenance had, he decided, given him a loose screw. The

smashed the chair was a nostalgic trace of a quelled rebellion, as absurd as politics in the suburbs. It was only now, in his work for the Church, that he realized loss of well-being didn't necessarily mean a change for the better. How could he have faulted his family? They were happy. Their edgy belief system had proven a self-fulfilling prophecy.

Fondly, he remembered a game played with his brother-in-law on his last visit, while his sisters pushed plastic squares around a new kind of canasta board. The object of the game was to identify a famous person from the first letter of their first and last name within a certain time-limit. Wayne thought the game stupid but wanted to please his brother -in-law. He had written, conversationally, on his score pad: IF AS WARHOL SAID, ALL PEOPLE WILL BE FAMOUS FOR 15 MINUTES ANY OF THESE NAMES ARE INTERCHANGEABLE.

"Just names we know," his brother-in law said. Wayne agreed. Love for esoteric objects mass produced was a common cultural denominator. It brought together couples, children, even estranged families. Wayne knew space hats and generations of Polaroids were a kind of social glue. Yet they were part of the oppressive sense of the "pleasant" which made his upbringing vacuous. It was a mind-set which prevented him from honestly defining his actions. He didn't live by acts but by chronicling the esoteric. Still, though he couldn't hear the sound, he HAD smashed the chair.

Now he understood his motivations for involvement in the Phoenix. Living with the involvement would be more difficult.

He would have to write three sets of reports: the "Helpful Hints" column, the Llama's AG report, and Sandy's reports on the Anarchist's project. He would also be assisting the Anarchist. Well, he consoled himself, the opposite of a vacuum was activity. Though he had overdone it. By declaring himself for the AG, he was in conflict with the Llama. Why did he choose this?

She had given him a sense of being an essence, a genuine person. What was the AG to herself? Emotion, perhaps an uncensored panorama of experience? A kaleidoscope of association related to the variety of life? Her source seemed infinitely unconscious. Wayne halted his speculations. He knew nothing about the AG. Did everyone project their sensibility onto her? For Sandy, she was a fool to dupe, for the Llama, a symbol of a religion he wanted to counterfeit? Wayne didn't want to entertain this. He slipped into his bed, enjoying the clean tucked sheets. It had been an interesting evening, not dull in the least.

The Anarchist, unaware that he still had on his black coat, lay down on his bed. He was glad to be solitary to mull over the meeting, his mission and his new assistant. Wayne Niebold appeared a likely lad; quiet, smart, eager. As far as trust (the question Sandy had posed for him), the Phoenix was already absurd. If leaked, who would take it seriously? He had heard murmurs at the 'opening' that the operation was a self-promotional event; a subversive act, whose purpose was be taped.

Was the Phoenix truly a grass-roots community action event? This applied only in a very limited way. Was he guilty of duplicity? Sandy had used his auspices but he hadn't misled anyone. One of the oddities of the urban culture elite was that they were so 'event' saturated, reality had disappeared from actuality. An event only existed in the interpretation and this was scrupulously left to critics. Why not? The task was awesome and many found it not to their measure.

The future of Wayne Niebold might be his own business, but the Anarchist could not ignore the danger in which he was involving the young man. His act, unlike Sandy's operation, was that of an Anarchist. As it progressed, conscience and action should meld to one consistent truth. Wayne would make his choices along the way, just as he had at the meeting. There would be plenty of chances for him to back out.

Filled with a tangible sense of purpose, the Anarchist dozed easily—the first time in weeks. He dreamt of confetti and tickertape falling out of windows on Wall Street. It was New Year's Day and brokers were dumping cartons of it. The Anarchist had forgotten about the New Year and was caught in miles of the stuff. Tripping and sliding, he couldn't find his way to the river. Ahead he vaguely saw the head of the George Washington statue on the steps of Federal Hall. Around it and the Anarchist was something so thick, he choked and gagged and ...

The Anarchist awoke to find a green paper on his eye. Closer focus identified it as a fifty-dollar bill. This recognition coincided with a giggle from the AG. The Anarchist found it hard to acknowledge the evidence of his eyes. The bed was filled with money. The AG continued to take more out of her marketing bag.

"AG! Where did you find all this?"

"We won the bank machine's cash game. It's legal, Anarchist! We can do so many things now!"

The Anarchist felt anxious. In the face of his recent commitment to the PHOENIX, the money could mean publicity he could not afford. Besides the AG had never wanted the joys of insularity that came with wealth. It was hers, in any case. In the aftermath of the PHOENIX, she could go and build herself a future. For now, for both their sakes, he would distance himself from her fortune.

"AG, I will not be a party to possession. How many account service charges, house foreclosures and car repossessions contributed to this bonanza? How many bankrupt families are represented by your windfall? Take the money and go or I will have to leave."

The Anarchist picked up a broom and began sweeping the green bills into a large pile.

"I'll hide it until you get used to the idea," the AG said. "You have wanted many things that are now possible."

"In the past. Give it away, AG."

As the Anarchist swept, the AG tried to tap into his thoughts. She was not completely blocked. He felt regret at having to reject the money. There was some decision which made it possible for him to detach his life from hers. His love for her was in conflict. Very twisted emotion, the AG decided, "You have a commitment," she said to the Anarchist, "that's making the money more than difficult. Please, forget it. Let us go away to a warm climate for a while."

The AG saw an image in her mind's eye, a desert with a small house and a miraculously sprouting garden. It was not a fantasy. There was something too tangible for that, something very changed in her Anarchist working that garden. The image provided a respite from the constant anxiety, which made her urgent and careless.

"Anarchist, something awful is going to happen. You've closed yourself to me!"

The Anarchist stopped sweeping. "AG, you have no right to pry!" The Anarchist felt afraid. He shouted, knowing he needed to break with the AG. He could not sleep next to her this night or any other (what if she found out about the Phoenix?). He swept quickly, realizing he did not want to lose her, knowing he had already given her up. He retreated into the age-old paradox of freedom and destiny. How did they interact? What was the story behind the AG's windfall? He believed there were no accidents, no true coincidences, just natural laws beyond common understanding. He was stubbornly committed to his destiny, and a little afraid it might not exist. The AG would not understand the necessity for immortality.

The Anarchist swept the bills into a neat pile, tied them

with a rubber band, and paused at the loft door before going down to his print shop. Adversity could not look at prosperity with less than contempt. He would not use the AG's money to finance his laser.

"AG, I will sleep in the shop. Please have the money removed when I return."

"You have a commitment," she said to the Anarchist, "that's making the money more than difficult. Please, forget it. Let us go away to a warm climate for a while." The AG felt devastated as she listened to his footfalls recede. She reviewed the evening for a clue to her error. She had not left the club at her usual time, eleven o'clock, because she had been too excited to stay past 10:45. She had been careful to hide her find from Joe and Rhonda, who would not understand. Joe would be disconcerted by her "easy money," suspicious that the Anarchist might have involved her in a criminal activity. Rhonda was superstitious. She would dwell on an impending social nemesis to descend on the AG, from a treasure gained without travail.

So the AG inconspicuously stowed her bag in its usual place under her mirror in the dressing room (though she did offer Rhonda a loan for a new costume). Soon as her act was over, she left to break her news to the Anarchist. Perhaps she had been insensitive? Showering him with cash was akin to her favorite luxury, wrapping her body in an incredibly precious silk. Money was just magic stuff. It could change their circumstances but only that. Obviously, the windfall meant something different to the Anarchist.

The AG wondered if she had been naïve. Many people thought money was life. Was the Anarchist such a one? Why else did he act, as though she had brought home something indecent, slightly obscene? He was a materialistic man by nature but he rarely wanted money. Only now for a specific purpose that was a mystery.

The AG's thoughts tumbled in confusion; her sensibility useless without her Anarchist. Lying on her bed, she sought a solution from her dreams. The AG had learned a method from a passing Sufi. He often discussed with his children over breakfast the content of their dreams. When a child was attacked by a tiger in a reoccurring nightmare, the Sufi instructed him to give himself a suggestion to combat the tiger, as he was falling asleep. When the tiger again attacked, the child woke up within the dream and vanquished the beast.

The AG understood how the two states of consciousness mirrored each other. She believed the dream life had more consistency, an emotional logic to the images and their sequences. Maybe she could use the Sufi's technique to dispel an amorphous dread of what was unfolding. She wanted to dream about the Anarchist and discover in what direction he was investing his destiny. She would wake in his dream, cognizant, and change the ending he had ordained. It was a tall order for a self-taught lucid dreamer. The AG closed herself to outside stimuli and gave it a try. She had had success in the past, awakening pink and happy with the outcomes.

First the sensation of consciousness in an immediate context – her body floating in an environment of rotating visions. She focused her attention with the exercises Sufis taught the rare "clairvoyant dreamer." She awoke in the dream context and prepared to place herself in the fourth dimension. The AG focused on clothes; patterns, textures, lines and colors. Using each concepts in turn (which she experienced on a daily basis) she was able to see the fabric of the future. Those concepts became invisible particles and waves, the texture of time. The AG sensed the play of the universe forming and dissolving. She was not ignorant of how the universe occurred but wasn't interested in the question. She was more practical. Her body was not meant for solitary space. Care had to be taken so she did not totally detach from gravity-bound existence.

The AG finished her psychic calisthenics, closed her eyes and visualized the Anarchist in sharp detail. Her dream sought its object but with little success. So much of her sensibility was invested in this subject, so much emotion present that she lost her dream state and could not sleep at all. That night, the AG discovered insomnia.

Desperate ambiguity awaited her, as night progressed to morning. Her feelings were only heightened by the knowledge of the Anarchist's movements more than five floors below.

Chapter 11

WHEELS TURN

The Llama eyed the contents of his In Box. The tray held a Pendaflex file with a typed tab reading DESTINY and a peculiar green folder left by Wayne Niebold. Though Wayne's report interested him more, he usually left rose-colored folders, but the Llama reached for the Pendaflex file. It held a punched paper roll and a report on the fallacies of daytime soap-opera psychology.

The report had been a factor in the Llama's concept of Denotational Drive-ins. It listed statistics from a recent poll. Soap fans were split 50/50 about whether human tragedy was due to random catastrophe or individual character flaws. Tragic incidents varied in number within specific time spans. Unexpected crisis was rarely linked to free will, yet outside the probability of random occurrence.

Crisis, the Llama reflected, is as mutable as personality, especially since free will was often inhibited by common sense. His drive-ins provided a medium for the exercise of the latter, since one could enjoy contemplation in the comfort of one's own time-frame and vehicle. Briefly, the Llama allowed himself to enjoy his own solid idea. Then he rotated the paper roll to the beginning.

The "DESTINY" roll contained a Denotational print-out on human aspiration. The print-out was the product of a "thought condensation machine" for organizing philosophical questions. The Llama found the device handy.

The print-outs simplified complex interactions, though it could also make them appear superficial. The editing on his word processor was worse. It convoluted his words and his thoughts could seem incomprehensible. He worried over the following paragraph, adding qualifiers:

HUMAN ASPIRATION DOES NOT **NECESSARILY** COINCIDE WITH THE NATURE OF REALITY.

HUMAN LIMITATIONS AND THE COMPROMISE OF **ACTUAL** CIRCUMSTANCES NEVER REALLY SATISFY INDIVIDUALS.

ASPIRATION CAN BE SATISFIED IF REALITY IS ASSESSED IN A **SPECIFIC** TIME FRAME. THE **CALCULATED** CERTAINTY OF PROBABILITY IS NOT A PROJECTION OR INTUITIVE GUESS.

PESSIMISM IS EQUALLY AS **IRRELEVANT** AS OPTIMISM.

A SKEPTIC LOSES **HEART WITHOUT** THE BALANCE OF ANALYSIS **TEM-**

PERED WITH EMOTIONAL RESPONSE.

HAPPINESS IS THE RESULT OF FELT KNOWLEDGE AND POSITIONED WITHIN THE LIFE STRUCTURE.

This was an infinite rewrite The Llama only too well appreciated the graphic form of this paradox between human compromise and aspiration. He put the roll away and opened Wayne's folder to a dated memo reading: FROM: WAYNE TO SANDY. RE: SUMMARY OF THEORY AND PROGRESS ON THE LASER ARM OF THE PHOENIX. EXCERPT: THE ANARCHIST'S WORK IN PROGRESS.

The Llama read down the page:

> Laser has been defined as Light Amplification by Stimulated Emission of Radiation.
>
> The word "laser" is an acronym formed by the first letter of each word of its definition. It means: "A light-emitting body with feedback for amplifying the emitted light."
>
> The Anarchist is assembling a chemically-powered laser once developed for experimental purposes by a company in California. It consists of a long, hollow tube with mirrors at either end. By burning hydrogen and fluorine gas within the tube, a bright flame is created. The light produced by the flame is then bounced back and forth by the mirrors at the

ends of the tube to produce a laser beam.

It is the "pointing technology" that worries the Anarchist. In addition to the two mirrors used to produce the laser beam, a third large mirror is required to reflect it to the target, and it will have to be "Q-Switched."

The Anarchist has decided against a ruby rod. They make a neater laser with more power but are harder to control and cost too much. The chemical laser burned with a flash lamp should work fine. The adjustments may be difficult, an angled window would take some fine grinding. And then, according to what he knows about the "Q-Switching" mechanism needed to control the "resonance" (as he says,) in such a way that the counteraction between the pumping and the laser action is eliminated.

This kind of laser would be of higher intensity because the conversion occurs in a matter of seconds. The stored high energy would burst out of the lasing element in a giant pulse with power up to gigawatts per square.

NOTE: The Anarchist just told me to add that the "Q–Switch" he will use is a rotating prism instead of a Kerr-cell tech-

> nique. The Anarchist says you should know that the most successful for pure continuous wave operation are the gaseous mixtures. He wants intensity. Still, it is possible to mix the gases, like argon and krypton, in which lasing might occur simultaneously at ten different wavelengths, ranging from violet through the red spectral region. A real "white light" laser.
>
> The most powerful and the most efficient is a CO_2 laser. The first glass one contained a helium-gas mixture. Although its first successful opera...

The Llama skipped from the technical information, available in the engineering section of New York's best public libraries, to the bottom paragraph which he circled for later contemplation. Implementation of the laser might imply its purpose.

> We are through with research and are accumulating apparatus. The Anarchist wishes the laser arm of the PHOENIX to be structurally independent, though, it will coordinate with the dust dump — just a half-hour before. It will be a dramatic forerunner. I will follow this report with further bulletins on our assemblage and general theory.
>
> You should realize the Anarchist has appreciable say in these reports, as he agreed to their

> existence with great reluctance. Since they are in evidence, you are under no circumstances to call him to account or comment on any aspect of his arm of the operation.
>
> IMPORTANT NOTE: DIO'S CHECKS ARE TO BE LEFT BLANK IN A WHITE ENVELOPE UNDER THE DOOR OF THE WORKSHOP.

The Llama put down the report with a feeling of acute betrayal. He had always thought Wayne a model disciple totally loyal to the Church and the Lama. What had gone awry? What had caused him to become associated with anarchists?

The report on the AG, yes! Wasn't it obvious? As the case took more hours, the quality of Wayne's reports had declined into obtuseness. Sandy and the Anarchist were connected with the AG. Wayne had become dangerously involved, split his priorities and personality. Only a "wash" would mend the fissure. The process of his defection would be unraveled, recorded, and stored for future reference.

The Llama pushed a small button inside his desk drawer which activated a teletype machine at the Inner City Villa. He spoke into the teletype mechanism:

"Tell the task force benevolence squad to send an 'invitational' telegram to Wayne Niebold, and pick him up for a wash. Immediately. I am to be informed."

The Llama, aware of Wayne's extreme sensitivity, was sorry

to give the order. But it was necessary for him to uncover the full meaning of the "Phoenix," including its timetable. If he didn't stop the operation, his centers with their blameless facades might not see the light. No one would see the Wes Mavine banner unfurled in the dark or....

Suddenly, he imagined a blonde girl, some clairvoyant dreamer LOST? NO! She would be saved from these anarchists, as well as his centers. Not an imaginative man, the Llama was shaken by this vision. Instead, he focused on Wayne. He consoled himself that Wayne intended for him to discover the operation. Why else would he have switched the color of the folders? THERE ARE NO ACCIDENTS he recalled as he pushed his button again to give a new order.

"Rescind the Wayne Niebold order. I want him in the field. Pick-up an anarchist called Sandy. Her description and habitats will be listed in the Niebold files marked AG."

The Llama eased back into his chair. The report was addressed to Sandy, the leader of the operation. She was the key, not Wayne. In fact, Wayne had expressed his loyalty by his subconscious exposure of the PHOENIX. He had proved his value, and, ultimately, he would lead the Llama to the AG.

The time-lapse between orders was only a few minutes but the Llama's Phone Alert crew coordinated schedules with the taped calls. The crew was already working on a batch of seizures and telegrammed "invitations," when they received the last tape of the day— the one ordering the seizure of Wayne

Niebold. The crew sent the telegram and assigned the follow-up, just as the machine closed down for the right. The rescind order and Sandy's seizure were unprocessed. Zeke, a temporary member of the crew, recently reoriented and awaiting release, received the name and address of Wayne Niebold with no small pleasure. Parts of his mind remained intact.

Wayne Niebold's apartment showed signs of accelerating chaos. Rings of paper were no longer identifiable among clothes dropped before. Piles of worn underwear, socks, shirts, and sheets filled the floor and a nearby chair beyond the limits of overflowing. Along with Wayne's peace of mind, he had lost consciousness of his immediate surroundings. His mental landscape was completely occupied by the Llama's report, Sandy's memos and his column. He lay on his couch in a kind of semi-conscious reverie, his exhausted psyche demanding respite. He let his mind wander through boyhood reverie of television long gone.

Wayne, age eleven, was watching "Saturday Night at the Movies" on the color set in his parents' bedroom, a large square room with two double beds welded together. Wooden end tables had cylindrical lamps of oriental rice paper with pressed leaves. Wayne's mother often remarked she had not bought ones with pressed butterflies, because they were barbaric. Wayne dutifully approved her sentiment, said he was sure he was okay alone to facilitate her exit. He wanted to explore the forbidden territory on the top shelf of his parents' closet.

Hidden by clothes was a back shelf of his father's "adult"

reading, his *Playboy* mags with *Justine*, *The Story of O*, *The Diary of a Victorian Gentleman*, and *Circus*, a lesbian pulp classic. Having read his mother's copy of *The Child from 5-11*, Wayne knew his curiosity was normal. Still he was careful to replace the books in the right places. If caught, he planned to say he only read them, like a soundtrack, while watching the movie. He never touched the *Playboys*. Seen one, seen them all.

On this evening, he didn't feel like reading. He had a high fever from chicken pox, though he didn't know it. His eyes were purplish and swollen. The images on the screen quickly skirted from the right to the left wings of the tube. Wayne wished he could slow them down. He wanted to read the actor's lips. After a while, he watched without trying.

The feature was an Alfred Hitchcock film with Doris Day and Jimmy Stewart. She was singing "Que Sera, Sera," tears in her eyes for her little kidnapped boy. In the final scene in an opera house, she screamed, thinking her boy lost. The fear in her face reflected Wayne's own feelings. He turned the set off, immediately jarred by the buzzy electronic quiet of his parents' room. Though he knew the boy was okay, he'd seen the film before, he was yet unsettled.

The room seemed to vibrate with the energy of the overhead lights. He turned them off and turned on the leaf lamps. Wayne still felt uneasy. Only movies turned out all right. Life would never wrap up like the movies. Real life, happiness forever, must only exist for a moment on the tube. Was Life a sham? Everything, including himself, was as inert as the objects in his parents' bedroom. Wayne wanted to put the TV in the closet and return to reality, but he knew his folks would miss it. Instead, he pulled a book from his dad's shelf and read the rhythms of eroticism on his own private soundtrack. He felt alive again. Wayne never watched TV after that, not really.

Now in his apartment, about twenty or so, he tried to visualize Doris Day. He saw not her but the AG with tears in her eyes. He wished he had a television. Over his image of the AG were printed the words: TO GET RID OF SINK ODORS, POUR STRONG SALTWATER SOLUTION OR A CUP OF BLEACH DOWN THE DRAIN. LET WATER RUN TO BE SURE NO BLEACH REMAINS TO ERODE THE PIPES.

Wayne got up to make some coffee. He didn't like the way tension and fatigue affected him, how his subconscious used Doris/the AG to work out residual emotion. He thought of comments by a scientist on the first photos of Saturn, "The commonplace is the bizarre." The Denotational corollary: "There are no mysteries."

To hell with introspection, better to deal with consistency in his reports. He had tried to make Sandy's terse and educational, though his loyalty to the Anarchist made him choose more jargon. For the Llama, he was repetitive detailing the AG's routine with hints of boredom and detachment, Wayne did not want to be accused of unpurged personal involvement. Only his "Helpful Hints" column remained a problem. Pragmatism was garbled with obscure ideas unrelated to basic household problems. Wayne was surprised the Llama hadn't commented on his incoherency. Recently he confused fixing a dishwasher with assembling the elements of a ruby red laser.

He had also mixed-up a description of the AG's latex column dress with directions on obtaining a mercury tube. That might have passed, since the AG's outfits were far-out. Wayne's problem lay in one area — thoughts lost all coherency in the image of Dio's cloud of Arizona Dust.

Wayne had assumed that somewhere down the line he would find the means to act as saboteur. Obviously he had underestimated Sandy's tight grasp of all facets of the PHOENIX. She gave no clear picture to anyone, except the mysterious Mr. Dio, as to how the operation was designed. Wayne had seen the mandala picture of the sites and an estimated timetable, but nothing else. When he delivered his reports, she never answered his questions about the rest of the operation.

Lately, ever since his mind had been functioning on overload, he wasn't sure what he had delivered to Sandy, or the Llama. This made him very nervous.

In his middle desk drawer, Wayne kept carbons of his reports in dye-cut folders color-coordinated with the delivery folders. This system was supposed to keep them properly separated but there was chance of mix-ups — especially for same-day deliveries. Wayne opened Sandy's green report to a carbon that read:

The AG wore a bubblegum pink dress

> with large yellow buttons. Her hat was a flat boater-type yellow straw with pale green ribbons. Her yellow open-work stocking and lime-green Mary Janes caused stares in Washington Square Park. She seemed not impervious to these, merely surprised, as though it was odd people stared at her when the colors of sunset could be seen shifting hue.

Wayne panicked. Not only had this report reached the wrong party, it wasn't even slightly objective! He had written as if he understood the AG's thoughts!

Staggered at this gross self-deception, he opened the rose-colored folder. It should have contained the Llama's report on the AG. Instead was a carbon entitled: LASER ARM OF THE PHOENIX OPERATION.

The title was all he had to read to know he was in trouble. Not wanting to think of the implications, he opened the last folder, kitchen yellow, and read:

> Are your crepe soles worn down with no hope of repair? Many shoemakers do not maintain rubber soles to substitute for worn shoes and heels. To fix your worn rubber footwear, use liquid rubber "Fix-It." Squeeze the substance from the tube to the level worn down on your crepe heel. Take a piece of cardboard and carefully plane off the excess. Dry with the heels up so the "Fix-It" doesn't

> run while it's curing. Soon your shoes will be good as new!

It was the correct carbon. One copy was okay. Who would react first, the Llama or Sandy? With luck the Llama had been too busy supervising the opening of his centers to read the report. Wayne could substitute the correct AG report. Sandy might think Wayne had developed a clothes fetish in regard to her roommate. Wayne realized neither of these outcomes were likely. Unsure how to rectify the potentially horrific consequences, he took refuge in editing his "Helpful Hints" column. He put on his Sony Walkman, turned the volume to max and felt the vibration in his temples—a musical rhythm. He tapped along with his pencil, reading the column.

> Natural kitty litter is more healthful for you and your pet than the commercially available brands. A simple, organic mixture of cut newspapers and regular potting soil is a good choice. Line the box with pebbles first, then the layer of cut papers. On the bed of papers, pour about an inch of absorbent potting soil. In this way you avoid exposure to the harmful additives contained in packaged litter.

Wayne crossed the column out as farfetched and tried to think of an alternative. All that came to mind was the AG, in a rhythm tangibly vibrating from his Walkman.

GOT ME AN ANGEL SENT TO EARTH, the pattern

went...

So much for automatic writing, Wayne thought, not believing he had spontaneously produced such corn. The words in the crossed-out column fairly rippled with emotion under the heart-felt "X." That act of censorship, he realized, was less about the column than his own fear of confronting Sandy or the Llama. Best to see Sandy first and explain the mix-up...

The door vibrated under the fist of someone knocking repeatedly? Pounding. Was it the Llama's proxy or Sandy about to blast him with some unimaginable weapon?

Wayne knew he had watched too many gangster episodes in his youth. The concept was almost prehistoric.

Wayne opened the door to a man in a Western Union uniform, holding out an envelope and a pink pad for him to initial. He asked who the sender was but the man in the uniform didn't know sign language. Wayne was writing in the margin of the pad, when he recognized Zeke. He changed his message: ARE YOU FROM THE LLAMA OR ON AN OUTSIDE JOB?

"Excuse me," Zeke said with no recognition, "I've never met you before."

Either Zeke's brains were scrambled from the "wash," or he had been trained to deny identification with the Llama. Wayne found little in his face, though the Llama's familiar logo was on the upper left-hand corner of the envelope. Wayne hid his increasing fear. Did an "invitational" mean

Zeke would attack Wayne, pin his arms behind his back and march him into a truck? He had heard but never experienced this and so decided it was best to go with procedure. If Zeke had suffered some brain damage, Wayne might as well use it to his advantage.

He signed the pink pad, took the letter and ushered Zeke out in a matter of seconds. He waited until the truck disappeared before opening the envelope:

CONGRATULATIONS DISCIPLE NIEBOLD. YOU HAVE BEEN SELECTED TO ATTEND A SPECIAL RETREAT IN THE EXCLUSIVE DENOTATIONAL INNER SANCTUM. VALUES WILL BE RENEWED AFTER ORIENTATION. SAUNA AND PUNCH PARTY AT THE LLAMA'S VILLA WITHIN THE NEXT 24 HOURS.

Sneaky to leave it ambiguous whether the invitation was for a "wash." If so, why did the Llama give him time to clear out— advance warning? His apartment was out. He would change his clothes for survival mode and beat it. The Llama WAS angry.

Wayne leaned out his window to enjoy the view for perhaps the last time. Other days, when he had problems, he went to the Bank Street dock. Today's problem demanded immediate action and yet Wayne saw that the day was fantastic, the sky a real robin's egg blue. The furthest point he could see was the white triangle tips of yachts bobbing around a shadowed

Statue of Lady Liberty.

Closer, now walking toward the dock, he saw rows of sightseers; bronzed men taking more sun, and an occasional woman. If he wanted, he could squeeze a space next to an old couple dressed in seedy resort clothes. Wayne noticed details of his open shirt, loose tie, and hat severely slouched over reading sunglasses. He liked how the woman's flowered silk dress fluttered over a pair of the nicest knees Wayne had seen lately, though she looked seventy. The woman was painting what Wayne took to be the harbor. She appeared irritated, when another bronzed man blocked her view. Moving his sight line back from the woman, Wayne noted two salad trucks, a Chinese food wagon, and numerous ice cream vans.

It was time to exit the crowded pier, yet it was as impossible to return to his apartment, as it was to comply with the Llama's order. Disappearance signaled refusal. He would file one last report and leave it behind for Zeke or another proxy. The report required the Llama to trust Wayne's information was correct and so his loyalty.

In the same way, the Llama outrageously expected Wayne to trust him. Even to the extent of placing himself in the Church's hands for a "wash!" Wayne owed the Llama this last report. It might yet be possible to stop Sandy.

Returned from the pier, clarity made his hands fly on the keys of his typewriter.

SIR, I AM NO LONGER A PRAGMATIST BUT I

HAVE LEARNED INDIVIDUAL RESPONSIBILITY FROM THE DENOTATIONAL CHURCH. YOU HAVE BEEN MY PSYCHOLOGICAL GUARDIAN, YET HAVE ORDERED A "WASH." I CANNOT REFUSE IN PERSON, SINCE YOU DO NOT OPENLY CONFRONT ME. I AM DISAPPEARING. BEFORE DOING SO, I FEEL OBLIGATED TO EXPLAIN SOME OF THE CIRCUMSTANCES OF THE REPORT YOU RECEIVED THAT WAS INTENDED FOR A NIHILIST NAMED SANDY. THE ANARCHIST, THE AG'S BOYFRIEND, HAS BEEN WORKING ON A LASER EVENT PART OF SANDY'S PHOENIX OPERATION. 6AM. ON MEMORIAL DAY IN MANHATTAN, DUST WILL BE DUMPED AT KEY ENTRY POINTS TO PARALYZE TRANSPORTATION AND MEDIA ARTERIES. ENCLOSED, SANDY'S TIMETABLE AND CONTACT INFO. DO AS YOU THINK RIGHT.

P.S.—DO NOT PICK-UP THE AG. SHE IS
IGNORANT OF THE OPERATION AND
SHOULD NOT BE HELD CAPTIVE. AS YOU
PROBABLY GUESS, SHE IS VERY SENSITIVE.

With this page on the table, Wayne hastily prepared to disappear in the underground of avant-garde culture in the East Village. He would contact the Anarchist at the health foods restaurant and avoid Sandy. Leaving the Church for the Anarchist was a step he first took the night of the meeting. He had kept one foot in The Llama's camp. Like many a prodigal, he was unsure if he would find home again.

With a thin blade, Wayne tore his shirt around the sleeve seam, making it look like the garb of a college boy gone wrong. It was a stupid stab, but he had to do it. Next, he safety-pinned the seams of his pants from the inside, pegging the shape. He took some kohl and rubbed it under his eyes. The total effect of his outfit was almost complete, the classic look of a cultural in-group of cultural outcasts. This particular uniform was the hair shirt of nonconformity to date.

Looking in his mirror, Wayne thought he totally understood the Anarchist's passion for vegetables. It was an aggressive act of renunciation of worldly values. Like the Anarchist, he was now renouncing his career, his home, his ambition, his stance of worldly sophistication. The Anarchist signaled this with the idiocy of a green thumb.

Wayne only had some fingers stained with washable ink. He wondered if the Anarchist would receive him favorably at the restaurant. Little emotion had passed between them.

Wayne entered the subway in an outfit no longer a disguise. He exited at St. Marks and made his way to the "Grass Roots," a leftover hippie bar. He noted the clientele, a mixture of hippies, college kids newly entering the work force, illegal aliens and transsexuals. They were all hanging out. Some were good at it, some were bad, some seasoned pros and some merely talented amateurs. It was all a matter of posture. Wayne discovered he could be very successful at being ignored.

The AG awoke suddenly and found herself in bed alone. She looked at her ceiling and thought of all the different kinds of ceilings she had seen in the city: high ceilings with ornate cornices, low ceilings with sound-proofing holes, sloped ceilings made of tin and plaster ceilings painted with shiny deck paint. The AG was especially fond of the white ceiling of her loft.

Unfortunately, on this night it made her feel lost in a large expanse. She would like to live somewhere else, she realized, a happy place again. Tonight she saw all the imperfections in her environment. Cracks which had never been spackled coated everything with dust. Bolts of fabric were stacked at random and the impression of disorder was not aided by the tawdry costumes she wore for clothes. Costumes cramped the makeshift rack used as an open closet.

Because of her disturbed sleep, such musings had become familiar. Fatigue prodded her from soft fantasies into a painful awareness of her surroundings. Her nerves, once nonexistent, had overtaken her playfully channeled sensibility. She missed the Anarchist and could not discover the reason for his absence. It was almost better not to know, bad enough she imagined the feel of him beside her, their legs entwined. The memory of his hair was a mockery of their present relations. He rebuffed her care and was hesitant to touch her, mourning, as if she were irredeemably lost.

The AG rolled into the dent left in the mattress by the Anarchist's body. It was as if the spot might yield some trace of his secret, one she dreaded discovering. Was the Anarchist punishing himself or her? Perhaps he should seek analysis, she thought, though the idea upset her. The Anarchist had always defied analysis, even his own. There were no ink stains on the spot he left in the mattress. His jaw was unaccustomedly slack. The AG knew he was making no posters, yet spent more time at the shop. He was quite guarded about that!

Once she had come to visit him unannounced. He had been cruel. She had stood timidly in the doorway of his shop. Her jacket was thin on her shoulders. He had been wild and terrible, his hair and beard seeming to have grayed. His eyes were mad before he masked them but it was his hands that upset her. They seemed autonomous objects, forming something insidious hidden from her sight.

"Get out of here!" he had yelled harshly, his voice a whip across her face.

Later, from a place by the stairwell, she had overheard Sandy and the Anarchist in conversation. The tone of their voices was very serious but all the AG could make out was "act of war," which for some silly reason made her visualize an etching of the Battle of Gettysburg. As the solemn voices continued, she recalled details of this work by an American primitive—the drawn swords, the cannon facing gray troops and Lee's face a wide-open frontal black.

Remembering that horrible afternoon, the AG rolled to her own side of the bed. She curled around herself.

How dreadful she looked. Purplish shadows circled her eyes, signs of time and strain. She would have to consciously control her worry or it would further deteriorate her energies. The AG was self-conscious. She felt her epidermis and dermis layers as pliant substances more tangible than the mattress underneath her.

She uncurled, stretched her legs and arms, wriggled her toes and rolled onto her back. She made herself less frail and slim, imagining her body a resilient cushion; a buoyant, springy place for her vibrating spirit. Her sorrows sank into the substance of her flesh. Release meant tangible joy throughout her being. The AG was ecstatic inside the fleshly coat of her skin. She could leave her body behind.

Not death but escape floating free, she had once done it just for fun. Now it could be useful to uncover what the Anarchist did, when he left her bed. But she was well aware of the dangers of out-of-body travel and the caution required. Two clients of the alcoholics' clinic summed it up, in a conversation overheard on her morning walk on the Bowery. "The human body is really something." Said the first one. "I've seen a man chopped up with knives, beaten within an inch of his life and he'll live but a weird slip, a quick fall on the head and he's gone. It's the oddest thing."

"Sure," said the second one. "We're only mothers' sons."

Threads that held body and soul together were delicate. The AG, who had no fear of death, found soul travel exhilarating. Even so, the similarity to death made her careful not to stray outside the loft. Who knew what snags might be encountered outside? She feared her present suffering far more. Imaginative control, enough to make a body rise, required intensive concentration. She was the process. The outline of her form heaved on the mattress. Gradually her weight receded into the depths of her flesh. She rose through her own dozing tissue.

Floating through layers, she listened to warm cells breathe, enjoying a placid dream cycle. The weight behind her, contained in the upward movement, she rose thinking of a transparent waterbed. At the point of separation, her body was buoyant, held within the framework of bones. She detached. With an act of will, the AG left her body behind.

She watched her sleeping shell with affection, finding it odd that death could decompose it. The idea made her sink a couple feet. There was danger of falling back into her form. The weight of her thoughts made her heavier than her last out-of-body ride. She would hover to adjust.

Separated from carnality, her substance was akin to an indirect light source. She flexed without limbs to respond. A wave of diffuse electrical particles, she pulsed to the other end of the loft at incredible speed. Unused to the motion, timid, she sank. Redoubling her control, she rose and executed a simple, lateral move.

The AG visualized herself as a blip on a computer screen and then a flash of bacteria in a Petri dish. Moving through a timeless medium, she was yet aware of the fine but resilient threads holding her to her body. As they effortlessly unraveled she recalled an ad with fiber optic threads, pulsing with impulses. I am like that she happily acknowledged.

The AG rose to the ceiling, got nicked in a crevice, and rolled around the rafters before sailing sideways out the kitchen windows and up a brick wall. She uprighted herself and took a long look at her body in the bed, seen through the window of the loft. Soon she saw a dot, the window of the loft from the top of a nearby water tower. She rose above the Bowery, parallel to an advertising blimp made visible by luminous computer graphics. She felt an electrical attraction to the powerful images and paused to soak up the vision.

RICHLAND – RICHLAND — A SAGA OF AMERICA

were letters on the blimp. A huge chunk of gleaming coal became a sun over a mountain range. Lakes filled-in. A derrick formed parallel to mountain peaks. Below it spread a lime green field and on it was a suburban home and a family fixing it. This became another field sprouting trees, many houses, flowers, and many families, hand in hand in front of sparkling housing units all lit up in runs of coded colors.

Intoxicated with the colors and lights, the AG suspended herself above the blimp with difficulty. Light components and spasms of sound sent her gliding. Down below, she saw the yellow dot of Phoebe's awning. She couldn't hear the words of Bowery men fighting but intuited the deep guttural sound of a man dying of a bullet wound — a soldier in the city's ever-present, unknown wars.

Out of body, she could do nothing to aid him and she feared other help would come too late. The man's pain was very intense. The AG unraveled for safety, where the air was thin and chilly. The higher she went, the more pleasurable was the sensation. The threads which held her, felt ticklish. She was newly conscious that their interference could be eliminated. The reality of this idea lowered her many sobering feet. Hovering over the injured man, she thought she could do something.

With her total being, she focused on a corner of Phoebe's canvas awning. A flame burst into life. A waiter, smelling smoke, discovered the man. The AG, uncomfortable with omniscience, zeroed in on what held her to Earth. Where was her Anarchist for whom she had risked this journey? The AG compressed downward to street level. She soared through the closed window of the Anarchist's shop.

The Anarchist, enraged, was talking to someone, pointing at a large glass tube and a case of lead. He was pressing an issue the AG couldn't make out, standing over two large mirrors and a prism, which hung near a basin. He played with the prism. Spectrum rays lit Sandy's rigid, angry face. She gestured toward a projector set up on the Anarchist's press bed. The AG heard her say, "If anyone understands the ironies of symbolism, it's me." Of the Anarchist's reply, she understood nothing. Her own emotions had short-circuited comprehension.

The AG attempted to rectify this but the argument grew more intense. She was blown around the room by the charged will of first one then the other. Like a weightless astronaut, she navigated with the wall as a ladder—hand over hand. The threads which held her to life could sever or melt in the hot war of threats and recriminations. Amidst the turmoil, the AG analyzed the specific objects of their contention.

Behind a funny wagon wheel design in magic marker was a map of Manhattan. Wall Street was outlined in a small, blue box. This box was the target of Sandy's wrath. The AG braced herself for the next attack.

"The amount of power you are capable of generating with that thing will do us little good at that target. I'll select a site that will yield some measurable damage."

The AG blocked her emotive feelings to hear the Anarchist's reply.

"I don't care about damage to property. I care about the icon of a great nation, a founding father long ignored. That musty building disgracefully hides a fine revolutionary tradition. It's a national shame! No one goes here but tourists. My laser will mark the blow of a refugee against American hypocrisy!"

Sandy smiled, a slight edge of contempt in her voice. "I am utilitarian. Your act has abstraction weighting it. It will mean nothing but a muddle. Who will hear your complicated idea of significance? Who will care?"

"You will be running the broadcast, Sandy. You could..."

"I won't. It's meaningless."

The AG, unsure what any of this meant, only knew the Anarchist was close to venting his violent temper. His hands, testing the prism, were becoming clumsy and forced. His sense of purpose was shaken. Yes, the AG thought, he needs a sign. I will move something, make some distraction to give him room for a rebuttal. Too many chemicals in the shop for a fire. Could she move an object at will? An attempt to move the projector sent her spinning dizzily, She was too light.

No better than an invisible cry, she thought, as she watched the Anarchist hold the glass tube. He explained about wave structures, about the force of the weapon, how larger and larger waves could decimate a whole building. He had planned a competent control mechanism with the help of his assistant, Wayne Niebold.

WAYNE NIEBOLD. The name in the Anarchist's mouth was a savior. If only she could find him! Wayne would help her. Perhaps his involvement was an answer to her request to watch her Anarchist? Disloyalty from Wayne was not an issue. He cared for her, she was sure.

The AG drifted with the Anarchist's excitement. As he explained his laser, diamond cutters, assemblers of silicon circuits, beams of electric eyes, and a sci-fi rifle were associations conjured for LASER.

"The site at Federal Hall or I'm out of this project," the Anarchist said.

"There is an agreement between us."

"I committed but only as an autonomous partner."

Sandy began to take off her clothes. "You threaten my authority, and, yet, you're committed to nothing but symbolism."

"Autonomy was my condition," the Anarchist replied. "Put on your clothes. I haven't enjoyed one night of love since my commitment."

Sandy stopped undressing, thoughtfully saying,

"You have sacrificed something more than ideas. The AG."

Fear, sorrow, betrayal ran through the AG's disembodied self. She crashed against the walls of the shop and shot back up to the now closed window.

Battered, she knew it wise to find her skin before the threads finally came undone. The AG could not listen to anymore words, nor could she leave the argument. She was diffused throughout the charged atmosphere of the shop. Not good, she thought. Imagination…

The AG assumed a stance above the Bowery, an entity beyond this immediate point in time. She imagined herself a handmade Japanese kite formed of translucent rice paper. Her owner, a loving child, carefully reeled in the string which held her, wanting to avoid a tear in the toy he had made with his own hands. She visualized this child in the loft, coaxing her back to her body, which rested so lonely in bed.

She felt a "click" as her circulatory system, her muscular layers. Good solid bones meshed with her spirit. She hovered an instant before sinking into the refuge of her slumbering body. Lulled into unconsciousness, she almost erased the Anarchist, Sandy; and the whole scene in the print shop.

There was an agitation that kept her from losing total consciousness. She could sleep through it but not obliterate it. The AG eased the sensation by channeling it. Unearthing elements from her memory, she constructed Wayne Niebold's clean features, the apartment he had described, the notepad he kept in an inside jacket pocket, close to his heart.

Details established, she endeavored to resume the psychic communication opened at Joe's Place. The AG had never tried to exercise her abilities over an indefinite stretch of time and space. Through motion-filled waves of sleep, she attempted to locate Wayne Niebold. Failing that, she would try to leave a message for him to come and see her. The AG only succeeded in waking her exhausted body with her efforts. Sweat all around her, she realized her agitation was less a spur than an impediment. Fear and sorrow had made psychic connection impossible.

***

In a bathhouse mirror, one door clown from the Grass Roots bar in the East Village, Wayne Niebold was enjoying the exaggerated points of his "outsider" clothes. His pants were sufficiently sleek, his sleeveless shirt was a classic, but he would have to do something about his hair, that emblem of eccentricity. He would have to make his Boho orthodox.

Wayne opened an ancient tube of Brylcreem hair cream he'd bought at a vintage 1950s store. He coaxed his hair, which was long on top, into a pompadour, and combed and cut-in the side for speed. When he finished, he had to admit the resemblance to a desert roadrunner.

Happy with the result, he exited the bathhouse for the street. He wanted to enjoy the effect of his hair design in the East Village (more girls with miniskirts looked at him than ever before).

Despite his homeless status, Wayne found this neighborhood very pleasant. Couples on stoops sat or stood with heads on each other's shoulders, exchanging coolly wistful smiles in the wind. Though stylish sophistication predominated, bodies melted together awkwardly – sways coordinated for a last desperate cling, a small clutch against time.

Wayne felt foreign in all that heat. In terms of women, he had never been awkward or adolescent. Women had always been available, but now he wanted to fall in love immediately, several times at least, especially if she had an apartment. His position might be precarious, but he'd fearlessly crash any party if it were possible he might meet a woman, if it were possible for him to fantasize about a woman's face held at a certain angle. Sometimes the conversation was provocative enough to activate his imagination, but nothing happened. He looked at the lovers in the East Village and felt envy for what appeared to be "easy affairs"—the "simplest thing" as a '50s song on an old jukebox would nostalgically chime in.

Wayne wondered if his preoccupation with women was due to his homeless state or his real feelings for the AG. Did he want to make love to her? No, he realized, strangely surprised. He wanted to make her tea, sit and talk with her, lose himself in her luminous presence.

Romance was what it added up to, not sex. She was the drifting focus of his thoughts, though his relationship with the Anarchist put him in a peculiar spot. The Anarchist might learn of Wayne's flight from Sandy, but he must never discover his connection with the AG. Besides, Wayne intended to ask him for asylum, a bunk in the Health Foods Restaurant. Suspicion would make life very difficult.

Despite this risk, adrift on the streets, he found it essential to inform the AG of his whereabouts. How, he wondered, was he to establish contact without the knowledge of either of her roommates?

Wayne decided to send a postcard so ambiguous, only she would understand its origin. The moment he made this decision, he was rewarded with a mind's eye image of the AG. With incredible clarity, he saw her mouth; the wide, softly puckered lips, the arc of the trembling upper lip.

Wayne was awed by the perfect consistency of color. He banished the image from his mind, knowing that mouth would feel lovely, and made his way to Unique Boutique. He would find just the right postcard there.

Rounding the corner of Astor Liquors, Wayne reviewed the exact information he had given the Llama about the Phoenix in his final report. His copy of the operations schedule was vaguely coded: TASK FORCE 9 AT TIMES SQUARE INTERSECTION AT 5 A.M. REINFORCE DUMP TRUCKS 1-8 FOR COMMUNICATIONS RADIO

BLOCKADE. Would such information make it possible for the Anarchist to seize control and reroute traffic along safer routes? Had Wayne wanted to help the Llama at the Anarchist's expense? Because of his confusion on the loyalty issue, he realized, he had given only half-hearted information. He hadn't wanted to be responsible for a rescue or an anarchist's act.

Wayne walked up Broadway, admitting his cowardice, but unsure what action would rectify it. Instead, he concentrated on the design of the postcard. As he had once noted in a fashion filler for *The Printed World*, Unique was a mass merchandiser of reasonably priced counter-culture fads gone mainstream. There were always bright colored T-shirts with various necklines and sleeve lengths. There were jeans of every conceivable leg width and length, as well as plastic geometric jewelry, belts, and high-tech scarves with a revival feel to them. Wayne especially liked the card kiosks. They were quite extensive.

He entered the clothing warehouse through a revolving door just past a chained park bench. An employee in a turquoise tux took his travel bag and stowed it in the top of a spray-painted locker. Wayne located the card kiosks in back of the polka dot and multi-media tights. He revolved past Man Ray's photograph of a woman bass fiddle, past scenes from Buñuel's *L'Age d'Or*. He paused at a row of black and white European surrealists. Classic or not, he didn't think the AG would like such contrivances.

For a thoughtful moment, Wayne considered a Walker-

Evans photo of miners, but eliminated that quickly. It was a genuine statement, but the AG might construe social commentary on a postcard as purely exploitative.

Wayne also looked at a trendy Warhol photo of Edie Sedgwick at her most decadent, and then some color Xeroxes of the Empire State Building. Edie had a nose resembling the AG's, but was inappropriate in style. The color Xeroxes were closer to the idea, but somehow uninspired. In this same fashion, Wayne considered a classical kiosk and almost bought a card of Ingres' Odalisque (before remembering Sandy's infamous alliance with the Anarchist, of which the AG needed no abstract hints). Finally, he settled on some montaged Xeroxes that had a freshness missing from the Empire State Building postcards. These were original and succeeded in being funny, which was more than Wayne had anticipated.

There were three types of montaged Xeroxes. In the first, the Statue of Liberty was being swallowed by the shark in *Jaws*. The second showed King Kong climbing the Empire State Building (which seemed reminiscent of the Anarchist's mission), and the third was a shiny idyllic convertible speeding through a fantastic 3D farm country. Freedom, affluence, innocence the significance of the image was widely understood. Wayne selected this upbeat, naive, shining postcard for its old-fashioned flavor. It was clean like the AG. It would communicate the idea that he was around but on the move, her shiny champion had not forgotten her. Wayne picked up his bag from the locker, located eighty cents, and waited briefly in a moderate sized line. He put his money on the counter glad he had exact change. There was little time to waste, if he wanted to catch the Anarchist at the restaurant.

Heading down St. Mark's, Wayne wondered if he should confess his love for the AG to the Anarchist, say that he respected him but his involvement with the project had little to do with politics. It was for the AG. Such a confession would be impossible. The Anarchist's involvement was not complex. He could never explain to this man, who was so fanatical about ideals, that he simply loved women, that the AG had made him believe in the existence of a soul, even his own. It would be as impossible for the Anarchist to understand Wayne's feelings, as it was for Wayne to understand the Anarchist's commitment to Sandy. It was better to let it ride. There was yet time before the laser was completed, time for him to influence the Anarchist in his madness.

How strange, Wayne thought. He had grown so fond of the Anarchist in such a short time. Was he substituting one mentor for another? His disillusionment with the Llama dated before the order for his "wash," about the time he had become involved with the Anarchist. He no longer thought of the Llama as a true visionary. He considered him a manipulator; a benevolent Machiavelli, a Freudian Bismarck savvy enough to pay attention to someone as unusual as the AG.

HE WHO PLACES A MAN ON A PEDESTAL WILL THROW THE FIRST STONE. In Denotational fashion, Wayne framed his question and tested it's accuracy concerning the Anarchist. The Anarchist defied his dictum about idols. They were equals. He proved this fact by remembering an intimate gesture of the Anarchist when Wayne and he were discussing the laser theory. The Anarchist philosophically tapped his finger along the bridge of his nose to indicate Wayne was right. This gesture was the acknowledgement of comrades. The two men were equal in radical activity and, though the Anarchist didn't know it, admirers of the AG. Wayne hoped he could trust the Anarchist to be consistent about their friendship. Wayne wanted to put him to the test and tell him everything, his connection with the Church, his mix-up with reports, his fear of Sandy. He wanted to spill everything so the Anarchist would be responsible for his destiny. It was a childish, self-destructive desire unworthy of equals, he realized. Such tendencies were the reason he had needed the Church's counseling. Instead, he would be adult. He would lie, since fabrications were less complex and more believable than truth. The Anarchist, rough-cut, had somehow evolved without being touched by modern socialization processes. This was why Sandy so easily manipulated him, but also, most probably, the reason the AG loved him. It was also why he would be more suspicious of a complex truth than a fabrication.

Fast approaching the restaurant, Wayne took out the postcard and wrote the number of the loft on the address section. On the other side he wrote the message: YOUR WORDS NEVER FALL ON DEAF EARS. FOR YOUR TOTAL PSYCHIC SELF REVEALED CONTACT MADAME ANNA WAYNE – FIRST LIGHT – TOUCH LATE IN THE WINDOW BOX, WHERE BEAN SPROUTS AND BACON BITS NEVER CEASE TO GROW.

Wayne dropped the card in the mailbox, hoping the Anarchist would not fail him. The AG was sure to get the message in a day. At the back of the tiny restaurant, the Anarchist wiped bacon bits off a counter. He regarded Wayne's underground get-up with some amusement.

"So you've picked up the regional garb?"

Wayne nodded, writing on his pad: EVICTED. I HAD NO FORMAL LEASE. NO HEAT, WATER, OR ELECTRICITY. DO YOU KNOW OF A PLACE I CAN STAY UNTIL I FIND SOMETHING?

"You have receipts for your rent checks, don't you!" the Anarchist exploded. "The realty company can't evict you without a hearing! Didn't they give you any notice?"

I WILL FIGHT IT. BUT CAN I STAY HERE TONIGHT?

The Anarchist patted Wayne's shoulder fraternally, considering options. "I'd ask you to my place, but it might provoke questions from my girl. Men like us should leave curious women behind. Serious matters sound childish in the daylight."

The Anarchist paused, looking out the storefront window of the restaurant. "Let me check with my boss about the bunk," he said, his thoughts obviously concerned with something else. Wayne placed himself in view of the Anarchist's boss, a round East Indian woman.

"Could he," the Anarchist said indicating Wayne, "sweep up for me in return for sleeping in the front window? He's safe and less expensive than a guard dog."

The Anarchist's boss, he had once said, was always ready for a laugh. This time, she tilted her head back to the limit and let one roar. This response, as it turned out, meant she liked the idea. She even supplied some large cushions, which made a comfortable bed when Wayne placed them across two chairs. Around this bunk, he arranged his change of clothes, note pads, toiletries, and the tube of Brylcreem. Then, he unbuttoned his shirt so the Anarchist would say good night. He wanted to be alone when the AG if the AG paid her visit.

"Aren't you going to help me with the project?" the Anarchist asked quizzically. "I found a bazooka case for the tube, and I've been waiting for you to assemble it. We'll go to the shop after I sweep up here and work most of the night."

Wayne took out his pad and wrote: I CAN'T RUN INTO SANDY. SHE HAD BEEN TRYING TO CONTROL THE PROJECT THROUGH MY REPORTS. I GAVE HER A PHONY ONE TO THROW HER OFF OUR TRACK BUT IT WAS TOO OFF. NOW SHE IS SUSPICIOUS OF ME, BUT IF SHE THINKS I'M MISSING, SHE'LL LAY OFF.

With concern, the Anarchist sat on a cushion. "Never wanted her to be checking up on us at all."

SHE'S ANGRY AT ME.

"Knock on the side window after you're through here, and I'll let you in. Wait until later, when Sandy's gone to work."

SHE WILL SAY ANYTHING TO INTERFERE WITH OUR OPERATION.

"Doesn't surprise me," said the Anarchist. "She can't confront me directly. We have our agreement. I'll have to keep you two apart."

The Anarchist stood and took a broom. "Now, I want to show you how to sweep up this place. You do a good job and come by the loft around eleven tonight. Sweeping's not as easy as it looks. You have to be careful to get the grains of rice that get stuck between the floor boards. After you wash them down, use a little boric acid to keep the roaches out."

Chapter 12

BLACK OUT

In his office at the shipping firm, Mr. Dio was cleaning out his desk. The top was clear except for carbons of trucks requisitioned and drivers hired. In the bottom drawer, he paused to cynically access all the bottles he had accumulated. Hard to believe the organization had let things get this far. Quite openly, he had asked his secretary to call drivers, carbon the requisition lists, and make location point maps showing each man where to dump his load of dust. She had done everything without comment, except for one pleasant remark that the drivers seemed a goodly crew. He had let her leave early for the weekend. By now, the drivers all had their instructions, pay in advance, and suggestions for dumping procedures to be used at various bridges, depending on localized construction techniques. It was only a matter of hours now before…

Mr. Dio took his bottles by the neck and placed them neatly in a plastic supermarket sack, mildly annoyed that it had no steadying cardboard bottom. He checked his office for personal effects and found none. In the beginning of his corporate life there had many photos and objects.

Gradually, that changed. He lived so long in so many offices the very atmosphere became as comforting as a home without the necessity of decoration. In fact, he had come to resent any intrusions into the indigenous office ecology; the personal touches of plastic frogs or onyx eggs. Even his apartment resembled the anonymity of his office. It bore none of the homey touches of compromise. White lights reflecting off white walls bore out the motto hung in his reproachless nursery: UTILITY IS BEAUTY. Always conciliatory, never anticipatory, was the way he had lived his life. NO MORE COMPROMISES, he thought with conviction Sandy had not inspired. At the end of his career, he could clearly see his origins in more than the spider ring incident. Obscure childhood memories were vague clues to what a certain character might choose for his fixation. He was the man he was born to be.

Psychology was barely adequate. Mr. Dio picked up the bottles in the plastic sack, turned out the lights, and closed the door of his office. He proceeded down the hall to a side door marked EXIT and descended steps into the alleyway in back of the building. There, with caring precision, he proceeded to smash each bottle.

The Anarchist met Wayne at the door of the shop. "We're changing our laser mode."

Wayne wrote his objection: THE HELIUM-NEON TYPE IS THE CHEAPEST. After he showed the Anarchist the note, he knew he should have said safest. Lately, economy had lost its priority with the Anarchist. Boxes had been arriving daily to the shop.

The Anarchist held out a pinkish metal rod, as if Wayne's note didn't exist.

"Pretty, isn't it? Aluminum oxide sapphire with five hundredth percent chromium, why it's pink."

MORE DANGEROUS.

"More powerful, too. One mm kilowatts. Let Sandy say we're ineffectual, now."

The Anarchist held up a glass cylinder and some sheets of tin. He talked about "oscillators," pointing out the place the bazooka shell would be fitted with tin reflectors. He indicated where the ruby rod would be held in place, and how an arc lamp would charge the whole thing.

It was this "oscillator" mechanism which worried Wayne. It was supposed to alternate the pulsing waves of the laser. But the mechanism seemed very makeshift, even for a workshop model.

SAFETY DEVICES, Wayne wrote, HAVE YOU CONSIDERED...

The Anarchist held his hand up to the pad for Wayne's attention. In it he held a box bearing an address in Plainsville, New York. Inside were two pairs of gloves and goggles. Wayne tried on a set and awkwardly wrote: IF THE LASER WORKS, DO YOU THINK THESE WILL BE SUFFICIENT?

"You're a pessimist, boy!" the Anarchist smiled. "If the mess explodes, we just run like hell was in back of us!"

Wayne didn't like it. He liked it even less when the Anarchist showed him the glass cylinder which went inside the black bazooka. It was beyond him to speculate how the cylinder would fit inside, how the Anarchist would secure mirrors on either side of the weapon case. What was a bazooka meant for anyway? Dictionary definitions always made Wayne feel secure. He reached for the Webster's near the printing press and read: BAZOOKA:

1. A crude musical instrument made of pipes and a funnel.
2. A light, portable shoulder weapon consisting of an open-breech smoothbore firing tube that launches armor-piercing rockets.

The definition was less than enlightening. No drawing illustrated the original appearance of a bazooka, and he couldn't imagine what an armor-piercing rocket was. Wayne would have to trust the Anarchist's ingenuity at adaptation, the same ingenuity with which he had obtained a genuine ruby crystal for the laser. From his own research, he knew the value of this type of laser; a peak power of one to one thousand megawatts. They would need it. Laser weapons functioned best in the vacuum of space, where beams could not be blocked by clouds or objects within the atmosphere. Still, how it would actually function at six A.M. at Federal Hall was beyond his calculation. The Anarchist might laugh, but Wayne would like to know just how they were to control the pulsing of the laser.

I DO NOT KNOW SPECIFICS ABOUT THE RUBY RED LASER. DO YOU HAVE AN OUTLINE?

The Anarchist handed Wayne some Xerox sheets newer than the Times' helium diagram. The heading of the first sheet read:

PROJECTION POINTS FOR RUBY RED

1. Excitation energy will be derived from a xenon arc flash lamp placed in a highly reflective housing so as to focus the lamp emission on to the ruby red.

2. The pulse of the normal mode laser output is, in the first approximation, about equal to the length of time that the xenon flash lamp would be excited.

3. The duration of the current pulse in the lamp is determined by the time constant of the inductive cap which derives the flash lamp circuit.

4. Two types of safety precautions have to be taken: against electrical shock and against laser radiation. The first type involves disconnecting all the electrical sources furnishing current

> to the laser system. The second is concerned with preventing exposure to a laser beam by looking directly at its reflections. All systems have to be grounded with safety interlocks. The tube is in danger of imploding if damaged or cracked by rough handling.

> NOTE: Laser beams are 10,000 times brighter than the sun's rays and much more hazardous.

When a beam of radiation from a laser is absorbed by living tissue, the extent of the damage caused is dependent on several things— the energy level of the radiation and the type of tissue, wave-length of the radiation, and the time of exposure to the radiation.

The Anarchist picked up the other pair of goggles and tapped the lenses under Wayne's nose for attention.

"The human eye," the Anarchist lectured, "is most vulnerable because it is not clothed. The tissue in the retina is particularly susceptible to damage, because the lens of the eyeball concentrates and focuses the laser beams on the retina. These goggles are the best!"

Wayne inspected the manufacturing label:

BROOMER RESEARCH CORPORATION MANUFACTURERS OF PRECISION OPTICS, BEAM SPLITTERS, REFLECTORS, AND COATINGS.

"The ruby rod with the flash-tube trigger electrifies from the reflector. It's really very neat."

Wayne read on, unconvinced by the Anarchist's precautions and enthusiasms and distrustful of his own fascination with the Ruby Red's potential power.

> 5. In a 3-level laser, the method of obtaining population inversion between the middle and ground state is somewhat inefficient. Very little of the electrical energy, which is supplied to the flash lamp, ends up as pumping photons. Carefully designed reflectors around the ruby rod are essential. The intense pumping flash is brief, and care must be taken to prevent it from overheating. Continuous pumping is possible if the device is cooled in liquid nitrogen.

Wayne wrote: WHAT'S THE DIFFERENCE BETWEEN THIS AND THE HELIUM SYSTEM WITH THE COOLING ACTION, I DON'T GET IT.

The Anarchist crumpled Wayne's note with an impatient gesture.

"The helium is a 4-level system, we're dealing with a 3-level, which is much simpler. All the elements are contained. The ruby rod is surrounded by the spiral of the flash lamp, the trigger electrode, and the reflectors on either side of the cylinder. Simple."

RIGHT, Wayne thought in large letters, reading down the page with increased confusion.

6. Voltage amplification is accomplished by an oscillation mechanism, which converts the DC voltage to a pulsation—pulsating in a direct current and then magnifies and feeds the high voltage to the flash lamp when the trigger mechanism is activated.

7. The ruby rod is about 1 centimeter in diameter and 15 centimeters long. When this ruby rod is illuminated by a high-intensity lamp light, such as that from a photoflash lamp, the rod fluoresces with a pink color. The fluorescence persists as long as the photoflash light persists. This is not a laser radiation, but an optical characteristic of the emitter, which is made of aluminum oxide (sapphire) coating. In laser radiation, the ends of the ruby rod are highly polished so that light can pass through almost without absorption.

Wayne wrote a note: I'M GETTING IT NOW. THIS LAST ONE MADE SOME DESCRIPTIVE SENSE.

"Good. Then while you're reading, you can polish this thing. Learn by doing and all that."

Wayne held the rod between his legs and took the finely-grounded metal dust that the Anarchist handed him and a pair of gloves. He began to rub the points of the rod.

8. A mirror is placed at each end of the rod and aligned perpendicularly to the principal axis. When the rod is illuminated with an intense photo flashlight, it emits a fluorescent light which reflects back and forth between the two mirrors with an increase in intensity. The phenomenon, known as light amplification, is produced by the oscillation of the ruby light with an optically resonant cavity formed by the rod and two reflecting surfaces of the mirrors. The light in this resonant cavity is known as a laser.

9. If the flashlight illumination (pumping) of the ruby rod continues for a few minutes, the energy cumulated within the rod will be so great it may crack or shatter into pieces. Accordingly, the laser energy must be removed as fast as it develops in the resonant cavity. The removal of the radiation from the resonant cavity is

> accomplished by making one mirror 100% reflective and the other mirror partially reflective. This allows some of the laser light generated within the resonant cavity to pass through as a laser beam of the same diameter as the ruby rod.

Wayne read no more. For the first time, amidst his murky conceptions of the weapon, he had a glimmer of what it was. He sat down on the unused press-bed stunned by the immensity of the weapon. He was joined by the Anarchist, who was exceedingly happy that the miscellaneous pieces of equipment would soon be united.

HOW DID YOU FIGURE IT OUT?

"Easy," the Anarchist said, "I was a wiz at fixing the fridge, and the telly, and..."

Wayne waved his pad, YOU ARE KIDDING.

The Anarchist looked at Wayne with no small self-doubt.

"Don't know that I have. Still, it's only words! Any printer knows words have two dimensions: what they mean and the space they occupy. That's all I had to know."

Wayne regarded the pieces to be assembled with new excitement, if not comprehension. The contraption was clever. It would appear like a hand-held missile launcher, but fit between their two shoulders, held in place with two long, black shoulder straps. It would look, on the street, like an old

WWII bazooka. The Plexi-molded cone at the head masked with a rubber nozzle would allow it to pass as an art object. Inside the apparatus would be the glass cylinder and the ruby rod in the center surrounded by...Wayne halted his enthusiasm, suddenly realizing that the whole project was active madness. His research, the Anarchist's enthusiasm, they were facets of a "can-do" ethic rendered wildly inappropriate. He would stop it, tell the Anarchist...

Well-coated in his black suit, with firm hands and total concentration, the Anarchist set about his task. The diagram might be simplistic, but the time was tight. He placed each object on the work bench in order of assembly and ceremoniously signaled Wayne to take a place by his side.

There were mystic overtones to the Anarchist's solemn, relaxed rhythm. He placed one object next to another in acts of perfect faith. Wayne couldn't stand the suspense, the timetable, and the Anarchist's obtuse ideology. He would confront him if he didn't get some hard explanations; statements of purpose, at least. He stared unseeingly at the Anarchist's diagram. The ideology was clear, though he had ignored that. Its form was imprinted on his memory.

Memory that played tricks, like now, when he was desperately trying to anticipate the Anarchist's next move. All he could think of was the Llama, Sandy, and the AG. Though the Llama's squad must have located him, he remained free. Maybe, Wayne speculated, the Llama had taken his report at face value and gone after Sandy. Yes, that was it! They would leave the basement and find their creation completely purposeless. With the Phoenix exposed, his remaining tasks would be to comfort the Anarchist and reunite him with the AG.

The idea that the laser would never be used soothed Wayne and steadied his hands. By second nature, he anticipated the Anarchist's gestures and allowed his mind to wander to the AG. Unaccountably, for something imagined, his image of her was very vivid. She was at the club, very tired and distraught. If she didn't contact him in another night, he would risk searching for her. Why hadn't she been in touch? She had read him easily enough in the past, why not now? Wayne calmed his feelings of estrangement, allowing his thoughts to glide with his hands over the objects the Anarchist was assembling. He was soon calm enough to visualize the AG again.

Her dancing was rhythmically way off. She was heavy footed, strained, and unable to escape her immediate timeframe. It was awful to watch her try and suffer.

Caught in her go-go cage, she was terribly aware of the stupidity of the act. Wayne could barely meet the pain in her insistent eyes.

"Where is he?" she asked, haunted.

"What do you mean?" he asked with a voice inside himself, despite the fact he was mute.

"Where is my Anarchist. You were going to watch over him. Instead, you've helped Sandy and encouraged him to a place from which he cannot return to me."

The AG's perfect mouth remained unchanged by her grief. Wayne kissed her mouth, as a tender statement of his own innocence. The point was well-taken.

"I'm sorry," said the AG. "It's confusing not to be able to tell what's going on. I didn't mean to accuse you, really. It just happened."

Wayne no longer saw the stage, but the atmosphere of the dressing room. He could smell the sweet creams and acrid sweat. He could almost feel the greasy blotches on the wall. He took her hand and found it tangibly in his.

"I am watching the Anarchist," he said, "but you must help me. Go the Pan-Am Building after Sandy is gone. Fix what she's started. I'm hoping it won't be necessary, but I won't know until tomorrow. Neither will you. It won't be easy to get there, AG! There will be dust everywhere!"

"You will watch the Anarchist?"

"That's why you must go to the Pan-Am Building, there's no other way I can be with him, all the way."

"But, I'm not sure what you mean..."

"The postcard! I sent one for you. Come see..."

"You've been waving thin air at me!" the Anarchist said, slapping Wayne lightly on the wrist. "Pay attention, please!"

The dressing room receded from Wayne's inner vision. He attempted to mask his preoccupation, but needn't have bothered. The Anarchist was very excited. He placed the curved coil of a flash tube on the press. He raised it upright and played with a wire.

"This is the trigger electrode. I'll wrap it around the coil. That other thing you're holding goes inside this lamp. It's beautiful. Let me show you."

Wayne, fascinated and frightened, moved off the press bed. The operation, he reminded himself, would never get off the ground. It was too ridiculous. He sat cross-legged on the cold floor of the shop, sorry for the Anarchist, who was dragging out a grounded electrical cord. After some minutes, the coil of the flash lamp glowed strangely. In the dark, Wayne sat watching below the press bed, looking upward. He felt the marvel of a crude giant observing a miniature spaceship.

SALVATION BY THE AG

The AG was so upset, she left Joe's Place without her customary refusal of Joe's offer of a ride. She left the club oblivious to her surroundings and entered the subway off Pearl Street, heading toward Houston. The train was empty except for two teenaged boys with roadrunner haircuts and '50s dress suits. They reminded her of Wayne's obscure rock' n' roll postcard, which she thought she might have understood. Poor Wayne, she thought, hiding made him terribly self-conscious. She could not decipher the mystery of his whereabouts from the card, but something of his presence had come through. She had been in her cage, trying to enter her trance state with little success, when she felt the grainy atmosphere of a strange storm lit like Christmas with red and green colored lights. Her cage was the vortex of that storm, and she was somehow at the command of someone else. Wayne had visualized 3D and given her a message about Sandy and the Pan-Am Building, but it was all very ambiguous. She found herself ambivalent about this vision, wondering if it were an active outgrowth of her suspicions of Sandy, or a genuine communication.

The element of doubt made her twist and grimace, overly aware of being isolated in a lonely train at an hour too late for safety.

The AG changed from the LL to the Lexington line since it was a nicer train and went directly to Astor Place. It was a familiar change, made strangely noisy by her hyper-awareness of the rat-a-tat-tat momentum of train on track past the station, plunging into a tunnel, turning a cavernous angle just before a red or white light suddenly appeared on a dim or brightly lit platform, reflecting off orange plastic or green wooden seats. She could feel every twist and turn teasing the long track. Anxiety made her catch herself in the faces around her, in the stances of bodies vying for inches in the car — in the odd cage that moved so electronically through space encased in heavy glass.

At Spring Street, the bored voice of the conductor announced, "Will the guy playing doorman please let the doors close so this train can leave the station?" The doors open and shut several times, but no one appeared to hold them back. The cabman, apparently satisfied, resumed the ride past stops the AG could easily anticipate. She got out at Astor Place as the conductor announced the train had inexplicably become an Express. Passengers going elsewhere were to wait for a local. In an infinitely tired voice he added to invisible adversaries, "Please don't play doorman! Let this train move!"

A boy, about twelve the AG guessed, jumped from the train onto the platform. He looked in his element, dressed in tight black jeans and a red satinette baseball jacket. An archivist of the subways, the AG fancied after noticing a spray gun barely concealed under his jacket, someone who knew the ages and origins of all the different trains. The boy was playing. He made a dodge over the yellow safety line and back. A friend in a blue satinette jacket rounded the corner from a trash dump. He dared him, saying, "Walk the edge, you can do it!" The boy teetered on the edge of the platform, enjoying his friend's approval, before the rushing wind blew him onto the track, scrambling to climb out of the fetid gulley.

The AG leapt onto the track. The skirt of her hot pink costume under her arm was a bright dot in the engineer's window. He saw it, thinking, that ain't no beacon, knowing he had only a few seconds to react. Luckily, he had not gotten stoned at a party hours before. He was no longer irritated by the MTA's wage scale. His reaction time would be okay if he decided to act quickly enough.

The AG knew death in the form of the train would painfully snap the threads which bound her to her body. She balanced one leg on the rails of the track, the other in the muck between. The boy said, "Say, babe, you crazy to come in here, let me help you get out..." The AG never laughed at bravado. She thought the comment was cute, especially since he could not touch the platform with his short arms. The AG tapped into the engineer's mind set.

Though he had forgone the Senegalese marijuana offered him earlier in the evening, he had taken enough methedrine to stay up the whole night. Speeding down the track, it was hard for him to judge distances. He was pure, high speed motion.

The boy's worried friend lay prone on the platform, extending his arm.

"Chas," he said, "you got to get out of there, man."

"No joke," said Chas. "I'm going to be the first human pancake."

Slippery with the oily muck, Chas tried to boost himself over the rail and up the wall of the platform, but he wasn't long enough to reach his friend's hand. The AG saw how it could be done. She was a small woman, but she knew the way to use her body as a stair. A foot on her knee, a grip on her shoulder, and a quick leap to the platform would be possible. She made herself a bridge between the two boys as the red light of the train drew closer. Chas panicked, slipping off her knee, crying, "We're dead!"

It might be true, the AG thought. The engineer's sensory state made him want to ride the tunnel into infinity—he had lost all sense of self in the sensation. She had to make him stop. She had to make him realize infinity did not depend on speed. With a mesmeric voice, she injected a few thoughts into the Engineer's mind.

"Do not rush, you may miss things. The time-space continuum is filled with unique phenomena. You will never be in this part of it again. This planet travelling through the universe will never pass the same star cluster, the same meteor shower. There are orbital shifts, but the voyage is never through the same terrain. You exist on one part of the spinning planet. I'm in your path. Have you ever seen me before? SLOW DOWN AND LOOK!"

The engineer focused on the shiny pink dot of the AG's costume. What or who, on this deadly boring night, was sending him a message? It wasn't methedrine paranoia, he decided, since the object was visible. If he wasn't loony, it was a UFO in his subway. He slowed down his car just in time to see the AG's ascent to the platform. Chas hit the platform a yard from his friend's outstretched arm.

"Some angel," thought the engineer of the AG leaping lightly onto the platform.

The AG saw his startled reflection through the window of the cab, knowing she had indeed entered his consciousness. She had experienced another's essence, which was also her own, in the way she believed all people had souls. The message from Wayne, she decided, must also be real. She would not contact him, but wait until it was time for her to go into action—-go to the Pan-Am Building and see what she was to do. She felt a small satisfaction that her ability was still in evidence. Sorrow and awareness of evil self-interest had taken a toll on her otherworldly self, but she remained, helpfully, the AG.

Chas and his friend stood shyly on the deserted platform trying to think of some way to thank the AG. He held his hand out. "Say, babe, even if you're nuts, you got nerve."

"They might be the same thing," the AG grinned. "Can I borrow that?" she said, pointing to the spray gun on the platform.

Chas' friend was annoyed. "How do I know if you run fast enough? You could get a few years for this."

"You have any pink paint?"

"Look, lady, that train's still here, and isn't it late for you to be out?"

The AG took the gun, though it was filled with lime green paint. She sprayed a line parallel to the yellow one on the edge of the platform.

"What's that for?" Chas asked.

"Safety. If you cross one, you don't have to fall over the edge. There's always the other."

WAYNE AND THE ANARCHIST ON WALL STREET

At four A.M., waiting for the Lexington Line, Wayne and

the Anarchist held the bazooka between them and hoped the damned train would arrive before a curious cop. They knew they looked suspicious, and worried that a delay increased their chances of being trapped underground by the dust dump at six A.M.

Train, come already! Get here! Wayne thought, annoyed at himself for forgetting how infrequent they were at this hour. He lit a cigarette from a pack he had bought as underground barter (cigarettes were always good tender for general info). Wayne was not a smoker, but he fervently wanted the old smokers' superstition to prove true, that a lit cigarette was sure to bring a train post-haste.

Wayne and the Anarchist didn't communicate beyond one man shifting more of his burden onto the other. The other redistributed his weight until it was his turn to shift. In this way, they passed the time, each alone with his thoughts. The Anarchist bewailed his foolishness in not investigating the trains available at four A.M. Wayne wished the Llama would stop the dust dump. He also persecuted himself for failing to prevent the Anarchist from building the laser.

The train that finally rattled to the Spring Street stop with one headlight missing brought much relief. The engineer, ready to speed down to the Brooklyn Bridge, had opened his doors at the last possible minute when he spied the two men on the platform. He noted the WWII bazooka and the two loonies with it, wishing the conductor wasn't at the front of the train working his way down. The skinny kid with the spiked-out pompadour and the ghoulish older guy could mean trouble. They looked like stupid rock 'n' roll, sci-fi, end of the world flicks. From experience, the engineer decided he hadn't seen anyone on the 4:15 train. It seemed the safest bet.

It was a clean dawn on Wall Street. The swept streets were still, except for the sea wind tumbling an evangelist's forgotten straw basket, a fast food flyer, a discount clothier's poster, and a bank receipt. Wayne noted these items with a sense of history heavy in his arm, he and the Anarchist carrying the laser lengthwise between them.

Wayne felt alive with the immediacy of a passing tabloid headline.

The Anarchist's vision was definitely catchy. It had influenced Wayne over the enthusiastic weeks of research and assemblage. Wayne, the passive recorder; Wayne, the would-be protector of the AG, had been converted to the Anarchist's cause without understanding it. He got Food for Vendettas, but the laser was a symbolic gesture of what? He saw himself carrying this bazooka clad laser to tumble—a founding father, in reality an ignored figurehead of an ignored museum? Damn Denotational Analysis, imagination, personal sympathies, and any other idiocy which had led to this situation. The root of the matter was that he MUST stop the Anarchist, for the sake of the affection he bore him, for the AG, and for that odd sentiment—patriotism. The figurehead might be the most he recollected from grade school, but he had to save it, the mystique of heritage. What else was left of the elementary facts?

Who was Washington? A farmer, a politician, a soldier, a statesman? A spirit of egalitarianism, maybe? Wayne knew he had no idea who George Washington was, but he had a clear idea of the Anarchist, who was trying to destroy the symbol of revolution in himself. A self-effacement ritual to end his rebellious struggles to come to terms with his world, obliterate the contradictions d his life. Wayne believed in contradictions. In a wave of epiphany which went with the sunrise, he realized he believed in contradictions in nature, in national consciousness, in individual personalities. He might not understand how the full circle of seeming contradictions meshed in life, but it no longer mattered. He had a sense of the wholeness of the world and would stop the Anarchist for love and life.

Walking down Wall Street, the Anarchist perceived the gray-rose light as that of a shooting squad on an execution morning, not unlike the one he had been exiled in on a boat so long ago. It was again a morning of nemesis.

He could almost imagine the mean goddess taunting him with his extravagant pride, fate and punishment. She held out a strong drink, a cup of megawatts travelling at the speed of light. The Anarchist shook off the doomful vision. The laser WAS necessary for political, not personal reasons. He didn't have much time left to execute it, either.

AFTERWARD? (The question arose despite his resistance.) Escape with the AG was no longer possible. No refuge existed for him. Anarchy didn't mean chaos, but self-government in the highest sense, no directives from higher-up. Washington knew that.

The Anarchist put the bazooka down on the steps of Federal Hall, easing Wayne's part of the load. He took a look at the water and decided drowning was definitely a possibility. Still, in his heart, he couldn't bear the risk of another boat picking him up and taking him somewhere else to live a useless life. The Anarchist believed in utility, but of an eccentric sort. His usefulness as a printer and farmer had never been sufficient. His definition of useful was probably closer to essential. Of what real use was his existence? The concrete mundane usefulness of his occupations did not contradict this feeling of inadequacy. He had fled a terrible war and offered clean vegetables. The only act which would resolve his life was the one he was about to execute.

The Anarchist saw Wayne's fear in the shaky way he erected the tripod for the weapon. The Anarchist straightened it easily, it was of his own design. He smiled encouragement and heartily remarked, "She'll be at the Pan-Am building by now.

"THE AG?" Wayne signed, unthinking.

"Sandy," the Anarchist answered, perplexed. How the AG had arisen in Wayne's mind. How did he even known her name? "The AG's home asleep with her fair self, I trust. We must hurry, Wayne. Soon the storm will be upon us. But gently, there, we've a dangerous charge."

Within the dull black bazooka lay the bright ruby rod surrounded by reflectors. Wayne had helped the Anarchist empower the rod with the flash lamp the night before. Even through the optical company shades, he had been impressed with the coiled lamp. The rod within it glowed and pulsed with energy, but how was it to be regulated? The Anarchist wasn't sure if the alternating device would work evenly, or at all. It was to control the force and direction of the laser waves, but was so crude Wayne couldn't imagine the rudder-like device would register such minute shifts.

"Move the tripod closer to the statue and steady it," the Anarchist ordered. Wayne stood the tripod within a few feet of Washington and rested it on a parallel step. The Anarchist hoisted the bazooka onto a horizontal position on top of it. He opened the box from Plainsville, New York and ceremoniously handed Wayne his goggles. Wayne looked as if they were alien items.

WHY BOTHER? (It won't work he wanted to say) "Wayne, put them on!" the Anarchist insisted,

excitedly putting the elastic band around Wayne's head. "We haven't a moment, ya know!"

Wayne shook his head to indicate he didn't understand the Anarchist.

"Don't play dumb now! I know you get everything!" Wayne wrote: I ONLY PRETEND TO. PUT ON YOUR GOGGLES.

The Anarchist was too tall for Wayne to force the elastic around his head. He placed his foot on the step above Wayne and reached for the manual lever. Wayne caught him around the ankle and sent him sprawling on the hard marble steps.

The Anarchist, blood on his mouth, jerked upward to the laser and threw the manual lever down. At an instant, Wayne knocked him aside and hurled the head of the weapon down onto the step. The Anarchist threw his arms around Wayne to send him after the weapon, when both men noticed nothing had happened.

"NOT A THING!" he groaned. The Anarchist's fighting hold became a tragic embrace. He broke loose, approaching his dud of a mechanism as if it were a false shrine — defying his dead god to do anything, wanting to see the real light of the laser.

The beam pulsed suddenly, strange and strong, instantaneously dissolving two steps. With no apparent alternator function, no hands on controls, the laser had a life of its own. It. swiveled crazily on its step, dissolving the base of the statue three steps above Wayne; then the statue itself, which toppled headlong to the bottom sidewalk on Wall Street. Wayne pulled the Anarchist out of the statue's way, using his body to cushion the impact of another fall.

"Where are you? I cannot see in the pain..." the Anarchist said, his face against Wayne's. Wayne felt the lips move, but had no way of answering. He turned his head.

Through the black glass of the goggles, he could see the thin beam of light cutting dents in marble, searing the air. 186,000 miles per hour, he thought. Does it kill long distance? Wayne crawled, legs first, out from under the Anarchist. Using arms and elbows, he inched his way, crawling toward the weapon. A good kick was all it took to send the bazooka down all the steps. He couldn't hear the crack of the glass cylinder, but thought he may have done the job.

Wayne found the Anarchist. He put his arms around him, holding his head against his chest. He was happy, glad they were unhurt, as he watched the bright explosion dissolve the sidewalk in front of Federal Hall.

Pain was all the Anarchist uttered. His retina was destroyed. He lay long against Wayne's chest, deciding he had died.

SANDY IN ACTION

At three A.M., Sandy woke up with a swollen eyelid, wondering if it were due to a bug bite, an allergy, or the beginnings of a fatal disease. This last worry amused her, especially when she considered the nihilistic content of this morning's activities. Sandy settled on delayed Rose Fever as the cause and took an antihistamine resting into the subtle fog of half sleep. She could afford to relax her internal analysis procedures for a while. The Anarchist and Wayne were already progressing to their site, laser in tow. All other aspects of the Phoenix were in operation with the exception of herself. She had to be at Ad-A-Live at four A.M., so there were a few minutes to spare. Sandy used the leisure time for reviewing information Ralph had compiled under the heading: PROJECTED IMPACT REPORT. He had identified the stages:

1. City Hall frequently fears that some kind of terrorist group is in operation. International organizations with local ethno-religious affiliations are the usual suspects until further information is uncovered. There is also, simultaneously, the suspicion that an organ in the Federal system may have enacted the operation as a demonstration of the incompetency of the mayor or the city government.

2. The PHOENIX, which is not totally unanticipated, is operating at a disadvantage. Still, if it is executed swiftly, it may be very effective. Not only is the city's communications network faulty under normal circumstances, but the police are spread out over a wide area. These systems will be fragmented by the nature of the PHOENIX. Strong winds will add to the commotion.

3. Local shows and national satellite broadcast systems will be dark. Still, the satellite systems will be the first to recover. They will use the word "situation," designate the PHOENIX as an incident, not a crisis. Disaster in the vocabulary of local politics would

be considered alarmist. It would also qualify the city for Federal funds, though such an "unnatural" disaster would be questionable. "Situation" is comforting, since it means something capable of being contained. I recommend we pirate network communications and project a specific image, like our cornucopia poster half-charred, reading: FOOD FOR VENDETTAS.

4. This image will identify our organization, our operation, and the scope of our influence. Disaster will then be appropriate terminology, no matter what satellite programming may designate. Especially if we make our media strike before they recover capability. We will then achieve the historical status of "disaster," invaluable for our intentions.

Sandy put aside the report. It was time to get dressed. She located her fatigue pants and camouflage shirt and put them on, relieved by the security of habit. Cost, availability, and general convenience had been the reason for her wardrobe of combat clothes that had, ironically, become very fashionable. Today, they were immeasurably appropriate. Sandy found her jacket and zipped it, surveying the city from her rooftop just once before she departed for the Pan-Am Building.

A carpet of crisscrossed roofs were laid out below her. The Phoenix, like the shadow of a big bird, rattled in a lone truck on a tiny side street. Sandy could make out one of her trucks, a dump rental, filled with fine Arizona dust. The truck could emit, she estimated, a cloud about four feet high with an immeasurable circumference. She could perhaps estimate the effusive circles arising from all the trucks under the Phoenix's wing, but such an activity would not be cost-effective. After sighting the truck, Sandy descended to the street. She knew it would be a good day.

The street in front of the loft was too quiet as she exited. Much interrupted construction was in evidence. Cranes had clumsily knocked down parts of buildings. A gargoyle from a cornice almost tripped her, but she didn't slow her stride. She would witness her event taking place. In a city of construction accidents, a country of technical failures, this was a planned incident that would succeed, no matter how it concluded. The fact it would take place was sufficient for Sandy's satisfaction. She had expected to feel triumphant this day. Instead, she felt the unsettling conviction that she was a tyrant. She had known this before, but never been shocked about it. There was no time for such weakness. The solution was an all-night diner and a good cup of coffee. Then she would tackle her task at Ad-A-Line. Butterflies were for ingénues. She had been around the block.

The greasy spoon was very adequate. It was the kind of Midtown place that rarely served anyone's mother, but wasn't isolated enough to attract the really rough trade. At this hour, with businesses still closed and disco-dwellers downtown, Sandy had the place to herself. No one bothered with her but the one-armed Greek who refilled her cup each time she slid a quarter over. They understood one another.

Sandy went over the list of stations that would have power failures at six A.M. Duncan had helped her install a transmitter onto the board at Ad-A-Live. She would be the only show in New York City. Sandy had prepared her statement and was sure of the content, if not the appropriate time of delivery.

The statement declared the PHOENIX to be an alliance of non-aligned, nonobjective interests gathered together to point up the imminent destruction of the world, because of the faulty cleaning apparatus built into guided missiles. Sandy hoped that her operation would change her deportation orders to extradition. She wanted the city planners to consider the effects of short-term planning that had resulted in faulty cleaning apparatus. She wanted the world to consider how something as miniscule as dust could clog a city.

At four A.M., on schedule, Sandy had exchanged the greasy spoon for the comfort of her dark switchboard. She had two hours before the dust dump and her broadcast.

Sandy brought out her map of the operation, the giant collage of flesh and geography. Motivation and desire, she thought, sounds like a supermarket romance. Yet it was real and she had plotted it!

All the pieces were in place. Sid's ladies with Georgeanne

in charge, rode the freeways to waylay officials. The Anarchist and Wayne were on Wall Street with the laser. Mr. Dio's trucks were rattling to their dump sites. Vendettas volunteers with their backpacks were stationed at the spokes of the mandala to aid pedestrians and redirect motorists. Everything was in order. She had even arranged for Ralph to release her speech at a certain time, if she experienced a communications foul-up. His tape was good broadcast quality.

Sandy didn't care, she admitted to herself, if Mr. Dio's message came across, or the Anarchist's. Who cared about missiles or the sacred nature of political icons? It was going to be her banshee voice on the air. Sandy, the mysterious lady behind the boards, the nihilist in love with negative potency. This operation was a kind of grisly compensation for her own deprivation, her own alienation from... remorse? Sandy felt a crisis upon her. Was there a cultural precedent? Medea and other femme fatales were insufficient, maybe later after their atrocious acts, not before. She hummed a bar of "Pirate Jenny," deciding to make herself a context; a collage of reality. She took some old magazines from a stack under her board and began to cut out representative figures and place them on her map in appropriate positions.

An image of a girl from *Oui* magazine served the West Side Highway quite pornographically. A priest from a homeowner's ad was easily substituted for the Anarchist on Wall Street. Mr. Dio's trucks: Mayflower, Ritter, Mr. Softee, were easy to find. A child from a Prudential ad served for Wayne. When she finished her collage, she wondered if she should represent the AG, but superstitiously decided against it. She hadn't seen the AG for a time, and wanted to keep it that way. It had been necessary to split up her relationship with the Anarchist, but she didn't enjoy the changes in the AG's face. Sandy had made her choices and was proud of them, though she couldn't stand the deep bags under the AG's eyes; the haunted vacancy that had replaced otherworldliness. Hopefully, the AG would sleep through the dust storm.

Sandy dismissed this sentiment for her collage. Self-actualization had become reality! Realizing her excitement bordered on hysteria, she put the collage away and calculated the next step in her part of the operation. Mr. Dio was to call from the Sherry Netherland Hotel. He would signal three times and hang up. This would mean his end of the operation was synched with the Vendettas crews.

The third time he rang, before he could hang up, Sandy plugged into the line full of impatience. "Mr. Dio!"

"Sandy, I didn't expect to talk to you in person." "How are things going?"

"All fronts are synchronized, if that's what you mean.

The trucks are in position and readied at GO."

"Great. Your message is represented on my tape."

"What exactly are you saying?" he said, displeased.

"That wasn't part of the deal," Sandy reminded Mr. Dio. "You gave me total control, so I don't need your approval."

"I'd like to know what you're going to say. It's my statement as well."

"Generally speaking, I stated this was a nonobjective demonstration underlining the real dangers of missiles and the absurdity of our safety balanced on something as inexact as Arizona Dust. The costs to the city will alert the nation to its real concerns."

Sandy paused, listening to the reaction of air. Mr. Dio had hung up. She must have been less than reassuring. But what did he matter? The PHOENIX was more profound than any of its parts. She had transcended her own limits with competent megalomania.

Sandy seized a cord and called Duncan to give him the okay for the station black-out. True to his word, he used his considerable technical means to jam frequencies. Sandy watched the first clouds of dust float by her window in the Pan-Am Building, while a few existing lights were extinguished. Power failure. Everything was coming apart by plan. What Sandy didn't plan was that Zeke had made it to the ninety-eighth floor of the Ad-A-Live headquarters past the wheelchair-bound vet who served as her guard.

Zeke opened the door without knocking and faced Sandy with an outstretched cheesecloth for only a brief, necessary second.

MR. DIO AT THE SHERRY NETHERLAND

Mr. Dio looked aimlessly out of his hotel room. It was four o'clock at the Sherry Netherland. He went into the bathroom and took a glass from the cabinet. The medicine cabinet was empty except for one other glass. It was wrapped, like Mr. Dio's, in a special paper wrapper, which signified that it had been hermetically sealed for hygiene.

Mr. Dio peeled off the wrapper and held the glass in the light, interested in perfection. A globule had formed on the side. Mr. Dio was more fascinated than disgusted. He thought of analyzing it by isolating its components. He tilted the glass in different directions but there seemed to be nothing unusual about it — nothing he could readily identify. Did it come in all the glasses? He examined the second one. The wrapper was the same, but the glass inside looked spotless. He put the two glasses side by side.

Which was the pure, which the impure? Ostensibly, Mr. Dio mused, the glass without globule, but not necessarily. A maid might have breathed on it, or a dishwasher or the hermetic machine might have coated the glass with a thin layer of silicone that remained uncured.

The globule might actually be a condensed purifying agent and not ordinary saliva. In any case, it represented a flaw, a snafu in the process, which somehow seemed significant to Mr. Dio. He put the precious glass on the sideboard with care. It was a special object, individual, and almost a relic.

Mr. Dio, early in his career, had designed precision ways to test precision devices. The "perfect" glass defied the rationale of reasonable doubt. He took the glass from the sideboard and held it to the light. The globule appeared to have evaporated to a smaller size. Otherwise, the surface of the glass was even throughout. Mr. Dio held it up to the light, enjoying its lovely reflective qualities for several seconds. His warm breath condensed in patterns on the surface before he crushed it with his hands.

He was surprised the glass was of fine enough quality for him to shatter it. He looked at the cut arteries, at his streaming hands, and saw no gesture of failure. Death was, after all, an anticlimax. This night, Mr. Dio looked through the windows of the Sherry Netherland with an objective. He would die.

The night lights were out all over the city. It was dawn and Sandy had blocked out communications; the dust was dumped. He watched the sky lighten as his blood drained into a clean towel. He was pleased his life wasn't flashing before his eyes. No thoughts of past guilt or feelings of past happiness prepared him for the cessation of life. No childhood Freudian memories purged his psyche, no Jungian reconciliations brought him full circle with new knowledge of prenatal universal meanings. Mr. Dio's thoughts centered on Sandy and the nature of the devil. He recalled some early Christian ethics, writings of Gnostic mystics, Dionysian cults. All these theologies seemed beyond the point. Evil was the flipside of good. Death didn't fit into either category. Despair was more to the point.

Despair was always an antisocial act.

Long before he met Sandy, he had declared the terms of its expiation. The cause was rooted in failed expectations, a life of unfulfilled meanings. Mr. Dio was a man caught passively negotiating change. He had loved a hometown sweetheart but let her marry someone else, a fellow comfortable with life happening around him. Occasionally she sent him a postcard from her home in Los Angeles. He never answered her silent question. Why did he abandon her? It was easier, he thought, somewhere he could never acknowledge or say to anyone.

Mr. Dio's suicide was not only an act of despair or disillusionment. He had carried his meanings inside himself, away from experience. Unfulfilled, he had no story to tell. Mirth, his own, uncensored, filled his being. At sunrise, Mr. Dio lay in a black lounge chair with a smile of beatitude on his face, Buddha-like, infinitely amused, if not joyous.

BLACK-OUT /THE OFFICE MAKES THE WOMAN

Out her kitchen window, the AG saw pigeons under the eaves of a neighboring roof. One sparrow-like bird landed heavily on the AG's windowsill and shook its wing, dispersing a puff of yellow dust. Leaden with the stuff, the bird could not fly. The AG leaned out the window and picked it up, holding its wings still, its bill out of pecking distance. She calmly held the frightened bird, until it too was calm, and carefully sponged-off its caked torso. Freed of its burden, the creature wanted flight. The AG placed it back on the sill and opened the window, hoping it would not plummet.

Unfortunately, the bird's lungs were filled with dust.

It hobbled unsteadily over the chasm under the eaves, between the sill and the nest. The AG's breath ceased with apprehension as she watched the bird's leg and wing attempt coordination. The bird flailed a brief second before it plunged. A wild burst of forward motion aborted the fall, and the bird attained the safety of the sill, unconscious.

The AG thought it might die. She could feel particles of dust choking it internally. Though she had done all that was possible, her empathy for the bird's condition had not diminished. Its very helplessness mirrored her feelings earlier that morning.

She had not gotten up, as her body dictated, nor had she slept as her mind craved. Instead, momentous images flashed through her consciousness. She had entered Sandy's timeframe for the PHOENIX. Trucks dumped dust. Communications lines were down, arteries leading into the city were clogged. The AG had to stop Sandy. She would go to the Pan-Am Building. Wayne's directive was clear, though Sandy's plan remained a mystery. The AG could see the city through Sandy's eyes, but she could not access her thoughts or physical whereabouts. After several minutes of limited insight, she pulled back to the loft and the small bird barely breathing. She visualized a tiny vacuum cleaner, miniscule suction tubes used to clear mucus from a newborn's nose. The AG looked around the loft, found a shiny white fabric in a basket of scraps. The rest, she remembered fondly, had been twisted into an aerodynamic hat. The scrap had enough bend to wrap around a lollypop stick. Her breath was a fine vacuum, sucking dust from the lungs of the limp bird and, at intervals, spitting into a paper cup. If he survived the shock, she thought, noting his rapid heartbeat as she put him in a shoebox, he would be all right. She placed the box by the window.

Outside, pigeons huddled under the eaves away from the dust. The AG realized the whole city was coated with the stuff. Were people dying? Would a simple handkerchief at the throat be sufficient? The AG closed the window and crossed the loft to her costume bins. She selected the mask of a Balinese warrior, because the mouth was hollowed to a round "O" shape. She taped acetate squares to the eye slits and attached a vacuum hose to a small skin-diving tank that was filled with oxygen. The Anarchist had used the tank for welding, but she guessed the oxygen was okay to breathe. The bizarre gas mask might even work for a while.

The AG put the mask on and zipped herself into her reinforced jumpsuit. The plastic had ventilation holes, which she decided posed little risk. The important factor was that the plastic was not porous. Another important thing was the strength of her psyche. She must be strong enough to remedy the mess and somehow save her city from complete disaster.

The streets were strange. Dogs jumped from bank to bank, as if the dust drifts were innocent snow. People cupped closed hands over noses and mouths. Out of half-mast eyelids, they furtively saw the shape of the block. In this way, the AG trudged from the Bowery to Astor Place, from Astor Place to Grand Central Station. She listened to tapes from various black box radios carried by cheerful teens elbowing their ways through the gritty subways with cries of "Cool dust!" The AG had been hoping to hear news, but had no such luck.

She discovered at Astor Place that the subways were not running. An amused youth told her of underground parties, taking exceptional interest in her Balinese warrior mask. The AG, thinking him too acquisitive, decided to risk an aboveground trek to the Pan-Am Building. She walked slowly, breathing with control, not wanting her small oxygen filter to clog before midtown. It was an efficient Japanese filter made for machinists, but insufficient for the dense dust particles filling the air. The AG was careful to slow her breath and pulse after the initial adrenaline propelled her hastily to Astor Place. The plunge of her energy level was potentially dangerous because her ESP was providing no compensation. That power had become as undependable as her Anarchist and the careful world they had constructed together. She would have to rely on her conscious will, no matter how undeveloped that faculty.

The AG concentrated on just walking, no further than three feet at a time. Then she would pause for rest and introspection inside the dark interior of her suit. Today, she thought, 'beauty, mystery, wonder, are not my priorities. I seem to be pulling inward to some dark base— some platform of iron I didn't know existed. Can I forge myself into a new creature? In this way, the AG conjured the strength she would need to fight Sandy's machinations. What, besides this horrible trek to the Pan-Am Building, would she need to do?

Absorbed along these lines of thought, the AG didn't see the elderly woman stuck in the gutter, her body rooted between dust and garbage. The woman, amidst her struggles, cried she lived in the streets, but never in the gutter. The AG heard this, somewhat muffled through the converted Balinese mask. She knelt beside the woman, balancing her body, clumsy in the suit, against a pile of compacted dust.

"Rock, please," the AG said, "slowly, a little more to the left every time, and we'll create some momentum. We'll knock the dust out and create air particles between the molecules and..."

"OOMPH!!" said the woman as she suddenly dislodged onto the street.

The AG helped her into a comfortable doorway and went on her way, pleased that conscious will could be effective.

A half hour later, the AG found herself burrowing horizontally to the entrance of Grand Central Station—a dusty battering ram. The inside of the station was intact. Even the down escalator worked, though the air (without her tank on) was more than a little stuffy. The AG removed her mask, which drew no comments from the permanent transients, the only inhabitants of the station. They shuffled indifferently from the waiting room benches to the restrooms and back.

The AG, assumed the station had an emergency generator somewhere. Had a guard had remained to operate it? She needed to know if the Pan-Am Building was open. The clock read eight when the AG questioned a transient about the electricity. It seemed the generator had been found by another waiting room habitué, a former electrician. Still, her informant insisted, it wasn't the end of the world, just a detour from reality. The AG thanked the unidentified transient, and replaced her mask and tank. She would need maximum energy and protection for her ordeal.

The escalator from Grand Central into the Pan-Am Building was not in operation. High as a small mountainside, the empty escalator provided an eerie means of ascent. At the top, the AG walked past an Urban Banking Center, looking for the side door of the Pan-Am Building, Wayne had referred to in his visualization.

TICKA-TICKA-TICK-A-TICK ... No sooner had she located the side door and a working elevator, when a vicious-looking man in a wheelchair raced straight at her. The AG's waning powers weren't sufficient to inform her why he wanted to run her over. But her physical courage was undiminished. The AG left the elevator door open until the chair was within striking range. She appeared paralyzed but quickly moved aside and let the chair smash into the rubber edge of the steel-cased door.

“Are you the welcoming committee?” she asked the stunned man, whose T-shirt bore the words “FOOD FOR VENDETTAS”.

The Vet spoke harshly, “Look, I’m paranoid, but I don’t kill needlessly. What’s your business here?”

“Oh,” said the AG, removing her mask.”You must know my Anarchist and Sandy if you know FOOD FOR VENDETTAS.”

“What is it to you?”

“I’m Sandy’s roommate.”

The Vet realigned his wheelchair so that it propped the elevator door open.

“What are you doing here?” he asked with less menace.

“Relief,” said the AG. “She’s been on this shift too many hours.”

The Vet wheeled his chair into the elevator and pushed the button for the ninety-eighth floor.

“Neat,” said the AG, “you know where the room is.”

When they reached ninety-eight, the AG tried to wheel the Vet, but he refused her attention. Turning his chair on “motor”, he raced down the hall to the door which read: AD-A-LIVE ANSWERING SERVICE.

The AG could feel in her sinus cavities the chloroform with which Zeke had saturated the cheesecloth. He had held it over Sandy's nose and mouth. The AG began to choke from the sensation, very nasty.

"Sandy's been drugged," she said to the Vet.

He rammed the door open with his chair, but the gesture was superfluous. The door swung open easily. Sandy's chair was overturned. Her map and cutouts were scattered over the floor. Several curved cords were in disarray on top of the board. The AG stroked her hair in a bird-like manner. Inwardly, she was effecting order out of disorientation. She would need such order to act.

"Who are you?" asked the Vet. "How'd you know what happened? You in on it?"

"The Anarchist's Girlfriend is what I'm called. It is obvious Sandy was kidnapped. There is evidence of a struggle."

The AG could see the Vet was very suspicious. She wanted to mitigate his feelings and let him know how much she respected his loyalty to Sandy. She looked into his Being. She realized he simply wanted her to tell him where she got her information and relieve his anxiety over his poor job performance. After all, it had been his duty to guard Sandy.

"I'm psychic," the AG said. "It's a political kidnapping, and the organization had prior knowledge of Sandy's whereabouts."

"What are you here for?" the Vet asked, wanting direction.

"To finish Sandy's plan. Does this mean anything to you?" she said, indicating the collage, which she had retrieved from the floor.

"Dunno," he said. "She never told anyone the whole story. I'll track her."

"Do that, and if you run into Wayne Niebold, tell him where I am. No one else!"

"Sure, Wayne Niebold," the Vet said, wheeling out. "Good luck with the board."

Sitting before Sandy's board, the AG could feel the darkened skyscrapers, the choked subways, the impassible streets, and the panic of the stranded. Hard urban people were familiar with temporary inconvenience and permanent disorientation. Delayed trains, housing hikes, job firings, divorces, shootouts, brown-outs, and torched neighborhoods were often handled with enviable equanimity.

New Yorkers were familiar with many events from vicarious or personal experience. Yet a dust storm imposed by a group of alien terrorists was strange. No one knew where the dust originated, and the jammed information networks were not forthcoming.

Without picking up a cord, the AG could hear the speculation chaotically filling the city outside the boardroom. Was the dust dump a tactic fostered by the Russians to heat up a refrozen war? Were the causes extraterrestrial? Was the dump a promotional campaign for a new movie that passed the limits of sane advertising? And if the latter were true, who in city government had issued the permits? Behind these possibilities, largely ignored, was fear that the dump was a nationwide event heralding a takeover by a terrorist organization.

These and other speculations circulated in the paralyzed city, anarchic without the controlling illusion of its media outlets.

Before the boards, the AG isolated the short waves that carried this chaos in its alternating particle-wave structures. Gathering her remaining paranormal abilities, she visualized the shapes of these molecules. Then, in a distancing exercise, she imagined herself and this crisis displaced in the time-space continuum. She learned that Sandy had really been convinced that cultural anarchy developed into a new kind of order if allowed to build momentum toward total destruction. Beautiful. She sees beauty in destruction. The Anarchist's name? She heard without understanding— nihilism, narcissistic nihilism, said with a sneer on his face. He hated Sandy.

The AG looked into the heart of her Anarchist but saw something else. Floating across his face were the words of an article yet to be written: THE PHOENIX WAS TO CATALYZE THE REPRESSED ANARCHY PRESENT IN THE URBAN STRUCTURE. THE RELEASED FORCES WERE TO COALESCE INTO A SELF-GOVERNING, DECENTRALIZED STRUCTURE THAT WOULD NOT BECOME AUTOCRATIC. STABILITY THROUGH SELF-RENEWAL. GROWTH. FOOD FOR VENDETTAS.

The AG felt the Anarchist was not presently writing. The

article seemed to come from him in some other time-frame. She scribbled down the word PHOENIX, glad to know the name of the operation and the Anarchist's reason for defection from her affections. Stasis was impossible for him, so he had chosen the PHOENIX.

Having removed her crisis from its context, the AG had the secret knowledge that she could use her conscious will to remedy the immediate situation. She must set a force in opposition to Sandy's will.

One by one, the AG plugged the curved cords into the holes in the three-tiered board. One by one, the red and green lights lit and blinked insistently with low buzzing sounds. The AG liked the noise, the din of people wanting a response. She got out the cigarette-pocked folder of Sandy's clients and read the names and box numbers to become familiar with some of the callers. It was a few minutes before she thought of answering calls. The prettily blinking lights resounded like Christmas lights multiplying all over the metropolis. It was this vital city that she would guide out of its danger. The AG curved the cord in her left hand and plugged into the network clearinghouse and Duncan's stark fear.

"Je-sus, do you have any idea of the damage, the sheer ... I said I'd help with the black-out, but..."

"This is not Sandy," said the AG, realizing how influential Duncan was. "This is the AG. I can tell things are jammed, but that has nothing to do with your facilities. Please return communication to your clearinghouse so ambulances can coordinate with Vendettas Volunteers on the walkie-talkies."

"I want my exclusive."

"On what?"

"The Phoenix and Sandy, or you. A blow-by-blow developmental piece."

"What is happening out there? I don't know."

"Neither do I but I'll start with the street dust; eyewitness accounts of the disaster and then a tentative urban impact report followed by an on-the-spot account of your activities. By the way, where is Sandy? She left a message with me and timing is most important."

"I don't know," the AG said. "When I got here, Sandy was gone. Her chair was knocked over, so it might not have been a pleasant encounter."

"I'm sure," said Duncan. "Do you know what organization was in back of Food for Vendettas?"

"There was a health foods store that took over after we went out of business."

"We?"

"The Anarchist and me."

'"What did you say your name was?"

"The Anarchist's Girlfriend. Can I call you back?

Before you release Sandy's message? I have some work to do."

"The message is due to air in an hour. I'll be in touch."

After Duncan unplugged, the AG felt a moment's uneasiness, knowing he would exploit the situation as best he could. Would he even continue the black-out if it were more newsworthy? The AG was soon relieved. She sensed him talking to the stranded employees about a new idea he had to unjam the network's TV and radio frequencies. He said an auxiliary energy source in the basement would do the trick, even without satellite reception. When the AG received this information, she unplugged her connection to Duncan's line. He would revive communications. All she had to do was coordinate the isolated rescue systems in the city.

Using Sandy's collage as a guide, the AG answered each light on her board. She gave out pertinent information referring to the mandala-shaped map of the PHOENIX, locating the dumping site near each client of Ad-A-Live.

After a while, outside individuals and organizations called, along with Vendettas Volunteers, requesting instructions.

While fielding the injured to hospitals, the AG noticed the only dark line on her board was the hole over De Long Shipping Co. She took a second to plug a cord into the hole and see what she could sense. She saw an image of a man collapsed in a chair, overturned on the floor of a room in the Sherry Netherland. Furnishing the information to an ambulance, she mentioned it might be a suicide and asked they contact a hotel doctor before speeding over.

Though Mr. Dio was unknown to the AG, she felt his death

as some kind of link with the event she was so embroiled in. This thought was her last private one as she fought to lead the city out of its deepening crisis—now dispatching medic teams, now coordinating snow removal units. Slowly, the debris from the unnatural storm was removed.

The officials at City Hall returned to their operations.

Some had stayed in bed too late to be waylaid by Georgeanne's girls. Others had spent the storm in their congenial company in the cozy heated van. A few were stranded in their offices with faithful members of their staff. None were pleased with the unexpected event. It made them appear negligent or guilty of a lack of vigilance, since local terrorists were involved. The AG was a likely newsworthy personality on which to deflect some of this responsibility. Circumstances surrounding her emergence were sufficiently peculiar. How had she come to be "just passing through" the Pan-Am building in the crisis? How did she know the way to coordinate the rescue attempts? It was logical, only if she were the unofficial leader of a terrorist organization, perhaps displaced in a purge, seeking retribution for her faithless comrades.

Officials prepared a statement of this kind with searching allegations and processed orders to establish the identity of the woman known as the AG. Police stood by to bring her in once the roads were clear. Then a cop on Pearl Street received a call from an old friend at an old hangout. It seemed the AG had popular favor on her side. Joe, a proprietor of the club, not too far from Wall Street, had given word the AG was "family." Joe kept a clean place and didn't like outsiders prying into his business. City Hall listened. Many campaigns were related to Joe's Family.

In the first hours of morning, a completely exhausted AG found herself in the office of Ad-A-Live answering service. Employing conscious will was more difficult than her "awareness," which at one time had flowed unchecked through her being. She was afraid of failing when so much more was at stake than her own personal situation. The mandala-shaped network was scrawled like graffiti across her beloved city. Sandy had marked it up with red Xs.

The AG took a royal blue highlighter. She colored across the Xs, making each a blurry purple star, as a bridge or thoroughfare was cleared. But all this quick-thinking activity was insufficient to make her forget her fear. As the switchboard filled with a maze of ever-changing cords, she answered, calm and automatic. "Vendettas center at Ad-A-Live, coordinating crisis relief. The bridge nearest you, the Triborough, is clogged at the northeast point. The central hut with snowmobile equipment and bulldozers is located at...please requisition local warehouse facilities for forklifts. Hardware stores will supply gas masks and shovels..."

Identified as just the AG, she gave specific instructions, finding on the map each marked bridge and the local facilities to clear it; the dumpsters, snow removal equipment and Vendettas Volunteers, who needed to be told where to direct the stranded, frightened, and injured. When Duncan McKenzie called in from the Network Clearinghouse, she was not as patient.

"AG, it's a mess out there."

"I have heard this."

"I have Sandy's statement, and I'm about to simultaneously broadcast to my affiliates."

"First, please connect the other networks that remain jammed."

"What do you care?"

"Please connect them. It is very dangerous. When people panic, they want the comfort of their favorite station."

"What about my exclusive?"

"You have Sandy's message and know who she is. I would think that's plenty."

The AG, unplugging the line to Duncan, realized she had no way to hear Sandy's message. Though she expected aimless rhetoric, there might be an explanation.

What was the source of Sandy's personal power? She was sincere, but was that enough to attract good people? For the AG, personal power was political. The PHOENIX had changed her existence. It was due to Sandy, though the Anarchist believed political will was a shining transcendent thing.

The AG summoned what was left of her paranormal abilities to sense Duncan's broadcast. Instead, she was beside Wayne, steps below the Anarchist, when a hot burst toppled marble down steps. The blast hurt her eyes and then...nothing. All vision was extinguished. No longer did she entertain the detached floating of her spirit. She was too engaged in the immediate pain of the Anarchist, Wayne, and the city itself.

She felt a horrible headache and laid her head clown on the board, amidst the buzzing lines. It was minutes before she opened her eyes again with the emotional realization that she had lost the psychic room of her private self. She was in a switchboard room, implicated in a terrorist operation, and she hadn't eaten for quite some time. Her head felt heavy on the board. I wonder, she thought, if Sandy rested her head in this same position, for nights on end, before exhaustion finally overtook her.

In the waiting room of the small airport, the Llama was struck by the strong resemblance between the unconscious girl on the padded seat and the AG. He asked his staff to make an extensive background check on Sandy before ordering his shuttle to take them to his private airstrip. The plane would have no other passengers. It only flew to the Llama's California headquarters on Stinson Beach. The Llama was aware of the fact that dust had been dumped in paralyzing quantities, and Sandy was responsible. He wanted to interrogate her in a non-pressured situation. He needed to determine her motives and the extent of her organization. He sought assurance it would not interfere with his own. A life's work, which affected the potential welfare of millions, demanded unusual sacrifices.

The Llama waited for the pilot, readying the plane for take-off. He played with the radio, pleased it functioned, surprised to hear the AG identified as the mysterious dispatcher responsible for coordinating the city's medical personnel and maintenance crew with Vendettas Volunteers. The commentator added that the authorities had not determined if the AG person was a ringleader or a savior, or just an average woman who happened to be in the right place at the right time.

The Llama carried a small battery run beeper-operated portable teletype with sufficient capacity to relay verbal commands as far as his inner city villa. He gave a command, which confirmed itself on a mini-printout: CONTACT ALL MEMBERS INFLUENTIAL AT CITY HALL. INSTRUCT A NEWS HOLD, POLITICAL BLIND, ON THE WOMAN KNOWN AS THE AG. WILL FOLLOW WITH NEW INSTRUCTIONS. The Llama would protect her until she came to him of her own volition. He assumed it wasn't wishful thinking that she would soon visit. He had something she wanted, maybe.

The Llama turned off the radio broadcast in favor of a wide-screen TV. The dust clean-up was in effect all over the city. The commentator spoke rapidly: "Replacing dark screens across the city tonight was this image: a yellow cornucopia bearing the half-charred words: FOOD FOR VENDETTAS. This unusual image is the emblem of an obscure terrorist organization. They bear the terrible responsibility for the operation known as the PHOENIX. The wings of this mythological bird, said to live up to three hundred and fifty years, darkened our city and our screens for almost fourteen hours as we struggled under pounds of a substance known as

Arizona Dust. Heroically, an unknown woman..."

The Llama turned off the sound of the television to answer his beeper. His staff had instantaneously assembled a report from Church members in City Hall. There was wide-ranging paranoia that the PHOENIX had been designed to demonstrate the incompetency of city government or the dangerous aspects of local initiatives or...

Officials most feared problems in designating the city a "disaster area" so it would qualify for state funds. The AG was a convenient scapegoat. It would cost him something to keep her out of the planning at City Hall. Their accusatory release awaited his concession. So far, her identity had not been disclosed on air. The Llama turned off his beeper and watched the television without sound. The cornucopia certainly beat the blank test pattern but seemed nonetheless ominous. The Llama turned up the sound just before take-off. He heard Sandy's message through Duncan McKenzie:

EGYPTIANS BELIEVED THE PHOENIX LIVED FIVE OR SIX CENTURIES BEFORE BEING CONSUMED IN FIRE BY ITS OWN ACTION. THEN IT AROSE FROM THE ASHES IN FRESHNESS AND YOUTH. OUR PHOENIX ARISES FROM THE DUST OF YOUR EXCESSIVE CONSUMPTION. THIS STORM IS MADE OF ARIZONA DUST, THE SAME MATERIAL USED TO TEST THE CLEANING APPARATUS OF OUR MISSILES. IN THE WRONG CREVICE, THEY WILL FIRE. DOOMSDAY IS ONLY A MATTER OF TIME. FROM DUST TO DUST. WITH SWEAT ON YOUR

BROW SHALL YOU EAT YOUR BREAD, UNTIL YOU RETURN TO THE SOIL FOR DUST YOU ARE, AND TO DUST YOU RETURN. A MISFIRE IS ASSURED.

Chapter 13

LIFE IN THE A-FRAME

There are a series of A-frame houses on a California hillside overlooking Stinson Beach. The houses were built for practicality by rich hippies and ecologists and various other people with sufficient funds and some imagination. The A-frames, almost hidden by erratic foliage, seem a sign of Descartian sanity on a hillside, blending raggedly into a perfect diagonal of beach. Nestled above that beach, where it curves into that hillside, sits one particular house.

The sun, glinting off the windowed front, reflected the ocean up to Sandy, hovering above in a helicopter. She could almost make out the refractory windows, but not quite. She was too stunned, especially with the chloroform still in her system.

"Where am I?" she mumbled in the direction of her unknown pilot, whom she fancied as some kind of high-tech angel.

"Above Stinson Beach on your way to the Llama's west coast retreat," the pilot replied, pointing with a look of pure benevolence. "That A-frame, there."

"Who's the Llama?"

The pilot smiled, humility wreaking havoc with his features, as he said, "God only knows."

Sandy didn't pursue it. Instead, she allowed herself to become mesmerized by white coastline against that inexpressible hillside. Descending, she could see iridescent waves against a sparkly, mica-filled beach. Sandy wanted to believe that she really was going to meet God at the A-frame. Such an idea would force her, with her existential dogma, to believe she was no longer in control of her destiny. The helicopter was, she decided, a hint in that direction. Surveying the beauty around her, she thought it might even be advantageous to abdicate her will in favor of whatever cosmic fluke had landed her in this paradise.

Reality had become more than she could comprehend from the narrow matrix of her switchboard. Tears, of real feeling, sniffles and a headache alerted her to the presence of her physicality. The dead did not cry. That she was sure of. Perhaps it was allergies, or…

"Is this some kind of power play? My being kidnapped?" she asked the pilot, who bore little resemblance, on second glance, to her idea of a celestial being.

The pilot seemed perplexed. "Power? That's energy in organic and inorganic substances on Earth, left over from the Big Bang. Depending on what you think is true, any theory you adopt will be serviceable. Differences depend solely on the environment in which it is adopted."

Sandy could not believe such inanities existed in Paradise. Before she could clear her mind for some type of escape strategy, the pilot leaned over, confidentially indicating the horizon line below.

"There are no accidents," he said cryptically.

Some propagandist, Sandy thought, searching the floor for her belongings. She was only able to locate a pair of men's sunglasses, which definitely weren't hers. She put them on to shield herself from the pilot, as well as the sun. In this way, she noted a square of a platform on the triangular roof of the A-frame. Practical solar heating panels pointed to places on the hillside for a possible escape. It might be crazy to perform unrehearsed physical feats, but she decided to try. Stinson Beach, if she guessed correctly, was in California. It was a feasible state to get lost in.

The helicopter dropped to the platform. Before Sandy could scramble, the pilot suddenly removed her glasses and held another soft handkerchief over her nose. Her eyes burned once again. Then, there was nothing.

The Llama sat on a large, flat cushion, watching what looked like an empty television set. He held a manila file on his lap and contemplated the dull gray field on the screen until he felt relaxed enough to grasp the subtle gradations that formed the logo of the Denotational Church. The dotted line of the highway within the circle always made him feel like a cosmic tracker. He drew confidence from the image and considered the contents of the folder.

It contained a charged secret that linked both Sandy and the AG. It also brought to question the foundations of the Denotational Church. Nature had denied his theory with an instance of universal duality. "Fragmentation," which he had always considered a psychological problem of modern society, had occurred in nature. The Llama formulated the mystery in a slogan: EVERY ENTITY THAT EXISTS CONTAINS ITS ANTITHESIS WHICH IS ENDOWED WITH AN EQUAL AND OPPOSITE FORCE.

If "fragmentation" was beyond a curable mental habit, denotation was powerless as a path to resolve such opposites. If the AG was one aspect of the phenomenon, Sandy was definitely the other — a doppelganger in effect.

The relation between the two had been established by his research staff. The synthesis, the way to wisdom, was beyond his grasp. The Llama knew this problem was fairly ancient. Even in Tibet, the paradox of opposites had infinite unsolvable precedents. Denotation was a generalized system for practical resolution— a way to externalize emotional logic, in a case by case system. Denotational technique was larger than individual psychology, but just as impotent in the face of a crisis like the PHOENIX. He may have kidnapped Sandy, but he hadn't succeeded in muting her destructive force. The AG had done that job with no support systems. What was her method?

The Llama stared moodily at the screen until the gradations of dots in the image unified into a smooth, opaque field. Each electrical dot was indistinct, yet essential in the pattern, an electrical cog. Vain with the success of his Denotational enterprises, was he just another kind of cog, ignorant of anything but administration? He was efficient at that chore and had extensive influence. Members of the church, highly placed in City Hall, would see themselves disgraced, careers in ruins, before they would allow the arrest of the AG for the PHOENIX.

His teletype confirmed the press would back-out. There would be an informational black-out regarding her identity and whereabouts. Only Wayne Niebold, his renegade disciple, was aware of the AG's true identity, as well as the Llama's deficits. He was at large on the streets of the East Village. For all the Llama's instincts for self-preservation, he would see Wayne prosper. He could not arrest him for a "wash" no matter what the consequences to his Church. A desire to become a genuine spiritual leader had arisen in the Llama. The dictatorial structure of the church might yet become a viable path to wisdom.

This alteration of his mission, not so far from his grasp, was tabled for the immediate problem of what to do with Sandy. The woman was murderous — monomaniacal, nihilistic, amoral, and dangerous, at the least. What could he expect from her, and how should he dispose of her?

Opening the file in his lap, the Llama considered Sandy's mandala-shaped map of the PHOENIX operation. He had obtained the Xerox with some trouble. Despite its intention, the Llama had to admire the beauty in its not-so-random structure. He could even admit an affinity to a mind with such an aesthetic.

He would offer Sandy guidance, remind her of her proclivities and potentials, and provide a haven for her to decide future direction. He would heartily suggest a "wash", perhaps a condition for the haven? Carefully, the Llama noted the distinction between Sandy's power urge and his own. Conquest, not mere influence and facility, were on her mind.

The Llama knew his course and felt its uncertainty. He turned off the set, full of paradoxes. He decided to take a walk among the erratic foliage that so reflected his inner turmoil. Not a small factor in his state was that Sandy's horrible success with the PHOENIX had meant the failure of the opening of his drive-in missions. Yet he had scooped Sandy from the scene of her triumph into anonymity.

Sandy found herself on a futon facing a window the length of a wall. On the other side of it was a hill and a blue moving shape she recognized as the ocean. If she was detained for deportation, they surely had upgraded the facilities. Unlikely, she decided, recalling the helicopter ride. What kind of freak had abducted her from midtown in the middle of a crisis?

A powerful one, she thought, before she caught sight of a short, squarely built man making his way down a nearby hillside. My keeper, she thought with sarcasm insufficient to cover her fear of a captor with an organizational facility superior to her own. Had she misjudged the impact of her operation?

Was simple father revolt, her primal reaction to her father's throwing her out of his house, a valid catalyst for political action? Had the PHOENIX transcended the usual Freudian clichés and achieved real significance? That was the essential thing to know. Survival had never been much of a consideration, more catch-as-can.

Cagily, Sandy noted her surroundings. She didn't much like the A-frame. Set-in steps led to a loft sleeping area. Otherwise, the multi-functional living room was wide-open, stuffed with more futons, mats, and too-sinkable pillows. Very New Age, she thought, uneasy with that style under the best of conditions.

Without acknowledging Sandy's presence, the short man entered the A-frame and formally removed his shoes. He seated himself contemplatively on a large cushion before what looked like a blank TV screen. Sandy was not sure if this procedure ruled life at the A-Frame.

"We're here to discuss business, correct?" she asked, pacing to establish her stride. When the Llama did not respond, she wished she had her video-cam. It was an excellent device in quirky social confrontations.

"I want a helicopter out of here," she began again. "Can we make some kind of arrangement?"

The Llama turned on the set and smiled as another kind of gray surface filled the screen.

Frustrated by the silent intimidation, Sandy fantasized about a confident Anarchist destroying Wall Street with his laser. Maybe she had achieved enough notoriety to rate prison in an A-frame? Stinson Beach wasn't a cattle boat, and this maniac, whoever he was, seemed a peaceable sort—the only one around. With some focus, she could reduce his advantage and escape.

The pilot had called him the "Llama." The closest she had ever come to a holy man was a Skinnerian whose lectures on "the behavioral nature of man" she had taped at Cooper Union. She recalled now fragments from that lecture series. THEMES: Autonomy, dignity and the good. How such attitudes were to be destroyed, if man were to survive on his already overcrowded planet. Also discarded, were archaic beliefs in the virtues of a consumer driven society, whose enduring products were frustration and violence.

Most of the series made little behavioral sense, more an outpouring of passion disguised as purification. Bored, Sandy caught the lecturer's face on tape, She zoomed in on the creased V's of his eyebrows, lips, nose, and chin, mechanically raving about "old conditioning." A pause to meet the eye of her video-cam, then down to her breasts below. She had left the lecture hall sure there were no real holy men, no matter how possessed. Later, in her copy of "The Lives of the Saints," she noted a holy man was, in the best sense, a man capable of order. Yet, she reminded herself, that did not mean incapable of desire.

Should she seduce the Llama? A glance at his square ascetic face was discouraging. Great logic and formality were essential in a person capable of extended celibacy. She had ignored controlling characteristics in her verbal approach. Had she breached his rules of conduct? Bowing, she spoke to the Llama with an exaggerated restraint.

"I am going to ask you a series of questions. You can answer or not, as you like. How did I get here and why? Who are you? When do I get out of here? Was the PHOENIX penultimate?" (Thinking, strategically, that he might answer the last one first)

The Llama did not change his expression, as though unfamiliar with her language.

"I ran an operation, a nihilistic act of terrorism, to point out larger acts less obvious and often sanctioned by institutions. Was my design effective?"

"The city moves forward," said the Llama, yawning and changing his position to lie prone before the television set.

"Were you in sympathy with the Food for Vendettas message on your set?"

"The city has no memory. Not even the Bowery."

He hinted at a knowledge of her past. Silently, Sandy stood on the edge of his futon in front of the screen, waiting...

"Most things only have meaning in context. Your event does not, in any general or specific sense, have a context. It is an act outside of nature so no triumph is possible. Only self-delusion and destruction."

"When will I be deported?"

"Your abilities are more useful out of prison. My suggestion? I can purge you of your patterns in a procedure called a "wash," a common requirement for criminal initiates new to the Denotational Church."

"Oh?" said Sandy, smiling politely, though confused by this obtuse suggestion.

The Llama pointed to the blank screen of his television set. "Care for some internal scrutiny on this question?"

"Not today."

The Llama raised his robe indifferently to the level of his knees. His calves bore the marks of a mosquito banquet. "I am unused to the insect population of Stinson Beach. Perhaps you are luckier—you are a practical existentialist?"

"Not in any mystical sense," Sandy said, taken aback at this assessment. "A personal nihilist would be more correct."

"Whose mission has affected an entire city?"

Sandy did not want to appear as if his information interested her. "Just a few hundred on my job. I'm a switchboard operator. I work the boards like any pavement pounder."

"I believe the intention of the PHOENIX is similar to my own goals..."

"I gather my operation was successful," Sandy interrupted abruptly, walking to the door of the A-frame, "so what's the point of listening to you?"

"If only to meet your sister," the Llama said, lying facedown on the mat. "Through introspection, some Denotational members have been known to develop an inverse of themselves in their choice of intimates—love object or friend. Humans are capable of psychic mitosis, you know. The modeling is exact enough for delusion, but the personality remains intact."

Could he mean it literally about the sister thing, Sandy wondered. "What do you know about me?"

The Llama handed Sandy the manila envelope he had placed under a pillow.

"After we have established the identity of your family, you will be in a better position to bargain for a life worth living," the Llama said. Sandy found him sanctimonious.

She seated herself on the futon and opened the file suspiciously.

The Llama opened the windows of the A-frame to experience the immediacy of ocean and beachfront. He acknowledged the taste of salt in his mouth and his shared affinity with Sandy's lust for conquest. He realized that his posturing was that of an administrator with no concrete ideology. All he had was his Denotational stance.

Situational relativity seemed an arbitrary premise, though before it had been truth itself. The AG seemed to embody nature's refutation of his posture. Sandy was his polemical daughter, and somehow the two were related. By reconciling this contradiction with his Denotational stance, perhaps he could form a philosophy to guide America into the next millennium? In his contradictory way, the Llama knew this notion was the abandonment of his grandiosity. No longer would he subliminally seek his name high on banners and tabloid headlines. By acknowledging the divinely eccentric AG, he and Sandy would conquer the fierce dogma of individualism.

While the Llama was deciding such ponderous issues, Sandy was shivering from the cold air and the surprising information in her folder. Her constitution was ill-prepared for nature and the resolution of her disturbed childhood. Fact or fabrication, it mattered little. The AG was a person who was only understood in context.

Everyone knew a different AG.

The Llama noticed her behavior and smiled reassuringly. "You will get used to the air very soon. Now, tell me about the AG."

"She is an innocent. I met her on the Bowery and found her to be useful. She doesn't notice being manipulated and... Does she know I've been taken?"

"No."

"Of course," Sandy said in some relief at the odd prick of conscience that made her wish to spare the AG's natural concern. Sandy took from the file a photograph of a work-worn faded blonde woman seated at a pedal-driven sewing machine.

"This is my mother," she said, more as a fact than a question. She had seen the strange machine on the island of her birth. There was something of herself in the squareness of the seamstress' body; the controlled pose of her hands—the straight, determined lines of her seams.

Sandy also that the woman's eyes, in their round shape, if not the faded green color, were like the AG; an impression borne out by the delicate limbs in the horribly plain, no-color dress. She studied the photograph, wondering about the genetic break-down of traits linked and traits acquired. She wanted to read a personality profile on the seamstress and as much exact information on her life as possible. Luckily, the file was most extensive, since without a doubt, this woman was the missing half of her family.

"You went to a lot of trouble."

"My staff actually. It was important, considering I am in the business of understanding spiritual phenomenon.

Your sister is one aspect and..."

"I'm the flip side," Sandy interrupted. She could not guess where the interview with this madman might lead.

"The Phoenix seems to have been a deadly try at synthesis."

"What about catharsis? As good a conjecture to me. What do you want from me?"

"You can go back to New York if you like. I'm not holding you here. I originally thought abduction would sabotage your operation and preserve my own. That's been proven absurd. You can do as you like. It's to your advantage to remain here, but you decide. I merely ask that you hear me out."

Sandy considered the Llama's offer and the miles of clean beach. She could be out the door and down the beach, negotiating a ride to the city and another American underground. A new name, another identity; a black-market green card? What were her possible options? How long would it be before she was caught or attempted another violent act? This one would have no pretense to political purpose. It would be personal in the way the Llama had inferred. She would be a fraud as her dad had been. Was she just repeating his alienation in her destiny?

The Llama spoke softly. "The screen is a good agent for thought."

Sandy sat on the futon before the Llama's television screen and contemplated the gray field. She had destroyed the city's peace of mind to duplicate her own inner chaos. She had destroyed the AG's love and life with the Anarchist. She had probably destroyed Wayne's future, and maybe the Anarchist himself. What was she but an agent of destruction?

The Llama's voice interrupted her gray searchings.

Sandy felt that he was more than her captor. He had revealed to her the secret of her birth—-a liberator.

"You are bargaining for peace," the Llama said. "That commodity is my stock in trade. I will absorb your organization into my own. You will receive a lifetime tenure here at the A-frame with a guaranteed non-anxiety clause."

"What does that include?"

"A reorganization and daily review of your life priorities. Peace as the actuality of continual regrouping."

"What do you want in return?"

"You will have to undergo a 'wash' that I will carefully arrange in accordance with your denotational profile."

WASH frightened Sandy. She would not bargain for a brainwash. A mental static screen was imposed between herself and the persuasive Llama. It helped her resist the Penetrating depth of his thought into her consciousness. She contemplated his gray field, maintaining an indifferent concentration. This was almost impossible as his voice intoned...

"You feel detached and ineffectual in your relationship to a society with superficial, self-serving priorities. You've decided to engineer its demise and your own, jolting yourself from the fashionable stance of disaffection. Using the remnants of what was at one time considered alternative culture, you strove to gain a foothold in the historical rising tides of one city. Fortunately, your plan was not as devastating as you had envisioned."

"Only a stunt," she said, as she shaped in her mind the rhetoric of her existential catechism.

"I was concerned with process, not result," she said, searching.

The Llama felt relieved. He had succeeded in penetrating her static. The batteries of resistance were running down. Soon his polemical daughter, a prodigal, would be coming home.

The Llama put his arm around Sandy, kneeling. "I promise you will be yourself in a superior form."

"I trust you," Sandy said, surprising herself. For possibly the first time in her life, she felt she could place her personality and total psyche in the care of another—this squarely-built, obtuse bald man.

The Llama assumed the "wash" would make a disciple of Sandy. A more standardized, less sophisticated mode of thought would benefit her and render her useful to the Church as well.

The Llama knelt. He placed both his arms around her in a ritual embrace. Gazing at the screen were two heads. Four arms intertwined in the dying light of a sun setting over an ocean as calm as this human Shiva. The Llama made a mental note that, if Sandy wished, he would set the "wash" at the earliest possible time.

Sandy lay down on the foam rubber mattress of the unrolled futon not frightened that her personality would be destroyed. "Altered" was the term the Llama had used. Some part would be irrevocably changed, in what way? Her "wash" instructions indicated that this could not be predicted. She thought perhaps some traits designated as "antisocial" had a positive flipside. Hypersensitivity that led to paranoid delusions and megalomania also made her a great recorder of the passing scene. Maybe aggression was linked with an unusual appetite for experiencing the intensity of life? Would a "wash" diminish these? Characteristics that make a great explorer, make a poor colonist. Great warriors rarely make decent governors.

Sandy was frightened of losing her individuality and with it, her newfound identity as the worldly sister of the AG. She combed her memory for a story of someone, who had successfully experimented with identity changes. She thought of a friend, an underground actress, grown up in a Connecticut suburb, who had lived in Arizona with a lawyer before her divorce. She moved to New York's bohemian fringes, where Sandy saw her in an avant-garde production.

Sandy enjoyed her performance, thought she found theater collectives guilty of the worst kind of class hypocrisy — pretensions to a proletariat they had only vicarious knowledge of. The actress supposedly had transcended her sexuality by playing a woman playing a man playing a woman. Sandy noticed the collective had shorn her long, rich, auburn hair.

The acting was as amazing as her friend's crew cut. She moved with a stiff, nervous tension full of the dynamics of emotional suppression. The actress held a twist in her mouth as she dry-humped a woman playing a horse. The production was appallingly lacking in substance, especially at the ticket price of ten dollars Sandy felt fortunate to avoid.

After, at a bar, the actress's role-carryover irritated Sandy. The booming, authoritative voice never did click back to her friend's rich, rolling tones. The actress's change lasted a little longer than the part. It was a dream, where she transcended her skin. Sandy had performed that through the PHOENIX, her waking dream of revenge. If it had not affected her identity, what could a "wash" do?

This matter settled, Sandy decided to follow the instruction in the booklet which said to visualize familiar surroundings. Sandy visualized her switchboard, allowing herself to drift into unconsciousness. Sleep, like a drug, filled Sandy with too welcome relief, she had avoided many nights into the PHOENIX.

The dream was tribal, her reoccurring theme. She was a Cro-Magnon creature painting a mural on a cave wall with a porcupine quill brush and berry dyes. The brush was too thick to delineate gazelles. She loosened the gut, selecting one quill. Dipping repeatedly, she painted delicate legs and hooves. The scene took shape. A herd of gazelle were chased by a herd of buffalo. The buffalo were chased by a herd of hunters with flat spear points.

A yell! A rough group of Cro-Magnon men entered sloughing a carcass on the packed dirt floor. One tore a limb, denuding the raw meat from the bone. It was a gazelle limb. Horrified, she lifted the carcass to throw it into a pot of boiling water when the seamstress appeared out of the frame of a large snapshot. The frame disappeared and the seamstress magically made the animal whole. The gazelle scampered out of the hole of the cave past the surprised horde of men. They turned to Sandy, each bearing the face of her father, sorrowful at her defection. The seamstress put her arm around Sandy and inner life fused between them.

Together they imposed their will on the horde of fishermen, making clear their familial connection. The men's faces became that of the Llama; then one Llama showing them politely to the entrance of the cave. Sandy turned to ask the seamstress where they were and found she was looking into the benevolent face of the AG. Sandy, the Llama, and the AG surveyed a lush plain full of the green grass reminiscent of the hill surrounding the A-frame. The AG found the edge of another snapshot and said to Sandy, "See you later. I'll be on another plane."

Sandy accepted what she didn't know and quietly watched the frame disappear before asking the Llama, "And what of the Anarchist?"

"He is no longer," the Llama said.

She had purposely omitted his existence from her consciousness, not wanting to know what happened to him. She woke herself up to find that she was not on the futon. Drab green paint on four walls absorbed the institutional light of a concave fixture overhead. Several men in beige uniforms that looked vaguely military indicated the seat Sandy was to take at a table. At closer range, she was unable to identify their uniforms, but had no recourse. She had to pick up the paper in front of her. With stark fear she read: DEPORTATION PROCEEDINGS AGAINST ALEXIS STANIFRAZ BY THE GOVERNMENT OF THE UNITED STATES OF AMERICA.

Outside this room, formerly a tool shed painted a perfect

green to camouflage with the hills, stood the Llama. Through a one-way mirror, he was able to observe Sandy's preliminary reactions. He noted them neatly on the form entitled WASH, which he had designed so long ago.

****

IN THE SHADOW OF FEDERAL HALL

The Anarchist's blindness was a practical horror for Wayne Niebold, in the choking hours that followed the dust dump. Gently leading the Anarchist to the shelter of Federal Hall, he stopped to rest and examined the Anarchist's eyes. There was no involuntary blinking of his eyelids, no pupil movement, and his retina was burnt white. The Anarchist, in pain, muttered randomly about how he was dead and was this hell, arguing angrily with himself that he had fulfilled his purpose, his destiny even, and didn't deserve to be damned.

The horror for Wayne was that he could not answer.

Repeatedly, he tapped letters into the Anarchist's palm, hoping he might get the idea that Wayne was still with him in this life. Unfortunately, the Anarchist had never learned to sign.

"Why is someone tickling my hand, yet saying nothing. Is this some cruel tease I can't understand or some hidden meaning I should know?"

"YES, YES BELIEVE THIS!" Wayne tapped exultantly.

"Nemesis is visiting me, saying to hell with your damned purpose. You have outlived it."

Wayne watched sprays of dust thickly whip down Wall Street on the breezes of the nearby ocean. Howling, he thought. Winds make a sound like that. HOWLING!!! he tapped into the Anarchist's hand, leading him into the rotunda of Federal Hall.

Convenient, Wayne thought, almost too convenient that no one locked this.

"Wanna die?" Wayne read on the lips of a boy walking out of a shadow with an outstretched knife in one hand and a black box in the other. "Say one word and..."

Wayne made his deaf-mute sign and the boy laughed, "Wrong party. Yes, I'm a survivalist, and if this is the end of the world—this part of it is mine!"

"I'm not dead?" the Anarchist asked.

Before the boy could react to the Anarchist, Wayne pointed to his own eyes. He opened them blankly and passed a hand over them to indicate a state of blindness.

The boy looked the strange pair up and down a second, laughing with a mixture of pity and contempt.

"Youse bums been fighting? Looks like you need some new clothes, but you're broke, right?"

Wayne, looking at the Anarchist's rags, realized how the boy might have assumed he was a derelict. It was a second before the idea penetrated that he was wearing the same disguise.

"Youse is harmless, I can see that. If you stay that way, I don't mind you hanging here until I tell you to get lost. It's creepy in here alone, know what I mean?"

Wayne smiled, deciding the boy must be about sixteen.

"Auxiliary power," the boy said, largely mouthing the words for Wayne. "Come on over and see this thing. We're in an emergency situation, they said about a half hour ago, no joke!"

The tough guy kid showed Wayne the way through the darkly echoing rotunda. Wayne followed, leading the Anarchist to a basement office, where a television was bolted high into the ceiling. On the screen was the Anarchist's cornucopia poster with the words: FOOD FOR VENDETTAS. A man, identified by a makeshift cardboard sign as DUNCAN MCKENZIE, talked with some confidence and misplaced hype.

"Aux powers unite! I am the exclusive coordinator between the Vendettas units and the city services, coordinating to remove the dust. I'm not usually on this side of the camera, I work for a network clearinghouse. By chance, I connected with the fabulous savior of our city. I am not at liberty to reveal her identity, but it's out that a woman is responsible. I can also say the criminals responsible for this crisis will be apprehended. Right now, we're working to get rid of all that dust, clear the thoroughfares, and get the city moving. 'Food for Vendettas,' in case you missed that, was founded by an anarchist who ran an east village co-op..."

"Look at that jerk," the boy said, "he's got the floor and don't know what to do with it. Man, if I had his gig, you'd know more about it. None of this protected name shit...I'd want..."

"She did it, didn't she?" the Anarchist said. "The AG. It's her who's saving the City."

"What do you know?" the boy asked the Anarchist.

Wayne tapped into the boy's hand to create a distraction and to possibly obtain a pencil.

"Away! You queer?" the boy said. "What do you know, old man?"

Wayne tried the drawer of the watchman's desk and found a few notepads and pencil stubs. He took one set.

NOTHING. HE'S CRAZY, Wayne wrote and passed it along. HE'S HARMLESS. LEAVE HIM ALONE.

"Why? Might have some fun provoked!"

The Anarchist smiled from memory. "Just a woman I know."

"Must be desperate to be with you," the boy said, moving his chair up from the Anarchist's to Wayne's.

"Are you queer?"

NO. HISTORY FREAK, Wayne wrote, pausing from his

scribbling about Duncan's editorial on the catastrophe, how the authorities were moving to normalize the city. So pretentious. Perhaps Wayne could give Duncan a little editorial competition. He began to record his own version of events with all the wit and experience he could recall or invent.

Notes didn't bind him to any ideology; not the Llama's or Sandy's or the Anarchist's. Nor was he tied to the specific purpose of news. He was entirely free, except for the imposition of time and accuracy. Hell, each sequence of the PHOENIX was history. Anyone could tell a story, but this one was uniquely his. There was yet time, with the network arteries clogged, to write a great piece on the miracle that had rescued the city, called the AG.

The boy held out a joint to Wayne, "Smoke? Could use some in this weather." He turned down the sound as Wayne took some of the joint into his lungs, "Don't mind if I turn this down?"

Wayne laughed and wrote, SAME TO ME. I JUST WANT TO GET THE GUY HOME TO HIS OLD LADY. KNOW WHAT I MEAN?

The boy laughed in friendship, "Well, good luck, man. Don't have to worry about cops looking for you tonight."

Wayne led the reluctant Anarchist out of the rotunda. He was equally tired but thought it important to return to the loft and the AG.

Progress was slow along the river. It was the fastest route, though the cold hurt and chapped his shoulder through the ripped fabric of his jacket. His skin itched from flapping shreds of cloth, especially where his pants had ceased to cover his calves. Yet a look at the Anarchist aroused enough pity that he almost forgot his own troubles. The Anarchist was clutching the piece of cloth Wayne had handed him for his mouth and nose. He tried to breathe through it. Bravely, he ignored the fine particles that settled in the creases of his face and were layering his beard. Wayne knew he looked equally pathetic; two mongrels searching for holes that once were homes.

At least, Wayne thought, the Anarchist had been a believer. He sought to fulfill his destiny with an act that made him part of a larger process—enough to stop the printing of the daily news. Wayne thought of the enormity of intention and how it had made them both Sandy's dupe. The Anarchist had paid for his misdirected idealism, aimed too high with lack of precision. He had paid literally. Lack of insight had cost him his eyes in an age without conscience.

The Anarchist, for his part, hoped Wayne would lead him home. He followed Wayne to a place where the concrete sidewalk became wood ties. He felt Wayne's hands steadying him, so he wouldn't fall in the odd places where ties narrowed to steps, then a half-step, then a rope ladder, and a small fall onto a boat bottom. The Anarchist felt the square-bottomed, upward slope of a rowboat. The lap of the waves against the dull wood put him to sleep. He knew he was finally going home.

Red /green, red/green—the lights on the board lit with the

constant monotony of Christmas lights. The AG stood for a break and stretched her cramped muscles, walking to the window where she could see the Pan-Am Building below her.

Streetlights were alive on Third Avenue and Forty-Second Street! Maybe, the AG speculated, on the other side of the Pan-Am Building and all over the city. She saw men uncover the necks and bases of the lamps. Trashcans, encased by dust, were unearthed by steadily burrowing bulldozers. It was not unlike a snowy late Saturday night, after the shoppers have gone and the plows gone out.

The midtown area was silent except for the steady clank of machinery moving intrepid snow. Tonight it was dust not snow, but almost normal. The AG felt as if some dire emotion had been exorcised from the city, leaving a new kind of joy, a new knowledge in the night air.

She, the AG, had done more than intuit the situation. She had taken charge! She allowed herself a quick flush of elation before the return of responsibility and a sense of personal failure. She had had no intimation about the Anarchist's fate. No sense but a painfully sharp light in her mind's eye, extinguished in the immediate anxiety of handling the phonelines. Insight, if it wasn't imagining, had been suppressed in the urgency to plug cords into the clogged arteries of urban vitality. It was some kind of sacrifice.

Buzz, buzz...an angry green light reminded her, who needed no reminding, that her mission was not ended.

"AG. It's Duncan from the clearinghouse. Aux circuits are

in operation. The test patterns are going off soon, and I'll make Sandy's broadcast. You better be going."

"Why?"

"With Sandy missing, you make a great fall guy. Split if you can. I won't give your identity away even though I was supposed to have exclusive rights to the story."

"That's nice of you. Journalists aren't noted for kindness."

"AG, I don't have any idea what those initials stand for."

"Anarchist's Girlfriend."

"I mean your real name, you must have a..."

The AG ignored the idea. She unplugged after wishing Duncan a happy broadcast. Was it was time for her to leave Ad-A-Live headquarters? She wondered if she were, indeed, in some danger from the police. The idea hadn't occurred to her before. She hadn't much thought about her world, except going home to her Anarchist. Now fear made her imagine her loft surrounded by police. Would she be hustled into a car, handcuffed on its roof, taken to some headquarters for questioning? Did such realities follow the patterns of television? The AG wished she had one. She would have to remember to observe TV rituals for procedures that mirrored real life. Since her second sight was failing, she would need a new way to live in the world.

Forgetting the miracle of her organization in the crisis, the triumph that might have bolstered her confidence, the AG felt like a criminal for the first time in her life. Was there anything in Sandy's desk that might be of later use? In the top drawer she found a plastic marketing sack. In the middle drawer she found Sandy's essential collage and propped it up on the switchboard, unaware of its meaning.

The AG simply found the thing horrifying. Jagged angles of model's flesh blended with chrome car bodies. Sky roofs mocking the dense claustrophobia of the composition made her short of breath. She disliked the paper surface of Sandy's world. Yet it was oily magazine stock filled with perfectly shot nightmare imagery. The AG exposed the cardboard back of the collage and with purposeful thought opened the third drawer for utilitarian goods.

Underneath a mound of plastic coffee spoons and stirrers and clear packets of napkins and sugar, she found a square object inside a plastic sack. The AG turned down the buzzer on the board, thinking it might be a momentous find, since it was hidden so well.

Inside the sack were Sandy's tape recorder and a small stack of tapes. Mechanical objects had never been a part of her life, but the AG thought the procedure might not be too difficult. She opened the clear window of the cassette player, placed a cassette into it, and closed the lid. Easy enough, she thought. Now if I can just figure out how to work the buttons. What did the gesture of playing a tape look like?

The AG recalled, with difficulty, an image of Sandy playing the tape. She had pressed two fingers simultaneously on two buttons. Were the two keys adjacent? No. There was one in-between. The AG pressed "Play" and "Start" vigorously. Unexpectedly, the voice that greeted her was her own. She recognized the baby-like gurgle so characteristic of her pleasurable sleep of former days. The AG felt acute embarrassment, a hot flush checked by Sandy's impatient voice.

"Alpha-level. Nothing discernible can break that flow.

She seems to operate on a low level of experience and comprehension. The AG as a subject is unintelligible but very reactive to auditory and tactile stimuli. Since she is so suggestible, she can be easily manipulated. To what advantage I haven't yet determined. The Anarchist, however, is a coherent sleeper. Fragments of stories and a repressed Irish are tantalizing aspects of his subconscious mind. They could be significant clues to his behavior, ideology, and the proper means for altering or interfering with his chosen routes...."

With much absorption, the AG listened to the rest of the tape. Then she lined up the rest of the boxes of tapes.

She checked the sides until she found the markings she was looking for. Dates. Months and months of tapes.

Where, the AG wondered, had she hidden the microphone?

BETRAYAL. Sandy's calculated purpose, her malicious intentions, were awesome to the AG. Sandy's assessment of her own perception had been too accurate. The AG had intimations of the existence of the PHOENIX, but was powerless to act on them. Second sight gave her a cosmic fatalism, a sense of the infinite that made her unable to interfere with destiny . She could offer aid to accident victims and animals, but not prevent their troubles any more than she could have stopped the PHOENIX. If she had been able to synthesize her instinctual feelings on a conscious level, she might have averted the terror that had paralyzed her city. This had been within her powers. But she had been lost in her instinctual overview, the realm from which she drew her inner sanctuary.

The AG walked to the window of the Pan-Am building and peered out into the night. Sandy's collage had accurately represented the landscape she had been blind to. The depths of Sandy's self-interest and betrayal of the AG's love, made a deep wound in her psyche. She wondered if she cared to leave Ad-A-Live for her "safety." Staring down at the city with new, somber thoughts on the useless nature of human life, the AG was only dimly aware of a faint buzzing from her board.

Sense of mission carried her back to the switchboard. She found her hand reach for the cord, her fingers curved around it, though her mind was still absorbing the stark shock of BETRAYAL. Was it necessary to hate someone to betray them, she wondered. Was it just a kind of extreme self-interest? An emotional form of cold steel? Something akin to the jagged sunroofs in car ads? What were the ethereal aspects of this evil?

Sitting in Sandy's chair, the AG thought, I was her friend. I will answer the line.

"AG?" a voice said.

It sounded like and unlike the Anarchist. She took a chance.

"Anarchist?"

"You're a brave girl to save the city."

"Did you want to destroy it?" the AG asked, realizing she had to know the depth of his involvement with Sandy.

"To destroy to save was Sandy's idea. I wanted to enlighten just a small part of it." The Anarchist said "enlighten" with a harsh twist of bitterness that seemed as foreign as his voice.

"Are you all right? You sound tired, what is wrong?

Tell me!"

"Soon enough," said the Anarchist with a stiffness that loosened her emotions.

"Do you love me, miss me? Will everything be okay?"

"Come soon," the Anarchist said in the same manner, "my love."

The AG replaced the cord into a hole on the switchboard. She opened the plastic sack and dropped the box of tapes and the recorder into it. Sandy's collage followed the tapes. The AG looked at the simple but frightening design and knew it probably revealed more than police were trained to read. Psychiatrists would generalize about it from other cases, the kind of speculative defilement the AG wouldn't wish on a fellow human, even Sandy.

Sandy's betrayal had been a less objective invasion of privacy.

The AG closed the sack and propped the map of the mandala-shaped operation on the switchboard. The police would appreciate the true value of that kind of strategy.

Then the AG put on her dust suit. She did not bother to hook up the diving tank. There would be no need. The streets were clear now.

Chapter 14

THE AG RETURNS TO HER ANARCHIST

The Anarchist sat in a chair by the kitchen table in his loft. He could hear Wayne's ballpoint scratching paper. He could also hear Wayne's typewriter tatting words with the varying speed of his passions. Occasionally, the machine would stop and the Anarchist would feel a cold, moist cloth bathing his still-swollen eyes.

The AG was not back. The Anarchist knew she was on her way, but feared she might have been detoured.

Especially since she was unaware of how excruciatingly difficult time had become for him. Maybe she had ceased to care for him? She seemed so serious and solidified on the phone, hard-sounding in a way most foreign to his experience. Had she been unable to reconcile his betrayal in her soul?

Over the sound of Wayne's typewriter, the Anarchist wondered how he could expect her to love him. Even if she had forgiven him, what could he offer her for the future? He was almost useless now, satisfied enough with his anarchist's act to welcome death before living past it. The AG's rejection of him would be just retribution for his betrayal of her love— the anticlimax of a life concluded. He only wished to hear her voice...to feel her hands on his face.

Irritably, he screamed for Wayne to stop his damn machine and read a section of whatever was in it. He had requested this several times, but Wayne had only patted him calmly on the shoulder in a gesture that urged patience. He would not ask again. Wayne could see his anxiety. Better to bear his horrible invisibility— stuck in the sightless walls of his mind. Absently, he ran the side of his hand against the wooden surface of the floor. Polyurethane or not, he felt a splinter lodge itself in his flesh and had the cynical thought; at least some part of him was tangibly alive! Moisture was in his dry eyes, before the slight breeze from the opening door prickled his skin. He felt a presence, a cool hand in his and a kiss.

The AG had run up the steps and entered the loft meaning to embrace her Anarchist, throwing her arms all around him. Instead, because he was so strangely solemn, she kissed his burnt, dusty beard, smoke-tinged cheeks, chin, and eyes, which he opened from habit to kiss her forehead.

"AG, my retina's fried from a laser blast," the Anarchist said.

The AG saw eyes that did not react to light. No response greeted her growing horror and a violent desire to destroy Sandy for what she had done to her Anarchist!

Such violence frightened the AG's gentle soul, unused to this extreme emotion. Her former peace had been detachment, she realized. That was sacrificed at the switchboard of active command. She would have to be conventionally cognizant of settings and time and the reactions of people. She would compensate for what nature had taken back from both of them.

The imprint of the AG's lips lifted the Anarchist's darkness. He could see their shape in his memory, suggesting the details of a face so familiar that he had almost forgotten it.

"Anarchist! You have a splinter in your hand. Let me sterilize a needle and ..."

"No. It'll work its way to the surface."

"You have me now," the AG said. "Where are the matches?"

The Anarchist had forgotten for a second there was someone else in the room. The typewriter stopped and he imagined Wayne taking the matches from the kitchen. The AG was making his memory a live thing!

The AG took his finger in her hands, "Still, just a second ..."

The needle gave a sharp sting and a smell of sulfur. A piece of cotton brought disinfectant sting and a pleasant medicinal smell.

"Now, let it get some air," the AG said, confirming for the Anarchist that his life was not over.

He was not necessarily a sad-faced, blind, prematurely aged man who had outlived his purpose. It might even be possible for him to mellow and live without incessant self-examination. Maybe he could think without censorship, give something of what remained inside him and have it be worthy!

"AG," said the Anarchist cautiously, since he still didn't believe in second guessing anyone's intentions, "Do you understand why I could not reveal the PHOENIX to you, but still had to follow through with it?"

"It was an act that was in your nature," the AG answered, "It was outside of mine."

The Anarchist wondered what that meant. He could sense nothing and imagine everything that was in her nature.

"AG, is there sadness? Do you no longer love?" he asked in courage and real anguish, knowing he cared too much about the answer.

The AG sat down on the floor of the loft, drawing the Anarchist beside her.

"Where is Wayne?" the Anarchist asked, suddenly self-conscious.

"He went into Sandy's room to leave us alone for a while."

The AG pulled his arms around her shoulder and sat within the circle of his lap, feeling her chest against his.

She felt huge with her vulnerable protector around her.

The Anarchist closed her into the triangle of his body. They emitted a joint sigh of pleasure and preciousness — timid like new lovers.

The AG broke the circle and stood to slide off her one-piece dust suit. She pushed the buttons of the Anarchist's pants through their holes and undid the zipper. She opened the ragged jacket and the buttons of the black shirt and sat within the inert tower of his body.

The Anarchist felt the shape of her toes, feet, ankles, and calves. He lifted her thighs until they were on top of his own and slowly eased his sex into the AG. The sensation was so foreign and familiar that he could not move for many seconds. He didn't want to move, actually, since the moment was complete.

It was the AG that began the circular dance that would spiral down inside her. The act made her envision radiant photography of gene structures, DNA double helices, the biological union she housed. Despite the loss of her second sight, the texture of sexuality was more palpable than ever. Nature did have its compensations, she thought, ecstatically.

As Wayne told it to the AG the next morning, there was a haul from the boat in Chinatown to the loft on the Bowery. Wayne tagged a ride for the sleepy Anarchist and himself by hailing a cab with a lit "on-duty" sign. The driver stopped, saying he was game for company, if they were game to test the dust. The Bowery seemed less pitiful covered in the stuff. Doorways were padded beds for the indigents and drunks, sleeping with their faces away from the street. Some nouveau arty types were shoveling out their front steps, as Wayne half-carried the Anarchist across the street from Phoebe's laden awning.

The AG read Wayne's gestures and explained them to the Anarchist. Between breaths, she indicated to Wayne to please slow down. When he was done, the Anarchist began.

"My objective," the .Anarchist said slowly, like a prayer, "is to adjust to the speed of sounds going by. Help me put them together as something more than disconnected ideas. I cannot see you, love. More's the shame, when I remember days I couldn't bear the sight of you. So afraid was I you knew my secret."

"That Sandy and you were lovers?" the AG asked with a harder tone.

"You do hate her, don't you?" he asked, surprised by her voice.

"Because of what she did to you. I had asked her to be kind."

"What?" the Anarchist fairly shrieked as Wayne's fist on his palm echoed his surprise.

"I had some insight into the situation I could not act on, so I bear a part also. Sandy cannot help being who she is. She didn't know what else she could become."

IS SHE ALIVE? DO YOU KNOW? Wayne wrote on a piece of scrap paper.

"Abducted or kidnapped," the AG said. "It might have been a client or police or anyone. She was gone when I got there, that's all I know."

Wayne wrote with some conviction, IT MIGHT HAVE BEEN ANYONE, BUT I'D BET IT WAS THE LLAMA.

"Who is he?" the AG asked, vaguely remembering a sleepy conversation on a subway train.

Wayne handed the AG a brochure. On one side of a glossy fold-out was the highway logo above a picture of a smiling young couple. On the end panel were copy blocks describing the Denotational Organization and how the drive-in churches and residencies worked. The rest of the end panel was filled with a cropped photo of the brownstone house of the east coast center and a cropped photo of the modern windowed A-frame that was the west coast center. The AG unfolded the brochure to the innermost panel, where she spied a broad, squat man identified in the caption as "The Llama."

"Where" said the AG with much concern, "would he have taken her?"

Wayne pointed to the A-frame and line of type which read: STINSON BEACH, CALIFORNIA.

"Why would he take Sandy?"

Wayne wrote, THE LLAMA WAS TAILING ME. I LEFT SOME NOTES ABOUT THE PHOENIX BEFORE ENTERING THE UNDERGROUND TO ESCAPE HIS "WASH." THAT'S HIS RESOCIALIZATION MODE. IF HE FOLLOWED ME, HE FOUND SANDY.

"I must find her," said the AG intensely. WHATEVER FOR?

The AG looked long at Wayne, but her words were for both men. Wayne noticed that her features, no longer luminous, had solidified into definite angles that didn't shift no matter how the light hit them. He saw no dreamy expression, but a clear, deep pool with visible rocks underneath.

The Anarchist heard a voice as frighteningly flat as any of the waitresses who ordered salads from him. The sound of playful wind chimes, her mysteriously random rhythms, were definitely missing.

AG acknowledged what was true. "Sandy is an unnatural horror. In my varying states, I've known this simple fact. Any creature that steps outside its own existence runs that risk. I accept this and must somehow..."

"Whatever she's brought on herself is small punishment!" the Anarchist practically screamed.

"The Llama may make her adapt to his system of reality and she will lose the essence of herself. Isn't that the point of the Llama's wash?"

Wayne had trouble following her lips. They had thinned with controlled emotion. He felt anger at the Llama and his church. They had attempted to standardize the soul of humanity. While not worse than many institutions, they never acknowledged their systems were highly idiosyncratic. Wayne did not know if religious truth was relative or eternal. It was the paths that needed scrutiny. The church's affairs were arbitrary.

Someone should make public complaint. In the face of

the AG's resolution to rescue Sandy, it seemed the least he could do. If the AG deserved historical credit for her part in saving the city, the Llama deserved condemnation for kidnapping Sandy for what purpose—to save his drive-in openings? Wayne would write an article about both. Who else was in a position to do so? New purpose filled Wayne with a desire to work on.

"It's not up to you alone," the Anarchist said. "I want you here."

"Where is our money, Anarchist?" the AG asked, kissing the crown of his head.

The Anarchist grew obstinate and crossed to the other side of the loft, feeling for the AG's bolts of fabric, where he guessed they'd be against the wall. Full of love and pity, the AG softly stood beside her Anarchist. She watched him pull the fabric taut on the bolts before stacking them close together in a neat row. The AG held his busy hands in hers. He tried to pull loose, but she held him fast and kissed him with a silent appeal. Then let go.

"Anarchist, I must find her. It's more than a sense of duty. I feel there is something unfinished between us, something in me she must also become reconciled with. It is important to what has happened and what will occur in the future."

"I used all our money on the laser, or rather your money. The costs were more than Sandy's backer had estimated. His resources diminished rapidly."

The AG's silence gave the Anarchist pause for thought. He

didn't understand the AG's appeal, but her arguments had never been logical. In this aspect of her personality, she was consistent. He feared she would not change the course she had set for herself. Reconciling Sandy's betrayal was almost as necessary as forgiving his own.

"I lied," he said. "Sandy kept Dio's money in the top of her video cam. There's a little left."

The AG found the video cam on Sandy's floor by the bed. She opened the top and took out a small roll of bills. Wayne counted them into a pile and wrote on his pad: IT IS SUFFICIENT FOR ONE ROUND-TRIP TO CALIFORNIA AND THEN SOME, BE CAREFUL.

"AG," the Anarchist called, "is it enough? Will you be coming back to me?"

The AG kissed Wayne on the cheek, fulfilling his ongoing fantasy. He wanted to return to his notes on her history, finding it reprehensible that he felt this desire in her presence. The AG put her hands on his shoulders and pushed him into his chair. "Work!" she said, fingers to her perfect lips.

The Anarchist had returned to the bolts of fabric, trying to lose himself in the imagined colors and patterns, trying to forget her quite unsatisfactorily. The AG took an Indian plaid out of his hands.

"AG," he said, "be aware. You have never been to California."

The AG kissed the Anarchist with as much confidence as she could assemble. "You will not worry."

The Anarchist ran his hands over her features to remember them, tangibly.

"AG, I will try to conceive of a future but you must come back. It's difficult to imagine a future when I'm living a life I've already passed."

The AG pressed her body against the Anarchist so he could feel her form. She fitted her face against his one brief moment and inhaled his quiet breath. Then she left the loft, clutching Mr. Dio's roll of bills.

It wasn't until she reached the streets of her beloved Bowery that she realized how little prepared she was for ordinary perception. Her familiar street seemed depressing, the way other people referred to it. She was also aware that, besides having no change of clothes, she had no idea how one got to the airport, what tickets cost or even a cab. In fact, she realized, she had never taken a cab in her whole life.

From habit, she tried to project a course of action, but nothing came to mind. She still had the ability to visualize, and so employed it. A memory of the Astor Place subway station seemed a logical start. The AG entered the uptown stop, thinking she'd ask at 42nd Street how to reach the airport. Instead, a billboard caught her eye, a subway car was surrounded by clouds. She read: TAKE THE TRAIN TO THE PLANE. The procedure seemed simple to try, though it might prove inconvenient for passengers hauling heavy luggage, she thought, relaxing into her subway seat.

Her course of action decided, she took notice of the car, hyperaware of other passengers, stops, and where her money rested in the pocket of her zippered flyer suit. With relief, the AG realized she might have lost one set one set of instincts but already nature was making compensation.

Chapter 15

CONFRONTATION AND REUNION

When the AG landed at the San Francisco airport she found virtually no ground transportation to Stinson Beach. There was, however, a ferry from San Francisco that would let her off in nearby Sausalito. The AG took a bus to the ferry and landed in the chic little tourist town, conscious that she had no change of outfit from her flyer suit. It would be hard to negotiate anything without appropriate clean clothes.

The AG stopped at a boutique, though she hadn't much money or any of the colored charge cards honored everywhere. She didn't much care about making an actual purchase She just wanted to feel the confidence of new clothes, after her plane and ferry rides. She also needed some diversion, as she tried to assess the requirements of her new circumstances.

She went into the dressing room of the cute boutique carrying a bathing suit and a Capri cruise-wear outfit. She spent quite some time getting used to the feel of them, walking between mirrors, swiveling and pivoting. The AG had lapsed into her old preoccupation with atmospheres—*what did the fabric feel like? What fantasy were the clothes realizing? What feelings did she get from them?* So immersed was she, that handclaps from a small crowd of watching shoppers came as a real surprise.

"It *is* darling on you," said the salesclerk, sincerely not thinking of a sale.

"Should I try on something else?" the AG speculated, pleased that she could entertain so easily; an enjoyable respite from her dire mission. There was something about the fantasy of this situation that made her long for the early visionary days of her go-go act. Urged on by the shoppers and sales help, the AG modeled cruise-wear, evening dresses, French designer swimsuits, off-the-shoulder pantsuits, accessories, nightgowns, and even shoes. After a while, she tired of walking and pivoting among the crowd mesmerized by off-the-rack make believe.

"I need a ride to Stinson Beach," said the AG to a salesgirl, who was part owner. "And please, can you can find my flyer suit? I must dress in it. I've got nothing else to wear.

"It's been a slow season," said the partial owner. "You just sold a month's merchandise for me, so take what you want. I'm closing now, so I'll drop you off at Stinson on my way home. If we hurry, we can still catch some rays off Mount Tam, Tamalpais to you."

The AG felt nautical. She chose the Capri cruise-wear and joined the partial owner in her dune buggy for a winding ride. Navigating, she asked her driver to halt at a green sign with an arrow pointing to the words STINSON BEACH.

She wanted to get her bearings, perhaps a sighting of the structure she had seen pictured in Wayne's brochure.

Having little confidence in her intuition, she was surprised when it directed her gaze upward to a hillside filled with spiky vegetation. In the fog rolls of late afternoon, she saw light bouncing off the metallic squares of a solar-heated structure. She asked her driver to continue up the road, until she saw the rich wood of a house with individual panels on its roof. The square back of a person emerged from the spiky scrub. She moved so deftly, despite her stocky build, that the AG was reminded of Sandy without her mad tension. Asking the partial owner to stop, the AG got out of the dune buggy with the plastic bag, which contained her flyer suit. She declined an offer of a sauna and dinner and wished the partial owner a pleasant evening and what was left of the afternoon. Then she faced the A-frame and Sandy with few doubts about her destination. She had definitely reached the West Coast headquarters of the Denotational Church.

"The Llama says we're related," said Sandy after a few seconds.

"We do look alike," said the AG. "That was true from the first time we met."

Sandy blissfully faced the ocean, aware that she must confess to the AG.

"I seduced the Anarchist for political purposes. Some personal perversity was also involved."

"I know."

"I invaded your privacy, the area of most telling vulnerability."

"I found the sleep tapes."

"I hated you, AG."

"I don't think I can," the AG replied. "And you don't know the worst. The Anarchist is blind."

"Hate me," Sandy cried with her old intensity. "Blind me! It would only be fair! DO..."

The Llama, a short distance from the women, hidden by another spiky scrub, gauged the escalating emotion. He approached an inch at a time so it appeared he came from nowhere.

She's like a kid, the AG, thought, her arms around Sandy's neck. Sandy abandoned herself to fearful sobs, which quickly changed to joyous smiles."

"You forgive Sandy now?"

The AG hugged her, fusing affection into leftover enmity.

"Please," said the Llama, "take her into my facility.

She is quite emotional."

His words were a signal. Sandy took the AG's hand and led her toward the A-frame. The AG was disturbed by a Sandy without self-possession. Somehow she must protect her from this man's manipulation. Sandy must reach a safe haven, where she could regain her personality. She must help...then reason silenced instinctive alarm.

What danger did the Llama really present? Studying his back, she found little menace. She would learn what power he wielded and why. Wayne had been his devotee for a long time before fleeing. The AG resolved to be cautious for her own sake and that of the Anarchist, who awaited her return. The Llama would need respect, she shrewdly decided. He would also require attention. Whether he was worth such considerations, had to be assumed. She must give him the benefit of her many doubts. The Anarchist awaited her return.

Sandy happily led the AG to the cushions in the meditation room and pulled her onto one saying, "This one is less lumpy than the others! The foam rubber isn't as old!"

The AG gracefully seated herself. Sandy lied down, resting her head in the AG's lap. Quietly, the AG waited while the Llama contemplated the imageless TV screen.

When he finally gave her his full attention, she spoke with measured ideas.

"Wayne informed me that you are the founder and leader of the Denotational Church. You believe that all men are related. Is that the sense Sandy meant about she and I?"

"No, silly!" said Sandy, raising an arm. "We have the same mother."

"In your case," said the Llama, "I'm being very specific. The seamstress, your mother, was the same disappointed woman, who once disappeared into the Aegean with a minor shipping magnate who became your father. You are Sandy's half-sister."

"What disappointed her?"

Sandy broke in with a distanced melancholy, "If you knew how inflexible my dad was, you wouldn't ask that question."

"Why did she leave the shipping magnate?" the AG asked, feeling strange talking about the unknown man who was her father.

"In time you will know," said the Llama. "It took a while to compile the report. It will take a while to digest it. Make yourself comfortable. Care for the screen?"

The AG agreed with the Llama. She knew the outlines of her origin, if not specific facts. Kneeling on the cushion in front of the video screen, she contemplated the grainy gray image. Soon she could distinguish the logo of the Church, and then other images superseding that.

The AG saw her mom, looking quite different than the pale, withdrawn seamstress, on the shore of a coastal town. She was just nineteen and very beautiful with blonde hair like the AG's and a build as stolid as Sandy's. Holding an infant in her arms, she swung in an arc, back and forth toward the sun. The pair were giggling and swaying as one bizarre form, quite moving to see. But it was the baby's feet that the AG was drawn to. They were as flat and leaf-like as Sandy's. The AG watched this confirmation of her sister, as the infant flailed its feet in the sand, kicking a bit of it just to watch it fly.

She heard the Llama's voice over the image on the screen,

continuing the report. "She apparently left the fisherman when a Greek in a small yacht offered to give her a ride to a neighboring island. She apparently did not return."

"Apparently," said Sandy, wondering what the AG might be visualizing on the opaque screen.

In a conscious act of will, the AG projected her emotion into reliving her mom's anxiety. The woman put the baby inside a neighbor's cottage with a contemptuous glance for Sandy's father, among the fishermen pulling in the nets. The seamstress loathed the counterfeit "working man" with his hidden Yank gentility. The AG felt her mother's guilt over abandonment battle with her desire to flee, as the schooner crept closer and closer.

A charming, gray-haired Greek smilingly offered his hand to her, "I am Nikos. You have read my letters or you would not be here. You have agreed to my terms?"

Contract? The AG saw her mother nod assent to this mystery, as she boarded the schooner, barefoot and thinking of her baby in the cottage. A waiter in a white uniform exited the cabin with a silver pitcher on a tray and two goblets. He said to the AG's mom, "Would madam like some sweet vermouth?"

As the shore receded, the AG's mom looked sorrowful. Nikos put his hand on her hip and said, "Soon you will have another. When I saw you in the town weeks ago, I knew only you would have my child."

"Why did she leave my father?" asked the AG, able to discern in Nikos a soul who valued individual eccentricity as much as she.

"I only know she was pregnant when she left him. She was careful about her anonymity in New York. Nikos was a wealthy man, but he never did find her— or you. Your mother's friend, Joe, was an efficient protector. Unfortunately, he never knew the investigators were for your benefit. You are an heiress, AG, if a modest one."

The AG had an essential question, which the Llama could not answer, and a task, she was unsure she could execute. Was there also a risk to her current psychic organization? The trip west had been a gamble and the terrain she was considering was not entirely unfamiliar. She found enough will to break through the pragmatic membrane, which sealed off her extra consciousness.

Detached violently, she hurled into an entirely unexpected place. Through the mind of a young soldier dying from a shattered spine, she saw a warm recess filled with liquid and a strange blonde woman, then a blonde baby with the AG's own face. The soldier and her mother melded together from her new womb view. She saw only her mother moving off a large, soft bed with a white lace coverlet. Back and forth, back and forth, she paced before a picture window Filled with an unforgettable ocean. Up and down, she raised and lowered her arms, placing items of clothing in a suitcase. Each gesture was punctuated with contained sobs.

Distancing herself further, the AG placed the scene in the

gray field of the TV screen. She placed herself back in the room with the Llama and Sandy. It was a delicate maneuver. She narrated her story for the Llama's records, unsure if the TV made her projections visible to the other two.

"Nikos wanted an heir, but he never loved the seamstress," said the AG. "Attractiveness and availability were his requisites. She thought he'd never forgive her when she gave birth to her girl-child. She also had discovered her dreams of luxury had little to do with peace, happiness or even self-satisfaction. She longed for the early days in her marriage with the American fisherman. She wished she could go back to him. Wished he could forgive her betrayal but suspected that would not be the case. No, she decided, it was her fate to do penance for her lack of faith. She would take her agreement money and go to the States with her baby. She would raise her daughter with love. Happiness for herself was an idea she would no longer entertain."

"I found out the facts," the Llama said, awed by the AG's projective capacity, "but not the content. It could not be deduced by my methods."

"It's gone," said the AG, as her projections faded from the TV screen. "I lost it for good this time."

The Llama disagreed. "Skills can be regained that were once instinctual talents. The true mystic absorbs himself in the stuff of consciousness."

The Llama's remark seemed to him shameful sophistry. It reeked of conceit. His ad campaign, with its posters and buttons, his mass membership strategies, his drive-in centers, were all concocted as clear signs of the extent of his influence—his empire. But what had he contributed to spiritual understanding? Denotation was just a method, a tool for understanding reality.

Years ago, he had decided that enlightenment was a story for others with more imagination, or merely the convenient invention of medieval campaigners who used conscience as their slogan. Still, he had just witnessed the AG's projections. If he could evolve to a state, where he could utilize his own abilities, if he could participate in the timeless dimension of the psyche and inspire not instruct his followers, might he not yet become a true leader?

"Thank you," he said to the AG, "for those images."

"You really saw them?" she asked in wonder.

"Yes. Externalization apparently exists."

With total control of her conscious intuition, the AG penetrated the self of the Llama. She experienced a complex man, devious in operation but with courage and a sincere intent. Unfortunately, his consciousness was incapable of any belief but that of its own existence. In fact, the Llama's mind was fascinated with its processes. It was this that prevented him from becoming much more than a spiritual administrator.

The AG kissed the Llama's wide forehead with an understanding that frightened the imposing man. He took her hand in his and turned the palm over for a brief kiss, begging her support in his new venture.

"I can see that Denotation has a limited context to understand reality. I end up distorting the texture of life, by making it conform to my system. Even though I am a sophisticated man, I would like to master the techniques of the sleepwalker. If I were absorbent of reality, if I were consciousness itself, perhaps I could serve as a real religious figure. How do I proceed?"

The AG didn't know. She was depleted.

"I feel blank," she told the Llama. "Somewhat cold as well."

"Sir," Sandy asked, concerned at the AG's diminished energy, "it is good to know my origin but, what am I supposed to do with that knowledge?"

"Shake hands, embrace," said the Llama. "You are kin. Sisters."

Sandy looked from the Llama to the AG with some confusion. She knew they were related, but was unsure what that meant.

"Llama," said the AG, "I want to take Sandy to New York to live with me and the Anarchist."

"It would not be safe for her or yourself. I contacted members of our Church in City Hall and was advised your status is under discussion. So far your identity is being kept secret, but the group doesn't know how long they can support that decision. A culpable party must be found if this administration is to survive. Even if my members were sufficiently dedicated to give up their jobs, that fellow from the clearinghouse knows you and Sandy."

Sandy's strangely detached smile made the AG uneasy. Ecstatically she cried, "What does it matter? If they want me, I will go to them!"

The AG addressed the Llama as though Sandy had not spoken. "Wayne told me you use a 'wash' technique to destroy idiosyncratic personalities?"

Sandy giggled inappropriately, "The Llama calls me his polemical daughter."

The Llama, embarrassed, walked to the window, where his face was away from the AG.

"Sandy's memory is not impaired. I saw myself in her machinations, the structure if not the content. I was careful to leave her potentials intact."

"Sandy," interrupted the AG, "did you do this voluntarily?"

"I needed some obliteration," Sandy said benignly. "I was, as you know, truly deranged."

The AG looked for some justification for Sandy's missing core. The Llama filled the window with his form. Though it was early evening, moonlight filling the glass glowed sufficiently to outline his body. The AG thought him impenetrable, as opaque as Sandy's reasons for becoming a disciple.

"The wash brings a state of grace," the Llama said. "You can't argue she's achieved a form of it."

Sandy happily joined the Llama. He made room, drawing

her into the window frame, his arm over her shoulder. The AG relived the horrors she had experienced because of this renegade, this wild girl from another continent, who had unknowingly shared her mother. She was so gentle now, so tamed. The Llama formed an unknown complement. Strangely, the AG felt superfluous. It was a family group.

Did my father ever love my mother? Did he want to know me? She asked those questions, wondering if there were answers. Was Nikos' search for her mother more than legal justice, her violation of their agreement? Was it about love and/or property loss? The inheritance was one kind of evidence. For another, she might question Joe about a persistent customer, a handsome Greek. He would, she speculated, be a practical genius with a gift for calculation, if little perception. The AG, watching the pair at the window, knew her questions belonged in a dimension irrelevant to their communion.

Unnoticed, she walked down the terraced hill, wondering what of the seamstress and what of the fisherman had combined in Sandy. Sandy's mad drive and her own ethereal qualities were clues to their mother, that quiet woman, whose real name remained as much a mystery as her own. At the bottom of the hill, halfway to the beach, the AG turned to look back at the A-frame. The pair at the window, twin dots, bid her silent goodbyes. She felt the weight of the Llama's unasked request. NO! She would never be a disciple or a priestess. She didn't want to aspire or lead those who did. She only wanted to walk to Stinson Beach. She only wanted to think about the practical problems of her return. It would be a long hike to Sausalito, since she would not hitchhike past sundown. Perhaps, she thought incorrectly, the beach will be a quiet place to assemble my thoughts.

The AG was unprepared for the noise of beach parties: black box radios, the smell of butane, hot dogs, potatoes, and chocolate. Stinson Beach was a busy place past sunset. The AG found a small, unoccupied spot and made herself unapproachable. She wasn't there to pay obeisance to nature. In her Capri outfit, she swam and felt the cold cloth adhere to her flesh. The experience contained no inkling of the past, but a cleansing of her worn emotion. Luckily, she had put her return ticket in a plastic bag. She had other worries to wash without that one.

What would happen when she arrived home? Would she find the Anarchist and Wayne arrested? For an hour, the AG gave her worries to the eager waves. It wasn't until much later, after the trip to the airport, that she allowed herself to collapse, tired, wet, and disheveled, into the warmth of the plane's cabin. The other passengers gave her a wide berth though the hostess was kind. She quickly brought the AG's special request for herbal tea.

The AG drank the brew, watching clouds from her window. She imagined what they would feel like, sheathed around a spirit unencumbered with flesh. She found the mere imaginings of an out-of-body sensation were enough. There was comfort in being a human confined to one plane. With that very basic feeling of security and satisfaction, she slept easily and had an unexpected dream. She was pregnant, living with the Anarchist on a wide, hot plain of land. They shared a canteen of city spring water, fresh from her old Bowery delicatessen.

Chapter 16

AFTERMATH

I SEIZE THE MOODS OF MY CITY, ASSUME THE SPIRIT OF AN AVIAN-MANHUNTER IN THIS DAUNTLESS METROPOLIS. I SPREAD MY HAWK WINGS, MAKE DARK SHADOWS OVER DARKER STREETS. I FEEL A KEELESS CRAFT TRAPPED IN NARROW CAUSEWAYS, STREETS THAT LEAD TO A NEAT WEDGE-SHAPED CENTER. THE TIDY DOWNTOWN HEART OF THIS ISLAND CITY IS OVERWHELMED BY OUTSIZE STRUCTURES, SKY DEVOURING METAL BOXES.

I AM CLAUSTROPHOBIC, LIKE IN THE WORST OF SUMMER HEAT. I SPREAD MY WING-ARMS AND TOUCH SMELLY SWEAT, THE CITY'S CONTAINMENT, AIR TOO THICK TO BREATHE. THE CONTAINER AND THE MISERABLY CONTAINED BECOME ONE THING, THE SPIRIT OF THE MANHUNTER IN THIS DAUNTING METROPOLIS.

It was five A.M. Wayne Niebold closed this last page in his journal, totally repulsed by his lapse into stream of consciousness. Poetic introspection was a useful tool for loosening one's analytical abilities. Beyond that it was pretty useless; indulgent, inactive, and nonproductive.

Idealism needed objective action! Would the Anarchist's tragedy have happened otherwise? If only he had been less introspective and the Llama more so.

Wayne felt hot in his apartment. He went to the window in search of a breeze. Leaves on a tree moved with an air current, though none of it reached his apartment. Totally unchanged. He sometimes marveled that the turmoil of events that had transformed his personality had affected little of his surroundings.

In the sameness of this apartment Wayne heard his real self for maybe the first time. It emerged with no reverb from the Llama's ideology. Denotation had proved the silliest nonsense. The Llama had merely invested homilies with meaning that was totally arbitrary. The church misled the confused into thinking things had intrinsic meanings. It created people, who were ignorant of their own proclivities.

Wayne had also discovered that his devotion to women was a lesser form of his wish to benefit all mankind. Modern hedonism had been a mask for an untapped activism. The church had exploited this. Now Wayne considered himself a realized man. The Llama, no matter how virtuous his original intentions, would have his business affairs exposed. The public also would learn the story behind the PHOENIX and the AG's role in rescuing the city. These objectives were Wayne's mission.

He opened a manila folder labelled LLAMA PROFILE. Wayne had found place of origin, legal name, etc. in the church's mainframe. Through a Denotational defector, he had a Xerox of the Llama's account of his highway vision, his usage of behavioral psychology, and specific mind manipulation methods he had learned in Tibet. There were also cost accounting of Wes Mavine's campaign for the drive-ins and the annual income from the Llama's non-salaried employees and various businesses. Wayne hoped to spark a federal investigation. He also hoped to learn the reason for the Llama's interest in the AG. What could that innocent have meant to this humanistic-Machiavelli, this Freudian-Bismarck, this.... To adequately describe the Llama, Wayne would have to invent phraseology. Hyphenation left too many gaps. The Llama was something more than a brilliant organizer and something less than a visionary. He had attempted to make the teeming morass of New York City his, and that was one hell of a game board.

Wayne closed the PROFILE for another folder which contained his unfinished article on the PHOENIX.

FUTURISTIC DESIGNER/GO-GO GIRL STEERS THE CITY OUT OF CRISIS

> The AG, self-named to protect her privacy, happened onto the information that her sometime roommate had enacted a plan to clog the arteries of Manhattan Island with a substance

> called Arizona Dust. During the emergency siege, armed only with a general map of her roommate's operation, called "The Phoenix," she single-handedly limited the damages to the city in human life and dollars. The AG successfully combated an organized terrorist activity by a band of nihilists acting under their general, Sandy…

Wayne stopped reading. He wished he knew Sandy's last name. It would definitely aid his credibility. He also wished he could interview the AG directly, though it was more important she remained ignorant of the article's existence. She would not like public exposure. Her natural reticence would forbid it, and the article was too important for that.

Since Duncan McKenzie's exclusive had been delayed by his arrest as a suspected terrorist, Wayne had begun developing his story as an independent feature. It was to serve many purposes. He wanted to clear the AG of possible criminal prosecution and net her the kind of celebrity that would widen her economic options beyond that of go-go dancer. He even hoped the story might net her a financial award her modesty would ordinarily prohibit. Also, if he were to be honest (and Wayne tried to be ruthlessly so), the story was to legitimize his own journalistic career. At the least, he thought as he gathered the file into his brief, the article was likely to result in a passing historical clarification and a limited vogue in the AG's clothing designs. Wayne put his brief under his arm and exited his apartment at 5:30 A.M., looking for an outlet.

The Times Square subway station led him to the Times building itself, located on Broadway and 42nd Street, which was not unexpectedly locked to the public. Wayne voiced some pounding protests to an invisible night watchman, before taking a downtown train to Broadway and 14th. The "Voice" was open, but filled with inarticulate reporters uninterested in Wayne. Impatient, he took a bus up Second Avenue to the Daily News Building. It was 6:30, and he was feeling downcast, when a laconic guard ordered him to remain in the lobby by the brass model of the solar system. Glaring at the Earth, he decided to disobey. A brief glance at the registry on the wall was all he needed to find the floor number of the UPI offices.

Wayne took the elevator to a highly polished, whitely lit hall and followed the arrows that said United Press International. Life came from two diehard operators, silently working in cubicles with half-Plexiglas walls. It was a twenty-four hour wire service, and they were so involved with the next metropolitan report, they didn't notice Wayne settle himself in an empty cubicle.

A word processor/teletype combo was all he needed. It took his bombshell feature amidst the operators' reports on the contained damage from the crisis and some far-out speculations on the identity of the girl known as the AG.

Wayne watched the copy to see if he was working the machinery right. He read as the words appeared:

SOMEWHERE ALONG THE BOWERY,

IN A BASEMENT, A RED-HAIRED ANARCHIST WEARS HIS ETERNAL BLACK SUIT. SOMEWHERE IN MIDTOWN MANHATTAN, A SWITCHBOARD OPERATOR WAS GOING ON HER NIGHT SHIFT. THEY ARE THE ROOMMATES OF THE AG, WHO WORKS AS A GO-GO DANCER FOR SIXTY DOLLARS A NIGHT. SHE ALSO MAKES CLOTHES FOR THE FUTURE, BUT HAD LITTLE IDEA THAT…

***

Hesitantly, the AG opened the door of her loft, hoping to avoid the mob of reporters, well-wishers, cranks, and curiosity-seekers who had made life so difficult since Wayne's article had appeared. She had never wanted to be famous. She wanted only to be able to take her customary walk and think about the news that her doctor had confirmed on the phone that morning. She was pregnant, without a doubt, and would need a refuge now that the Bowery had gone public.

The Anarchist, inside the loft, was feeling the soil he had placed around a plant in a large rubber bucket. It was odd, but the six foot corn stalk was thriving with almost no light.

"Anarchist," said the AG, moving inside, "we're going to have a child."

The Anarchist was somehow not surprised. The AG had changed in so many ways. A child was an extension of a union that had renewed itself doubly, like a plant recovering from a long frost—or growing almost in the dark.

"We'll leave then," he said. "A move has been in the air for some time now."

"But where?" the AG said in perplexity. "What place can we go to?"

The Anarchist eagerly put his hands in a plastic bag full of rich, chocolate-colored potting soil. The stuff felt as alive as electrical current. It could just as easily be sand, he thought confidently. I can grow food anywhere.

Simultaneous with this idea, the AG was remembering the shape of the future she had visualized on the plane. There was herself and the Anarchist on horseback, then just herself with the Anarchist leading her through the Mojave Desert. Cheerfully, they passed and swilled a jug of spring water she had brought from New York.

"I don't know where we'll live," she said. "How will I have a baby in the middle of a desert?"

"Desert? Wherever did you get that idea?" the Anarchist asked, kissing her hand serenely. "This baby is an externalization of what we are, my love. Don't worry, he'll grow up strong."

"The baby is no extension or externalization or anything but himself or herself!" the AG argued, knowing the outburst was unreasonable.

"Wayne will find us a fine home," the Anarchist said soothingly. "He owes us one for this unexpected exposure, this violation of our private lives."

Adobe, the AG considered thoughtfully, is a good material for desert homes. It is used in bricks and rolls that can be cut.

"Anarchist," she said, "Think about the move seriously and then, when I get back, maybe we can both contact Wayne. Perhaps he won't be too busy."

The AG decided to take a chance on a solitary walk.

It was one of the last times she would really see her Bowery. She descended the steps of the loft to the street and wasn't even recognized by the aspiring journalist from NYU. The AG did not much resemble the blonde in the student's photograph. Her hair was long and dark.

Slightly purplish shadows around her eyes gave her a wary expression unknown to his photograph of the old AG.

She was pleased to go unrecognized and, in truth, would not be sorry to walk elsewhere in the future. The Bowery had witnessed the wreck of her old self. It had seemed a different street in that time. With some emotion, she looked at the garbage strewn road. Clearly, she could distinguish all the details of an empty plastic water jug, a smashed soda can, several methadone vials, and a cement-fossilized pigeon—all strewn like broken toys in the gutter. Her neighbor, the ranting socialist, had disappeared.

His corner apartment was dark, the red light long extinguished from his ceiling. The socialist had died in a fire, the AG had learned from the garage owner next door. His apartment had been charred to the foundation, a mere shell. The windows were frameless eyeholes. His cigar, she guessed, had remained lit and slid from his special ashtray, a pewter remnant of World War II. In a lucid moment, he had explained to the AG how very bored he had been in an army outpost in Germany. He had melted down bullets and poured the metal into molds to make souvenir ashtrays.

The ashtray never held his cigar well. The molds were designed for thinner cigars from a newer source.

The AG gave him these passing thoughts as she continued her walk down the length of the Bowery. Arizona, she reasoned, is just another kind of desert. Perhaps more sparsely populated than the newly gentrified Bowery, but that would be okay. Clubs, with decor befitting bombed-out basements, were crowding the blocks. Even the Anarchist's shop had been closed as the owners of the building negotiated co-op lofts. Few traces of the jerry-made remained in that near-famous basement, though scraps of yellowed cornucopia posters, now a valuable item, peeked out of various St. Marks shops.

The AG took care where she walked. In her body beat the heart of a living embryo, a child waiting for itself to be. An Anarchist junior, a blonde AG, a throwback to the seamstress, the Greek Nikos, or a soldier completely unknown? The future of this disciple, tyrant, or Buddha was a faceless wonder.

All the AG knew for sure was that in a couple of days, his eyes would move center and register REM movement.

What they saw, she imagined, would be the interior world of a rudimentary mind. The AG fed her child all the imaginings, desires, and sensations she could. Her newly fierce posture protected him from a world not yet too old.

The AG turned down the Bowery toward her home. She saw the clock on Cooper Square which read 5:00 P.M. She saw the crowd of strap-hangers emerge from the Astor Place station to fan out toward St. Marks, Soho and the W. Village. She felt strong and able to embrace the universe in good and evil. She had even embraced Sandy, the woman who had tried to appropriate that universe. She was, she realized, well-rounded. She would be a good mother.

There was also the business of the inheritance she might claim for her son or daughter. The AG had not used her perception to discover the sex of her child. She liked a surprise or two, and the Anarchist wanted to take the future in its own time. Perception, she had learned, could be compartmentalized without losing flexibility. It was tiring but good. Her child would have her gift and would need her learning. This child would provide the cutting edge for the new age.

****

The Llama agreed to abdicate his position at the Church. His decision was sparked by a series of articles by Wayne Niebold, after his PHOENIX series. He had paralleled the growth of the PHOENIX with that of the Denotational Church. He had inferred a connection.

Both organizations exploited the emotional lag humans

experienced in the age of high-tech. One operation was aimed at immediacy of meaning-purpose, the other at long-range maintenance. Weren't these phases of the same process? Where had the funding come from for the PHOENIX? The last had proved a costly inference for the Llama personally and his now struggling Denotational Church.

On Stinson Beach, in the A-frame, Sandy sat at the Llama's feet taking dictation. She wrote notes about the new conversion of the Church's holdings into a non-profit foundation devoted to the documentation of parapsychological effects associated with esoteric religions. Participation would be through exclusive invitation or exchanges with other aligned organizations. As Sandy wrote, she wondered if the Llama's introversion might be based on the current federal investigation sparked by Wayne's articles. She found it hard to believe the Llama could take the series seriously. They were based on nothing but the wildest conjecture.

****

When the openings of the drive-in churches were cancelled, Ray and Zeke were pleased. They had wanted more control of their operation. The Llama settled the garage on them, recognizing Zeke's role in bringing Sandy safely to him. His only condition was that they run a legitimate business. Ray and Zeke gave the ritual answers, neglecting to inform him of their new consultant firm which specialized in finding the flaws in scams with objectives.

Ray had begged the board of the Church for a reduced subscription, when the Church went exclusive. The board had agreed and granted Ray, as a member, the right to obtain Denotational situation print-outs from the computer service. The privilege was, she rationalized, something, though it didn't make up for lack of access to the Llama. Zeke was very much consoled with the large success of their business.

****

The Llama, finishing his dictation, waved Sandy to her lunch and went to the front window of the A-frame to contemplate the ocean. Actually, he wanted to think about Wayne Niebold. He didn't associate betrayal or a sense of injustice with the actions of his former disciple. On the contrary, the inferences had been made by the kind of reasoning he most admired. Proof had little to do with that kind of truth. Wayne, he mused, had gone beyond Denotation. He might not care, but the Llama considered the triumph of Wayne's article series also his own. The Llama believed his own work had reached its zenith. He felt fortunate to have escaped the grandiose imaginings of his planned expansion. Knowledge, he felt assured by his foundation, would continue.

****

In an office at UPI, behind a real door and not in an open editorial cluster, Wayne Niebold took a break. He looked at a recent photograph of the AG taken on the border of the Mojave Desert. She stood in front of her adobe cabin on the plot of ground, which Wayne had located. The deal originated with a dare from a chamber of commerce skeptical of the fertility of unirrigated desert. Miraculously, the Anarchist had grown corn, tomatoes, soy beans, and some varieties of high protein grains.

In the photo Wayne held, the Anarchist posed in a red shirt. He was no longer thin. Dark glasses protected his damaged eyes, but his beard and hair clashed gaily with the shirt. He gestured, in raptures, at his model farm. The AG, sweet by his side, had apple cheeks and long blonde hair piled loosely on top of her head.

No longer slight, her figure had rounded with the child and gardening work. Her eyes, no longer wary, were as crisp as the white bleached fabric of her sundress. Proudly, she wrote that the garment was all she wore these days. She had woven the material and the baby's shirts from cactus fiber.

These changes in the AG were surprising to Wayne, but less so than her offspring. The baby she held was a red-head with otherworldly eyes and the angular jaw line of her aunt, Sandy. She gazed at the camera, quite composed.

Wayne put the photo away, glad the AG had found some happiness. For many weeks, she had suffered turmoil and anxiety for an indifferent city. The schizophrenic inflation-recession had accelerated, but overall the accelerating events — Sandy's coup and the AG's rescue— had affected nothing. Nemesis was possible only within a specific time frame. In the ever-changing city, focus on the AG's personal sacrifice was short-lived, forgotten in stories about economic insecurity, which had become a status quo. The city was moving forward to the millennium, charting economic flutters and its reflections in lifestyle. No other memory existed, except the silent Bowery.

Wayne found this idea oppressive. He retired behind a screen, which shielded a Japanese futon in a built-in wooden frame. Wayne sank into it. Fresh air from an open window wafted over his tight muscles as he thought, as he often did, of the Llama. The man knew more about what "grounded" an individual than anyone. Wayne was almost sorry about his investigation ruining his business. But he could not allow regret to interfere with his professional stance. He had a stake in knowing there was no one answer.

It was a cynical but perhaps necessary posture, he thought. Otherwise, he would report nothing but his own preconceptions. Still, he would like to reconcile with the Llama someday. In truth, he owed him one. In criticizing the Llama's stance, he had discovered his own.

Tired of thinking, Wayne practiced an obscurely personal meditation technique. He kicked off his shoes and fixated on an abstract image made by a blob of plaster on the wall. The shape resembled the AG's mouth. The connection was enough. His heart beat less fitfully. He was aware of a quick, hot sensation, fluid rushing through his body. The course it took became that of every child's first smile, every hillside and lake he had ever loved on a fantastic day, when he knew nothing but the color of the sky.

THE END

About the Author

Susan I. Weinstein is a writer, playwright, and painter. Her novel, *The Anarchist's Girlfriend*, was developed in the art bars of late 1970's New York and excerpted in the 1984 debut issue of *The Portable Lower East Side*. That literary magazine is in NYU's collection of the lower east side art and literary movement. Besides the new Pelekinesis edition of *The Anarchist's Girlfriend*, the novel was serialized by maglomaniac.com. *Paradise Gardens*. an Orwellian speculative fiction, and *Tales of the Mer Family Onyx: Mermaid stories on land and under the Sea* will also appear in new editions by Pelekinesis. Susan's short fiction and poetry have appeared in literary magazines, such as *The Metric*. Currently, she is at work on a WW2 novel, based on letters.

A graduate of Temple University's Tyler School of Art, Susan's Arte Povera piece, "Play Without Words," was presented at Sara Lawrence College. While pursuing commercial illustration, she wrote "Rabies," a new language play produced by A.C.T. in Squaw Valley. "Stakes," a vampire play, led to a scholarship to Iowa City's Playwrights Workshop. Later, she developed "White-Walled Babes" at The Public Theater and Samuel French selected her green card play, "Something About That Face" for a production at the Harold Clurman Theater. In 2014, her adaptation of Hans Christian Anderson's "The Little Mermaid," a Bunraku version, was produced in Williamsberg, NY. In 2016, "The Wapshot Whatever," a computer play, was accepted for a festival. She is also developing a new play, "The Making of ADD/ADHD."

Susan's oil painting, "Portal" was shown at Gallery Brooklyn, selected in the 2014 Curate NYC program. She also received a special Achievement award from the LBI Foundation of Art, where she's exhibited. Her drawing series of Pier 41, pre and post hurricane Sandy was exhibited at the PATH Cafe in 2015. She has received painting commissions and an illustration appears in the NYU Press book, *Up Is Up, But So Is Down, New York's Downtown Literary Scene, 1974-1992.* Whenever possible, she paints what she sees.

Susan has made her living publicizing books. often on arts, political and social issues. Once she initiated a "Plays are Literature" campaign on a TCG grant to see if scripts might be reviewed. A review for the script of "Angels in America, Part 2" did appear in the Los Angeles Times.

Susan I. Weinstein is married and lives in NYC. She has made her living publicizing books on arts, social and political issues, among other topics, for a variety of publishers—mainstream, small and university presses. Her review blog is www.notanotherbookreview.blogspot.com.

About the Cover Artist

C. Saksa-Mydlowski is a painter and shows regularly in the Princeton, NJ and New Hope, PA areas. She is active in her community and has work acquired by The Mercer County Heritage Foundation. Previously Saksa-Mydlowski was an award winning collage illustrator and book jacket designer in NYC. She presently lives with her husband and daughter in farm country near Princeton.

A Reader's Guide to *The Anarchist's Girlfriend*

Talking Points for "Paul the Book Guy" podcast and "Cindy Rakowitz on Voice of America talk radio."

Q. What inspired *The Anarchist's Girlfriend?*

A. Around 1977, I moved to New York. I was living on the Bowery in a loft, which looked into the men's dressing room of The Public Theater. Hartz Mountain was renting "raw space," previously used to store birdfeed. This meant I, and my two roommates, had to go to Orchid St. and buy sinks, toilet and a bath tub and carry home. I was writing plays and working odd publishing jobs. I kept thinking of Mishkin in Dostoyevsky's *The Idiot* and wondered in this era what a divine "idiot" might be. He was not quite of this earth and a blank screen for other people to project onto. He reflects his world, as does the AG. I wrote about what I saw around me. People think the novel is fantasy, but actually many characters and their New York were real.

Q. Does the AG parallel The Idiot?

A. It's set in 1980, in NYC, a time of arts and politics not unlike St. Peterburg in *The Idiot*. People are both passionate and hypocritical. The New York of late '70s-'80s was full of creative people; artists, writers, Swiss filmmakers, and yes, an Irish Anarchist, who silk-screened peace posters. Many of the characters are based on real people in a NYC, where politics, arts, fashion, music mixed and were international. Philosophy was discussed in bars. Manhattan was the Left Bank of the World.

Q. What do you mean?

A. The "scene" mixed high and low culture. Money was not the only currency. Wit, ideology, vision held court with beauty. Fashion was often tongue-in-cheek, even Dada—especially at the downtown Mudd Club. St. Petersburg was also a kind of "Left Bank" city where the bohemian underground spiced up rich salons.

Q. You didn't write equivalencies?

A. No that's why it's inspired, not based upon. The ideology of my characters is intrinsic to their personalities. As their destinies unfold, there is an inevitable quality. Character is destiny and people change in the process, but that predates Shakespeare. The otherworldly AG is an unconscious force for what we think of as good, who also inevitably changes. The movies *Zelig* and *Being There* were fatalistic "take-offs" on *The Idiot*. They even reference names and dialogue. Here I started with the idea of the divine fool and did something else.

Q. Can you explain?

A. Like Mishkin, the Anarchist's Girlfriend is an unworldly mystic. The story is told by Wayne, a deaf-mute journalist for the cultish News World. Wayne is very like the narrator of *The Idiot*, in his search for a moral compass. Wayne works for The Llama, whose existential religion is the basis of a business empire. The Llama could also be compared to the businessman in The Idiot, but similarities are accidental. The Idiot was only a jumping off point.

Q. How did this become a serial?

A. It evolved. I read first the intro and then chapters at art bars and clubs, like Darinka, and benefits for zines, like *The Portable Lower East Side*, which had the AG in its debut issue. (It's now part of NYU's collection of the downtown art lit scene.) Audiences came weekly to see a chapter read-performed. For new people, I summarized previous chapters and went on from there—ending with a cliffhanger. It was great fun. I read in one benefit, where *Slaves of New York* was also read. That depiction of real estate, money, status and drugs was alongside the idealism and political passion that brought creative people to the city. The AG's side needed to be heard. Politics were as serious then as "Occupy Wall Street" is now. Rent was cheaper, but living on the edge in survival jobs was already reality for many people. Temp was becoming permanent in the AG.

Q. What role did politics play in the AG?

A. Sandy's drive for power and the Anarchist's need for a meaningful political statement are catalysts for an act in front of Federal Hall on Wall Street. Though set in 1980, it reflects the frustration and hopelessness felt in the U.S. and much of the West after the recession of 1973. Here's bit of economic history.

Wikipedia: The recession in the United States lasted from November 1973 (the Richard Nixon presidency) to March 1975 (the Gerald Ford presidency), although its effects on the US were felt through the Jimmy Carter presidency until the mid-term of Ronald Reagan's first term as president, characterized by low economic growth. Although the economy was expanding from 1975 to the first recession of the early 1980s, which began in January 1980, inflation remained extremely high until the early years of the 1980s.

Q. Would the AG fit into 2016 New York?

A. She probably could not rent a Bowery loft, even with roommates. In 2016, she might make a living as a designer but more likely would be a bohemian "Muse" for a designer or a Brand, who would capitalize on her lack of worldliness. She might quietly run a prosperous mail order business. She would certainly avoid selfies. She might know it was idiotic, yet believe souls could be stolen by cameras.

www.ingramcontent.com/pod-product-compliance
Lightning Source LLC
Chambersburg PA
CBHW031137020726
PP18521300001B/1

* 9 7 8 1 9 3 8 3 4 9 5 2 2 *